Praise for

HOUSE ᵒꜰ ODYSSEUS

"A superb sequel to the brilliant *Ithaca*, this is another clever, vivid reimagining of myth told in North's indomitable style—with wit, attention to detail, and exquisite characterization. Ancient myth becomes real and urgent, the world of the divine and the mortal expertly balanced throughout the unfolding twists and turns that will leave the reader eagerly anticipating the final installment of the trilogy!"
　　　　　　　—Jennifer Saint, author of *Ariadne*

"Claire North has the most original voice—every page is an absolute joy. I loved *Ithaca*, but *House of Odysseus* is even better. I cannot wait for the final book in the series!"
　　　　　　　—Elodie Harper, author of *The Wolf Den*

"North's writing is evocative, vibrant, and delightfully witty—capable of rending your heart in two with only a few words from a scathing and surprisingly ardent godly narrator."
　　　　　　　—Bea Fitzgerald, author of *Girl, Goddess, Queen*

"North's novels are triumphs of conception and execution.... Her prose here is elegant, poetic, and gorgeously descriptive.... This is a stunning novel."　　　　　　　—*Booklist*

Praise for

ITHACA

"Richly poetic.... An impassioned plea for the lost, disenfranchised queens of ancient Greece, a love letter to the silenced women of history who had to hide their pain behind their eyes and their skills, capabilities, and power behind false incompetence and ignorance." —*Booklist* (starred review)

"North breathes new life into an ancient story you would think had nothing left to tell. Instead, she shines a light on all the stories that were always there but never told. She gives voice to the voiceless and their message was a joy to read. This is a story as entertaining as it is thought-provoking, as witty as it is intelligent. If you're going to delve into Greek-retellings, let it absolutely be this one." —*Fantasy Hive*

"A dazzlingly complex, twisting tale. Claire North breathes life into a cast of mythical characters from goddesses to queens to slave women in a richly nuanced portrayal of human life."
—Jennifer Saint, author of *Ariadne*

"Like Penelope at her loom, North both weaves and unweaves, teasing out the threads of Homeric myth to recombine them into something unique, wonderful, and urgently contemporary."
—M. R. Carey, author of
The Girl With All the Gifts

"The queen of the gods narrates a crackling tale of secrets and intrigue.... This is a ground-up view of Greek myth populated by spying maids, crafty merchants, and conniving queens. It's taut, suspenseful, and full of Hera's delightfully dyspeptic attitude. A thoroughly enjoyable exploration of Penelope's side of the ancient story." —*Kirkus*

"Told in the arresting voice of the goddess Hera.... *Ithaca* conjures up a world in which women, abandoned by their men, must weave their own destinies." —*The Times*

"North gives a fresh voice and point of view to the tale narrated by Hera.... Women shine in this tribute." —*Historical Novels Review*

"A gorgeous, emotive feminist retelling of the classic Greek myth of Penelope." —*Belfast Telegraph*

CLAIRE NORTH

HOUSE ^{OF} ODYSSEUS

A SONGS OF
PENELOPE NOVEL

REDHOOK

Copyright © 2023 by Claire North
Excerpt from *The Last Song of Penelope* copyright © 2024 by Claire North

Cover design by Lisa Marie Pompilio
Cover illustrations by Shutterstock
Cover copyright © 2023 by Hachette Book Group, Inc.
Author photograph by Siobhan Watts

Redhook Books/Orbit
Hachette Book Group
1290 Avenue of the Americas
New York, NY 10104
hachettebookgroup.com

First Paperback Edition: March 2024
Originally published in hardcover and ebook in Great Britain by Orbit and in the U.S. by Redhook in August 2023

Redhook is an imprint of Orbit, a division of Hachette Book Group.
The Redhook name and logo are registered trademarks of Hachette Book Group, Inc.

The publisher is not responsible for websites (or their content) that are not owned by the publisher.

The Hachette Speakers Bureau provides a wide range of authors for speaking events. To find out more, go to hachettespeakersbureau.com or email HachetteSpeakers@hbgusa.com.

Redhook books may be purchased in bulk for business, educational, or promotional use. For information, please contact your local bookseller or the Hachette Book Group Special Markets Department at special.markets@hbgusa.com.

Library of Congress Control Number: 2022952189

ISBNs: 9780316668835 (trade paperback), 9780316668811 (ebook)

Printed in the United States of America

LSC-C

Printing 1, 2023

DRAMATIS PERSONAE

⤜⤜⤜⤜⤜⤜⤜⤜⤜⤜⤜⤜⤜⤜⤜⤜⤜⤜⤜⤜⤜⤜⤜⤜⤜⤜

The Family of Odysseus

Penelope – wife of Odysseus, queen of Ithaca
Odysseus – husband of Penelope, king of Ithaca
Telemachus – son of Odysseus and Penelope
Laertes – father of Odysseus
Anticlea – mother of Odysseus

Councillors of Odysseus

Medon – an old friendly councillor
Aegyptius – an old, less friendly councillor
Peisenor – a former warrior of Odysseus

Suitors of Penelope and Their Kin

Antinous – son of Eupheithes
Eupheithes – master of the docks, father of Antinous
Eurymachus – son of Polybus
Polybus – master of the granaries, father of Eurymachus
Amphinomous – a warrior of Greece
Kenamon – an Egyptian

Maids and Commoners

Eos – maid of Penelope, comber of hair
Autonoe – maid of Penelope, keeper of the kitchen
Melantho – maid of Penelope, chopper of wood

Melitta – maid of Penelope, scrubber of tunics
Phiobe – maid of Penelope, friendly to all
Euracleia – Odysseus's old nursemaid
Otonia – Laertes' maid

Women of Ithaca and Beyond

Priene – a warrior from the east
Teodora – an orphan of Ithaca
Anaitis – priestess of Artemis
Ourania – spymaster of Penelope

Mycenaeans

Elektra – daughter of Agamemnon and Clytemnestra
Orestes – son of Agamemnon and Clytemnestra
Clytemnestra – wife of Agamemnon, cousin of Penelope
Agamemnon – conqueror of Troy, killed by Clytemnestra
Iphigenia – daughter of Agamemnon and Clytemnestra, sacrificed to the goddess Artemis
Pylades – sworn brother to Orestes
Iason – a soldier of Mycenae
Rhene – maid of Elektra
Kleitos – priest of Apollo

Spartans

Menelaus – king of Sparta, brother of Agamemnon
Helen – queen of Sparta, cousin of Penelope
Nicostratus – son of Menelaus
Lefteris – captain of Menelaus's guard
Zosime – maid of Helen
Tryphosa – maid of Helen
Icarius – father of Penelope
Polycaste – Icarius's wife, Penelope's adopted mother

Assorted Mortals Living or Deceased

Paris – prince of Troy
Deiphobus – prince of Troy
Xanthippe – priestess of Aphrodite

The Gods and Assorted Divinities

Aphrodite – goddess of love and desire
Hera – goddess of mothers and wives
Athena – goddess of wisdom and war
Artemis – goddess of the hunt
Eris – goddess of discord
The Furies – vengeance personified
Calypso – a nymph
Thetis – a nymph, mother of Achilles

CHAPTER 1

>>

They came at sunset to my temple door, torches burning. The fire they carried was thin against the scarlet west and picked the bronze lines of their helmets out in gold. The last of the devoted scattered before them as the shield-hearted men climbed the thin path along the curve of the hill, piling the scent of jasmine and evening rose with the heaving of their really rather lovely contoured chests. Such a fanfare of oiled arm and curving leg could not help but be noticed from a valley away, and so it was that my priestess, fair Xanthippe, was waiting for them at the top of the three rough steps that rose to the columned portico. Her hair was set high above her face, her gown low about her bosom. She had sent one of the younger girls to grab a bunch of yellow flowers from the shrine that she might hold in her arms as a mother could coddle her babe, but alas, the girl was slow on her feet and did not make it back in time to complete the pleasing image, and instead had to huddle at the back of the priestly assemblage gripping her petals between twisting fingers as if there were a scorpion in the bouquet.

"Welcome, fair travellers," Xanthippe called when the first men of the approaching column were within reach of her low voice. It is not acceptable to ask a lady her age, but she had grown well into her beauty, wearing the lines about her eyes with mirth, a twist about her smile and a flash of her fragrant wrist as though to say "I may not be young, but what merry tricks have I learned!" Yet the approaching men did not return her courtesy, but instead lined up in a half-circle a few paces from where the women stood, encasing the mouth of the temple as if it might belch snakes. Below, to the west, the last of the setting day pricked pink and gold off the thin waiting sea. The town that rested beneath the shadow of my altar was crowned with gulls, and the bright banners stretched from column to pine about my temple twitched and strained against their string.

Then, with no word spoken, the men in bronze, helmets upon their brows and hands upon their swords, moved towards the women. I was having a bath at the time in my lofty Olympian bower, enjoying the nectar pooled in my belly button – but the instant their heavy sandals slapped upon the sacred timbers of my sacred temple below, I raised my eyes from contemplation of my fairer parts and bade my naiads cease their cavorting, which they did with some reluctance, and turned my gaze to earth. In credit to her priestliness, Xanthippe immediately stepped forward to block the passage of the nearest man, her nose coming up to a little below the round lip of his breastplate, her smile giving way to something tinged almost with disappointment.

"Good travellers," she proclaimed, "if you have come here to give thanks to the bountiful goddess Aphrodite, then you are welcome. But we do not profane her shrine with weapons, nor offer anything in her name save with the greatest piety, friendship and delight."

The soldier who led this group – a man of notched chin and significant thigh that under normal circumstances I'd find really quite enthralling – considered this a moment. Then he laid his hand upon my priestess's shoulder and shoved her – he actually

2

shoved my priestess, upon *my* sacred hearth! – so hard she lost her footing and half fell, caught by one of the waiting women before she could tumble entirely.

Golden nectar splashed around the lip of the bath, spilling in shimmering pools about the white marble floor as I sat upright, the bones of my long, silken hand standing out white. I cursed the soldier who so dared touch my devoted one, barely noticing what I did: he would love and he would bind his heart to passion and when he had given his all, then he would be betrayed. And *then* genital disfigurement. One does not cross Aphrodite without some thoroughly explicit consequences.

When the next man crossed the threshold of my shrine, and the next, oblivious to the sacred rites and duties owed to me, I bade the earth tremble a little beneath their feet, and lo, it was so, for though I am no earth-shaker, the soil beneath my worshippers knows better than to resist the will of even the loveliest of the gods. Yet these fools continued on, and when all men had crossed and were looking round the inner sanctum of my temple as one might inspect a sheep at market, I raised my fingers, still pouring golden fluid, and prepared to smite them with doom unnameable, heartbreak perpetual, with broken soul and broken body so vile that even Hera, who has a knack for the grotesque, might turn her face away.

Yet before I could obliterate them all, transform every cursed man who dared knock the flowers set upon the altar with their grubby hands or pull back the covers on the warm beds where was celebrated that most sacred communion of body and flesh, another voice rang out from the dusty webbing of paths and crooked houses that surrounded my shrine.

"Men of Sparta!" he cried, and how well he said it, a lovely ring to the sound, a sonorous quality that spoke of a captain of the seas, or a soldier upon the falling ramparts of war. "Profaners of this sacred space, it is us you seek!"

The men within the shrine ceased their searching and, hands upon blades, emerged again, the bloody sunset burning through the plumes of their high helmets. I cursed them all anyway to a weeping of vilest fluid from their nethers, which condition would come upon them slow yet unstoppable until they flung themselves at the feet of one of my ladies and implored mercy. This done, I permitted myself a little curiosity as to the scene unfolding before my shrine; what petty mortal malady was it that was bringing such disturbance to my evening bath?

Where there had been one line of armoured men stomping about my shrine, now there were two. The first, the cursed men armoured in bronze, arrayed themselves in a straight line of soldiery with fading sun at their backs, mouths set and visages part hidden by the helmets that still weighed upon their brows. The second wore cloaks of dusty brown and green, and no helmets, but were gathered in a loose knot about the mouth of the path from which they had emerged. "Men of Sparta," continued the lovely leader of this second pack – *unyielding*, that was an excellent word for him, so very unyielding in both tone and the furrowing of his brow; I do sometimes appreciate a fellow of that sort – "why have you come here with weapons? Why have you committed sacrilege in this most peaceful of places?"

One of the armed men – one of those who would shortly be finding his manliness bursting into a misshapen swollen protuberance beneath his tunic – stepped forward. "Iason, is it not? Iason of Mycenae."

Iason – a very pretty name, I decided – had one hand on his sword beneath his cloak and did not dignify these impudent men with a smile or a nod of courtesy. "I will ask you one last time, and then I will bid you leave. Sparta has no authority here. Consider yourselves lucky you still breathe."

Hands tightened on hilts. Breath slowed in the lungs of those who knew how to fight, grew a little faster in those who were not yet familiar with the bloody course of violence. Xanthippe was already ushering her people into the shrine, pushing shut and barring the heavy doors against the outside world. The last curve of the setting sun hung for a moment too long on the horizon, a little curiosity perhaps overwhelming the sacred duty of the celestial charioteers, before it dropped beneath the western sea, leaving firelight and the last scarlet echoes of the fading day.

Iason's hand tightened on his hilt and I throbbed in his heart, yes, yes, do it, yes! He shuddered with my celestial touch, as all people do when Aphrodite walks among them, honing desire to a single point within his breast. Draw your blade, I bade him, strike down these defilers! His heart beat a little faster; does he feel the strength of my hand upon his wrist, does he quiver with an arousal that he cannot place, the rushing of blood, the clenching of muscles in his chest? Many a man of war there is who has felt the place where fear, rage, panic and lust meet; when I am slighted, I will joyfully meet them there.

Then another voice spoke, cutting through the busy, raging silence of hand tightening upon sword, breath rushing in chest – one both new and familiar. I started with surprise to hear it, and felt too the shock of recognition in Iason's chest as the speaker's words spilled like oil through the dusk.

"Good friends," he said, "this is a place of love. And it is with love that we have come."

Then stepped forward another man. He wore no armour, but a cloak the colour of the rich wine that had fattened him since he sailed from Troy. A crown of thick dark curls adorned his head, traced with grey, and his skull sat upon a neck that expanded in a triangle down to his shoulders, so that head, throat, chest all seemed to be of one matter, rather than three distinct organs. He was no taller than any other man, but his hands – such hands! So thick and wide they could crush a blacksmith's face within his palm. Spear-throwing, heart-rending, sword-swinging hands of the kind that I do not think we shall see in Greece again. His hands were the first thing all observers might note, but when he spoke again, their eyes would rise to meet his and then immediately look away, for in that wintry gaze was something only the Furies might name. His lips pulled into a smile, but his eyes did not; nor could I, whose memory is boundless as the starry sky, recall a time when I had seen them smile, save once or twice when he was but a mewling babe, before the time of ancient curses and newest wars.

Iason's grip did not loosen on the hilt of his sword, but even he, my brave little warrior, felt his footing shift before the gaze of this open-armed figure slipping through the defilers' ranks. And for a moment, even I did not know whether his smile portended worship or sacrilegious burning; whether he was about to offer incense and grain to my glory or bid the timbers of my shrine be set alight. I searched his soul for an answer, and could not see it. I, born of sacred foam and the south wind, *I* gazed into his heart and could not know it, for in truth he did not know it himself; but only I was afraid.

Then he turned that smile again upon Iason and, in the manner of a scholar who wishes his pupil might form some great idea on his own, said: "Good Iason. Your honour is spoken about even in our little, little Sparta. I had not thought to find you in a place so . . . quaint . . . as this, but clearly there has been some miscommunication. When one is concerned for the welfare of those one loves – for the good of a kingdom, for the very heart of Greece, for the blessed land that fathered us – one must learn to cast aside all expectations. All normal expectations, if those normal things stand between a man and his duty, his honour even. I think you understand these things, yes?"

Iason did not answer. That was fine – very few people did when this man spoke.

"The truth is, my men are tired. They shouldn't be, embarrassing really; there was a time when men, real men, could march without food or drink for five nights and still fight and win a battle at the end of it, but I fear that this time is over, and we must reconcile ourselves to a weaker sort of man. A foolish sort of man. For they are fools to have come here in such a provocative, thoughtless manner. I will give you ... three of their lives, if you wish, in recompense. Chose whoever you will."

The men of Sparta, if perturbed by their leader offering up three of them to immediate dishonourable death, did not show it. This was perhaps something their king had done before – or maybe they were too preoccupied with the growing sense of discomfort about their groins to fully appreciate the matter unfolding.

Iason was slow to understand the sincerity of this moment, but at last shook his head. Yet this was not answer enough. The other man stood with head on one side as though to say "Will you not choose?" so at last Iason blurted: "I ... no. Your word is enough. Your word is ... more than sufficient."

"My word? My word." The man tasted the idea, tried it out in heart and mind, relished the flavour of it, spat it back out. "Good Iason, it is a comfort to me to know that Mycenae has men such as you in it. Men who trust in ... words. My nephew is blessed with your loyalty. He needs that now. He needs the loyalty of all of us in these times. Such times." Again he paused, and there was a place where Iason could speak, and a place where again, Iason had nothing to say. The man sighed – this was a disappointing conversation, but hardly a surprising one. He was used to the sound of his own voice, though had yet to work out why. He stepped closer to Iason, and when the younger man did not recoil, moved closer again, put his hand on Iason's shoulder, smiled, squeezed. He cracks walnut shells between two fingers, once twisted the head of a man so far that his neck snapped, barely marking what he did. But Iason was brave; Iason did not flinch. This pleased the man. Very little pleases him these days that is not expressed in a language of pain.

"Well," he breathed at last. "Iason. Iason of Mycenae. My good friend Iason. Well then. Let me ask you – as a loving uncle, as a loyal servant, humble supplicant to our great king of kings, Orestes of Mycenae, your noble master, my dear nephew. Let me ask you then. Let me ask." Menelaus, king of Sparta, husband of Helen, brother of Agamemnon, he who stood in burning Troy and stamped on the heads of babes; a man who in the most secret place of his soul every night swears himself my enemy as if the oaths of mortals have any meaning to the gods – now he leans into the sweating soldier of Mycenae, now he whispers in his ear with a voice that has commanded the world to break: *Where the fuck is Orestes?*

CHAPTER 2

>>>

Off the western coast of this land of Greece there is an island dribbled into the sea like the last liquids of an unsatisfactory encounter with a premature lover. Hera would look shocked if I expressed it to her in those terms, but once she had berated me about my choice of language, she would cast her eyes down from Olympus to survey the little spew of geography to which I refer, and she would not in fact disagree.

This isle is Ithaca, seat of kings. There are other islands nearby that are far less wretched and unpleasant. A tiny worm of water separates it from the lovely hills of Kephalonia, where olives grow abundant and lovers may lie upon the western sands, pure as the salt water that tickles their bare, tangling toes. Yet it was on Ithaca, that backwater little nowhere land, that the family of Odysseus, wiliest of all the Greeks, decided to build their palace – a scrubby insignificance of black rocks, secret coves, thorns and foul-smelling goats. Athena would intervene at this point and harp on about its strategic importance, about tin and silver and trade blah blah blah, but Athena is not the teller of this tale, and for that we can all rejoice. I am a far more tender poet, studied in the subtle art of human passion and desire, and though I would never be seen on Ithaca in any guise, mortal or divine, it being so utterly unfashionable and lacking any of the luxuries one might require, yet there is now a question asked whose outcome could affect the gods themselves – and whose answer must bring even one as cultivated as myself to these miserable isles.

Where is Orestes?

Or perhaps more precisely: *Where the fuck is Orestes?* for Menelaus, king of Sparta, is not above a certain blunt crudity in his words and deeds.

Where the fuck indeed?

Where is the newly crowned king of Mycenae, son of Agamemnon, greatest ruler of the greatest land in all of Greece?

These are not questions that would bother one such as myself. Kings come, kings go, but love remains, and so really these matters of politics and monarchs should be directed to Athena, or even Zeus if he could be bothered to raise his head from his cup to answer them. Yet I will admit that when it is Menelaus who makes such an enquiry, husband of my dear, lovely Helen, even I will raise one perfectly sculpted brow to contemplate its answer.

Come – take my hand. I am not vengeful Hera or Cousin Artemis; I will not transform you into a boar for daring to brush your skin against mine. My divine presence is of course overwhelming, I do understand – even my attending nymphs and naiads are often overcome by my fragrance, and many is the night I have to fetch my own hot milk, finding my staff preoccupied past the point of usefulness. But keep your eyes fixed on a certain distant point, and you may journey with me through matters past, present – maybe even some of those yet to come – and return again, your body and mind mostly intact.

There is a place on Ithaca called Phenera.

Even by Ithaca's very low standards, it is a miserable little dive. It was once a smugglers' cove, framed by grey rocks against which the sea grinds like a drunken bawd, squat houses of mud and dung set back from a shingle shore. Then raiders came, men driven by ambition and petty schemes of mortal men, and what little there was of note in the place was plundered, pillaged or burned to the ground. Some still sleep among the few shacks that hold against the wind – fisherwomen and the hard-faced old ladies who carve mussels and scrambling creatures from the deep. But mostly it stands as a monument to what happens when an island is not defended by a king – dust, ashes and the salt wind off the bitter sea.

I would not normally deign to look twice at such a place, no, not even for the prayers of the young lovers who used to fumble crudely at each other by the shore. My prayers should be carried by panting breath, caught in secret whispers or sung in delight at the golden touch of dawn upon a lover's back; not twisted into a muttered "Go on, get your tackle out." Yet on this night, with the moon half full across the bay, even I turn my celestial vision to the earth to see a ship powered by the beating of oars and the thrust of the waves drive prow-first up onto the shore at Phenera.

It is a curious vessel; neither smuggler's bark nor Illyrian pirate come to plunder Ithaca's land. Though the sail is plain and unmarked, at the prow of the ship is carved a roaring lion, and the first men who jump from it to the wet sand below are wound in fine dyed wool and lit by the dim light of oil burning within bronze.

They are grateful to reach land, for their nights upon the sea have been plagued with restless dreams, with gasping awake and crying out for those lost, with the taste of blood between their lips though they have not eaten meat, and with violent waves that seemed to lurch and buckle most incongruously as they made their way beneath a bruised grey sky. The sweet water tasted of salt, and the salted fish they dined upon had worms in it; and though they could not see it with mortal eyes, there was a black cloud spinning about them that rose up to the vaults of heaven and squeaked, higher than human hearing, in the tongue of the blood-drinking bat.

For some minutes these same men, flesh still warm from their pleasing exertions on the oars, make to securing their ship against tide and wind, in a manner not befitting any pirate, while others set out with torches to explore a little the ruined edges of Phenera. A startled cat shrieks and hisses and runs from their passage. Busy burbling birds chatter at each other from the sleepy rocks, disturbed by this unexpected arrival of humanity and its firelight, though even they fall silent as the darker presence that lurks above the deck makes itself known. A fire pit is dug on the beach, fuelled by smoky timber gathered loosely about the shore. A canopy is swung above it, some chairs produced, and boxes on which others sit – women too now descending from the ship to join the men, their eyes sunk from sleepless worry. The moon turns towards the horizon, the stars spin around their celestial point, and on the very edge of ruined Phenera, more than just wolf eyes watch.

Come – it is best not to linger too long by the ship. There are those upon it who even I, born of the foaming scrotum of Uranus himself and thus really rather remarkable in my potency, would rather avoid.

Two men of this vessel prick their way through the ashes of the town, one holding a torch, the other a spear. They are set to guard the edge of this place, but they cannot imagine what they are guarding against – Ithaca is an island of women and goats, nothing more. One pauses to relieve himself while the other politely turns his back, and in doing so, he sees the warrior.

She is dressed in leather and knives. The knives are the most prominent feature, for she has one on her left hip, one across her back, one on her right wrist, and one in either boot. She also wears a sword upon her right hip, and carries a javelin. If one can briefly overcome the distracting failure of fashion that is her garb, one might notice her short, dusty hair, her delightful hazel eyes, and, should one get a little more intimate, the enthralling tapestry of scars both ridged and silvered traced across her poised, muscled flesh.

"Um ..." begins the soldier who is not occupied with his bladder.

"You will tell me who you are, and where you are from," the woman declares, loud and sharp enough to make the preoccupied soldier jump, sprinkling himself with his own urine before scurrying to hide his flaccid shame.

"Who in Zeus's name ..."

The woman does not move, does not blink. The arrow comes from the darkness at her back, passes over her shoulder and embeds itself in a crumbling muddy wall a palm-print away from the head of the nearer soldier.

"Who are you, and where are you from?" repeats the woman, and when neither man answers immediately she adds, an afterthought that someone else has told her to remember: "Ithaca is under the protection of Artemis, the sacred huntress. If you are foes to her, you will not live to tell others to fear her name."

The men look from the woman to the arrow lodged beside their head, to the darkness from which it has come. Then, rather wisely, the man who a moment ago was performing an act of nature blurts: "She said you would come."

"Who said? Said what?"

"You must come with us to the ship." And a moment later, perhaps understanding that this is not a woman for whom "must" is a sensible choice of verb: "We can explain all there."

"No. This is Ithaca. You come to me."

These men are not Menelaus's Spartans. They are Mycenaean, and they stood with eyes open when Queen Clytemnestra ruled

13

her husband's lands. They are unusually accustomed to women saying no. "We must fetch our captain."

The woman gives a sharp nod of assent, and the men scurry away.

It does not take them long to return. The threat of an unknown, potentially celestial archer or archers waiting in the fading dark provokes a certain haste among even – if not especially – the most seasoned veterans. When they return to the edge of Phenera, to the place where torchlight meets darkness and the thin, muddy path, the woman is still waiting there, a statue baked in bronze and the skins of animals. Did she blink? Why, yes – she blinked, paced, flapped, exchanged a brief conversation with one of the hidden watchers arrayed in muddy garb about the edge of the village; and then, on hearing the soldiers return, assumed again her fixed position, to create the impression that no thunder nor volcano might rouse her from her duty. Let me assure you, as one who watched the heroes of Troy most particularly, that sometimes even Paris had to take a shit in the bushes, and lovely Hector with his adorable button nose snored like a bear and farted like an ox. So much for the stiff dignity of marbled heroes.

The soldiers have brought with them two others, and those others are wisely unarmed. One is a man dressed much as the men who summoned him, in breastplate and greaves, a sea-battered cloak upon his back, his hair salty and battered around his tired face. His name is Pylades, and his love is of that tragic sort that blazes so bright he fears to express it, lest it be extinguished in rejection and thus snuff out the brightness of his life. The other is a woman, crow-faced and black-feather-souled, her hair long and wildly set free by the tossing of her sea journey, her face pinched with hunger and hands clenched in fists at her sides. It is she who steps towards the knife-armed woman, and without fear holds out her right hand, opens her fingers and reveals within a golden ring.

"I am Elektra," she proclaims. "Daughter of Agamemnon. This ring belonged to my mother, Clytemnestra. Take it to your queen."

The woman with knives observes the gold suspiciously, as if it might uncoil at any moment into a mystic snake. "I am Priene, and I serve only Artemis," she replies, and might have said more if Elektra hadn't cut in with a mocking snort.

"I am Elektra," she repeats, "daughter of Agamemnon. My brother is Orestes, king of kings, the greatest of the Greeks, ruler of Mycenae. On this island he slew our mother in vengeance for her crimes, while your queen, Penelope, stood by, betrayer of her own kin. Make all the speeches you want about gods and goddesses and such, but do it quickly, and when you are done, take this secretly, take it fast, and give it to Penelope."

Priene considers both the ring – which in her way she regards as a somewhat inferior work, nothing like the moving horses of gold the people of her homeland could beat and curl from even the smallest nugget of metal – and the woman who holds it. She already knows that she despises Elektra and would happily kill them all and be done with the matter, but alas – alas. There are women at her back to whom she feels a certain obligation, and whose lives would be inconvenienced to say the least should all of Ithaca burn in a war of fiery retribution. The seas are full of angry men these days, veterans of Troy who did not get their due, and their sons, who are beginning to understand that they will never be accounted as great as their fathers.

With all this in mind, she takes the ring, slips it into her garb nearest her bosom, watches Elektra to see if this intimacy might arouse a reaction that would justify the unleashing of blade and arrow, and when it does not, nods. "Do not leave the beach," she barks. "If you do, you will die."

15

"I have never feared the forgetful river of Hades," Elektra replies, soft as a mountain stream, and Priene is familiar enough with killing to see the truth of it, and wise enough to wonder why.

Priene turns her back without fear on the men of Mycenae and their queen, and walks into the darkness, which watches still.

CHAPTER 3

I n the palace of Odysseus, a queen lies dreaming.

These are the things the poets say she shall dream of:

Her husband, as she saw him last nearly twenty years ago,
with an added gloss of heroism perhaps that broadens his chest,
puts a sheen of gold into his hair, puffs up his archer's arms
and sets laughter upon his lips. They were still young when
he sailed, she younger than he, and in the nights before the
Mycenaeans came to summon Odysseus to Troy, she would find
him holding their newborn son and gurgling all his hopes in
the chubby baby's bewildered face, *coo-coo-ee, yes, coo-ee, who's a
little hero, yes, you're a little hero, cooooo-eee!*

Or if she does not dream of Odysseus, which surely she must,
perhaps she dreams of:

Telemachus, that same baby boy now nearly grown. He has
set sail to find his father, or his father's corpse – either has its pros
and cons. He is a little taller than his father was – that would
be his Spartan grandfather's blood – but fairer too, infused
with a pallor that verges on the winter sea. That would be the
influence of his grandmother, the naiad who bore Penelope
and thrust her into her father's arms with a merry cry of "She's
yours, byeeeee!"

Telemachus did not tell Penelope he was leaving Ithaca. He would not believe that she wept to see him go, though she did, red eyes and runny nose, an ugly kind of crying that only a mother would appreciate.

These are the two dreams most acceptable for a queen. There is of course a third dream that some of the more naughty poets might speak of, should things go terribly, terribly wrong. For in the crooked halls of the palace, in little back rooms built over a sheer cliff edge, in shacks dressed up as abodes worthy of a guest, and throughout the scattered villas, hostels and hovels of the town below, the suitors slumber in their drunken fugue, the young men of Greece all gathered to win the hand – and the crown – of the lady of Ithaca. Does she dream of these strutting fellows? The pious poet cries no, no! Not the wife of Odysseus, not her! Chaste contemplation of wiping her husband's furrowed brow, nothing more. The poet of the cheaper sort, though – why, he bends in and whispers: *it has been a long time to lie in a cold and empty bed* . . .

Penelope knows – why, even Penelope's dreams understand – that should she fail to be anything other than an immaculately chaste queen, the poets will absolutely sing of her as a whore.

And what does she actually dream of, this sleeping woman upon her lonely bed?

I lean into the tangle of her thoughts to catch the spinning spider's thread, and there, quivering in its net, she dreams of . . .

Shearing sheep.

In her dreams, the sheep sits, legs up, bum down, clasped between Penelope's knees as she cuts through its shaggy woollen coat, revealing the slender summer creature beneath. Her maids collect the wool and pile it up in baskets, and no sooner is the first animal finished, with its huge yellow eyes gazing up at her in confusion, than it's on to the next, and the next, and the next, and . . .

This is, perhaps, some metaphor?

But no. As I am a goddess of desire, let me state that there is no peculiarity or predilection in her mind, no amorous shepherds standing by nor thrilling undertone of thwarted passion. Penelope dreams of sheep because when all is said and done, she has a kingdom to run, and being unable to manage it on the traditional pastime of plunder, pillage and thievery that is the kingly sort of business, she has been forced to fall back on such lesser matters as agriculture, industry and trade. Thus, for every moment spent pining and gazing upon the stirring waters that keep from her both husband and child, there are twenty given over to matters of sewage, manure and the quality of the land, thirty-five to the business of goat-rearing, forty to the tin and amber that flow through her ports, twenty-three to the olive groves, twenty-two to household affairs, five to the beehives, fifteen to the various industries of weaving, sewing and beading practised by the women about her house, twelve to questions of timber and nearly fifty to fishing. The stench of fish upon the island is such that even my celestial perfume is tainted by it.

Alas, whatever dream posterity may claim Penelope dreams this night, it is sorely and soundly broken by the act of Priene climbing through her bedroom window.

How many wonderful encounters have begun this way! Be still, my little fluttering heart; and yet how disappointingly Priene declares her presence as the thin light of dawn slips across Ithaca's grey stones, with a resoundingly mundane "Hey! Wake up!"

Penelope wakes, and though her mind is still suffused with the smell of wool and the bleating of shaven animals, her hand goes at once to the knife she keeps always secreted beneath the woven blankets of her bed, drawing it from its sheath to thrust towards the shadowed darkness of the woman who has so rudely roused her from her slumbers.

Priene regards the weapon without fear or surprise, well beyond range of the queen's wandering arm, then, waiting a little moment longer for Penelope to blink some semblance of awareness into her eyes, blurts: "There's a Mycenaean ship hidden in the smugglers' cove at Phenera. Twenty-nine men, armed, ten women. This girl says she's Elektra, daughter of Agamemnon, gives me this ring. Shall we kill them all?"

Penelope is at the turning age of life where a woman has either found that sense of herself that makes any creature radiant, beautiful, a splendour to the heart and the eye; or in her flailing and thrashing about for identity has reverted fitfully to some younger time, painting her face with wax and lead and rubbing henna into her hair in the hope perhaps of buying a little more time to learn to love the changing visage she sees in the reflecting pool.

Penelope doesn't much gaze upon her own face. She is a cousin of Helen herself, distant enough to have none of that queen's fairness but near enough that her plainness is therefore remarkable when viewed side by side. When she was a young bride, she pushed her dark hair back from her brow and worried that her pale cheeks were not flushed enough for her husband's liking, or that the sun as it beat upon her shoulders might make her an unattractive lobster hue. Twenty years of chasing cattle across the rugged isles of her scattered kingdom, of sail and tackle and salt and dung, has dented this aspect of her nature, and not even – or perhaps especially – the arrival of the suitors can rekindle it. So it is that a profoundly dishevelled Penelope sits up in bed, knife waving through the empty air, her hair a broken nest about her skull, her eyes popping bright in a face smothered in grey, the aquatic tone of her skin somewhat chafed beneath the rough erosions of a summer sky, cheeks worn down by the wind from the sea, which qualities she attributes to womanly grief whenever she remembers to do so.

A pause while consciousness catches up with event, until at last she blurts: "Priene?"

Priene, captain of an army that should not exist, waits by the window, arms folded. She knows where the door is, and how to use stairs, Penelope is certain. Yet this warrior of the east took an early dislike to the secret ways of the palace, guarded by Penelope's maids, and prefers a more direct form of access to her sometime-employer, maybe-queen.

"The ring," she declares, dropping the fat gold band into Penelope's startled palm, utterly oblivious to the blade still waving loosely in the direction of her face.

Penelope blinks, lowers the dagger slowly, as if forgetting now that she held it, stares at the ring, holds it up, cranes to see it more closely against the thin dawn light, cannot get a good enough look at it, rises, a tangle of gown draping with a rather fetching looseness about her curling shoulders, walks to the window, holds the ring up again, studies it, takes in a sharp, fast breath.

This is the biggest reaction she will show for a while, and it startles even Priene, who draws a little nearer. "Well?" she asks. "Is it war?"

"You're sure it's Elektra?" Penelope replies. "Small, angry, prone to wearing ashes as a fashion statement?"

"Her men were Mycenaean." Priene has killed a lot of Mycenaeans; she knows the type. "And I don't see why anyone would lie about being the daughter of the cursed tyrant."

"Please tell me now if you killed any of them," sighs Penelope. "I would rather not be embarrassed by the revelation later." Her voice sits in a carefully judged place; she is hardly going to tell her captain of the isles not to slay armed men who unexpectedly land upon her shores – she will merely be disappointed if this action was taken imprudently.

"I was restrained," grumbles Priene. "Though the night is

21

dark and accidents happen when ships land in smugglers' coves. You know the ring?"

"Wake Eos and Autonoe," replies Penelope, folding the ring, still warm with Priene's touch, into her fist. "Tell them we need horses."

CHAPTER 4

>>>

O nce there was a wedding feast.
I have mixed feelings about weddings. On the one
hand, I blubber all the way through the ceremony, and though
my tears are always diamonds brimming in the perfect silvers
of my eyes, it is poor form for a guest to distract from the more
performative and important emotions of the groom, the bride
and of course, everyone's mothers-in-law. What can I say? I am
a very empathetic soul.

Now, some might tell you that a wedding is a celebration of
true love, of pious coming together and the weaving of a knot
for the ages, but let me assure you that the main function of a
feast of this nature is its unfailing ability to produce break-ups
among courting couples who had unto that moment thought
that perhaps they were on to something with each other. It's all
very well holding hands and sneaking a tender kiss when the
west wind blows across a midnight sea, but there is something
about observing the reality of commitment, not to mention the
profuse consumption of rich food and strong wine, to throw
a relationship into harsh relief. Thus no wedding is complete
without a corner beneath a tree hanging with heavy fruit where
young women sit and weep, abandoned by their lovers and their

dreams. Yet I would far rather they suffer a quick rejection from false desire than the slow heartache of a life lived without truest, purest love.

Weddings also contain within them two of the most dreadful, most excruciating processes to be endured: speeches given by old bores who are only interested in themselves, and dire small talk with one's relatives.

So it was that I found myself at the wedding of Peleus and Thetis, sitting at a table with Hera and Athena.

Hera, goddess of queens and mothers. She has in recent months been accused by her husband, Zeus, of meddling in mortal matters – always meddling, he says, always interfering in the realms of men! Men, specifically, are out of bounds to her. She may dally with women, with mothers, with lesser creatures such as they to her heart's content – no one will notice or care. It is the *men* that Zeus objects to. Women who seek to interfere in the business of a man always make things worse, and Hera, as the goddess who stands above all of her sex, must take this to heart. Whether she wishes to or no.

Her beauty is a diminished, beaten-upon thing. To please her husband she must be radiant, glorious, a creature of the highest divinity. But if she shines too brightly, Zeus cries out that she is a harlot, a hussy, a whore – just like Aphrodite, indeed. He does not know where this line is, between one whose beauty is merely pleasing and one whose beauty is an unacceptable fanfare, but he absolutely knows it when he sees it, and so today Hera's hair is too lustrous, tomorrow too flat. Today her lips smile too brightly, tomorrow she has a frown that makes her look like an ageing misery. Yesterday her bosom was too exposed, grotesque. Now she is frigid, a barren wife whose only beloved child is my beautiful Hephaestus, who the others call a disfigured fool.

So it is in this manner that Hera's beauty fades, plucked from her body by others' hands, carved from her flesh one cut at a time, leaving only a painted statue behind. There was a time when all this was not so – a time when she rebelled against Zeus himself – but he bound her in chains after Thetis, mother of Achilles, exposed her plans. Hera's invitation to the wedding of the nymph who betrayed her was therefore, one might say, something of an imposition.

To say that the conversation did not flow freely from Mother Hera sitting to my left-hand side would be akin to suggesting that a man who has had his parts bathed in ice while the principles of mummification are explained to him might not be feeling the rising fire of sensual passion. True, the blossom billowed from the trees and the fair grass was mottled with perfumed dew and all things were as perfect as can be in the garden of the Hesperides, but that was absolutely not going to dent Hera's foul, simmering mood.

What then of the conversation to my right hand?

Alas, here there was also a lack of entertainment, for there sat Athena, goddess of war and wisdom. It being a wedding, she had left her breastplate and shield on Olympus, but her sword was slung across the back of her chair where other women might have draped a becoming shawl. She picked at the food that was served her, eating precisely enough to show courtesy to the host and not a morsel more, for she too had very little time for Thetis. Strangers beholding her might not know this, for she was always good at a polite "may your children bring you glory in their victories" and so forth, but as Zeus droned through a self-congratulatory speech, I glanced into my cousin Athena's eyes and saw only the gleam of the blade set above the smile of the shark.

"Well, isn't this lovely?" I opined, and because a table of three women sitting in sullen silence at a wedding will ruin the mood for everyone, I burbled about nothing much and this and that, resolving that should Hera and Athena wish to either silence me or join in, they were perfectly capable of exercising agency in that regard. I also enjoyed the liberty to speak with – I should more honestly say *at* – my female family knowing that the men paid us no regard, for at the feasts on Olympus I can hardly open my mouth without Zeus snorting at the slightest thing I say as though it were lewd, or Hermes making a poor joke about genitalia.

Even so, with the best will in the world, I must say the whole wedding feast was getting really rather unbearable by the time Eris played her little trick. The centaurs were deep in their cups and nearing the point of inebriation where everyone agreed it would be wisest that the bride was removed before conversations could begin about "testing" – let alone "proving" – anyone's manliness on the nearby females, and Ares had summoned his favourite bull and was blathering on about its steaming rump or some such. I do enjoy a bit of Ares every now and then. My poor darling husband Hephaestus has spent so long being assured that he is half a man, worthless, diminutive and fit only for mockery, that he now believes it unto himself, and though I have tried to encourage him to have faith in his romantic and sensual prowess, whenever he does come to my side, he covers my eyes with his hands as if too ashamed to have me gaze upon him while he performs the act, and cries out that I am disgusting whenever I touch him in those tender ways a lover can. I understand that it is not I myself who am disgusting. He is disgusted by himself, and so he is disgusted by one who could see him as beautiful. And so it goes.

Given those circumstances, fifteen minutes of Ares after dinner is if nothing else a different sensual experience to stimulate the senses, even though it can get a little tedious being with a man who will insist vocally that he has nothing to prove, and thus has to spend a great deal of time proving himself in ever more hasty and thrusting ways. Gracious, I once tried to say, it isn't a race! If he heard me, he pretended he didn't.

Well then, this was the situation, and my goodness it was all getting rather loud. Athena, Hera and myself were heading towards the golden gates that frame the blessed garden of the Hesperides with a "thank you lovely evening goodnight" – leaving a wedding always takes an age – when Eris, goddess of discord, lobbed her golden apple through the door. Personally I think Eris is an absolute treat at any wedding, especially when the dancing gets going, but Thetis, the smug little prude, had refused to invite her. Well whoops to her, and whoosh goes the golden apple, with "to the fairest" written on its glistening flesh, and bump it goes against the sandal of Athena, and "oh dear" say our eyes as the three of us look from it to each other, and before you could mutter "best not to get involved, darling", Hermes, the vapid boy-child of the assembly, has grabbed it and is holding it up for all to see.

"Ho ho ho!" says he, or words to that effect. "For the fairest! Who might that be?"

Now naturally, and of course, the fairest is me. But I will concede that the way Hera straightened her back was not merely the resilience of a queen, but the defiance of a survivor, of one who has been conquered and conquered and conquered again and will yet still rise. And Athena, lady of bronze and ice, who gave the olive tree to her people and who alone besides Zeus can wield the thunder and the lightning, has in the corner of her eye a power and a presence that the Titans themselves would quake at. And I? Even Zeus fears me, for my power is the greatest of them all, the maker and unmaker of the broken heart, the bringer of desire, the lady of love.

We should all have demurred. Charmingly, delightfully, we should have held hands and said no, but you, fair cousin – oh no, but you, my good sister! It would have been very fetching, especially at a wedding. We could have made it cutting, witty, barbed, but also delightful, an intimate thing that no man could ever understand. Instead we stood dumb an instant too long, and so Zeus, turning his attentions briefly from a quavering naiad, exclaimed, "Who indeed? We must decide!"

At once, of course, everyone began insisting that only Zeus could judge, being the king of the gods, but he, with a sparkle in his eye, declined, saying he would of course have to choose Hera, being his wife, and thus was far too prejudiced in the matter, renowned arbiter of moderation that he is. No no no, they needed an independent adjudicator, someone who was entirely separate from matters of the celestial and the kinship of the divine. You over there – the nice young man who was complimenting Ares' bull – you pick one!

At my side, I felt Athena stiffen like her spear. I heard a little breath from Hera; but the old queen showed no more, did not bend, did not break as this mortal boy, barely more than a child, stepped forward.

He should have begged. He should have cowered. He should have wept and grovelled for having the temerity to look a goddess up and down, let alone in the eye. He should have kissed our feet. Instead, this petty mortal walked from one to the other and inspected us like prize sheep, while the centaurs broke from their rutting to applaud and the guests cheered and bellowed out their personal opinions and advice.

Did I love Paris then?

Not really. I have seen enough men who will tell a woman "you are not really my type" in an attempt to trick that woman into prostrating herself before him, playing upon the fear of rejection to conquer and control her. There is a power in that arrogance, a strength to it that is fascinating, even to the gods – but only ever for a little, little while.

Yet here was some small redemption for Paris, some glimmer

of the charms that were to go some way to redeem him to me, to keep him mildly interesting to my fair eye. For having made a show of examining us all, he stepped back, bowed, and with a flourish turned to the crowd. "They are all too fair, too majestic, too alike in wonder. I cannot choose between such creatures of perfection!"

I felt Hera relax a hair next to me, and I too was ready to clap the boy on the shoulder and congratulate him on not having made himself an absolute fool. But Athena remained stiff and frozen, fingers clenched at her sides as if she would grasp a blade, and that should have warned me.

"Cannot choose?" Zeus mused. "Then clearly you have not seen enough of them!"

The menfolk understood before we did what this might entail, for they roared their approval and laughed and clapped and said it was the best idea ever. What sport, what an absolutely brilliant notion!

"No, I . . . " Hera began, but the roar of voices drowned her out, and she turned her face to the wind before any could see the tears prickle across her beautiful burning eyes. Athena's breath was fast and shallow, but she did not speak, did not grace these men with her voice, sanctify their barbarities with anything but what must be done.

Then Hermes guided us, Paris carried upon his back, to the sacred spring that rises at the base of Mount Ida, and with his little piggy eyes glistening in his puggish face invited us to strip. Paris hung somewhat back, doing his best to be if not discreet then at least mildly respectful, Zeus beside him, a hand upon his shoulder. The moon was full overhead, blotting out the watchful stars, the water of the pool a perfect shimmer of skin-scintillating cool on a warm evening, as all the evenings are warm when three goddesses bathe beneath the mountain's shadow.

I called out to my blessed assistants, the ladies of the seasons and joy. They came at once, unpinned my hair, eased my gown back from my shoulders, took the golden clasp from about my neck, rested the bangles from my wrists and ankles on cushions of woven silver and silk, and stood back as I descended into the pool. The water shivered at my touch, as if reflecting the pleasure of my flesh. I watched the curve of my leg as I broke through the surface, let the shock of the coolness upon my navel run all the way up my arching neck and back through the bend of my skull, then with another little step allowed myself to sink away from the edge and into the night-kissed waters themselves.

Behind me, I heard the breathing of Paris, faster than he knew, inaudible to any but divine ears. And more than that, I felt his blood, the hotness of his skin, the rousing of his parts and knew that he blamed me for this, thought it was in some way my magic, my divinity that made him this way, instead of a piece of his humanity stirring from within.

So be it – the water was beautiful and so was I. I drifted a little, careful to keep my hair swirled about me so that it might be a halo of gold, rather than tangle most unfortunately across my brow – a fetching look only when one emerges from the water, where hopefully another waits who will delight in pushing one's damp curls back from one's eyes. Then I looked back to shore.

Hera and Athena both still stood there, fully garbed. Hera's face was near crimson, her lips slightly parted as if she was not sure she could hold back breath, voice, cry, scream. Athena was the wintry opposite, shivering as if blasted by the cold wind, eyes pressed narrow against the storm. I reached out to them with both my hands, and smiled.

Come, sisters, I whispered in the voice only women can hear.
Forget the eyes of men.
You are not whatever it is you think they see.

30

Come.

Come, my glorious ladies, goddesses of fire and ice.

You are beautiful. I love you both.

They did not move. I do not to this day even know if they could hear me, so far was tenderness barred from them.

I thought I heard Zeus stifle a chuckle, but his eyes were all hunger. Not for me – he averted his gaze from me, for I was too beautiful, too powerful even for him. His greatness was nothing before mine, while the moon kissed my body and the spring of Ida washed against my crystal skin. Flesh may be stolen, savagely stripped and conquered with blood and cruelty, but love was beyond even his power to take.

Nor did he look upon his wife, whose nudity was nothing more nor less to him than another manifestation of his power, and a little one at that. There was no part of her he had not derided before, no piece of her he could not mock even when he lay upon her in the marriage bed. Rather, he gazed upon Athena, upon the lines of her stiff, straight robe, which always so well masked the sensuous curves of her breasts and buttocks. Of all the creatures in all the worlds, only two there are I cannot influence with my great divinity – Athena and Artemis, the chaste goddesses, those who kill rather than yield to desire. Zeus tried to rape Athena once, and she showed him that day why she was a goddess of war as well as wisdom. Well, he would never have another chance to take her again, but he would certainly make her pay for her sanctity, make her suffer for not being entirely his.

Again I reached to them; again extended my arms.

My sisters, I called. *My lovely ones. My fairest ladies. They do not own us with their eyes. Your beauty is yours, and yours alone. Come, my lovely ones, my sisters, my fairest queens. You are beautiful.*

It was Hera who moved, not towards me, but turning fast on the spot and fixing Paris with the full force of her gaze. I felt her

31

power stir, often so hidden, so shadowed, now blazing with a tiny taste of the great queen she had been, the goddess of earth and fire set above them all. *"Choose me,"* she roared, *"and I will make you a king of men!"*

Immediately Athena spun, and fixing Paris with the same look that stood just a blink between divinity and death, thundered: *"Choose me, and you will be the wisest man upon this earth!"*

As Paris reeled from the force of two divine interventions, I splashed a little this way and that, flicked droplets up onto my chest and watched how they wriggled back down to the surface of the water, how they mingled and divided upon my skin. It took me a moment to realise that the young Trojan was gazing my way, expectant, waiting. That was when I became absolutely convinced he would be trouble, but what can I say? Everyone seemed to be waiting for something, all eyes upon me – and not just in their usual way.

"Fine," I breathed into the waiting ears of destiny. *"Pick me, and I will give you the most beautiful woman who ever lived."*

Now. With the wisdom of hindsight, I will admit that there is a lot about this sentiment that one might consider a bit of an error of judgement. Things that with just a hair more consideration, I think I should really have seen we'd all come to regret. But what can I say? In the moment there just seemed to be a bit of an expectation, and well, one doesn't want to disappoint.

"Her," Paris said, levelling a mortal finger towards my celestial sculling form. "I pick her."

And so began the journey to the war that would unmake the world.

CHAPTER 5

>>

D awn over Ithaca.
      I suppose it is a perfectly pleasing affair, if you like that
sort of thing. The sea is so much greater than the land that we
hardly need speak of the stretching shadows from the battered
trees or the gentle warming of cruel, jagged rocks. Rather we
can talk of silvered mirage and that golden line in the east where
sea and sky become one, so bright that even the gods shield their
eyes from its illumination. Gulls rouse themselves in spinning
flocks and the midnight buds unseal themselves from their tight-
fisted knots, the dawn perfume rising like woman's delight.

   For my part, I prefer the dawn across Corinth, where the
early light may drift through billowing gauze to spill its golden
touch upon the upturned backside of a waking lover or two;
where the warmth of the day mingles most pleasingly with
the gentle stirring of the inland sea to goosebump flesh still
warm from an evening of pleasing exertions. There are few
such matters in Ithaca, for the men of the isles sailed away some
twenty years ago to Troy, and not one of them has returned.
The widows waited as long as they could, while their daughters
grew old and loveless, and in time weariness became habit and
survival became mundane. Not for these women the caress of

a man's tender fingers down their spine to rouse them with the calling of the morning birds; rather the chopping of wood and the hauling in of nets, the catching of crabs and the turning of the night soil greets the ladies of the isle. Of the men who stir at dawn's rosy touch, there are but a few elders left – men like Aegyptius and Medon, councillors of Odysseus too old – or too conveniently enfeebled before their time – to sail to Troy. Of the younger sort, not a native son who is not barely out of his boyhood; and the rowdy suitors who snuffle and snort in drunken slumber around Penelope's halls are touched with as many youthful pimples as manly beards.

And yet, if I am fair, let us not entirely presume that the western isles are without their dawn pleasures. On Zakynthos, the smell of yellow flowers may brush the nose of a maid whose breath tangles with that of another girl who never knew her father's name as they rouse themselves from their straw-laden bed. Or above the rich ports of Hyrie, a sailor from Crete kisses his lover tenderly and breathes: *I will return*, and thinks he means it, poor lamb, until the harshness of Poseidon's seas and the distance between them brings a certain ending to their tale.

Pray to me, I whisper in the ears of slumbering Antinous and lazy Eurymachus as I drift across the palace halls, the wine still sticky on the suitors' parted lips. *Pray to me*, I murmur to brave Amphinomous and foolish Leiodes, *for I am the one who gave fair Helen to Paris; it was I, not Zeus, who brought about the end of the age of heroes. Ajax, Penthesilea, Priam, Patroclus, Achilles and Hector – they died for me, so pray. Pray to love.*

The suitors do not stir. Their hearts are fled far from divinity, even a power as potent as mine. Their fathers sailed to Troy and they were raised by mothers. What kind of men will they be, they ask, when they have only women to teach them the blade?

I scatter rosy delights with the flick of my wrist across the minds of those still dreaming, that when they wake their hearts are full of longing that pleases, and yearning too that aches a little on the edges of their souls.

Then I must be off, following four horses as they slip from the palace of Odysseus by the rising light and gallop north, towards the ashes of Phenera and the unwelcome vessel that waits upon their shore.

Penelope rides with Priene and two of her maids, trusted Eos and light-laughing Autonoe, though no one laughs now. The night hid the archers who huddled in the dark above Phenera, but as day rises, they too must retreat, Priene's hidden guardian women of the night slipping back to the farms and fishing huts they call home, and which they will fight to defend. Their departure is not noted, as their arrival was not either. The men who guard the Mycenaean boat stand anxious, spears in hand, at Penelope's approach.

She takes her time dismounting; her time surveying the scene, before, with a polite nod to the men who await her, declares: "I am Penelope, wife of Odysseus, queen of Ithaca." This latter title must follow the first – for what is a queen, in this day and age? Fair Helen, in whose name died the last of the heroes? Or murderous Clytemnestra, who took being queen a little too much to heart and forgot that she was a woman first? Penelope has taken note of both these lessons – she is a wife, maybe a widow, who happens through the coincidence of these states to also be a queen. "And you," she adds, "appear to have come unbidden yet armed to my dear husband's isles."

In another woman's voice, this could be a fawning declaration of anxiety, a dread enquiry into terrible things yet to come. But an arrow still quivers in the wall near the soldiers' heads, and so the men scurry to fetch their captain from within the shadowed bowels of the ship – shadows that even I shudder to disturb – and out comes Pylades, long hair really rather charmingly stirred by the sea, and Elektra, less charming in all things.

When last they came to these islands, it was with an escort of many vessels, fanfare and pomp. They departed with the body of Clytemnestra, a triumphant monument to their endeavours, all of Greece hailing their deed and name. Yet what do we see now? A ragtag crow and her salt-scarred escort, hidden in a smugglers' cove? You do not need a soothsayer to read the innards of a calf to see that something here bodes ill.

"Cousin," Elektra calls, before Penelope has a chance to make her feelings on all this known. "I am grateful you came so quickly, and with such ... discretion."

Elektra's eyes move from Penelope to Eos and Autonoe, their faces hidden beneath the accustomed veils of the palace maids. None of them are appropriately attired to meet a queen, but I think their hasty garb and quick departure adds a certain dishevelled authenticity to the whole affair, a comely spontaneous-tumble-in-the-barn sensibility that is really rather fetching, seen in the right light. Elektra does not look at Priene. A surfeit of knives can discourage contemplation.

"My honoured cousin," Penelope replies, walking quickly through the Mycenaean men, who part as beetles before the spider as the women approach beneath the shadow of the ship. "I would say that you are welcome to Ithaca, but traditionally a princess of your nobility is greeted with triumphant drums, speeches and a great amount of cooking. So I have to wonder – why am I welcoming you to this plucked place of crows; why a message sent with this?" She unfolds her fist and there is the ring, gripped so tight it has left its mark on her palm, the blood fled to leave just the hollow burning of clenched gold. It is Clytemnestra's ring, of course – Elektra will never wear it, accounts it practically cursed, and knows also the value of cursed things.

As Penelope draws near to Elektra, the younger woman does something that is entirely unexpected.

She darts towards her cousin, and with a sudden ferocity that startles even Penelope, clasps both the queen's hands between her own. She holds them tight as if she has never before felt such human warmth through her icy flesh, and for a moment it seems she might even embrace Penelope, might throw her arms around her and hold on to her tight, as an orphan might cleave unto a mother, long lost. Such an act would be inexplicable, astounding. The last time Elektra held that tight to any living creature that was not her horse, she was seven years old, and her mother was taking her little sister Iphigenia to see their father on the sacred cliffs above the sea, from which trip only the mother would return. She has not known the comfort of a familial embrace since that day, and were the moment longer and I a more maternal sort, I might have gently touched her on the shoulder and bade her cling to Penelope and weep, as only the lost may.

She does not, and the moment passes, and at once releasing the grasp about her cousin's hand as if suddenly burned, Elektra draws back, stands up straight and proclaims: "I need you to see."

There is very little room within the innards of the Mycenaean ship. What space there is has been packed with water and salted fish, with timber to repair a broken mast or shattered beam, with amphorae of wine and chests of cloth and copper to trade. The darkness is a thin, slotted thing, broken only by the little lines of light that crawl through the floor above, or down the open hatch. There are no fires allowed below; its occupants must huddle in darkness, with only the pounding of the sea and the scurrying of the rats for company.

Oh, but more, how much more than rats lurks within, for I see the three women that mortal eyes cannot perceive, hear the leather of their wings as they shift and stir at my divine approach, see their bloody eyes glowing in the deepest dark of the further shadow of the ship, in that patch of icy cold where no mortal goes, though they themselves know not why.

I would not go near these three hidden hags for even the love of mighty Ares, yet Penelope follows Elektra into the belly of the ship oblivious to the cruel profanity that lurks below, and so I follow too, doing my best to ignore the laughter of the foul ones whose fetid touch is rotting even the newest timbers of the ship from within.

One more creature lurks below – a man, visible to mortal eyes though barely, for he is so swathed in rancid cloth and shadow that Penelope must catch herself a long moment while her eyes adjust to the gloom before she can pick him out in the dark. The blood of Clytemnestra, born as it was from a touch of divinity, was always stronger than the cursed lineage of Agamemnon. Thus in Orestes one may see his mother's dark hair, flecked only a little with a reddish hue from his father; also his mother's full lips, brown eyes so dark they are inclined to char, the skinniness of a woman about his shoulder; and of his father, merely some stiffness in the spine, hooked nose and proud, jutting chin with which he would have battered down the very gates of Troy. He is young enough that he should be busy wooing queens for his new kingdom, and yet old enough that his wooing should be sophisticated and charming, studied in the excellence not merely of his own worth, but the worth of she he would entice.

Alas, Orestes has not wooed a creature of any degree for many, many years, and nor do I think it likely he shall ever woo again.

Instead, curled up in his own rancorous filth, hands clinging to the foul blanket twined about his body, his eyes spin wild into the darkness and spittle foams at his mouth as he grunts and groans and rocks and shudders. Now he howls like an injured pup. Now he turns his face away from even the meagre trickled light of day, and rocks and tries to beat his head against the wall. Now he gibbers and the words are a tangled mess that no one can unpick – though perhaps Elektra hears a word repeated, *Mother, Mother, Mother* – and now he grinds his teeth so hard I fear they will break in his jaw, swallowed bone and blood and flecks of gum.

There he is.

Orestes, son of Agamemnon, king of kings, the mighty lord of Mycenae, nephew of Menelaus, killer of his own mother.

There the fuck he is, pissing himself in some hidden corner of a secret ship.

Elektra stands at the foot of the steep, splintering steps that lead to the dark, as if she dare not go any further within, her back turned to the invisible hags on whom, whether they know it or not, all mortals will turn their backs in time.

Penelope approaches a little closer, mouth agape, to study her cousin, who seems for a moment to see her, seems for a moment to be almost glad, then closes his red-rimmed eyes to shriek again, "Mother!" or perhaps not Mother, perhaps murder, perhaps madness, perhaps just a protracted shriek that began and ended around a sound of puckered lip and tip-of-the-tongue. His cry is loud enough to stop Penelope in her tracks, to make her recoil a few paces, hand reaching out to steady herself against the cross-beamed solidity of the ship.

"How long has he been like this?" she demands at last.

"Nearly three moons," Elektra replies. "It comes and goes from him in fits and starts – but it is getting worse."

Slowly Penelope nods. There are a great many questions – and a great many unwelcome conclusions that could be arrived at. None of them are good. There is not a single outcome right now that she enjoys considering. Instead she goes with practical matters. "Who knows you're here?"

"Only the people on this ship. I told no one where we sailed."

"And in Mycenae? Do the people know that your brother is ... like this?" Elektra does not answer, which is a fluent enough reply. Penelope pulls back a sigh. It is too early in the morning for matters such as these. "Menelaus?" she asks at last, eyes half closed against the visions of disaster unfolding before her imagination. "Does he know?"

"My uncle has spies everywhere."

Now finally Penelope turns her gaze from contemplation of the young, shivering man, fully to Elektra. "Cousin," she murmurs, "what thrice-cursed new disaster have you brought upon me now?"

Elektra learned how to glare like a queen from her mother, who accounted herself the greatest woman in all the lands. She would not admit to having acquired such a skill from one she believes herself to hate, but now, for almost the first time, it falters, and she turns her head down, before raising it again, a child, barely more than a girl, afraid. "My uncle cannot find Orestes in this condition. He will use it to take Mycenae for himself. He will be ... I do not think you or I would enjoy his rule."

When the poets speak of this moment – and they will not – I believe they would depict the two women at once joining in a weeping embrace, united by grief and terror for the men they love. Oh my poor brother, might wail Elektra; and oh dear cousin, might weep Penelope.

What the poets will not report is that other moment – that fleeting yet profound moment – where Penelope contemplates the alternative. For a second her mind races back to the palace, and she is summoning Ourania, that secretive former maid who sometimes goes about business for the queen around the western seas, and she is sending word to Menelaus to come at once to these islands. "Oh protect me, good friend of my husband!" she is crying out, as the great warrior of Troy lands upon her shores. "For Orestes is mad!"

Menelaus likes it when women cry at his feet while begging for protection. Their tears help fill the leaking hollows of his fractured soul. This is something Penelope is going to keep in mind through much of what is to come.

Yet for now, the queen of Ithaca will keep her options open. She lets out a quick breath, straightens up, nearly hits her head on the confinement of the timbers, stoops again, and in a busy, brisk voice begins to command. "How many souls are there upon this ship? Thirty, forty?"

"Near forty. But we left Mycenae with over two hundred."

"Where are the others now?"

"They took shelter at a shrine to Aphrodite, a day's march from Calydon. We let it be known that my brother was travelling to the temples of all the gods to ask their blessings for his reign."

"Good. If – or when – your brother is found here, that will be our story. There are no shrines on Ithaca worth his time, but he can be visiting the place where his mother perished to give thanks to Athena. Everyone likes it when people give thanks to Athena on Ithaca. Do you trust the captain of the ship?"

"I trust no one. But Pylades is . . . close to my brother."

"Fine. He will take the ship and all the finery you can muster and sail to port." Elektra opens her mouth to object, but Penelope cuts her off. Elektra has not had anyone cut her off since her mother, and it is a feeling of both indignity and strange comfort for her. "We cannot hide a whole ship of Mycenaeans in this place. They will be found. Better that they are discovered on our terms. Pylades is . . . an ambassador. A goodwill friend. Sent by Orestes to show his unwavering support for myself and my son. If we are lucky, that little lie may even keep the suitors meek for a few days – that'll be something."

"What about my brother?" murmurs Elektra. And then softer, the fatigue the only thing keeping her voice from the edge of a whine: "What about me?"

"Your brother cannot be seen at my palace in this condition. Ships sail from Ithaca all the time; word would spread in an instant. We must hide him."

"Where?"

Penelope stares long at the twitching, groaning king, before closing her eyes to the inevitability of this outcome. "I have a place. How many of your maids and servants do you require?"

"None."

This surprises even Penelope. "That is wise, although I do not have many I can send to wait on you – not without attracting the interest of the suitors."

"I came to this place especially to keep my brother far away from the ones who know him."

Penelope learned at a very young age not to show surprise, nor let her mouth hang agape too rudely. Her adopted mother would put two fingers beneath her jaw whenever it was flapping and gently ease it shut with a murmur of "A queen shows her teeth only to smile or to bite, dear." Instead, she brushes down the front of her faded gown, presses her left hand over her right across her belly, turns her head up and a little to the side as if she can see through the timbers of the ship to the far-off heavens themselves, before at last proclaiming: "Well then, cousin. I suppose I must welcome you and your brother to Ithaca."

In the shadows of the ship, the three hags laugh and clap their taloned hands together, and Penelope seems to feel the chill of their foul merriment brush through her like the first wind of winter, for she unclasps her hands and instead draws her arms a little tighter about her. Elektra half closes her eyes, for she, even she who learned in the empty palaces of Mycenae how to ignore the cold and the laughter of her enemies, cannot quite shut out the mockery of the hidden ones who lurk in bloody dark at her back. I would reach out to her, comfort her with a golden caress of my inner light, but I shine low in this place, my eyes turned

42

from the hags, my divine radiance dimmed to invisibility in the cramped confines of this wretched place.

Orestes, though – Orestes sees. At the laughter of the cursed women, he raises his head, then lifts his hand to point, finger uncurled as Zeus might smite with his thunderbolt, to accuse his accusers, and now he beholds them, and he screams and screams and screams until Elektra calls Pylades, who helps drag him, still shrieking in his terror, up into the light of day.

The three women, the Furies, blood of lava and wings of the bat, eyes of blood and fingers clawed, dance together in delight at their sport, before turning upwards and, with a single beating of their blackened wings, rising through the boat itself and into the sky high above, to spin tempests and ebony clouds above Orestes' head. Called by the shedding of a mother's blood – brought up from the pits of the earth by the madness of the son, perhaps – the Furies are in no hurry to tear their prey apart. They will watch and they will wait and they will howl in their merry games at Orestes in his madness. They will let him linger as his sister weeps, they will let him piss himself in the halls of kings and drool in Menelaus's arms, and only then, only when there is nothing left of the king of Mycenae save hollow insanity and broken pride, will they finally eat his flesh.

I watch them, and do not intervene. The ancient Erinyes were born of earth long before the Olympians tamed the skies. Even Zeus himself thinks twice before whispering their name to the thunder. There are things that can be done, of course – bargains to be struck – but the price is always high, and though my curiosity is piqued, the time is not right.

Not yet.

CHAPTER 6

>>

A Mycenaean ship sets sail from a hidden cove in Ithaca, to make its reappearance in more pompous state at the harbour of the city around the nose of the isle. Pylades splutters when told the plan.

"I must be near Orestes! He is my brother!"

Pylades has a heart that beats so large and loud in his chest he sometimes can hear nothing else. Eos, though she is small, knows how to fill a space with her presence, and now she faces up to the fuming Mycenaean and exclaims: "We will keep your brother safe; we know how to protect the king."

"Protect? With your blessings of Artemis and your women's prayers? I was with him when he killed Aegisthus, I have been by his side since Athens, since he was just a boy. I will—"

"Pylades!" It is Elektra's voice that settles it, and by Elektra's command that he finally obeys. "Your loyalty is valiant, but misplaced. I will tend to my brother now."

For a moment they lock eyes, the warrior and the princess, and Eos stands a little back lest the furnace of their gazes scorch her gown. But it is Pylades who bends first, turning his back – so rude! – on his master's sister and storming towards the prow of the ship to join with the really rather lovely sight of men with calves and shoulders exercising both as they push the vessel back into the choppy waters of the bay.

Elektra turns away, and it is only Eos who sees her shudder.

The chief of Elektra's maids, Rhene, puts a hand on the princess's shoulder. It is a touch that from anyone else would be immediately punished. But Rhene was a child when Elektra was too, a few years older but still near enough in age to have something of a companionship about her. She will never of course be a friend – slaves are not friends with their mistresses – but neither will she be whipped for showing the slightest glimmer of a caring heart.

"Let me come," she murmurs. "I . . . understand if you do not want me near your brother, but you . . . you have . . ."

Rhene is on the verge of saying something unforgivable. She is perhaps about to suggest that Elektra has needs, feels pain, yearns for company, has vulnerability within her soul. If she says any of this, Elektra will break, which is unforgivable; and yet how deeply she yearns to hear these words spoken from another's lips.

Rhene hesitates. Rhene knows all of this without having put it in any conscious form of words. She seals her lips and says no more.

Elektra squeezes her hand, and nods once. "Watch Pylades," she whispers in the maid's ear. "Watch him well."

Rhene steps away from her mistress's side, returning to the ship and her duty, and does not look back, and does not let Pylades see that she is watching.

As the proud ship returns again to the water, an Ithacan maid rides to the temple of Artemis in its sacred grove away from the beating of Poseidon's sea. The maid's name is Autonoe, and when she was a child she considered running away, yearned for power, freedom and the worship of men. Then she learned that the only freedom the free women of the isles had was to be

45

wed, or piously abstinent and shunned for it, and so she stayed in Penelope's service, where there was, she found to her delight, a different kind of power to be wielded in the dusty halls of the palace.

As a young woman, men tried to own her. They saw her beauty, the brightness in her eyes, and they wanted it for themselves. She was told to be flattered by their attention; informed how lucky she was to be a thing possessed. But when the reality of what possession meant was shown to her, she nearly gouged out the eyes of that foolish man who tried to force himself upon her, and was thus judged broken and beyond repair. An un-woman; a barren, wasted thing. Even her fellow maids clicked their tongues in the roofs of their mouths and said she was wrong to fight, for of course, if Autonoe refused to be silent in her suffering, then what worth was the suffering of all those beaten mothers who had gone before?

Autonoe has very little interest in men these days. Looking back on her life, she is pretty confident she never had much interest in them to begin with – it was just the thing that everyone expected, that the world at large seemed to require. She's not averse to the idea if someone came along who made her feel warm inside, but until that most unlikely of days, there are plenty of other ways to find power in pleasure. And that's what pleasure means to Autonoe, of course. The power to control when she experiences ecstasy. The power to choose her own delights. The power to choose to be delighted, in her own way, at her own time, with whomsoever she pleases. No matter what else the world may give or take away, this will always still be hers. She has sworn it.

Now Autonoe rides to the temple of Artemis. She rides like a man, bent low over her horse, enjoys the secrets she carries on her tongue, the wind in her hair, the responsibilities that are hers to honour or betray. She wishes her father could see her now, an unsupervised woman who laughs as she says no. She thinks he would be appalled, and she revels in it, all the way to the temple doors.

Artemis's sacred shrine lies deep in the scrubby woods of Ithaca. There have been many odd "sacred feasts" held at this place in recent years. Many women used to chopping their own firewood, digging their own wells, protecting their sheep from wolves, skinning their own bears – these are the ladies most frequently seen at the huntress's porch, bows in hand and axes by their side, eyes of stone fixed upon the cowering gaze of any stranger who dare scamper into their midst. The men who visit Ithaca's ports mutter among themselves at this strange isle of widows and unwed wives, and conclude that it is best not to enquire too deeply into their private, personal beliefs.

The priestess of the temple is called Anaitis, and she has just the most fabulous line in earthy, hunky sexiness that you will ever see. My goodness, if ever there was a woman for caressing in a field of barley it is her – but alas, she does not see herself in that way, for as Autonoe approaches the lady with autumn hair who stands in the porch of the shrine, Anaitis folds her arms and tuts: "What's happened now?"

Away from the temple, from Anaitis and Autonoe and their shared whispered secrets, four travellers with two horses trudge east across the island in silence. Elektra rides Penelope's horse. She didn't ask whether this was apt, since she is the daughter of Agamemnon and taking other people's horses is practically the family business. But she is learning – oh, she is learning – for not a second after bum hit saddle it occurred to her that she was technically performing a gross violation of her role as a guest, and such a vulnerable guest too. The next stage in her redemption would be to splutter an apology, to beg forgiveness for this transgression, but though Elektra is doing much better at thinking about the needs of others than is traditional in her family, she hasn't quite made it far enough in her personal journey to ever say sorry. So instead, awkward, frozen and stiff she rides, mortified, stubborn, afraid and small.

Orestes is bundled onto the back of Eos's steed. He is just about capable of holding the pommel by himself, but Eos has positioned herself near enough to his side that should he fall, she could definitely be seen to make an effort to catch him, while also being far enough away that she can leap to safety and thus avoid a dangerous concussion. In this way, the maid remains entirely consistent and true to her nature, for she has studied her mistress for many years, drinking in hungrily every aspect of Penelope's rule, and knows now how to be not quite one thing nor another, pleasing no one entirely nor angering anyone too far. Her little square body is strong from days walking between groves of olives or fields of sheep; her fingers are worn and quick – she is Penelope's favourite weaver of hair, even though she's not particularly good at it. Several other maids – Euracleia in particular – have offered to teach Eos many extraordinary ways of weaving hair quickly and well, but she has always politely declined. The slow comb, the long, careful winding as they talk of secret things – this is more important to both mistress and maid than the final result on Penelope's head. Intimate things and whispered truths are more arousing to Eos than any brush of finger down her spine. Foolish suitors think she is cold, unstirred by their cavorting. If only they knew how she might moan with pleasure at the murmur of some deepest, darkest secret.

These travellers now follow a thin, grubby path picked out with biting stones and busy thorns, with shrubs that catch at trailing gowns and morning insects fat and curious that cling to nostril and hair, inland and up, climbing away from the sea towards a little farmhouse far from temple or shrine. A meagre olive grove runs behind it on a low rump of sloping land, and there are a few pigs stirring in the yard, fat and pale, black-spotted and curly-tailed. Some signs of ongoing renovation are still apparent, from a freshly built high wall more suited to a fortress than a farm, to new clay tiles upon the roof and the trappings of a wooden gate, not yet suspended from its hinges but rather sitting on the ground, waiting for the working women to come and complete their labours.

In the courtyard beyond the would-be barrier to entrance, an old woman stands by a well, one bucket already filled by her feet, another vanished into the black interior. She starts back, more annoyed than afraid, as Elektra rides within, opens her mouth to cry out something rude, something thoroughly disrespectful, then stops when Penelope enters the yard, and nearly rolls her eyes.

"Penelope's here!" she hollers to the dusky interior of the farm, and this duty done, goes back to her labours about the well.

The smile on Penelope's face is the thin lip of the snake that startles when it gapes and reveals its fang, her eyes barely wider in their contemplation of this introduction. Yet someone stirs within the farm, a man pushing back a freshly hung door of fine timber from the northern isles, and at once Penelope stands a little straighter, clasps her hands, forces her chin down and her eyes up in polite deference to the old man who emerges from within. Laertes, father of Odysseus, sometime king of Ithaca, may live in a farm freshly rebuilt from the ashes of the old, new clay and stone, but he makes few enough endeavours to match the manner of his accommodation. An old grubby gown, muddy at the hem and flecked with stains of food and other bodily matters, hangs about his skinny frame. His nails are black and his white hair grown long, stooped as if all of him were bending, bending towards the earth that waited for him. A one-time Argonaut, he was never much for the normal way of things when he was a king, proclaiming that the storm did not care if you had polished your helmet to greet it, nor justice give one fig for the smell of perfume. In his way, he was right, but his wife, Anticlea, had enforced some basic standards of propriety and common deportment, proclaiming that a king might rule justly and be wise, but he would be just and wise significantly longer if he also looked after his teeth and said "oh how nice" to powerful strangers occasionally.

Anticlea is dead, of course.

She died pining for her son, lost so far from home.

Motherly love is Hera's domain, but even I felt a golden tear tickle the corner of my eye as the old queen raised her cup of wine, laced with poppy, bidding her pain be drowned. Laertes did not cry at the funeral, and snapped and barked and said that to weep was a womanly affair. Instead his legs swelled up to near two times their natural inclination, and hives broke out upon his back, and for six months afterwards he limped about in pain, decrying grief as a foolish notion, not fit for heroes. Sometimes, you see, we gods are not to blame for the things men do after all.

This then is the old man who steps from his house to see his daughter-in-law and her guests, and in a voice like rain falling from a dirty roof barks: "What do you want?"

"Good father," Penelope begins, and at once Laertes' face curls into a scowl, for nothing pleasing ever comes from the words "good father". "May I present to you Elektra, daughter of Agamemnon, and Orestes, king of all the Greeks."

High above, the Furies are spinning, spinning, spinning. Dead birds will be found on the morrow, dropped from the heavens in a perfect circle all around Laertes' farm, their eyes still open as if surprised by their fall. The Furies do not have the power to smite those who care for their prey, but goodness that has never stopped them letting their feelings be known in signs and portents as subtle as a blade to the throat. Laertes stares at the rocking, shaking, quivering Orestes, then at his stiff-backed, tight-lipped sister, before blurting: "What in the name of almighty Zeus are you people playing at?!"

CHAPTER 7

>>

O restes is laid in the bed of Laertes' maid Otonia. He
should take Laertes' bed, of course, being a king above
all other kings, but dammit, Laertes was an Argonaut! Golden
fleeces, terrible curses, skeleton warriors – and his back has been
giving him grief ever since those damn pirates tried to burn his
house down!

"This bed is perfectly satisfactory, thank you," intones
Elektra. "And I will sleep on the floor by my brother."

Quite where Otonia is to go, no one really asks. I pat her
gently on the back as she stands by the door. She is old now,
and unseen in her age. Once, when she was young, she tangled
in the arms of a man whose voice seemed to sing in perfect
harmony with hers, their lives a perpetual celebration of each
other's glory. He died in Troy, and she has not loved since, but
his memory still shines within her bosom, and she is mine.

"What's the matter with him?" demands Laertes from the
door, as Elektra wipes sweat from the brow of her brother.
None of the women answer, so he throws his hands up and
blurts: "Fine! Ignore the wisest of the ancient heroes!" Then he
turns and marches back to his room, and attempts to slam the
door with the same dramatic flair his grandson Telemachus has

sometimes been known to use in his more petulant displays; but the door is new, the timbers not yet settled into their final shape, so it drags painful and slow across the floor as he attempts to heave it shut.

In the stillness of the room he leaves behind, Penelope raises her head to her maid, Eos, who gently takes the arm of Otonia and leads her from that place.

For a little while, Elektra and Penelope wait alone, watching Orestes turn in his little bed. Then Elektra straightens her back – she has always been straightening her back – and says: "There is nothing we can do for him now. He will sleep for a while, then wake in a fitful state, then sleep again."

"Very well. Shall we talk?"

CHAPTER 8

≫≫≫≫≫≫≫≫≫≫≫≫≫≫≫≫≫≫≫≫≫≫≫≫≫≫≫≫≫≫

T wo women walk around the edge of Laertes' farm as the sun rises hot and bright over Ithaca. A ditch has been dug to separate the wall from the fields that frame it; the old king of Ithaca was insistent. "No point having a fort without a ditch," he would proclaim. "No point at all!"

"But honoured father," sighed his daughter-in-law, "what use is a ditch if the only people defending the walls are yourself and Otonia?"

"When the suitors finally kick off and that big fancy palace you're in is burned to the ground, you'll be thanking me for my digging!"

There was, Penelope was grudgingly forced to concede, a certain wisdom to the old man's argument.

Now the queen of Ithaca walks along the edge of this fresh-dug hollow, Elektra at her side.

She waits for Elektra to speak.

Penelope is supremely gifted at waiting.

"It began a few moons ago," Elektra says at last, and stops, as if doubting her own recollection. Then finding again that certainty is a gift of her blood, continues. "After we left Ithaca . . . after the rogue queen was dealt with . . ." She will not say her mother's name out loud, and so neither will anyone else in the royal court. *Clytemnestra*, I breathe in her ear, and am pleased to see her shudder. *Clytemnestra*, who taught her lover Aegisthus how to worship at the altar of her skin. *Clytemnestra*. Hera loved Clytemnestra far more than I, for she was a woman who revelled in being a queen. I have no interest in such fatuous displays of power – but I have always liked a woman who values her own pleasure.

High above, the Furies are spinning up a whirlwind in the heavens, the clouds scudding fast, the land below spilling in shades of grey and black as their busy tumult darkens the sun. Mortals across the western isle shudder and murmur that the weather has turned, and look up, but do not see. Only Orestes knows, and he cries out again in anguish, his voice disturbing prowling Laertes, who snarls and spits and hears his dead wife chiding still against profanity.

On the tawny ground outside, Elektra and Penelope walk, heads down, voices low. "We returned to Mycenae," Elektra says. "My brother was crowned, celebrated by all the Greeks. He had slain the killer of Agamemnon, brought justice, proven himself worthy. I thought no man would dare challenge a king so brave he would kill his own ... Then the dreams started. He would wake weeping, run to my room, did not eat unless reminded to, grew pale and quiet. He was not vicious in his melancholy, maintained decorum in public. But the priests were restless. They said there were signs and portents. Animals died in the streets, their innards rotted and bursting with maggots, which split and tumbled from their ruined flesh where they lay; no rain fell upon the young harvest until there fell too much rain, a month of downpour that drove every man in the streets to their houses, a cloying, pestilential moisture in every corner from which you could never be free. Bats swarmed about the palace at sundown, drained the blood of the horses in the stables with their fangs – but in the morning they could not be found. The people spoke of Furies, foul and malignant rumours against my brother – but he wore it all. He was shaken and weary, yes, I do not pretend otherwise. Grieving, perhaps, maybe even that. But he was not mad. Not mad."

In the secret hollows of the night, when Elektra slept and Orestes lay awake in his father's bed in the Mycenaean palace, he sometimes pressed his hands over his eyes and cried out, Mother, Mother, Mother!

He never cried out for his father. Orestes was only five years old when Agamemnon left him to bring back his brother's wife from Troy. On the walls of the palace the Furies lurked, laughing at their merry game. Not for them the meagre disembowelling of their prey, nor the crude punishments of the unimaginative gods. Nothing was as sweet as the madman who begged for death, and for whom death did not come.

"A few moons ago, he began to change. I thought at first it was his melancholy, but what melancholy leads men to start gibbering and crying out in strange voices in the company of their friends? What melancholy makes your eyes start from your skull, heart beat loud in your chest, sweat stand out from your skin like the sea, convulsions rack your poor, wretched limbs and bile spew from your mouth? I was slow to recognise it. Too slow. Until I found one of my maids lying on the floor in the same condition. That was when I knew. This was no malady sent by the gods." It takes her a while to say the word, but it is so close to having already been said that she may as well go through with it now. So in the voice of a tiny, frightened child, she whispers: "Poison."

Penelope nods; the whole thing seems entirely logical to her. "Did the maid live?"

"Yes. And I questioned her. Demanded to know her every step, suspected her, had her sent far from my brother. She confessed to having drunk some of the wine he did not finish, begged my forgiveness, said she would take any punishment – but by then, of course, the wine was gone. And then Pylades too fell sick – a mild malady, but still a similar sort, for a day, maybe two. Pylades has ... many faults ... he is not ... but I do believe him loyal to my brother. Then the messenger came from Sparta, saying my uncle was on his way. Menelaus had heard of my brother's distemper and was rushing to his aid."

"How thoughtful of him."

"He could not see Orestes in this state. He could not. He would have summoned the kings of all Greece, laid out his right to the Mycenaean throne in his brother's name, spoken of battle and honour and Troy, and how there could not be some ... mad mother-killer as king of kings of all the Greeks. He would have called a council of men, and who would have spoken for Orestes there?"

No one, of course. Maybe Nestor might have put in a good word, feeling a little embarrassed about the way the whole thing was playing out, but Leucas had a fondness for usurpers and Diomedes would stand by his bloody brother in battle through blood and sacrilege, no matter what. Elektra would wait at the door, peeping in, barred from entry or voice, while her brother babbled madness from the middle of the room. So fall the children of Agamemnon.

"Funny how Menelaus knew your brother was sick, all the way from Sparta," muses Penelope, as they turn again and turn about the farm.

"He has eyes everywhere. He says he will always be loyal to his brother's son, but in private he calls my brother 'boy'. As if a 'boy' could kill the traitor queen and her lover! As if a 'boy' could hunt her across the seas, as if a 'boy' could ..." She shudders a moment, like a duck shaking water off its back, eyes front, hands clasped in fists. "I knew we had to leave. Before my uncle arrived. We couldn't slip away, of course – that would have looked like we had something to hide. I had a man called Iason organise the matters of soldiery, drum and goods to trade and sacrifice, as fast and as secret as he dared, and then we left. First to Aegium, offering sacrifices to Athena and Artemis as we went, then by sea to Chalcis to make offerings to Zeus."

"Who knew where you were going?"

"No one."

"Iason? Pylades?"

"No. I told them what to arrange, that we would be travelling for some time, but no one knew where. But it is hard to disguise the march of three hundred soldiers, priests, servants and maids through the land."

"I imagine it is. What of Orestes? Did he recover?"

"For a few days, yes. When we camped at night, I prepared his food with my own hands, fed him water that only I had tasted first, and for a little while I believed this was helping. It *was* helping. But whenever we stopped around a city, some petty king would insist on welcoming us, and I would have to say my brother was in pious prayer, secluded from the world, while I – to keep the pretence up – would eat at the lordly table and say needful words of peace and solemnity. Each time I returned to my brother from these diplomatic efforts, he would be sickening again. I could not watch him every moment of every day; I feared sleep. Dreaded the end of the day.

"Then, a few days from Chalcis, I received word: Menelaus was in Aegium. He had come to Mycenae as promised and, finding us gone, had embarked at once to find his nephew – to support us, he said, in our pious journey, and offer such devotions to our good cause as a mere king of Sparta could. If he found us, I would never be able to free my brother from his afflictions. He would be paraded about before all the kings of Greece; he would lose his throne. We had to run. I divided our forces. The majority I sent to a town in the hills above the sea where there is a temple to Aphrodite, to make noise with drum and trumpet as though Orestes were still present and in prayer. Then with those I trust the most, my most faithful servants and maids, I set sail for Ithaca."

This declaration seems the end of Elektra's story, and for a while longer the women trudge through turned-up mud about the high walls of Laertes' land. I drift along behind them, impatient for their speech but enjoying at least the busy tumult of their respective souls as words rise and fall like lust. Finally Penelope says: "All right, cousin. All right. You are here. I was hoping when you came to these isles again – if you came – it would be with a wealth of stately gifts and long speeches to the suitors about how they must stay in line lest the wrath of Mycenae descend upon them and so on ... but I suppose that was a little naïve, all things considered. Do please keep in mind for future visitations, however, that we are particularly appreciative of copper ingots and barrels of salt. For now, assuming such things are unreachable, what would you have from Ithaca?"

"No more than you have already provided. A place of safety, secrecy for my brother."

"You make it sound so simple."

"Is it not? Ithaca hides things well."

Penelope sighs, but cannot entirely disagree. "You think the one who poisons him – if he is being poisoned and this is not just some malady of guilt ... "

"There is no guilt!" snaps Elektra, voice higher and sharper than she intends – a voice, Penelope feels, very much like the voice of Clytemnestra. Perhaps Elektra hears it too, for she recoils a little, and softer adds: "There is no guilt."

" ... you think the one who poisons him sails with you still. That you have not escaped their clutches."

"I do. I had thought by leaving Mycenae ... but that was not enough. I had thought by leaving the majority of my train . . . but that also was not enough. At every step I find that the betrayal, the violation of my faith, goes deeper."

Penelope does not answer; these things Elektra speaks of with such outrage are merely an evening hobby in the house of Odysseus. Instead: "I have sent for a priestess of the island. She is good with certain herbs, and of the women who enter her care, only the average number die, which is an excellent record for a physician."

"A priestess – not a priest? Are there no servants of Apollo on Ithaca?"

"There is one, but he dines regularly with the master of the docks, whose son Antinous is a suitor at my palace. I cannot imagine you want word spreading to those quarters. Besides, he finds it distasteful to tend to women's maladies, and as most of the island are women, this has left him relatively few patients to practise on."

"Do you trust this priestess?"

"As much as I trust anyone. She is the lady of the temple of Artemis."

Elektra lets out a little breath, a puff of air at the name. "They say the western isles are protected by the huntress. Some business of Illyrians – or were they Argives? – raiding your land? Ships found set ablaze, corpses riddled with arrows, an intervention from the gods, no? What good fortune that your piety can conjure the goddess's most useful favour."

Is that a hint of spite in Elektra's voice? When she was twelve years old, she snuck into the armoury of her mother's palace and stole a sword, was found waving it around in the courtyard, both hands clutching the hilt as it flopped in her grasp like a gasping fish. If she had been born a man, she would have killed Clytemnestra, instead of making her brother do it.

"I presume nothing." Penelope's reply is tight, sharp, an

ending of this line of enquiry before it can progress any further. Elektra recognises it, and stiffens too. For a moment, two would-be queens stomp like the heavy-footed hippo through the mud about Laertes' house, but it is Penelope who softens first, if only a little. Penelope never wanted to be a man. Achilles could only prove his worth by dying, heartbroken, in some bloody field. Heracles slaughtered his wife and babes, and even those heroes who made it through relatively unscathed too often died wretched as their legend passed. "May we speak frankly, Cousin Elektra? I think it is perhaps good if we are clear with each other, talk with perfect trust and honesty."

"That is not the fashion, cousin. But if you wish, since we are alone."

A sharp nod: she does wish it. The novelty of it is thrilling to her lips, a hot arousal on her skin. "There are certain matters between us. Matters of your mother, of course – pacts and understandings made. I will seek to honour these, of course I will. I will do so for the blood we share, for your brother – who seems if nothing else to be no worse a king than any other – and for certain accords we have. I will do it for you, cousin. I will do that too. But if you have brought Menelaus to my shores – if my people are endangered or my kingdom threatened – I will not flinch in my duty. I am queen, and you are in my dominion. Whatever may come, whenever it comes, remember that."

To her surprise – to my surprise – perhaps even to the surprise of Elektra herself, the younger woman nods. Is that a hint of humility in her eye? I find it intensely displeasing; perhaps one day Elektra will make a coy and comely wife after all. "I understand, cousin," she replies, and for a while more they walk together, in silence.

Then Eos stands in the gateway that guards the walled farm, and waves to them across the field. "He's awake," she says.

CHAPTER 9

>>

Once, Zeus tricked me into lying with a mortal.

"Tricked" is his word, of course. He was incredibly proud of the whole affair. "Look at the little whore, fucking a mortal man!" he cackled.

He did it, of course, to prove that he held power over me. It was very important to him to demonstrate this point as publicly and viciously as he could, to dispel the gossip common among the gods that he cowered from me for fear of the punishment I might unleash upon his soul. That even the father of the gods was not immune from the power of desire and love. As if love were merely lust, and desire could only lend itself to conquest.

Anyway, bewitched I was into believing that I lay with another of the divines, and a really rather juicy night we had together, Anchises and I. By the time the enchantment wore thin, I had already suspected that it was a mortal I lay with, for he worshipped at my body, exulted in my grace with a humility and a gratitude that exceeds anything I have ever received from my celestial peers, and a thoroughly wholesome and lovely experience it was too. Afterwards, of course, things were hard for him. He proclaimed that no woman would ever satisfy him as I had done, which was self-aggrandising rot, and though I warned him not to mention the business to any other mortal, he couldn't really stop himself and Zeus struck him blind with a thunderbolt for his sins. Such a shame.

I always kept an eye out for Anchises, of course, and especially our beautiful boy, Aeneas, who I knew was going to do wonderful things. The gods laughed at me, found it outrageous, absurd that the hussy whore should feel a shimmering of affection for the mortal who ravished her; but Anchises was as bewitched as I, and our lovely child bore no sin from our copulations. This too caused much confusion among the Olympians, for what manner of foolish deity permitted a child to live as if he were his own man, free from the legacy of his parents, and yet loved him still? Absurd, they cried. Ridiculous! Yet more proof of Aphrodite's empty little skull.

I never loved Anchises, though I felt some lingering sympathy and affection for him. I loved Aeneas, our boy, with a ferocity that drew even I, the fairest of the gods, to the battlefield. The gods said I loved Paris, and if they want to believe that, they may; but in truth there is but one other mortal I have ever loved as fiercely as I love Aeneas, and she now is sailing straight for Ithaca.

CHAPTER 10

>>

In the house of Laertes, Orestes stirs.

Penelope and Elektra stand by his side, hands clasped like mourners already gathered for the funeral.

When he blinks open his eyes, they are rimmed with gum, as if his lids were sealed with ancient wax. The whites are shot with red, and at once Elektra draws in a little breath and reaches for a bowl of clay laid nearby, daubing a hempen rag in it to wash the crabby dew from his eyelashes, wipe the salt from his brow. She has a comb of carved shell with which she caresses the hair across his scalp; the movement seems to bring him some respite, some gentle ease. Perhaps his mother combed his hair so too, when he was a child, before his childhood was soaked in blood.

"My brother," she whispers, and he seems to recognise her, claws one hand of whitened bone around her skinny arm as she pads gentle liquid into the burning skin of his cheeks and the pulsing redness of his throat. She smiles, squeezes his hand. "I am here."

He sees her, tries to smile, teeth flecked with yellow. His pupils are wide and dark, irises thin lines of deepest grey pressed so tight it is as if the darkness in his vision might burst, might consume his whole gaze. His eyes flicker to Penelope, strain to see.

"Mother?" he asks.

This is perhaps the single most awkward identification he can make. Penelope shifts a little where she stands, but moves no nearer.

"No, brother," Elektra whispers, dribbling a little water into his mouth. "It is Penelope."

A moment of confusion – who in his life is Penelope? Ah, but then he remembers, and the answer absolutely does not help alleviate his distress. "Penelope," he repeats, digesting it as a starving man might digest rotten fruit. "Then . . . Ithaca?"

"Yes, brother. We are on Ithaca. You were ill. Do you remember?"

A little nod. A little turning away of his head; he is done with water, done with the mopping of his brow, the combing of his hair. He now wishes to stare into the wall, into the darkness, to close his aching eyes.

Penelope finally shuffles a little closer, displacing the reluctant Elektra at his side. "Your majesty," she begins, and when this produces no reply: "Cousin. You are in Laertes' house, father of Odysseus." The barest nod – or perhaps she imagined it? In the gloom it is hard to tell. "Elektra thinks someone is trying to harm you. Trying to poison you. Do you know who would do this? Do you know how?"

Orestes shakes his head, curls his knees closer to his chest. "Forgive me," he whispers. And then again: "Forgive me."

Above, the Furies cackle, black tongues over scarlet lips, but only Orestes hears. He presses his hands to his ears, squeezes his eyes until they weep, whimpers: *forgive me, forgive me, forgive me* – until his words drown in the encroaching dark.

Anaitis, priestess of Artemis, throws open the shutters.

"Light! Air!"

Elektra flinches. Orestes cowers, lost in a half-shrouded daze.

Laertes stands in the door, arms folded. He does not approve of all these women prowling across his property – bad enough that his daughter-in-law has brought a half-mad king to his farmhouse, disturbing what was otherwise a perfectly adequate morning, but to have brought the maid Eos, the priestess Anaitis as well as Orestes' gloomy sister Elektra is just serving to make the place feel cramped.

But now! Now Anaitis is in her element, barking instructions and commanding clean water, fresh bread to be dipped in it and eased into the mouth of Orestes like mulch to a babe. There is something really rather magnificent about a woman who knows what she is doing, Laertes decides, but damned if he will ever say as much.

"He must eat," barks the priestess. "Nothing hard on the stomach." She sits and feels the blood rushing through Orestes' neck, peers into his eyes, sniffs his breath, tugs at his hair, which to her mild disappointment doesn't fall out when she pulls.

"What manner of physician are you?" demands Elektra, at this minor insult.

"I was helping the ewes birth when I was five," retorts Anaitis. "Humans aren't much different."

"My brother isn't pregnant."

Anaitis turns a glower on Elektra that has very little time for royalty. She has just about mastered the art of regal deference when Penelope comes calling, but even that is a bit of a stretch. This Mycenaean scrap of a girl is another matter entirely.

Penelope clears her throat. "Do you have any sense of Orestes' malady, Anaitis? Would you say that his condition is – and I speculate loosely here – immediately curable with a single common and readily available herb that will have him up and about in no time and ready to return to ruling Mycenae before the situation can deteriorate further, for example?"

Anaitis turns from Elektra to the Ithacan queen. "He reminds me of a horse when it has eaten of certain plants that grow by the stream. Also there is that in his ravings—"

"He is not raving!" snaps Elektra.

"He *is* raving, why does she say he isn't?"

"Familial affection," explains Penelope, cool as a mountain spring. "Please continue."

"Fine. His ravings are like the priests who inhale too much of the divine smoke – they are not oblivious to the world around them, but neither do they speak of it coherently. Has anyone else shown signs like these?"

Elektra shifts a little, eyes fixed on another place. "In Mycenae, before we left. One night, at the very beginning, a maid drank of his wine. In the morning she was hot, breathless, eyes wide, seeing things that were not there. And Pylades too."

"Pylades?"

"A captain of Mycenae who I believe should imminently be making port at the city and acting as if everything were entirely normal and under control," explains Penelope, to Anaitis's only mild interest. They gaze upon the king, while Anaitis presses her hand to his brow again, a little frown across her broad, eloquent face. "Who prepares Orestes' food? His drink?"

"I do."

"In every way? You draw the water from the well? You stir the gruel for his bowl?"

"I ... no. But in Mycenae, the moment I suspected he was being poisoned, I ordered that the kitchen prepare all meals the same, all served in the same way, and had them laid out before me. I would choose one dish from the table, and the rest would be eaten by our guests, servants and slaves. I alone would carry Orestes' cup, and I ensured that everyone in the house shared the wine and the water that was poured into it. There was no way to poison my brother that did not risk poisoning all others too."

Penelope attempts to raise one eyebrow, but her features are not quite agile enough that she cannot help but raise both. "That is a fantastically dangerous gambit; what if the poisoner did not care who they killed?"

Elektra's eyes flash – oh, just like her mother's did, she'd hate it if she knew that. "So? If everyone must die so my brother lives – is that not what it is to be a king?"

Elektra is Agamemnon's daughter too, we must always remember. Her father killed her sister so he could have his war, and forgot about Iphigenia's bloody corpse as readily as he grew used to the smell of the funeral pyres on the beach of Troy. Penelope saw a lot of would-be kings when she was a girl in the court of Sparta. In many ways the unfashionable end of the western isles has been a pleasant relief from having to endure too much of their company.

"I take it your brother did not improve?"

"Sometimes he did, and then he did not. It came in fits and starts. By the time we fled, I was certain that my actions were not enough. But what could I do? He is king. He must be seen to be king – to hold audience and pass judgements. He cannot be locked in his room; that would be just as dangerous as if he were dead already. Maybe more so."

"If they wanted him dead, he'd be dead," pipes up Anaitis with the casual cheer of one who knows their business and thinks nothing of it. Eyes turn to her, and she is briefly aware that others may not feel as detached about this statement as she. She shrugs – as a young priestess she was slapped across the shoulders for the gesture, but now that she is in charge of her own shrine, she'll have none of this nonsense about deportment or decorum ruining the pure essence of Artemis's worship. "There are many flowers, mushrooms and herbs that if mixed into a dish, or crushed into a drink, or distilled into an oil and taken on the tongue can kill in less than a day. If I wanted this man dead," a loose wave towards Orestes, who is still of only limited interest to Anaitis in his capacity as king of kings, "I can think of three or four herbs within easy reach of this farm that I might feed to him that would be more effective than this gibbering nonsense."

"A mad king," muses Penelope, "can be as useful as a dead one." Penelope is an expert in matters of ambiguous royalty; peerless in the nuance of absent kings. "What would happen if Orestes died?"

"A council of kings. The elder statesmen of the land would gather. The greatest warriors. Menelaus, of course. Anyone who felt they had a claim to the throne."

"And who would be crowned?" Elektra half closes her eyes, shakes her head. She cannot think about this; she must. "Menelaus?" asks Penelope softly.

"No. His claim to the throne is the strongest, of course. He is Agamemnon's brother. But the others would never allow it. They would unite behind someone else – some candidate weak enough to be controlled by the old families of Mycenae, strong enough to resist Menelaus should he refuse to accept the result. There cannot be one king in both Sparta and Mycenae – such a man would be able to conquer all."

"A man both weak and strong – and you?"

"I? I would be the one who seals the bargain. I would marry whoever they choose, to keep Menelaus from the throne."

"Would you?"

Elektra does not know. Her duty is clear, and she believes above all other things in duty. But she is wise enough to know her heart, and she fears that like the heart of her mother, the heart of her cousin Helen, she is treacherous. She fears that she is capable of loving, and that is the greatest danger of all. It is one of the reasons she has come to Penelope. The queen of Ithaca, she is sure, has banished all love in the name of duty.

This is what Elektra must be, a woman of ice and stone. I stroke her cheek, plant a gentle kiss upon her brow. Elektra has only really seen love once – when her mother loved Aegisthus, and he loved her – and it was poison to her heart. She does not believe that this can ever be remedied. Yet another of her mistakes.

"What if Orestes *is* mad?" Penelope asks, and at once Elektra is back in this present place, cheeks flushing crimson fury, eyes rising hard. Penelope meets her gaze, does not flinch before it. "It is an entirely reasonable political question, cousin," she muses. "Indeed, if the poisoner has not killed your brother, it must be for a reason. Madness . . . raises questions, does it not?"

"If . . . *if* it was judged that my brother was in any way . . . unable to rule," Elektra growls, barely able to seethe the words between her teeth, "it would be chaos. Some would attempt to form a council of elders, but those who were willing to defend my brother's claim would not stand by it. Pylades would raise men in Orestes' name, Menelaus too – though what they meant by it would be entirely different. As with your husband, the problem would be this: what happens if you take up arms to claim the throne, and then Orestes – or Odysseus – comes back? It is . . . incomparably dangerous."

"And as with my husband," Penelope muses, "some weight would be thrown behind whoever you married."

"I will marry no one who seeks to usurp my brother!"

"Even if he is mad?"

"He is not mad!"

Elektra puts her fist in her mouth. She has not done this since she was a child. She bites nearly hard enough to draw blood, then at once whips her hand away as if others might not have noticed the movement. Penelope sits, fingers folded in her lap, and has the grace to pretend she did not. Anaitis blinks, bewildered, looks from one to the other. Is this what royalty is like?

70

she wonders. Just like people? No wonder nothing much ever seems to get done.

"Well," Penelope breathes at last. And then: "Well." She rises, moves towards the door, stops, turns back. "Whoever is poisoning your brother – however they are doing it – they clearly do not intend for him to be dead. That means they have a master who has a great deal to gain from confusion. There are very few people who thrive in chaos, cousin. And one above all others. Think on that, when Menelaus comes."

Elektra says nothing, and turns her face to the wall.

CHAPTER 11

>>

There are matters only a queen may attend to.

Or rather, there are matters that a queen must be seen to be attending to, lest anyone consider that she is not doing her queening appropriately.

A little after the sun kisses the highest tip of the sky, as Elektra stands guard over her brother's twisted form, Penelope is returning to the up-and-down miserable little "city" that the people of Ithaca acclaim their capital. Barely one good road runs through it, along which priests must process at an excruciating shuffle to drag out the solemnity of their rites over so small a patch of land. From this single path break off alleys and stairs that wind round the cracked buildings and little houses grown like crooked teeth from the rocky earth, each knocking against its neighbour. There are no defensive walls about the place, but the palace of Odysseus at least has some walls raised by Laertes' father, mostly to impress the many strangers and loose-lipped poets who reported of Ithaca to its peers that the people smelled of fish and talked only of goats. "Go forth and proclaim that though we do love a goat and a nice mussel or two for dinner, what this makes us is fearlessly rugged and resilient!" quoth Laertes' father, and lo and behold

72

if his children did not pay the price for the successful dissemination of this notion.

The murals that line the innards of the palace – at least those innards where prying foreign eyes might go – used to be of Laertes on the *Argo*, valiant warrior king sailing with the greatest men of Greece. But the salty air from the harbour will wear away even the finest art, so Penelope acquired the services of the third-greatest artists from some of the most moderately cultured corners of the land to refresh those daubs of white, red and black with images of her husband's exploits. Here: Odysseus slaying a fierce wild boar. There: Odysseus beating against the walls of Troy, or fighting to defend the body of fallen Patroclus. The image of the wooden horse dominates most of the main hall where the suitors drunkenly gather, and Penelope has invited the carpenters of her house to carve horses' heads or the lines of their flowing bodies into any ornamental surface that they may discover, both as homage to Poseidon (who doesn't care), and to gently remind any and all visitors of the cunning of her absent husband.

And where is Odysseus now?

Why, he rolls in Calypso's arms on her little island in the shrouded sea, and she is a fabulous lover – I would, I absolutely would, and perhaps when this is done and she is pining for her loss, I will, lucky little nymph. He is aroused by pleasing her, excited by her groans of ecstasy, by the taste of her upon his lips, and resents that she has this power upon him. And when he is not richly wound between her legs, he sits upon the rock that faces (he thinks) towards Ithaca, and weeps. So much for Odysseus. The most I send him is a conciliatory pat on the back, when I can be bothered to remember.

Within this painted palace there are a great many features of a proper princely abode you will not find. There is a lack of golden tubs within which a conqueror may bathe while being

73

pleasured by his concubines. There is a dearth of gently billowing drapery behind which the loose giggle of a charming maid may be heard at an inappropriate hour. There are far too few beds of feather and soft down in corners scented with jasmine and honey, but rather rooms of hard pallets pressed in tight to accommodate the poorest of the suitors, the most meagre of the maids. Incense should be burned every morning and every night, the aroma floral and light in summer, rich and full of woody nectars in winter, and the sweet sound of a lute heard from some soft courtyard beneath heavy vines would be a pleasing addition at any time of the year, but most especially on long, hot evenings when the sea breeze may carry the notes, or in deepest winter when the north wind bruises the land. Long corridors with great tall columns behind which one might see a distant lover dart to shadow are essential. Heavy doors that one may close with a solid thud, sealing up the night to this private intimacy, are also very important to a proper palace, but the walls should never be too thick that one cannot hear a moan of ecstasy from another room – merely thick enough that one can never be quite certain where said cry came from.

Instead, the palace is much as the town – a tangle of confusing dead ends and stairs to unusual corners, rooms added and divided and added again so that the whole thing leans towards the edge of the cliff as if its growth has turned into a slow, suicidal shuffle. In the morning it smells of the pigs that snuffle the yard; in the afternoon of the fish gutted in the kitchen. At night it fills with the roar of drunken men who have ceased pretending to woo, and instead gorge themselves on meat and grain, hoping perhaps to starve the Ithacan queen into submission; and when the wind blows from the east, the smell of the manure and compost heaps is washed in through the unshuttered windows, enough I swear to put even the most intent lover off their business.

In short: it is a dump. Only the occasional passing presence of foreigners swept up by the busy trade that runs through the ports of the western isles would induce me to even glance its way, hoping perhaps for some flame-haired barbarian from the north, all furs and pounding chest, or a beautiful fellow of the southern lands with midnight skin and a rich, deep voice that has bartered in many tongues, wooed in a few more too. *Come to me*, I whisper into these strangers' ears. *Leave your trader's bark and lie with me in a bed of flowers. The land here is mellow and mild, the harshest of the seasons gentler than your burning sun or icy forest. You are far from the lands of your gods; you would be wise to do homage to the greatest in these parts. Worship me.*

Sometimes they listen. Sometimes they do not, the pattern of their native speech and familiar worship deafening them to the more pleasurable path I offer. Here is one – look, here. Here is a man from far-off Egypt come to woo Ithaca's queen. He has been sent, he says, by his brother, whose trade is dependent on the flow of amber from the northern ports, which trade must be kept safe as it passes through the western seas. He lies on this point, but on all other matters is remarkably honest. His hair is curling and black around his sunset face; his garb has grown more and more like that of the Greeks with whom he spends his days, though there is still gold about his wrists and upper arms, a reminder of the value of his suit. When he is in the palace, he wears no weapon, as courtesy to his host. But this afternoon he walks, as he has so often walked, along the ridged spine of Ithaca, eyes to the south, wind pounding in his ears, his mind in two places at once – his home, long lost, and here too, in ways he did not anticipate.

His name is Kenamon. There was a time when he walked upon these hills with the son of a king, winning favour from Telemachus himself, until that young man set sail in secret to find his father. Now he walks alone, save for those rare precious moments when he might stumble on another between the ragged pastures and crooked olive groves. He did not think his heart would ever flutter with love. How naïve men can be. Of him we shall have more to say.

For now, though, there is business to attend to. Penelope returns to the palace, Eos at her side, as loyal Eos always is. If asked where she has been this morning, Penelope will give her usual pious answer: "I walked upon the cliffs and wept for my missing husband"; or perhaps, if she is feeling particularly irritated at the people who constantly enquire unto where she treads in her own land: "I was so overcome with sorrow for my husband and now my wandering son that I fell upon the hard earth and rent my garments and scratched at my bosom until I bled, oh woe, do not speak to me lest the ague come again!"

The first time she delivered this statement, she somewhat misjudged the manner of it, and the listeners were forced to do a significant amount of labour to interpret the angry impatience in her voice as blazing womanly grief. Now she rattles these sentiments off briskly and without too much effort, and people nod and smile and say, ah yes, that's our Penelope, that is. Nice bit of pre-lunch wailing, back in time for supper.

Her council is already assembled by the time she has entered the palace gates, removed her veil, pushed her sea-shaken hair back from her face and eaten a mouthful of cheese and garlic plucked from a ready plate. Or rather we should say it is the council of her husband that has gathered, an assemblage of the menfolk Odysseus deemed suitable to leave behind when he sailed for Troy. She attends these meetings to watch without remarking, so that when Odysseus returns she may report, "Ah yes, the men you trusted met and spoke and said sagely things," and then return to being silent again. Today, however, as the men speak of matters of business – a row in the harbour over the value of tin, an embassy from the north come to barter free access to the narrow seaways guarded by Ithaca, reports from the farmers of Hyrie and a dispute between two old great men in Kephalonia over some stolen cows – she hardly even pretends to listen. Sits, chin in her palm, and stares at nothing much. She is waiting. Penelope is always waiting.

Two of her council – and they are only three strong now that Telemachus has gone – do not appear to notice. Peisenor and Aegyptius would fancy themselves men of war and action, if only they had sailed to Troy. Old soldier Peisenor, one arm ending in a stump, his chin a tarnished gristle of scar and stubble, was ordered by Odysseus to see to the defences of this land in the absence of his wandering king. The recent revelation that Artemis's blessed arrows do more to defend the western isles than any militia of grubby boys he could raise has somewhat dented this would-be warrior's sense of worth. He has not stopped to enquire too particularly into just how pirates are slain at Ithaca's doors without his involvement, and never will. Odysseus, for all his talk, was not someone who liked to promote questioning types.

Aegyptius, a string of a man who if plucked like a harp would twang with a discordant note, *has* on occasion wondered exactly how Ithaca defends itself. The conclusion he has reached is in many ways a wise one: that the knowing of the answer might bring him into some personal danger, and thus it is best not to dwell too particularly.

" . . . the shipload of timber was delayed, the master at Patrae again no longer a suitable supplier . . . "

The third councillor, loyal Medon, who loved and loved and loved until death at last took his wife, and still loves her ghost as though she were living, glorious in his heart, spies Penelope from the corner of his eye, and unlike most of the men in these halls, he sees her. Not some grieving queen, but Penelope herself, whole and true.

" . . . and now of course they are demanding gold for amber – gold! As if they really expect any sort of meaningful trade if they open with those terms . . . "

These are necessary men. It is important that they are seen to be in charge, even if they are not. They are another veil that the queen draws across her brow, another little wall that has sprung up around her crooked palace.

"This morning a Mycenaean arrived, a fellow by the name of Pylades." Aegyptius is the one who breaks this news. He is somewhat smug that he is the first to know this thing – he had it from Eupheithes, father of Antinous, whose family is master of the docks and don't they like to remind people of it. Aegyptius has always been careful to be friendly to the fathers of the suitors, saying it is for Penelope's good that he labours through the toil of many dinners and cups of wine, his own future a mere secondary consideration in this game.

"A Mycenaean?" Penelope's voice is the soft brush of the concerned hostess, nothing more. "Perhaps he has some news of my son."

Aegyptius and Peisenor exchange weary looks. For nearly twenty years Penelope has offered up the phrase "perhaps he has some news of my husband" as an excuse to engage in borderline-improper chat with every merchant, sailor and dreg of the seas come to her house. After barely fifteen years it was wearing a little thin, and now this – another vanished relative, another piteous look in the corner of her eye as she homes in on anyone who may have intelligence of her absent kin.

It is only Medon who looks upon Penelope as she says these words and understands the difference. She is a wife who can barely remember her husband, but she is also a mother, who always knew that one day her son would leave but did not think it would be in cruel secrecy in the dead of night, sailing away across dangerous seas without so much as a by-your-leave.

Sometimes even Penelope is caught having needs of her own, he concludes.

"Pylades is Orestes' chap, isn't he?" grumbles Peisenor, quick to avoid even the slightest whiff of sentiment in a conversation. "Close to the king."

"There have been rumours coming from the mainland." Aegyptius loves a rumour from the mainland. "They say Orestes hasn't been well."

"What kind of not well? Not diseased?"

"The kind of not well that one might expect of a man who kills his own mother."

The room falls into an uncomfortable silence. It is embarrassing enough that Clytemnestra was killed on their isle; worse still that no one can find anything to say that would let everyone involved feel thoroughly satisfied about their part in her demise. Nuance is not something these wise elders of Ithaca are kept in grain for.

It is Aegyptius who clears his throat, eager to move on. "In somewhat ... other news ... excellent word from Polybus and Eupheithes, who have finally agreed to work together and contribute two good crewed ships to the defence of the island."

Penelope freezes, even as Peisenor nearly bends double with relief. "Finally!" sighs the old soldier, and: "They have what?" blurts Medon.

Aegyptius looks from one to the other, not quite sure how to address this contradiction. It is Peisenor who comes to his aid. "If two of the most powerful fathers of two of the most powerful suitors in the land are finally collaborating in the protection of the kingdom they hope their sons might one day rule, this can only be a good thing! Taking responsibility! Showing willing! Not to mention helping with pirates in the local waters – all good stuff!"

"Those two despise each other nearly as much as their sons do," retorts Medon. "Only one of their sons can be king ..."

"*If* my husband's body is found," corrects Penelope, a habit more than anything, a common piping bird.

Medon breezes straight through – nearly everyone is now in the habit of breezing though such sentiments. " . . . and as sure as anything, Antinous son of Eupheithes and Eurymachus son of Polybus will have just one mission, which is to slaughter the other. And you say their fathers have suddenly discovered that they're willing to be friends again? To . . . what? To serve Ithaca as if they were not the bitterest of rivals who would rather see the islands torn apart than their enemy on the throne? I don't believe it."

"Believe it or not," Aegyptius retorts, uncurling the stoop in his spine to stand a little higher above the round old man, "it is happening."

Medon's jaw works like a suffocating fish for a moment, but he makes no sound. It is Peisenor who decides to take responsibility for a conclusion, stirring enough to bark: "No harm in more ships in the water, more men at sea. We are seafarers – this is what we should do!"

It is a sentiment of such utter banality that for a moment even Peisenor seems surprised that he's uttered it, but too late now. The old soldier thought he was in love once, with a woman who seemed willing to listen – to really listen – to everything he had to say. But one day she spoke up and suggested, gentle as the sparrow, an alternative interpretation of some great and swelling tale he spoke, and then he realised he didn't love her after all. Peisenor, like so many others of the warring kind, never dared love lest it give him something unassailably potent to live for, and thus he found himself afraid to die.

So the council disperses, until just Penelope and Medon remain. That is acceptable – he is far too old, far too familiar to be considered a proper man, and thus may be in the company of this woman he has known since she was a girl. No doubt, the others say, he is comforting her while she weeps again for the fate of her lost husband, her absent son. Medon's robes must be rimed with the salt of womanly tears.

Instead, however, she blurts as soon as the door is closed: "Polybus and Eupheithes have ships now?"

"I am as shocked as you."

"I need to know everything about this as quickly as possible. How was this agreement reached? What are their intentions? Why haven't the other suitors rebelled against it? Why didn't we know?"

"Ask your woman Eos – she seems to know more about the suitors than any of my eyes and ears," retorts Medon.

Penelope just about hides her scowl – a queen must never show displeasure unless she can act on it immediately in the most demonstrative, preferably violent of ways. "I will have the maids enquire, but if this sudden alliance is a threat, it must be dealt with as quickly as possible."

"You don't seem overly concerned by the arrival of Pylades," points out Medon, hands folded across his curving belly. "I would have thought you'd be straight to the great hall for some glad tidings and pouring of wine."

"You find me a little put out by matters nearer to home."

"If you are certain." Medon is not. Medon has not been certain of very much at all where his queen is concerned for a long time. He loves her, of course – more perhaps than even her own somewhat disinterested father did – and his love is strangely reaffirmed every day by the realisation that he does not fully understand her, will never be entirely trusted by her, and yet would die for her in an instant, if that was what was required. He hopes it will not be. "I trust you will find the time to be at least a little cordial to this Pylades. If the suitors are planning something, you will need the support of Mycenae. Unless the time has come . . . ?" Penelope's frown is a sharpened battering ram across her face. He raises his hands in polite deference. "I merely suggest that if there was ever a time to marry a suitor, it could well be now, when Antinous and Eurymachus seem to be practically friends and the new king of Mycenae will defend your choice." She doesn't answer, and an ugly thought flickers through Medon's mind. "The new king of Mycenae *will* defend your choice, won't he? Unless there is something you know that I do not?"

Penelope rises in a swirl of slightly faded robe, smiles, kisses the old man on the cheek as she walks by him. "Immeasurable things, good councillor. But would knowing bring you joy?"

"Probably not," he concedes, as she glides out the room.

Pylades is waiting in a room to one side of the great hall where nightly the suitors feast. This is both a polite and practical choice, for the hall itself is being swept again of the encrusted remnants of the prior night's meal, the hearth set with fresh kindling, chairs righted, tables scrubbed and all things restored as if a hundred drunkards would not again at sundown descend upon the palace demanding meat! Fresh meat, fresh meat and also, yes, meat that is also metaphor, so tasty, yum yum.

A stool is set aside for the waiting soldier, and fresh drink and the finest fruit that the isles can provide is laid out beneath a window that faces the sea. The breeze is one of salt and fish, which Pylades dislikes, not realising that the alternative smell that might assail him from the other side of the palace is pig shit and goat skins. He has been attended to by maids – he has not bothered to learn their names, though he is polite enough to say thank you when they refill his cup. This is less because of who they are, and more in deference to his host, who he suspects has very strong feelings about the welfare of the women who serve in her household, and who he would strive not to offend even if she were not currently privy to certain secrets. Pylades considers himself a good man. This is a confusing self-judgement for any man in his position to hold.

He has been kept waiting far too long, he thinks, before Penelope arrives. She is veiled, as she always is when she enters a room with one who is not her husband or the three males of her council, and has taken some care to ensure that the soft gown that drifts around her when she comes to a halt before him is utterly shapeless in a way that suggests not that it hides a sensual form at all, but rather that it is designed to obscure a medley of physical defects both profound and unfashionable. It does not. Penelope's beauty is of the thigh that walks many hours upon the rugged ground, of the hand that holds the throat of the sheep as the knife is drawn across it, of the back that must not bend and the curves of womanhood that change as women age, flesh moving here and there of its own accord to create new contours that the nymphs mock and deride, not understanding what it is to live in a body that is the mirror to your soul.

Pylades sees none of this – just a veiled widowed woman, her state ever more precarious the further she grows from child-bearing years. So it is that with somewhat less than regal regard he half whispers, half shrills: "Where is Orestes?" as soon as the maids have closed the door behind their queen. Penelope attempts an arched eyebrow. It is something her mother-in-law did masterfully and she does not. Pylades is in no fit condition to heed the effort, as he adds: "I should be with him! I should be by his side!"

"The king is safe, and the princess is with him."

"Where?"

"I will not tell you."

Pylades bristles, he sweats, he turns crimson as the sunset sky. "He is my sworn brother, he is my care, he is—"

"Poisoned," Penelope murmurs softly, and the word is a

punch to the soldier's gut that he has almost never felt before. "Your king is poisoned."

"How?"

"We don't know. But when a man is bitten constantly by a snake, one cannot expect him to recover with the snake so near."

Pylades was not always quick to anger, but these times have been taxing, and so . . . "You cannot suggest that I—"

"I suggest nothing. Merely that Orestes was poisoned when at his own court, and then he was poisoned when away from it. He was poisoned on the road, he was poisoned on the seas. The serpent, it seems, has never been far from his side."

Pylades sits – or at least he seems no longer able to stand, and there is at least a helpful stool behind him. Penelope watches a moment, then drifts towards the window to enjoy a little of the smell of the sea, the wide ocean below her palace walls. At last: "I will need information on every soul who travelled with you from Mycenae to Ithaca. I need to know the name and quality of every man and woman on Orestes' ship. I also need to search your vessel."

"Why?"

"To see if the drug that has been used to poison Orestes remains on board."

"If Ithacans are seen searching a Mycenaean ship . . . "

"We will be discreet. I have a woman who has several cousins who work for her on the docks. They can board to help fix some loose timbers perhaps, or to help reseal a join? Tedious work, time-consuming. You can ensure they are not disrupted in their labours?"

He nods, and seems to have no more words to say.

She turns to him again, surprised perhaps by his quiet, and adds: "Elektra tells me you too were poisoned. In Mycenae."

"I . . . I was ill."

"In the same manner as Orestes?"

"It was . . . there was a night . . . I was ill."

"What did you do that night? Do you remember? What you touched, what you drank, what you ate?" He shakes his head, and she tuts. "This is your king's life."

"I . . . don't recall. We ate together, but there were many people eating. I touched nothing he touched, he drank from his own cup, we retired – he went to his room – and that is all I know."

Pylades is lying. Penelope suspects it too. But without the wisdom of the gods, she is not sure how to question it. "Do you have any idea of how your king is being so affected?" A shaking of his head. He is suddenly young. He is suddenly tired. Neither he nor Orestes were meant to be men so soon in their boyhoods; neither really had time to learn how to grow up. "Well," breathes Penelope at last, "you will be welcomed here as an ambassador to Ithaca. If you need anything, just . . ."

His hand curls out and catches at her wrist. He is holding too tight – this is how you hold the wrist of a maid, not a queen – and at once he loosens his grip. "Can I see him? Just for a moment? Can I see him?"

Penelope shakes her head, and leaves him alone in the silver light of the reflected sea.

CHAPTER 12

>>

A feast! But of course and always: a feast.

Here are some of the names of those who regularly attend this meal, served in the great hall of the palace of Odysseus:

Antinous, son of Eupheithes, his dark hair held in the most ridiculous of preened-out fashions with beeswax and oil. He heard that this is how the young men of Athens and Sparta, Corinth and Mycenae wear their locks, but having nothing more than some crude scratching on clay by which to model the effect, he has ended up with a mess of styles that would be laughed at in all places of culture across the isles. Thankfully Ithaca is not a place of culture, and those who would mock Antinous do so behind his back.

Eurymachus, son of Polybus. Golden-haired and pale-skinned, he has in recent months tried to acquire something of a more warrior-like physique, prompted no doubt by the really rather exceptional arms of the warrior Amphinomous, son of a king, or even the beautiful hint of chest and back that one may sometimes catch from Kenamon, the lovely Egyptian with the deep, scrummy eyes. Eurymachus is doing reasonably well on the toned arms of the discus thrower, albeit with the inevitable disparity between right and left that comes from such a sport, but alas, a truly manly chin brushed with soft beard that one might caress fondly after a turn between the sheets will always evade him.

Usually Antinous and Eurymachus are at each other's throats. Tonight they are not. Rather, a sullen mutual silence sits between them. That is strange indeed.

Serving the feast are the maids of the house – gorgeous Autonoe of the hollow laugh, quiet Eos who meets no one's eye until she does, and then it is as if one were struck blind by the force of her grey gaze. Others too – Melantho, broad-shouldered and wide-hipped, who carries grain on her back from the granary to the kitchen as if she were flinging sacks of fluffy cloud around, and light-footed, giggling Phiobe, who secretly sings at night songs that are meant only for the men, and long ago learned to rejoice in the sensuality of her own body. Of all of them, Phiobe is the only one who offers her prayers to me, and though I rarely heed the calls of maids and lesser sorts, tonight I kiss her soft brow with my crimson lips and give her my blessing. I will not curse her with an enforced love, nor promise her the fulfilment of some fantastic, ludicrous dream. Such things always end badly, and of all the gods, I know how carefully my powers must be used. But I can give her those gifts for which I am most often derided – a delight in the words of others spoken to her in praise, a joy in the beauty of her body, an ecstasy that lingers in warm contentment when she presses herself to another's flesh, a trust in a tryst that tonight at least no one will betray.

Pray to me, I whisper to the room. *Pray to Aphrodite.*

In corridors about the hall, when the menfolk are apart, the maids approach the suitors. In the early years, when the first suitors arrived, the maids kept distant, aloof. For one to crack, for one to dare whisper to a man that she too might be a being of sexual desires, let alone dream of such foolish notions as companionship, friendship, love of another who would choose to be by her side with joy in their heart – that endangered them all. For though the law said that any man who touched a maid could be punished most extraordinarily, if it was so much as whispered that the maid first cried out "yes, yes, yes!" – well, that was another matter entirely. So the maids kept themselves encased in ice, as their mistress was, Athena-like in chastity, the only safety a woman could own.

Yet a creature of warm blood and beating heart cannot live on ice alone for ever. And as more suitors filled the halls, there were really some quite dishy specimens starting to arrive, men who wooed the Ithacan queen with their eyes to her kingdom, not her flesh, and yet who were themselves also made of mortal parts. It was a nobody suitor – a man by the name of Thriasus – who first wooed a maid. He had been sent to Ithaca to try and make himself king, but his heart was not in it and he knew he had no hope of a crown. Yet neither could he leave, admit himself a smaller, lesser man than his peers, and so grumbling he remained until at last his eyes fell upon a maid by the name of Iros, and her eyes met his, and for a while – oh, for a while – it was love. They tumbled in moonlight, bathed in the sea, rubbed oil into each other's skin, each worshipped upon their lover's lips. Their young enrapturement faded after a while, crushed beneath these words: duty, honour, manliness, fear, secrets, dread. But it was enough to open the door, and from then on the maids and the suitors entangled with every form of desire, from the whims of the flesh through to the throbbing of hearts that beat only for each other.

Nothing could come of it, of course. If a maid grew fat-bellied, she was sent to one of Penelope's houses across the western isles to be a mother away from the eyes and wagging tongues of men. If a man sought to take a maid without consent, word would fly back to Penelope's ears, and though she could not punish that man publicly – not when it was known to all the isle that the womenfolk of her house were that most unhallowed of things, sexual beings – yet he would be punished. Stomach cramps would assail him from any dish he ate, his wine would always be bitter, his sleep disturbed by biting insects from filthy straw, and if at last, driven to distraction, he fled Penelope's house to take refuge in the town below, that would not end his torment. Even there those strange and peculiar plagues – wet wood smoking in the hearth, foul garments, and cruel rumours as to every aspect of his manhood – would pursue him, until into exile he went, laughter at his back and silence upon the lips of the women who waved him farewell.

Priene, captain of Penelope's secret army, considered this an entirely inadequate punishment. Death was what she sought for any such fellow – but a wrathful hostess may not murder even her most wayward of guests.

Euracleia, the old nursemaid of Odysseus, was of a different mind. "If a woman will bare her skin, smile, laugh, talk boldly, be loud, be seen, make herself known, then what does she expect? Men will be men, they can't help it, it's their nature. It's the woman's fault if she puts herself in a bad situation!"

Euracleia was a sexual being once, a long, long time ago. This single act of coitus had her whipped by her then-queen, Anticlea, and sent to the shadows of the palace, where she was called whore, slut, lowest of the low. When she gave birth, the child was sent away – she was told it died – but the milk from her breast was useful to the queen when her own ran dry, Odysseus being then but a babe. Euracleia has not permitted herself to think of the touch of a man – let alone a woman – since.

The nursemaid despises what Penelope has let her maids become, and yet her growling cannot prevent it. Nor would it even if Euracleia were of the more persuasive sort, for if

Penelope has learned one thing, it is that the occasional companionship between a maid and a suitor can be very, very useful.

And so:

"How are you tonight, Eurymachus?" asks bright-eyed Autonoe, as she passes him another cup of wine.

"Antinous, did you oil your hair just for me?" giggles Phiobe, leaning down low to spread another dish before him.

"Amphinomous, may I tempt you to something more?" wonders Melantho of the generous hips.

There was another maid here not long ago, a Trojan by the name of Leaneira, who also played this game. But the game went too far, and now she is gone. When the word "freedom" was whispered, Eos was appalled.

"Leaneira free?" she gasped. "How will she survive?"

In her quieter moments, Penelope thinks upon this question, and feels ashamed.

Usually the soft enquiries of the maids would produce a giddy response of male enthusiasm, as each suitor feels assured that he – why yes, even Eurymachus – has with his manly attributes won the adoration of a woman of the house. And why wouldn't he? He has many qualities such as . . . well, you know . . . there's this one thing he can do with a fig . . .

Tonight, however, the suitors are distant, distracted. They do not respond to the gentle brush of a finger across their backs. Do not turn their heads when invited to talk some easy talk in the moonlit garden, do not glance up from their bowls as elegant wrists refill them. It is baffling to Eos, frankly insulting to Autonoe, and a source of great discomfort for the Ithacan queen.

Pylades sits near Penelope in the place of honour at the top of the hall as the poets sing and no one stirs. He is a sullen guest, picking at his food, another discordant note in the shadowed room. Behind them is the chair that Odysseus would sit in were he here. Penelope has never sat in her husband's seat – that's the kind of thing Clytemnestra might do, the kind of act that people might look at and go "she's got some ideas above herself, that one has". Instead she sits a little below and to the side of it, a guardian of this empty place, her husband's ancient dog Argos at her side.

The poet has been invited to sing songs of Agamemnon tonight. It is always good form to sing something that might make your guest feel at ease, but Pylades appears not to notice. Penelope makes some effort at small talk – she is very poor at the art, relying on the willingness of others to talk about themselves to get by – but to no effect.

The suitors do not look at her, and this is unusual, so she takes the opportunity to stare straight at them, examining every man from beneath her veil with a boldness that the rules of modesty usually deny her. They are a shrunken, hunched lot tonight. They are vultures, curled behind their feathered wings. They are hiding something, she is sure of it.

All except one. Kenamon, the Egyptian, an outcast to both his people and this hall, looks up as her gaze pauses upon him, and smiles.

His reaction is shocking, unacceptable. Penelope's head whips away, a sudden movement that still is not enough to rouse Pylades from his misery, though Eos's hand flies to her mistress's shoulder, enquiring, supporting.

Men do not smile at Penelope.

They smirk. They leer. They ingratiate. They whine. They bargain.

They do not smile as if they were genuinely pleased to see her. Even Odysseus, when they first met all those many, many years ago, had to learn what it was to be happy to meet his wife. She was a princess of Sparta, she was the mother of his child, she was a queen of Ithaca, and these duties left little time in the day to be anyone else, let alone a woman, whole and true.

Kenamon smiles, and when he does, it is as if he is smiling at her. At the woman beneath the veil. At Penelope. This is as disturbing and strange as the coldness and quiet of the usually boisterous suitors.

I move through the hall, run my fingers through Kenamon's hair. He smells of salt and cedar, the memories of old loves and broken hearts clinging to him still from his far-off land. He has done his duty, he thinks – he has sailed to Ithaca as his brother commanded, to woo a queen – and now he can return home, a failure again. Why doesn't he? He does not know.

Pray to me, I whisper in his ear. *Pray to Aphrodite. I will teach you to know the truth of yourself, to love yourself, to love the world.*

He does not hear me. His prayers are to the falcon, Horus, who travelled far and wide before returning with sword and justice to his homeland. I met Horus once on an island swallowed by the sea, and though the beak made for an unusual experience, it was still a fascinating and thoroughly worthwhile afternoon. But for all his many positive qualities, I have no doubt the protector god does not heed the prayers of this mortal from so far across the sea.

Pray to me, I breathe. *Pray to . . .*

Then I sense the power of another.

Soft and silver, she moves through the hall both visible and invisible to mortal eyes.

She is dressed as an old shepherd, and should a mortal glance up and behold her, he will see a crooked man smiling with broken teeth. Then he will look away, and he will forget that he saw anything at all, and thus both here and not here, Athena, lady of war and wisdom, comes to the feast.

I straighten at once, resisting the temptation to adjust my gown, to flick my hair from my face and pull my shoulders back to match her divine hauteur. No one can out-Athena Athena, so I do not try, but rather rest contentedly in my own strength and beauty, my shrouded radiance hidden from the eyes of men lest the whole meal around us descend into a rather thrilling yet ultimately messy orgy at the merest whiff of my perfume. Her eyes settle on me for the barest moment, then she turns away, moves towards the fireplace near where the poets sing, imbuing the music with a clearer note, a curious turn of phrase as she passes. A line that should have been sung to the glory of Ares twists on itself and instead praises the mighty spear of Athena. Ares, though mighty, is not wise. He has not spent as much time as Athena has dallying with the souls of those who sing a warrior's praises.

She settles on a stool by the hearth, and I unfold myself one elegant limb at a time on a seat before her, resisting the temptation to blow her a gentle kiss across the gulf between us. Such a display of affection would only rile her. This is her tragedy, and mine.

"Athena," I chirrup, holding in a waft of glorious scent from my settling gown lest it set off a bawdy ballad from the singing man nearby. "How lovely to see you."

"Cousin," she replies. "I did not think to find you on Ithaca. I thought maybe the temples of Corinth, or some pet-alled bower?"

"And is there not love in the western isles?" I reply. "Is there not some really rather juicy passion? Take Penelope, for example." Her eyes flash, but she is hiding her thunder, her might, her roar of flame – unusual for Athena. "How enthralling it is to see a woman who as a young bride took such delight in learning and exploring the contours of her own body," I continue, head a little to one side, studying my cousin's visage, "who remembers what it was to be held, to be loved, who knows its soft breath, and who yet denies herself. There was a time when she touched herself while remembering these things, but even that has faded, is not allowed, is not permitted, because of the danger in it, such danger in love, such power in it! She understands that better I think than some of our peers. It is enthralling, is it not? When she finally lets herself go, my goodness it will be a sight to see, it will be a prayer of ecstasy to set Olympus on fire, it will be—"

"That's enough, cousin!" Athena barks, and there it is again, her hidden flame that she will not let burn. I smile brightly at her, resting my chin in the palm of my hand. Athena does not meet my eyes.

"And how is Odysseus?" I ask. "I saw you watching Ogygia again a few nights ago. Calypso is astonishingly flexible – and imaginative too! It is refreshing, is it not, to see a man wholly release himself, wholly trust his body to a woman; submit you might say to the wisdom of one whose sensuality is of such honed and delightful quality, to the benefit of both."

"Odysseus will be freed." She is on the verge of growling, spitting the words through gritted teeth, though I do not know if she knows that she does it. "Poseidon is visiting the people of the southern seas; he will not return for several moons. I have arranged everything. Father will agree. Hermes will fly to Calypso, she will help him build a raft . . . "

"And then what? He returns to this lovely little palace to find a hundred men waiting for him who are less than enamoured at his return? Is that why you are here, cousin? Having a look at what's in store for your handsome hairy Odysseus? Not that I mind a bit of hair, lovely chest he's got, lovely legs, that scar! I could trace that scar for hours . . . "

"Why are you here, cousin?" She is a breath away from snapping the words, a goddess of wisdom who does not have the answer, who cannot meet my delightful eye. I let out a little breath, understanding, lean forward, catch her hand in mine. She flinches, but does not pull away. Of all the gods, only she and Artemis can resist my power, even if Athena doubts, doubts in her heart, oh, but how she doubts that is true.

"Oh dearest one," I breathe. "You are afraid." She bristles, prepares to roar, to blaze, but I put a finger to my lips. "Not of me. Not of me. Never of me. How long has Odysseus been on Ogygia? Six, seven years? A hero who wouldn't die, who must therefore suffer, and keep on suffering until the gods decide his story is done. You have fought for him so hard. I've seen you on Olympus, plotting, scheming, whispering in corners just like Penelope. And now that you are so close to achieving your end, of freeing your favourite, you are afraid. Of what? That if you shine too brightly, that if you reveal your love for this man – yes, it is love; love is more rich and more splendid than any of our brothers will ever know – Zeus will keep him imprisoned for ever? Your affection has made you weak. Vulnerable. You have shown loyalty. You have shown passion. This means you can be hurt. Our brothers will hurt you, if they know they can. It's just what they do. That's why you hide your fire. You are afraid."

Athena pulls her hand from mine, squeezes it into a fist as if stung, but does not flinch away, nor meet my eye. "Hera came to Ithaca," she murmurs. "She came because Clytemnestra was here. Her favourite queen. The last of the great queens of Greece. Clytemnestra . . . had to die. Hera knew it. But she wept for her. All the gods saw Hera weep. And where is she now? Trapped on Olympus, watched every day and every night by the servants of Zeus. He said, 'Dammit, she loves that dead mortal bitch more than she loves me!' He made it funny. Everyone laughed at Hera, stood and laughed, because she had shown herself to be weak. She had shown that she could love. But not Zeus. He will punish her for that. *Is* punishing her for that. He will never forgive her for loving someone who isn't him."

Again I reach for her hand, but this time she snatches it away. "My poor owl," I sigh. "My lovely Athena. Of all the heroes you could have chosen in all of Greece to take to your bosom, you had to choose the soppiest. Don't worry – I won't tell. No one would believe me if I did. You want to know why I am on Ithaca? It is because someone *I* love – very much – is coming to this island."

Athena's eyes dart to Pylades, and in her gaze I see her also looking beyond, to where Elektra slumbers by her brother's side, then up to where the Furies still circle high above Orestes' sweating brow. But no – she is wise, and so she looks beyond, beyond again, and then at last she understands. "Oh," she breathes. "*She* is coming."

"Of course she is," I murmur. "He never goes anywhere without her these days."

She straightens a little, and what moment there was of a woman swathed in silver is gone, and only the goddess-warrior remains stiffly seated before me. "These matters are more complicated than you understand," she barks. "They are—"

"Oh, that," I interrupt with a waft of my silken hand. "I wouldn't want to trouble my poor fuzzy little brain with all these ... *political* things. Who is going to be master of Mycenae, king of kings, all that dreadful tedious stuff. Don't worry – Aphrodite leaves all that big, important business to people who really care about it. Which I imagine you do, a little. I imagine that it would be less than thrilling for you if Menelaus seized Orestes' throne, crowned himself king of kings. I imagine you would be not entirely titillated to see a man whose only deity is Ares, the cup and the spear, made master of all the Greeks. Why, a man like Menelaus, if he had enough power, wouldn't give a damn about Odysseus or who was king in the west – he'd just take it all for himself. Gobble up every last isle and kill any poet who sang any name but his own. That would be dreadful, wouldn't it? One man set above all the rest, only his name remembered through the ages, only his story told – not Odysseus's. Not yours. Even thinking about it makes my dear little head ache. And of course, that doesn't even cover what between sky and sea you are going to do about the Furies."

Athena's lips thin, imperceptible to all but the most divine of eyes. I resist the urge to run my finger along the line of her mouth, to explore those contours and see if her flesh is indeed as cool as her voice. I am so enthralled by contemplation of this expedition that I nearly miss her words, delivered as if they were the most obvious thing in the world.

"Clytemnestra did not set the Furies upon her son."

"I . . . What?"

"Clytemnestra. No doubt she will be blamed for summoning the Furies to avenge her, but she did not set them upon Orestes. She drinks of the river of forgetfulness until it washes away the memories of her slain children, her slaughtered lover, until only Orestes' name remains. She clutches at the wound through her chest that he made, and it bleeds, and keeps on bleeding, and she cries out, 'My lovely boy!' as she wanders through fields of mist. As I am the lady of wisdom, I say this: Clytemnestra did not summon the Furies."

"Then who?" I ask, and at once think I know the answer. "Goodness. What a state."

"You see now why these matters are beyond you?"

"Oh yes, dear cousin," I chirrup brightly. "Hera is stuck on Olympus watched over by her husband, you are hiding every part of yourself from sight of mortal and immortal alike lest someone think to mention to Poseidon that you are within a whisper of having Odysseus freed. Hermes is doubtless off stealing cattle, Apollo strumming his lyre and Artemis having a lovely time in her forest grove. Why, it seems that really the only one of your kin who might be of any use to you at all in preventing Menelaus burning these islands to the ground is the most ditsy, air-headed and useless of them all!"

It takes a lot to surprise the goddess of wisdom. When she is surprised, it shows only as the slightest intake of breath, so soft and gentle you might think it nothing more than a little inhalation after a fat black fly landed on the tip of her nose. It is the same breath she drew when she accidentally drove her spear into Pallas's heart when they were sparring, saying of it after: "I have learned much from the experience." Pallas had often dreamed of their fights together, and of how at the end of a turn about the dusty field they would fall, swords at each other's throats, lips at each other's lips, legs scrabbling against each other for purchase as they tumbled and tumbled and tumbled, sweat and blood mingling on their brows, fingers unhooking the armour from off each other's backs. That dream died when Pallas did, and Athena breathes slightly – so slightly – even when her heart is breaking.

So she steadies herself.

Athena is nothing if not steady.

She says, without looking directly at me – very few of my kin ever look directly at me – "There may be a time. When I must call upon you."

These words are hard for her. I want to tell her that it's all right, that I'm here for her, that I love her. Those words would be impossible for her to hear. So instead I nod, and let that be enough, and she is gone in a breath, in a flicker of silver, in the beating of white-feathered wings.

In the night, after the feast, Penelope goes to her bedroom window and thinks she hears singing.

It is in a strange language, yet one she can now at least place even if she does not understand the words.

Kenamon, the Egyptian. He is sitting in her secret garden – the garden where really the menfolk should not go, not that she can ban them outright should they demand to walk its narrow confines. She showed it to him one day after Telemachus had sailed, told him he was always welcome in it, in thanks for some few services he had performed in her son's aid. Naturally he could never be in it at the same time as she – that would be impossible, dangerous beyond belief – but she hoped the sweet fragrance of the flowers might bring him a little contentment, seeing as he was so far from home.

My husband, you see, is also far from home.

She felt she should add these words, muttered out of the corner of her mouth, her eye not meeting his.

Of course, the Egyptian replied. I am sure his every thought is of coming back to you.

Now he sits in her garden, and he sings songs in a language she does not understand.

He knows that she can hear, though of course he has never asked.

She knows he knows, though of course she will never say so. A man singing for the queen of Ithaca? It cannot be allowed. But a stranger, ignorant of the proper way of things, who happens to sing in a fragrant garden beneath an open window?

Well.

Sometimes these charming coincidences.

They will happen.

So they will.

And so to the darkness, and to the darkness alone, Kenamon sings.

Two days later, the Spartans came.

CHAPTER 13

‣‣‣

The Spartan ships have crimson sails, and if you did not see them as they approached the bay, you would hear their drums.

They beat out a steady rhythm, each one ringing to the strain of sinew, to the gritting of teeth, to the thrusting of arms and bending of backs as the sailors pull against their oars. *Boom – boom – boom – boom.*

They come at first light from the south, pushing up towards Ithaca's harbour. Fishing boats scatter before them, their crews of widows and daughters hiding their faces beneath their cloaks as they pull for shore, the morning catch flopping at their bare shell-scarred feet.

Boom – boom – boom – boom.

The largest of the vessels has an awning set out at the stern, draped silks that billow in the breeze. They are woven with golden thread, and some still bear the image of the horse, the sea, the fallen city from which they were stolen, taken from a royal bedchamber to now bedeck a ship at sea. Maids with golden bangles on their arms and faded white scars across their backs hold up platters of figs and dates, grapes and pickled fish for their masters' hands to pluck, while the drummer, clad only in a really rather charming loincloth that leaves little to the imagination, maintains his rhythm. Not many men can get away with displaying so much buttock while on the job, but Spartans have always had very strong opinions about male beauty, and though it can lead to some socially toxic long-term consequences, right now I am here for it.

Boom – boom – boom – boom.

The soldiers who mill about the deck are also chosen for their beauty, though the ideal that sculpts such a word is never simple. "Beauty" in a veteran of Troy must encompass scars; there must be an eye that looks darkly upon the world, a mouth that is rarely inclined to laughter. Height and width of shoulder are prioritised over smaller, speedier men who did just as well at surviving the war as their hunky counterparts – for a sharp blade and a quick mind will sever a man's arm as surely as a strong swing from a hunky bicep. Yet that is not how the poets speak of war – their discourse is of giants and lions, the clash of shields and the roar of mighty men – and in Sparta, for all that they pretend not to have much time for the poets, they nevertheless have taken this message to heart. So it is that a giant surfeit of manhood, an enormous bulk of muscular masculinity stands upon the decks of the six red-sailed ships as they approach Ithaca, to the pounding of the ox-skinned drums.

Boom – boom – boom – boom!

Penelope is woken by Autonoe, who has already set much of the household in motion. Eos is on her way to Laertes' farm with a warning to the Mycenaeans huddled within; Melantho is rousing Pylades.

"You are sure it is Sparta?" asks Penelope, already knowing the answer.

"Unless any other king plans on visiting with sails like blood and ships decked out in spears," Autonoe replies, as Penelope is pinned into her veil.

*

For all that there are some really mighty biceps pulling on the oars of the Spartan ships, it takes them until the sun is well above the horizon, the sea turned from silver to gold, to enter Ithaca's port. The harbour mouth is not wide, nor the quays truly built for so many substantial vessels. Other smaller ships, merchants from the north and purveyors of amber and tin, are forced to cast off and shuffle aside to make way for the royal fleet. This would usually induce a litany of complaining and bitter reproach – today it does not. Even the saltiest of the sea-faring sort keep their mouths in check when warships such as these come into port.

The jostling back and forth, the shuffling in and out does rather detract from the regality of the moment. The more cynical might suspect that this is somewhat satisfying to the Ithacans as they assemble on the edge of the water. "No point having a big ship if you can't sail it," mutters Peisenor, the old councillor dragged from his bed far sooner than he would wish, his finest robe a little grubby about the knees.

"I heard Menelaus 'acquired' his navy from Tiryns," muses Medon, as the drums beat on despite the clearly now less than rhythmic motion of the vessels. "Suggested to the king there that what would be best for his city would be the loving protection and generous support of Sparta, and that Sparta could best support said city if it took command of Tiryns' navy, granaries and lumberyards. In a friendly, neighbourly fashion."

"Are you surprised?" tuts Aegyptius. "Even before Agamemnon appointed himself king of all the Greeks, those brothers were pulling that trick. The only thing that stopped them was the lesser kings banding in alliance, and alliances these days are . . . " His voice trails off. Aegyptius doesn't really know what to make of the alliances of Greece today, but he's pretty sure they weren't like that when he was young.

Penelope says nothing. When men talk, this is her usual

position. There was a time when her son, Telemachus, would stand by the docks with her and ask questions – *Mummy, what's that big ship?* Or, *Mummy, why is Agamemnon the king of kings? Is he really really wise and good or is he just strong?*

Under those circumstances, Penelope would answer – not as a queen, of course, but as a mother. Her voice was acceptable and she never said anything too controversial, and thus, in a way, the merest presence of her son gave her a chance to be audible. But Telemachus is gone, and today, as the sun rises higher over Ithaca, his absence is a knot in her belly. She knows she should fear these crimson ships, she should be trembling inside with what they entail, with who and what they may bear, and yet now – oh, now – she reaches out her hand to where her son would have been, and he is not there, and it sickens her to her very centre.

Pylades arrives as the largest and greatest of the Spartan ships finally positions itself and ropes are thrown to the shore. He is fully armoured, his helmet polished, his greaves glistening in the sun, a sword at his hip. Aegyptius looks at him as one might regard a child with a wooden blade. Peisenor appears mildly envious of the young man, chin up and back straight. Penelope glances at him once, then away, and is grateful that the veil hides the rolling of her eyes.

Behind him, the suitors. Antinous and his father; Eurymachus and his. Even Kenamon has come to see what portent these scarlet sails might bring. He has heard great rumours of this Menelaus – many people who have not seen lions have compared the man and the beast, and Kenamon, who has indeed seen a lion and understood that the long grass around it hid the hunting females who he saw not, is fascinated to learn what the poets are going on about.

The drumming stops.

It has been such a recurring theme of the morning that

the people of the town had almost forgotten it was there, the noise blending into the background of voices, creaking and the squawk of gulls. Its silence silences them, which is precisely the effect intended. A ramp is lowered from the side, and a troop of men in bright bronze armour and red plumes in their helmets jog – actually jog, it's all so *very* manly – onto the quay. There they array themselves in two lines down either side, their heels threatening to tip backwards over the water as they try to leave enough space on the narrow walkway. Thus assembled, they raise their spears three times to the heavens and give their cry: "Menelaus! Menelaus! Menelaus!"

There are two ways an entrance such as this may go. In many cities across many lands, such a roar of hearty breath would be followed by wild and rapturous applause, cheering, stamping of feet and cries of "Long live Menelaus, hero of Troy!" This is perhaps the desired effect. But the people of Ithaca are nothing if not a little backwards, and all but a tiny handful of assembled women and one Mycenaean man at the harbourside are frankly astonished by this pronouncement. Menelaus? King of Sparta, hero of Troy? What could possibly bring him *here*? Thus, rather than cries of celebration and general ecstatic brouhaha, it is instead to a hush marred only by the heavy flapping of sheets tied down in the breeze and the billowing of slightly grubby gowns that Menelaus descends from his ship.

Menelaus.

There he is.

I remember him when he was a young man, fighting with Agamemnon to win back his kingdom and, incidentally, any other kingdoms nearby that no one seemed particularly willing to defend. Neither he nor his brother would be painted on the side of an amphora any time, but that was because they had not yet accrued enough power to really make their mark on fashion. Only once they had slain their enemies, claimed their crowns, declared themselves kings above all the rest did the ideal of manhood start to move from the taller, skinnier type with a honed but fairly mighty chest to the somewhat shorter rectangles of thrusting humanity that the brothers represented. That was when I began to understand their power – they had grown so great that even beauty bent and changed to honour their whim.

And so there he is. A man who was once considered really rather ugly, and became through power and might and force of arms one of the most handsome men in the world. Time has swagged his belly down but holds no power over his shoulders, his slab neck, his jutting chin and hooked nose. His dark curls, flecked with that same bloody hue as his crimson flag, are greying about the temples, and he does not bother over-much with tending to his beard. True Spartans, you see, do not need to *work* on their physique. They are born perfect, or they are not – that too is the myth Menelaus has created. He wears a robe the colour of the evening sky. It was Priam's robe, king of Troy, plucked from his body, the blood still a little mottled around the hem. Menelaus says it has never been washed, and doesn't realise that he lies – it has in fact been cleaned eleven times since the fall of Troy, twice by accident and nine times when it began to reek, and he doesn't notice and wouldn't care.

He doesn't wear armour.

Menelaus of Sparta doesn't need armour. He didn't wear it when the Trojans burned the Greek ships, rushing into the melee straight from his cot in little more than a loincloth and sheet to lay waste to his enemies. Observing his breastplate when he returned from Troy, he concluded that of all the dents and bumps it had received, none would have been fatal, so what really was the point, but he travels everywhere with it, suspended always above the throne wherein he sits, so that he can explain his reasoning to anyone who might deign to ask. Everyone makes sure they do.

This is the man who steps from the ship onto the dock at Ithaca, in the silence of only a busy breeze. This is the man who walks down the alley created by his warriors, his eyes taking in it all – the crowd, the suitors, the councillors, the queen. This is he, who burned the towers, who slew the babes, who stood upon the corpses of fallen kings, who plucked his rogue queen by the hair and dragged her back to Sparta, this is he, *this is he* – Menelaus, Menelaus, Menelaus!

He approaches Penelope in silence.

Other nobles and dignitaries, when they come to Ithaca, might approach her councillors first, the representatives of the isle's missing king. Menelaus has no time for old men like these – his gaze is fixed firmly upon the queen, flanked by her maids in shrouded veils. His eyes flicker to Pylades – barely – then dance away. His smile grows as he nears the ladies – what might these little white teeth in rolling crimson lips entail? they wonder. Will he pluck off their veils, kiss their cheeks, strike them down? What would the butcher of Troy not do to a woman whose man has left her far behind?

Penelope has not seen Menelaus for over twenty years, when all the daughters of Sparta were married off to their various princes and kings. Then he spoke to her only once, to say: "So you're the one who hatched from a duck instead of a swan?" and everyone laughed and thought it was very funny, and Penelope smiled and simpered and only later, being barely more than a child, hid in her room to cry.

Now he nears.

Now he slows.

Now he beams into her eyes as if the veil that covers them and the distance of more than twenty years, of war and sea and blood and the forging and breaking of every vow that could ever matter, were nothing – nothing! A thing that happened at last full moon, a little sneeze lost to the wind.

106

Now he opens his arms.

"Penelope!" he exclaims.

And in a single swoop of sand-scorched limb, the king of Sparta gives his cousin a great big squishy hug.

Cloth flaps heavy in the breeze. Water laps thick against the harbour walls. A gull shrieks indignantly. I pinch its beak shut, gesture at it and its kin to be gone, silence the shrilling of a flock of cliff-hugging birds that chatter and hop together on walls of ragged stone. Glance around to see if any other gods are watching – think for the briefest instant I see a flash of Athena's spear among the crowd, but she is as hidden as quickly as she is found.

No man has touched Penelope for nearly twenty years. Her child, of course, Telemachus – when he was too young to understand what it was to be a man, he would hold her hand, hide behind her gown, run to her for comfort. But those days are gone, even if he remains still a boy trying to grow a man's beard.

And besides, no man has *hugged* Penelope for as long as she can remember. Odysseus "he gives lovely hugs" is not how her husband is generally renowned. But Menelaus – he wraps his arms around her, presses his beard into her neck, his chest against her chest – not with a hint of sexuality, not a single jot of desire or stirring of nether parts – and just holds her tight, as if by his touch he might help carry the burden of all things that sit upon her.

It goes on for an age. It is over far too soon.

Menelaus steps back, hands still clasping the tops of Penelope's arms. Beams, squeezes and seems for a moment so pleased to see her that he might just give her another great big hug again, unable to contain his lovely fluffy delight. Looks around and takes in the elder statesmen of the isle, the massed suitors, the maids – Pylades. Now he lets his eye fall a moment longer on the Mycenaean, and he smiles and smiles again, and nods once in recognition, if not perhaps in friendship.

"Penelope!" he repeats, letting his voice carry with the ease of a general across the silent crowd. "Penelope – your majesty, I should say! Goodness, so rude, so thoughtless, forgive an old soldier." He releases his grip at last, executes a little bow – a far greater bow than anyone has given this shocked queen since . . . goodness, since when? (*Since the lovely Egyptian came to your land*, I whisper. *He bowed to you, not knowing any better, and my word, wasn't it delightful?*) "I'm getting so thoughtless," Menelaus continues, in much the same manner as a man might confess to sometimes not bothering to secure his robe tight about the loins. "I keep saying to my sons that all this peace will be the death of me!"

He laughs. In the crowd, a couple of suitors attempt to laugh with him, and at once Menelaus's eyes dart to them, and they fall silent again, staring at the ground and shuffling their toes – nothing to see here. This laugh, it appears, was his to have alone. He will inform you when merriment is to be shared.

"My lord," Penelope begins, a little speech she has had a while to prepare, a piece of modest oratory, precisely and exactly judged. "You are most welcome to Ithaca, where—"

He cuts her off. Clytemnestra's jaw would have dropped; she would have been furious at the brisk dismissal, the sharp swipe of a man's hand through her words. Penelope merely closes her lips. Penelope is not Clytemnestra. "You needn't bother with all that!" Menelaus proclaims, wrapping an arm about her shoulders and pulling her a little way from her entourage, as if it were for the maids or the assembled men of Ithaca that she is now needlessly performing, rather than him, good old Menelaus. "May I call you sister? I know it's presumptuous, but your husband was my sworn brother, a great man – a great man – and I've been dreadful in all these years he's been missing. I feel terrible about it, leaving you out here alone. If Odysseus could see me now, he'd be furious at my letting his wife put up with all this by herself. I feel ashamed. Utterly ashamed. I hope you can forgive me, sister?"

His eyes are wide, round, flecked with green in his sun-drenched fruit of a face. Penelope was trained as a girl to meet no man's eyes, then as a queen to meet some eyes some of the time, but mostly to aspire to look up and a little to the left of any questioning gazes that might fall upon hers, as though to say "ah, look, I am contemplating some distantly queenly matter you cannot comprehend" without risking the full confrontation of visage gazing upon visage. With Menelaus, there is no escape. He is a battering ram; his shoulder pressed to hers like ladder to wall.

"There is nothing to forgive . . . brother," she manages at last. "Rather it is I who should apologise to you. Ithaca and Sparta have long been the nearest of allies, but with my husband lost, I have been too weak, too foolish to honour and uphold our ancient accords as I know he would have wished. I can only hope that in this happy hour . . . "

It is then that she sees her.

The rest of Menelaus's entourage are standing upon the deck of his ship, waiting their turn to descend.

There are some she does not recognise. Warriors, a prince, a priest. A noble assemblage to accompany a king.

But there is also one she knows well.

She stands upon the edge of the ramp to the quay, her arms held loosely by her sides, fingertips resting in the palms of the two maids who steady her, as if even this light motion of the ship at harbour might be too much, overbalance her dainty little limbs. Her golden hair is woven with silver and pearl; her face is painted with white lead, brows stained with wax and charcoal to darken and elongate their already perfect form. Her lips are pricked with crimson, which also is smeared into her cheeks, and she holds her chin high so that all might appreciate how even after all these years, all the children she has born, her neck is like the long white limb of the sacred swan that made her. There are wrinkles about her eyes, soft folds of flesh near her hips and about the tops of her arms that she has tried to hide with binding, with concoctions of oil and ground-up metals, with painted ochre and the way she draws her shoulders back, but they are there nonetheless, mortality weighing down even upon one whose life should be an immortal myth. If a reckless sniffing stranger drew near, they would find that her hair smells of marjoram, her arms of roses. I breathe the lightest divinity upon her, to elevate the sweet perfume that wafts about her, so that even those on the dock think they catch the faintest trace of jasmine on the air, detect the shimmer of perfection in her tiny flashing smile. Whisper in her ear: *welcome, my love. Welcome.*

Penelope seeing her seems to create an arrow-straight line that others may follow. A little gasp runs through the crowd, a ripple, a stirring of men and women alike as people behold the woman on the deck, growing as they understand. But surely it cannot be, they wonder; surely this thing is not possible? Not on Ithaca, not on these islands smelling of fish where the most interesting thing that happens is sometimes finding an exceptionally large squid. Is it her? Is it she?

It is Peisenor who is the first to crack and give hushed voice to this enquiry, leaning over to Aegyptius to mutter: "That's not . . . ?"

"It is," Aegyptius mutters back. "Zeus save us all."

As if she had been waiting for that little ripple of recognition as an orator awaits their cue, the woman descends, still guarded by her maids as if the slightest step might turn into a fatal fall. The prince, the soldiers and the priest follow behind, making no effort at all to try and outshine the majesty of this female's descent, a shuffling clank of manhood drifting in her wake.

Menelaus stands by Penelope's side, arms folded now, his

smile a crooked thing that presses against one side of his jaw as if it is contemplating making an escape from his face altogether. They wait for the woman to approach, which she does at no great speed. Wait for her to bow before the queen of Ithaca. Wait for her to straighten up, smile, simper, turn her eyes demurely to the ground.

"Penelope," Menelaus says. "You remember my wife Helen, don't you?"

CHAPTER 14

>>

Once, there were three princesses in Sparta.

Clytemnestra and Helen were daughters of Zeus, after he took a fancy to Leda, the king's wife, and descended upon her in the form of a swan. Now I'm open-minded about basically everything in the realms of consensual bodily exploration, and I can see where Zeus was coming from, but even so, I doubt the execution of the act was half as exciting in reality as he thought it was going to be in his overactive imagination. He swore blind on his return to Olympus that it was really all rather fantastic and he'd absolutely do it again. Leda's opinion on the matter was not sought.

Penelope was the daughter of Icarius, brother of Tyndareus, whose wife it was who had such an unexpected ornithological encounter. Icarius was married to Polycaste, a really rather decent woman, but that didn't stop him having a night of acrobatic and somewhat damp sexual ecstasy with a nymph of the river and the sea who didn't have anything else going on that evening and wasn't too bothered either way. When nine months later, said nymph arrived with a babe and deposited her at Icarius's door, the Spartan prince took one look at the child, nodded with a firm, warrior-like resolve, waited for her mother

112

to depart, scooped up the slumbering infant and threw her off the nearest cliff.

This should have been the end of it, but what can one say? Sometimes the sea and the river take offence when one seeks to drown their progeny, and with much quacking and falling of feather, no sooner had the babe been chucked to her doom than she was lifted back up to her father's side by a flock of ducks.

Usually in such tales the rule of three might apply, and Icarius should have sought to murder his daughter twice more. However, there is something about the sight of your infant child being borne aloft by more than a dozen paddling birds of various sorts that sends a clear and decisive message, and so with a remarkably level head, Icarius nodded once, picked up his babe, marched back to the palace, deposited her on his wife's lap and said, "Fantastic news, dearest! I found this beautiful orphan child and have decided we should adopt her, isn't that top notch good-o?"

Much like Leda, Polycaste's view on all of this was not sought. Yet unlike Leda, who on giving birth to eggs after a night of being ravished by a swan was hardly in the nurturing mood, Polycaste was disinclined to punish the child for the sin of her origin. "She shall be loved," she declared, holding the infant Penelope unto her bosom, and to everyone's surprise, this turned out to be true.

Thus these children were raised together – the daughters of a god, and the child saved by a flock of protective ducks. Traditionally your Spartan king is more interested in sons than daughters, but after Tyndareus's precious twins, Castor and Pollux, kidnapped the betrothed daughters of his brother Aphareus and whisked them away bound and gagged on the back of two horses with a cry of "We told you we were the better choice of husband!" a messy feud ensued that resulted in a great deal of spilled blood and a rapid loss of available menfolk to really get invested in. Thus Tyndareus spent an unusual amount of effort to ensure that the marriage of his female family members was a great event, in which all the kings of Greece came to compete for the privilege and honour of their hand. Clytemnestra was married off to Tantalus first, which was considered a perfectly adequate match that helped secure a long-time ally of Sparta on the country's northern border. Agamemnon, however, had taken a bit of a shine to Clytemnestra, which he manifested by slaughtering her husband and infant babe in front of her before claiming her as his wife, just to make it clear how strongly he felt.

Helen, however, was the real prize. So beautiful that even as an infant she had been kidnapped and stowed away by Theseus until she was of marriageable age, her reputation fast outgrew itself to the point where her actual charms were of very little relevance to the conversation. What mattered about Helen was that someone *else* wanted her. Another man. Another king. And thus, to truly show your manliness, to truly prove that *he* was greater than *him*, and that *he* was the mightier specimen than *that man over there*, it became something of a test of kingship to be the one who successfully captured the hand of this Spartan princess. This presented a problem for Tyndareus, who had hoped he could get her married off to Menelaus as quickly as possible, and thus help ensure that the crown of Sparta passed to his favourite drinking buddy on Tyndareus's death. But suddenly all the manhood of Greece was swaggering around Sparta, demanding to be fed and watered and explaining in the most emphatic of ways that no, but seriously, *he* was the better match.

This was roughly the time when Odysseus, a nobody prince from a fairly insignificant splat of grimy islands, offered Tyndareus a helpful plan. Have all the suitors swear that no matter who married Helen, the others would all support that man and defend his claim. Since every man there firmly believes *he* is the right choice for Helen, they won't hesitate to swear, imagining that the oath will ultimately benefit themselves. When only one man can win, it is remarkable how many men will consider themselves the guaranteed winner, whispered Odysseus.

This was a fine plan, as far as Tyndareus was concerned, and when Odysseus named his price for his cunning, though it was cheeky and somewhat steep, the king was in such a good mood that he didn't really argue.

"What, Penelope?" he blurted. "You want my brother's daughter?"

"Indeed," Odysseus replied. "A match with one as noble as she would bring great honour to my house."

"First we get Helen wed," Tyndareus agreed, "and then we talk."

I attended the wedding of Helen and Menelaus, of course. Many gods did. Zeus had run his fingers through his beard and mused over dinner: "I see Helen is getting married to Prince Menelaus. So nice to see young people doing well," and his gaze had swept the room and the assembled divinities had got the idea pretty quickly as to the right kind of noises they should make.

I probably would have gone anyway, if only because as weddings went, it was one of the most lavish, most spectacular the mortals could throw, and at events like that there always comes a point after the moon's silver orb has set where people really let themselves go.

Helen had met Menelaus only once before the wedding. She was fourteen years old, and very excited. Everyone had made it clear to her what a strong, handsome, brave, magnificent chap this young prince was and how lucky she would be. On their one encounter before vows were made, she had been so nervous she'd hardly been able to look at him, and he had been so thoroughly disappointed in her little giggles and shallow mono-syllables that afterwards he'd gone and found himself a devotee of my temple to ease his anxieties with, enjoying a thoroughly fabulous night with an experienced older lady who knew pre-cisely how to hold two bodies on the very edge of ecstasy, the pinnacle of tortured delight as you cry no, yes, no, please, yes, no, yes! Menelaus was by then already a warrior, a soldier at his brother's side. He had no interest in conquering weeping vir-gins when there were cities to raze, princes to slaughter – real battles to win.

On the wedding night, Helen lay down on a bed of petals, having been told by her mother what to expect. "A man will do things to you," Leda had explained, her eyes fixed on some distant place. "As his wife, it is your duty to put up with it."

Though she was still but a child, Helen was already coming into her womanhood, into fluttering feelings in her belly, a dampness between her legs. Clytemnestra had whispered to her: *here is how you touch yourself*, and Helen had been shocked, horrified, fascinated. For months she had refused to listen to her sister's advice, until at last she cracked and felt ... things she was certain a woman was not meant to feel. And yet she hoped. Even when Menelaus strode into the bedroom and saw her lying there, sizing her up with the same expression he used when considering the height of some enemy's wall, she had prayed. And her prayer had been for joy, and ecstasy, and love. And her prayer had been to me.

It did not take Menelaus long to do his business. He did not look up to check whether her little cries were of agony or ecstasy. He didn't wish to know, and it was easier for everyone in a marriage to simply assume the latter. When he was done, when he was gone, Helen touched herself to see if that would take away a little of the pain. To see if she could transform this experience into what she knew it needed to be – purest, happiest, most wondrous love. I stroked her brow, lay beside her, held her tight.

My lovely one, I breathed, as she tried to pleasure herself into believing that her life would be a joyous one, that her body had flowed with that of her husband in perfect harmony. That she was not merely flesh to be used. *I am here. You are not alone.*

Helen was pregnant from that very first encounter, and she was glad. She swore she would love her child, and when Hermione was born, she held the tiny squirming infant and felt . . . nothing. Shame, perhaps. Shame that she did not love the babe. Shame that she was a failure as a wife, and as a mother. Perhaps with her next child. Perhaps then she would feel something more. Menelaus told her that childbirth had made her feel less good inside, so sixteen-year-old Helen kneeled day and night before my shrine and implored me to make her a better wife, a better lover, better able to please her husband.

My love, I whispered back, *you could be the greatest wife in the world, and still he will not worship you.*

And of course there was the business with the apple, the Garden of the Hesperides, my slightly reckless offer to Paris, prince of Troy. I still feel a little embarrassed about it now, but what can I say? In the heat of the moment, it didn't seem so bad, all things considered.

Helen was twenty-two when Paris came to Sparta, and still a child. Being a child was her greatest safety, for if she was a woman or a mother, she knew that she would be a failure as both. A woman should satisfy a man. A mother should love her children. But if she was still a child – well then, that rather let her off the hook, didn't it?

Yet Paris – ah, Paris. He had grown up a shepherd before he was a prince, and had about him still the fragrance of the field and the forest, of damp wool and rugged nights on cold mountains. He was like nothing she had ever seen before, but still — but still. She knew her duty. She knew the rules that bounded her life.

But he's such a dish, isn't he? I whispered, as she watched him watch her over the lip of his cup of wine. *The way he looks at you — it's like he sees the real you inside.*

I had made a promise to Paris. An oath sworn on divine power. I would keep it, no matter the cost. Even we divinities have rules.

"You seem to be the kind of woman," Paris murmured, "who hides what she is feeling deep inside."

This is the kind of aphorism that Paris had used a lot in his wooing career. It is much like saying to someone: "I see you have sometimes been sad," or "I know that when you are happy, you laugh." The odds of these statements being false are basically none, but if you are a lonely woman starved of the bare minimum of conversation, they take on a profound depth of insight and meaning that can really be quite a thrill.

Do it, I breathed. *Do it. Be seen. Be a woman. Be free.*

Paris, for his part, was a tender lover. Helen had not known there could be such a thing.

So this is what it feels like, she thought, as he gazed into her eyes and promised to always listen to her words, honour her desires, *to be a woman after all.*

CHAPTER 15

>>

Helen of Troy – or one should say, Helen of Sparta – has two maids who never leave her side. Their names are Tryphosa and Zosime. They are not like the other women of Menelaus's house. His palace is full of captured mothers and enslaved daughters, of beaten sisters about whom he would say: "They don't need to speak to work, do they?" For a slave to be heard speaking the dialects of Troy is death; for a maid to be heard speaking anything much at all there are a range of punishments that grow steadily more severe.

Tryphosa and Zosime are not like these women. There are no scars upon their backs. Their necks are as perfumed as that of their charge. Their gowns are soft and delicate, they wear gold upon their wrists and upper arms. And when Eos and Autonoe approach and introduce themselves as the chief maids of Penelope's household, here to serve, here to ensure that their mistress receives whatever she might require, Tryphosa looks Eos up and down once, tuts, and turns her back on the Ithacan maid. Eos is briefly outraged – angry even. Then she is angry at herself for allowing even the slightest flicker of indignation to pass across her features, and is stone again. Autonoe just smiles in the corner of her mouth. These fine ladies of Sparta, dressed in pearls and pride – they may think themselves raised above all the other women of all the other houses, but Autonoe recognises slavery when she sees it, even if it is not so officially named. She knows how to spot women whose greatest pride is in how well they bear their suffering, and with that knowledge, she turns away, for Tryphosa and Zosime are of no further interest to her.

In public, Helen is radiant, demure, waving at the people gathered on the dock as if they had turned out just for her, dipping the tips of her fingers in a tiny motion as one might greet a child. No one waves back. In the end, in a moment of wisdom, Medon elbows one of the very, very few Ithacan men they've managed to find who can carry a shield and a spear. "Sound the horn and bang the drum!"

The horn makes a sound like a Titan passing wind, but it is at least loud and ceremonial enough to break the spell of silence that has settled on the staring harbour. The drums are old and saggy, dragged out only for rare festivals when the priests of the temple of Athena think it might be worthwhile to wake the town up early and remind them of just which goddess has really got their backs.

They process to the palace. The Ithacans don't have much in the way of order. Everyone agrees that Penelope should probably be somewhere near the front, but no, she also needs to be somewhere near the back to keep up a lovely litany of small talk with Menelaus. Thankfully he does most of the work in this regard.

"Fantastic place you've got here," he proclaims, as they pass through the market, stinking of fish, and the winding whorl of crooked houses built upon each other like an old beehive in a stooping tree. "Odysseus used to bang on about it like you wouldn't believe: oh, Ithaca, he'd say, amazing place, the wind, the sea, the sky – he had a whole thing about the sky, golden, he'd say, golden! We were all like yes yes yes, of course the sky is lovely but what about the women, *the women*, and you know what, I feel like I know you so well, so well, I do, goodness, the way he talked, it's like you were on that beach with us."

It occurs to Penelope that Menelaus technically has had a far longer and quite possibly far more intricate relationship with her husband than she has. She only knew Odysseus a few years before he shipped off to war, and a significant part of that time was spent acquainting herself with her royal work – the cultivation of olive groves, the management of sheep and how best to barter with the lumber traders from the north – with only the odd romantic dinner punctuating the labours of the day. Whereas Menelaus sat on a sandy dune with Odysseus by his side for ten years defined by either prolonged bouts of boredom in which they waited for something to happen, or extraordinary flares of life-threatening violence. Either might induce a quality of relationship that, if she is honest with herself, Penelope has not experienced with her husband.

This feeling is unsettling, if not exactly surprising.

"And your palace! Wonderful. Wonderful! You can really see the workmanship, can't you? The history! Other kings would always say, gold, marble, art – *art*! But Odysseus insisted, he always insisted, a palace should be a fortress first, send the right message, make it clear what your priorities are, you have to admire that, don't you? Have to admire the tenacity – that's the word, *tenacity*. Ithacans are so damn tenacious!"

There are others with Menelaus, besides his wife and her maids.

His son, who is probably a prince, but the matter has never been entirely settled. Nicostratus walks a polite distance behind Helen and her maids, a spear in one hand, plumed helmet tucked under his arm. You would not know he was Menelaus's son when you first glanced at him – he has his slave mother's wine-dark skin and a thick furrow of a brow that seems to always slope down, down, down. But once it has been pointed out to you that he carries his father's blood, there it is, in the curve of his nose, the smallness of his ears, the shortness of his strong legs. His father came as close to loving his mother as Menelaus has ever loved, exulting in her defiance, the flash of her eye, the sharpness of her tongue, until one day after he had lain with her, she laughed and said: "Not your best performance, was it?" and her body was found strangled that very night at the doors of the palace.

Nicostratus was three years old when Helen fled to Troy, and even at that tender age he had learned to despise the woman who was not his mother. Her departure merely formalised and gave permission to his hatred. His understanding of love is merely a physical thing. Love is sex. Sex is power. Power conquers the submissive. Conquest is desire. That is all there is for Nicostratus to say about that.

At Menelaus's side, a soldier, head of his personal guard. It is a silly thing really that I need a personal guard, he tuts, but the men of Sparta do insist, they're such old women, so precious, so here he is – say hello, Lefteris. Say hello to our nice Ithacan friends.

Lefteris, veteran of Troy, warrior forged in blood and stone, long hair grown wild about his shoulders, nails worn down to nubs on his spear-grasping fingers, says hello, nice Ithacan friends. None of the nice Ithacan friends say much in reply.

Next: a priest. His name is Kleitos, and he is not Spartan at all. His body is made of angles, as if someone had pieced together a whole series of triangles to try and create a man. Knees and elbows, ribs and collarbone, jaw and sharply pointed grey beard. He is treated with some honour, as befits his station – but less honour than he feels he should really be receiving, all things considered. He travelled from Mycenae with Orestes in those first few weeks of the king's unexpected "pilgrimage". He muttered all the way along the road that he didn't like being bossed around then, and he doesn't like being bossed around now. Don't they know who he is?

He does not express any of this to Menelaus, of course. He is sullen, not suicidal.

At his side is one we already know. Lovely Iason with that really rather fascinating lump that moves up and down his throat as he swallows, mighty shoulders and firm-set jaw. We saw you last, did we not, at my gorgeous temple tended to by Xanthippe, guarding your secrets by firelight? I kiss your cheek – it is of course a terrible portent that you are now here, on Ithaca, but so nice to see old friends.

These are but some of those who progress from the ships to the palace, of whom we shall have more later to say. The Spartans do their best to make a show of it – all marching together, feet stamping the ground in unison – but the twists and the turns of the tight winding streets somewhat limit the drama of the effect, and by the time the last of their crew begin to arrive at the palace gates, they are giving up on the whole thing and just walk like normal people on their way to a normal place.

The interior of the palace is a whirlwind of preparation. It was already fit to bursting with the weight of the suitors, but now – now – the king of Sparta has arrived! Every corner must be cleaned, every surface scrubbed, every nook of space eked out to give room for these noblest of men.

Menelaus is having none of it. "Nonsense – nonsense! You are already having to do so much – I hear these things, you know, suitors, *suitors*, the absolute cheek of it! As if you didn't have enough to worry about! We won't be a burden at all, you won't have to worry for anything, look, look!"

He clicks his fingers, and when this does not elicit an immediate response, clicks again, fast, impatient, about to turn on his own people and roar when two slaves rush forward carrying a chest between them, and lay it on the ground at Penelope's feet with a heavy thunk. Menelaus opens it, taking his time, enjoying the weight of its lid as it rocks back on the thick hinges. Those few onlookers who can see its interior produce a satisfactory intake of breath, a gasp of awe. Penelope considers the contents of the chest, but does not touch. She is not superstitious about these things – golden plate and silver cups marked by the slaughtered craftsmen of Troy are no different from the gold her husband stole from the westerners or her father-in-law pillaged from the south all those years ago. But she still has duties as a hostess, so at once begins a little speech.

"Majesty, no, we cannot accept this, of course we cannot, you are our guest, the most honoured, the most—"

"Sister," he barks, cutting her off, hard as a blade. "You will take my gift." An afterthought, a thing to be thrown in with a wide, delightful smile and a little bobbing of his head. "Please. It is the least we can do, for the trouble."

Penelope was never going to say no, of course. She has a kingdom to run. But she also knows that a full treasury can bring as many problems as it does solutions, and it is the suitors who watch the chest most attentively as it is borne away.

Most of the Spartans set up camp on the edge of the city, or remain on their ships. A few of the finer sort are billeted in the town, with families who do not meet their eyes as they welcome them in. Even so, by the time the afternoon breeze has turned from the south, Penelope estimates that there are more armed Spartans in her palace than there are Ithacan men. It is Eos who finally gives this hypothesis voice, whispering in her mistress's ear: "It would appear we have been conquered."

They stand by as Helen is put in the room of old Anticlea, Odysseus's dead mother. This process requires an inordinate amount of labour, for she has come with every concoction and scent that can be conceived, from the furthest reaches of the

Nile to the northern forests of the barbarians. She has mirrors of polished silver, chests of gowns – for walking, for dining, for reclining, for listening to sweet music – and an array of devices that Penelope has never seen before for the perfect creation of the most elaborate styles of hair.

"Oh, you don't know these?" Helen asks, as Penelope and her maids stand by the door, hands wringing and expressions dumb. "Well I suppose Ithaca always was going to be the last place to learn about fashion!"

She laughs.

Her laugh is the high, brittle cracking of a songbird, shrill enough to make bystanders wince. It starts and it stops as suddenly as the cry of the raven, as if the humour in her heart that has fluttered down all at once flies away.

"I'll have Zosime teach some of your little ladies if you like – oh, *Zosime*! Zosime, where are you – oh, there you are, goodness, yes, do you mind awfully? I know our Ithacan hosts would just *love* to learn a little bit about hair!"

Does Zosime mind?

Her lips curl in displeasure and she does not say either yes or no. This is, Penelope thinks, remarkably rude, but Helen doesn't seem to notice or care.

"Now where's that gown – oh, *fabulous*!"

Penelope can barely move through her own palace without bumping into another maid, another man, another slave, another soldier. She tries to make it to her bedroom, with its bed grown from the olive tree, but at every stage someone is approaching, demanding her attention.

"Nicostratus is not happy being in his room he says he has to be near to Helen, and Menelaus says he can't possibly sleep in Laertes' old room he wouldn't want to sully the old king's honour by daring to . . ."

". . . sent for more sheep to slaughter for the feast but they're not going to arrive until tomorrow, the tides for Kephalonia are all wrong and even if the messenger arrives in time . . ."

" . . . our last amphora of oil and after that I don't know what we're going to do!"

"The Spartans say they must keep their armour and their swords with them in their rooms but we don't have space for both the men to sleep and their armour to be stowed unless they put it in the actual armoury now I suggested we turn the armoury into another sleeping quarters but they say it's too cold and dark down there so what we need are fifteen oil lamps, five crates from the port and a . . ."

"Penelope! You didn't tell me Pylades was here!"

Menelaus catches her as she tries to cross the great hall, the fire already being stoked for the evening's feast. He has found Pylades in the throng, wrapped a great big friendly arm across the Mycenaean's shoulder, is walking with him as if he has found his long-lost brother at last. "Pylades, when did I see you last? You're such a loyal friend to my nephew, it means so much to me to know that he has someone like you by his side."

Kleitos and Iason, the other Mycenaeans in the room, stand aside quietly, heads down, Spartan men by their side. The Spartans are not *guarding* these two, of course. Not at all. It's just very, very important to Menelaus that their every need is attended to, and that means they need attending.

"How is Orestes?" Menelaus asks, gently squeezing Pylades as if he might shake some hilarious secret from the man's flaring nostrils. "I heard my poor nephew was taken ill – a terrible thing! He's well now, of course?"

"When last I saw him, the king was well," Pylades replies. He would meet Menelaus's eye if he could – very few men have the guts, but Pylades is willing to give it a go. But Menelaus is constantly moving, moving, pacing round the hall as if he has lost something that he now cannot remember, dragging Pylades with him, a convivial companion on this epic domestic quest. To stop now, to turn now, to confront the Spartan now would require more steps and more aggression than even Pylades with his lovely brave courage can muster.

"Good, good! Not in Mycenae, though? Neither he nor that niece of mine have been seen there for several moons, I heard? Forgive a nosy old man, but Orestes is so dear to me, my brother's only son, precious – a precious boy. My brother always told me that if anything was to happen to him, I had to do my duty and see that Orestes was safe. Family. You know how it is with family."

There it is again, that flash of a smile like oil catching fire. Penelope sees it, and though she does not flinch, her fingers flicker into fists for just a moment by her sides.

"He is visiting the sacred temples of the gods," Pylades manages to reply, the words dropping like stones from his lips. "To seek auspicious blessings for his reign."

"Good lad – good lad! Wonderful stuff. Peace and friendship, that's all my brother ever wanted, all he ever dreamed of. Good lad to be really committed, really following through. And you are in Ithaca because . . . ?"

Pylades struggles for words, eyes casting all around, so Penelope slips in with a flutter of veil and the barest breath. "I of course leave conversations of honour and matters of diplomacy to my husband's chosen council, as they have the wiser and more experienced heads – but I would be remiss if I did not value the trade in silver, amber and tin that my husband's people have with the people of Mycenae, and Sparta too, I believe? These things are never static – the value of these goods waxes and wanes – and I get the impression that Orestes means to ensure that all trade is fair to all."

Menelaus has stopped dead in his pacing, and for the first time looks at her – looks through her veil and straight at her, as if seeing the woman, not the story, standing before him. His smile this time is slow, a curling outwards of his lips, as he lets Pylades go and steps instead towards the queen of Ithaca. He holds out his arm. She takes it. Slower now they progress, as if he does not wish to trip the feet of this delicate creature.

"My brother's son, a trader," he muses as they wander. "When I was growing up, we took what we needed, plundered where we must – but that was then. Troy – well, Troy brought us together. A union of kings. Oaths sworn. Blood shed. And when we came back, I know it was my brother's deepest wish, his most profound wish, that we not return to Greek against Greek. But this 'trade' – I'm not going to pretend that my soldier's brain has much time for it. I leave it to others. People more suited to the task. I suppose that makes me a terrible king."

"You are a mighty king," she replies. "A hero."

"I'm getting old." A sigh – a rebuke, even. "An old man. See this belly? Too much meat, getting old, getting fat. And when I think about my legacy, about what I'm going to leave behind ..." A shaking of his head, a little sigh. "That's why family is so important. My daughter, Hermione – you know she was betrothed to Orestes when they were both just babes? Queen of Mycenae she was meant to be, but then there was all that business with Achilles' son and it got messy and I feel bad about that, I really do, but I know she's always held out hope that she'll be with my nephew, that they'll be able to cement the family bond between them for good, Sparta and Mycenae as one. Maybe Elektra and my Nicostratus too – it's just an old man's dream, of course, but ... well, we let go of our dreams last of all, don't we?"

Lefteris, Menelaus's captain of the guard, is standing in a corner picking at his teeth, lounging against a wall on which is painted some image of Odysseus, obscuring the face of the Ithacan king, a slouching armoured grin of a man, enjoying

128

watching his master at work. Penelope is ice. Penelope is stone. In Sparta, Polycaste, the woman who raised her as if she was her own, took her daughter by the hand and whispered: "The only one who can tell you what to feel is you."

In Ithaca, Anticlea, wife of Laertes, mother of Odysseus, in those days before she finally drank herself to death, would stare into her reflection in the water and proclaim: "No one else must be permitted to put words in your mouth."

Anticlea was raped the day before she married Laertes, in vengeance for the deeds of her father. The next night she made sure that Laertes did his duty by the marriage bed, so that no questions might be asked, no trouble raised, and no one else need ever know.

Now her daughter-in-law walks arm in arm with Menelaus, king of Sparta; forces herself to turn from the leers of Lefteris, and murmurs: "You are right, of course. Of course you are right. I have tried so hard to be worthy of my husband. I have not seen him for nearly twenty years, and now my son has set sail to find his father and I . . . I fear that I cling to foolish hopes. To reckless dreams. Even when I thought I was free of them, they return to plague me. Is that not absurd?"

Menelaus gives her arm a gentle squeeze. No man has been so near to her as he is now for so, so long – but that's fine. Menelaus is the husband of Helen. He is a king, sworn blood brother of Odysseus. The normal rules do not apply to one such as he. "I saw your son," he says, and Penelope nearly trips on her own toes. He steadies her without blinking, without losing a step or a breath, an easy thing – an expected, predictable thing. "Young Telemachus, nice lad – he came to Sparta, looking for news of his father. You've done so well with him, all things considered. Lovely firm voice, good manners, strong spear arm – you'd hardly think he was raised by women at all! Of course we couldn't help him. But even seeing the boy I felt myself come over all emotional. All fuzzy. I really miss your husband – we all do. We had our disagreements, of course, but at the end of the day, Odysseus – you could really rely on him to get the job done. I'm only sorry we couldn't give your son better news – any news, I mean. Not bad news. Just any news of your husband at all."

Penelope's body is moving, and she is in it, and for now that will have to be enough. A head of lead nods once on a neck of straw. "I see," she breathes. "And this was . . . recently?"

"Not five moons since."

"Five moons. Yes. Thank you. I am glad that . . . It is a comfort to know Telemachus is well. Thank you."

He stops, so suddenly that Penelope nearly bumps into him as he turns, taking both her hands in his. He stares through her veil, straight into her eyes, squishes her fingers between his, bows. "I am your husband's brother," he proclaims. "And Ithaca will always be safe with me."

He kisses her fingers.

Lips on skin.

The moisture of his mouth lingers when he is done. It is the single most sensual act any man has performed for her in nearly twenty years, and when she is finally back in her bedroom, Penelope washes her hands three times and changes her gown.

CHAPTER 16

>>

A feast.

Menelaus has brought his own wine.

This is an outrage – an insult! No host would ever dream of letting a guest bring a sip of drink, a mouthful of food to their table. It is a violation of the most sacred traditions of the land, unspeakable. But Menelaus is no ordinary guest, and Penelope, why, she . . .

"You've gone through so much, so much hardship, more than any woman should," soothes Menelaus, as his servants bring the amphorae from the ships into the hall. "All alone without your husband, without a man to keep you safe, and I have neglected you. I really have – no, not a word! I won't hear a word, I have neglected you, failed Odysseus, failed my blood brother by letting his wife suffer all this time on this rock, and you a princess of Sparta too. Not all the wine of all the groves of Laconia can make up for my failures to you, and so you see, good sister, I must make amends. I must. If you refuse me, you will surely damn me. I mean to make sure that the western isles are neglected no more. I mean to make sure you are properly looked after."

The wine is potent, even when water is added, and has beneath the sweetness a strong, hot tang of sour.

*

131

Eos whispers in Penelope's ear, as she refills her cup: "Spartan soldiers are spreading across the isle."

"Have they hurt anyone?"

"Not yet."

"Send word to Priene. Tell the women to hide their spears and their bows."

The bards in the hall are Spartan too.

"The finest – the finest in all Greece!" Menelaus explains, at Penelope's little intake of breath, her flutter of indignation to see her own musicians displaced. "I had them from Athens, they make music – just the sweetest music – you will ever hear. I mean no disrespect to your local sort, of course, but you really must hear – and if you dislike them then I will have them drowned immediately, not a question asked, I swear!"

Menelaus has sworn it. Clearly it must be true. They listen to the musicians of Athens sing to save their lives, and Penelope knows she is defeated. Clytemnestra would have declared that she found the music distasteful, just to make her point, and stood on the side of the quay as the men were hurried to the bottom of the ocean with stones about their ankles. But Clytemnestra is dead, murdered for being too much like a man, and Penelope cannot help but think how inconvenient it will be to have to fetch out the corpses of the dead bards once the Spartans are gone, lest they contaminate the water with their putrefaction.

The songs they sing are not about Menelaus. He barely features in a single line. Instead they sing of Agamemnon, his great brother, the king of kings. They sing of the unity he brought, of the peace won by power solely wielded, of the heroes who came together beneath his crown, of the purpose of one people, together at last. Menelaus hums along at the good bits, out of tune and only half interested, a familiar ditty he has heard so many times that now he barely hears it at all.

Menelaus sits in the place of highest honour – next to Odysseus's empty chair. Penelope's chair is set a little below his, but he barks: "I can't possibly talk to you if you're down there. Here, join me, join me!" And as it is either put her chair next to his or sit in his lap, Autonoe and Eos move the queen's chair next to the king's.

Helen sits below, flanked by her maids. Nicostratus is opposite, playing with his food. Pylades sits among the suitors, the soldier Iason and priest Kleitos besides him, there being nowhere else to put these otherwise worthy guests. Lefteris prowls the edge of the hall, a sword at his side. He is a friendly wolf, a grinning salute, a knife-edge smile. No one meets his eye and no one objects when he takes the food from their plate – friendly like, of course. Sharing as brothers, sharing as friends – all so very friendly.

"What are you then?" he asks the Egyptian.

"I am Kenamon," Kenamon replies, and there is an unusual coldness in his voice, an unexpected distance that he has never shown even to his greatest rivals, the other suitors in the hall. Where has this come from? Ah yes – it is the sound of soldiers meeting who cannot quite imagine that they meet in a time of peace. Lefteris looks at Kenamon, and Kenamon looks at Lefteris, and each sees in the other's eye a man who knows what it is to pull his blade from the insides of a still-beating heart while the blood runs warm down bronze. Other men may prate of chariots and glorious charges. Lefteris and Kenamon smile the icy smile of recognition of men who would rather kill their opponents while they lie sleeping than ever walk into bloody battle again. Such a smile is unusual in this hall of vain boasters and prattling fools; they linger a moment too long in each other's gaze before Lefteris moves on about his prowling of the hall.

Every suitor is dressed in his finest. Robes edged with beetle dyes and bangles of gold have been produced from some secret place; hair is oiled and curls artfully arranged, fingers washed and the dirt scrubbed from between toes. For one night only, the royal palace of Ithaca looks as if it might almost deserve the name.

Helen talks. It is an unrelenting burble of light noise, consequential as the beating of a dove's feathered wing, busy as the sound of seabirds nested upon the cliff. "Goodness, does this have crab in it? Oh, how lovely, I don't usually eat . . . but I'm sure it's delicious, isn't it? We never have crab in Sparta, you know, and in Troy we had it only occasionally when a raiding party managed to get out of the seaward gate and back without losing too many men. Such a treat! Such a treat – though I suppose for you, Cousin Penelope, you must have this all the time. How lovely. You know, I do envy you sometimes, out in this little palace, a simple life, so simple, it must be such a relief not having to worry about things. Back in Sparta we are constantly having to entertain, all those dignitaries, all those kings, and one can never quite remember which one is which, can one?"

Her laugh is not the laugh that caught Paris's attention. That laugh was rich and round and had beneath it a hint of dirtiness, a deep burst of lung and a hint of snorting nose. That laugh was the laugh of a woman who has briefly dared to be seen, briefly dared to be something more than just a simpering child – dared perhaps to have a heart beating beneath her lily chest. That laugh was if anything more seductive than even the perfection of her flesh – perfection that I will admit I did set off a little with an added dose of divine radiance. But it was that laugh, a promise of secrets, a promise of hidden places where no one else but he might go – that was what really caught the ear of Paris of Troy.

This is not that laugh. This is the laugh she relearned in her room in Sparta, staring at the tarnished reflection of herself in a muddy bronze mirror. Her voice fluttered up and down in search of the perfect pitch, perfect tone, and then she would experiment in front of her husband when he said something that people seemed to find amusing, testing out which response produced a frown and which a sigh, and which he could ignore entirely. This laugh is the last of those three, a sound that Menelaus barely seems to know exists, as if the part of his ear that might acknowledge it has died, clattered into silence perhaps by ten years of the rattle of sword on shield – even though the sound causes nothing but distress and confusion to all other hearers.

Very few of the suitors can hear what Helen says, though not for want of straining. Penelope envies them that.

"Saw your lovely Telemachus, oh, he's such a fine boy, isn't he? He was travelling with one of Nestor's sons, striking lad, but you know what Nestor is like – well, they're all just a bit dry, aren't they? A bit dull, I dare say, terribly naughty of me, oh!" She puts her fingers to her lips, a naughty girl caught saying something she shouldn't. Then smiles and goes straight on, the child at once forgiven. "Everyone got dreadfully emotional at the feast, of course. So many of the best are lost – Agamemnon, Achilles, Odysseus – and you know what, actually for all that he chewed with his mouth open, Hector really was a very thought-ful man, very thoughtful, I'm glad Achilles didn't desecrate his corpse too badly, you know – it's not just about how one treats an enemy, but what one thinks about oneself inside. Who one wishes to be. Whatever happens, cousin ..." Helen reaches out to Penelope, but is too far to bridge the distance between them, so leaves her hand hanging in the air, "I know you will always choose love."

Penelope has absolutely nothing to say. She is flabbergasted. She looks to Menelaus, but if he has heard a word his wife says, he shows no sign. She looks to Nicostratus, who is sprawled so far back in his chair it is a wonder he doesn't just plop straight out of it, skull back, bum up, whoosh! She looks to the suitors, who are all very much doing their best not to be seen to be watching the royal group, and finally back to Helen, whose hand still hangs there, a little smile on her face as though to say, *come, dear one, come.*

She thinks perhaps this is a test. She is good at tests – the answers she is meant to give have always been very clear to her. So, smiling, she ignores the hand, ignores Helen's wide, glistening eyes, pupils fat and black, and says: "Of course, cousin. And what love is there that is greater than a wife's love for her husband?"

Helen's smile does not flicker. But she pulls back, slowly, rests fingers palm-up on her lap, folds her other hand over the top as if she might hide some stain, stares into the middle of nothing, does not eat, and for a little while says nothing more, only sips the wine that is poured for her by Zosime from a golden carafe.

The musicians play, more meat is brought to the table. Helen's lips are crimson as she drinks, her eyes focused on some far-off place. Penelope leans over a little to Menelaus.

"I hear some of your men are travelling across Ithaca," she breathes.

He doesn't meet her eye as he takes little sips from his cup. "Your womenfolk tell you that?"

Penelope smiles. She smiles because there are several meanings to the word "womenfolk" when it comes to the ladies of Ithaca, and she has no idea how many of these Menelaus might know. It is possible that he understands more than he says, in which case all is lost – her home, her kingdom, her hope – but it is equally possible he uses the word as a loose insult, a breezy dismissal of all that she is, and all who serve her. Either way, Penelope will smile. Smiling hides the fear, the outrage, the sickness inside. Kings don't need to smile, but for a queen it is a most useful tool to have at your disposal.

"Is there something your men need? Something we have not provided?"

"I believe there is good hunting on the isle," Menelaus replies, still not looking at her, not deigning to give her the grace of his eye. "Odysseus had this story about hunting a boar when he was a lad – showed us all the scar too, great fat thing, he was so proud of that scar you'd think he wasn't even a proper warrior about a warrior's work! Plenty of scars you'll have soon, don't you worry, I said to him, but no, he just kept going on about Ithaca and that damn boar. Anyway. Seeing as how you don't have much in the way of menfolk on the isle, I imagine you've got plenty of game running around. Women can trap rabbits, of course, but a proper boar ... with your permission, that is. I'd love to see just how much of Odysseus's story was like all his others – more words than tusks."

Penelope has chosen this smile well. It has crinkled the corners of her eyes and everything. She does not have mirrors of the same high quality that Helen used to practise in, but sat with Ourania, her lady of secrets and spies, rehearsing the look until it came as instinct. "Of course," she murmurs. "I can think of nothing better than a royal hunt on Ithaca after all this time. But your men need not risk their comfort by straying too far in the dark. The island is small – we have people who can show you the best hunting grounds."

"Not at all, sister." He pats her gently on the back of her hand, isn't she sweet for thinking about these things? "We mustn't inconvenience you any more than we already have. Wouldn't dream of it."

And that appears to be the end of that.

"Well, Priam, Priam! I mean, he always told the same three stories. There was that one about the horse, there was the one about the prophecy and there was this dreadful story about the time he went to Colchis ... "

Helen talks.

It is baffling to Penelope that one voice can maintain such an inordinate flow of meaningless noise. It is baffling to her that her cousin can speak so easily about Troy, about a thing that broke the world in two, and yet somehow say so little. That there can be so many words tumbling from Helen's lips, with so little actual content.

" . . . remarkable what they do with their hair. So when a southern girl becomes a woman, she will shave it all off and wear a wig instead, but in other places you get these braids that are symbols of the knot between husband and wife and go all the way round like this – Penelope, are you looking – all the way round, but also they have these dyes, a dreadful reddish brown, ghastly really but they say it symbolises fidelity and loyalty towards . . . "

As Helen talks, there is movement in the palace.

It is harmless, nothing to remark on. Just the maids of Penelope – of Odysseus, one should say – about their business. Most are occupied downstairs, with the feast, but there are some, led by light-stepping Autonoe, who now drift through the rooms of the visiting Spartans, ensuring that when they come to bed, they will find basins of cool water waiting beneath the window, that the rough woollen blankets are as smooth as they may be, that there are no rat droppings or scurrying beetles to be seen in even the most meagre of the rooms. Autonoe is accompanied by Phiobe and Melantho as she goes from room to room, buckets of water in hand, a polite smile upon their faces, eyes down to the ground. There are some Spartans set to guard the doors, but they merely stand and watch as the women work. There is no harm, after all. And what can slave women possibly see that might be of interest to them?

In Nicostratus's room, which was once the childhood room of Telemachus, nearly as much space is taken by a suit of burnished golden armour beside the door as by his actual bed. Nicostratus was born too late to fight at Troy. He knows this, and the day after his fifteenth birthday instead threw himself into any and every battle he could find against pirate and raider. This task took some contrivance, for the peace of Agamemnon still held and it was considered uncouth for the young warrior to plunder Sparta's neighbour kings. Instead he had to sail south, all the way to the lands of the Pharaohs and the bearded Hittites, in search of glory and gold. Sparta didn't need gold, but Nicostratus needed glory, even if the only way to obtain it was through the slaughter of fleeing children. His armour, he claims, was taken from a great warrior on a chariot whom he fought single-handed near the city of Ashdod. Its chief feature is a tower shield that could easily be used as a roof for a family of three, it is so cumbersome and oversized. Nicostratus did kill a man on a chariot near that place, but he was attempting to flee, and the armour was found buried beneath a widow's house. He thinks that one day he may be king, and if he is, he will dedicate his life to warrior Ares and see that all women in his house know their place. This latter is a recurring motif in the conversations of the men-children of Menelaus.

Autonoe and the women light the oil lamp that burns by the side of the bed, so that Nicostratus need not return to his room in darkness.

Menelaus's room is, by comparison with his son's, far plainer. Certainly there are chests of gold and arms for generous disbursement to all who please the mighty king, and his bed has already been draped with stolen silks hemmed in the Trojan style. But he does not need to leave his armour on a stand, a great shield propped by the door. He does not need flummery to show the world who he is – he is Menelaus! There is a quality about his eye, a majesty to his step that should be quite enough to communicate this, thank you very much.

The Spartans watch as Autonoe fills the golden basin by his bed with water from the well. The basin is not from Ithaca – not that Menelaus would mind washing himself with tools of tin and clay, not at all, he's a warrior, you see, a warrior first! It's just that someone in his household thought it perhaps fitting he be surrounded by gold, and well, the staff, the staff – you have to indulge them sometimes, even when you're king.

Helen's room is dominated by mirrors. A small mirror for examining her face; a magnificent mirror in which she might assess her majestic final look. A mirror that can be held up so she can see the back of her head; a bronze mirror that a servant might carry if she needs to check her appearance on the go. The largest and finest of these all is polished silver, the reflection a brilliant, baffling thing that Phiobe finds quite hypnotic. Helen did not take any mirrors with her when she went to Troy. It was only after Paris died and his brothers stood around arguing over who should own her now that she finally allowed herself to gaze deep and long into the looking glass.

"Good news," proclaimed Deiphobus, son of Priam, brother of slain Hector and slaughtered Paris, as he stood in the bedroom door, hands already working to unhitch the belt about his hips. "I won."

"This is where that man raped me, good husband," Helen explained, smooth as pearl, as Menelaus stood in Deiphobus's room before the cowering, wounded prince as the city burned. "He did it. That man there."

Menelaus took nearly two days to kill Deiphobus, while Helen watched. As Deiphobus screamed, Menelaus imagined that it was Paris he mutilated, Paris whose limbs he tore asunder. What Helen imagined as the prince of Troy died is for only she and I to know.

Since then she has never been more than a few seconds from a mirror, adjusting a curl, ensuring the drawn line of her brow has not smudged, checking to see how the light falls across the subtle wrinkles upon her forehead, the little lines etched in the corner of her jaw.

On a table there stand jars. Ointments and concoctions, potions and pastes, formulas both tested and speculative. Autonoe has never seen so many pots of cream and vials of perfume, sniffed so many scents floral and earthy all at once rising from this place. She leans in to examine one, the oil lamp she carries cupped safely, and a voice from the door barks: "Move away!"

A maid of Sparta – Tryphosa – storms into the room, face flushing crimson. "Move away!" she repeats, flapping at Autonoe and the Ithacan women. "You are not wanted here!"

If any other slave had dared speak to her in that way, in the house where she is one of Penelope's most favoured, most regarded, Autonoe would have thrown a pot in her face. But tonight she is a woman on a mission, so she bobs and smiles and says, "So sorry, we were lighting the lanterns and bringing water for our guests ... "

"We will see to that!" shrills Tryphosa, turning her body so she might drive the Ithacans like foam before the wave out of the door. "We will see to everything!"

Thus Autonoe is banished from the room.

In the hall below: " ... I don't eat eggs, of course, terrible for the skin, and bloating too, I find, don't you find that, Cousin Penelope, don't you find that eggs give you just the most dreadful feeling? I have to be so careful with what I eat these days, my stomach has become quite refined ... "

Helen witters on, the musicians play, the suitors sit sullen below.

At least, nearly all the suitors. There is one who is about to make a mistake.

Antinous rises.

This is unexpected, even to a goddess of my incisive power. This suitor, son of Eupheithes, detaches himself from his table, wine upon his tongue, and turns to the assembled royalty at the head of the room. He has been commanded to this by his father, of course, otherwise he would never have dared. Two fears have warred within him and delayed this action until the feast is nearly done – terror of his father weighed against terror of the Spartan king. Remarkably, terror of his father just about edges out his mortal dread of Menelaus, and so Antinous steps from his place and approaches the regal court.

At first, no one notices. He is presumably heading somewhere to relieve himself, or is drunk and will shortly be abed. The notion that this suitor, even being one of the more senior among the group, would dare speak to the conqueror of Troy is clearly absurd. But no, he nears – he stops – he bows – he waits for someone to notice him.

Penelope does first, and for the first and nearly last time in her life feels a pang of fear for the boy standing before them. Beneath the sprawled open legs of Nicostratus, son of Menelaus; before the grim wall of Pylades and Iason; below the chair where Menelaus himself sits, Antinous is suddenly no longer a man who would be king of Ithaca, but a child. A boy dressed up in his father's clothes, sent to do his duty, obeying in absence of his own common sense.

Penelope's attention draws Menelaus's. Menelaus's focus finally silences Helen. Nicostratus rouses himself a little from his slouch, curious as to where this might go. The musicians fall silent. Antinous clears his throat.

"Mighty Menelaus, king of Sparta," he begins. He has practised this speech in front of his father nearly non-stop since the crimson sails were first seen upon the ocean's thin horizon. "Greatest of the Greeks, king of kings—"

"Who's this?" Menelaus cuts through, addressing his enquiry to Penelope. "Not one of your suitors, is it?"

"This is Antinous, son of Eupheithes," replies Penelope, in a voice like fallen feathers. "He is indeed one of the many men who would look to protect Ithaca in her weakest hour."

Menelaus snorts. "You mean sit on your husband's empty throne and cuckold him in his own damn bed!"

Antinous has already lost the thread of his already short speech, but tries to pull it back. "Great king, greatest of all the Greeks—"

A finger thrusts forward from Menelaus's hand. "You! Boy! Did you fight at Troy?"

"I . . . I unfortunately was born too late . . ."

"Ever killed a man?"

Antinous has not, but can hardly say so before this assemblage. Menelaus leans down a little, punctuating his question with a stabbing digit towards Antinous's quivering nose. "Have you met Odysseus?"

"I . . . did not have that honour."

"You did not have that honour. Of course you didn't have that honour – your nose was still being wiped by some milky nursemaid when the king, my brother, sailed to Troy. You have no idea of the quality of man you're seeking to usurp, no idea at all. It would be despicable if it wasn't so absurd. And I hear that you spend all your time eating from this good woman's plate" – a wave towards Penelope, rigid by his side – "and drinking her wine and taking liberties with her maids – I hear things, so I do, word of your depravity comes even to Sparta – and why? Because you think you have the legs to walk one step in the footsteps of her husband. By all the gods, if it weren't against my nature for the lion to slaughter the rabbits, I would strike you down and no one would complain. You're all lucky that I've grown mellow in my older years."

Antinous stands agape. Then – a rare moment of wisdom – he closes his mouth. This is an astonishing turn of events. Penelope has to stop herself from leaning forward to savour it. Antinous, son of Eupheithes, gives a little bow, steps back once, steps back twice, makes to turn and . . .

"So what was it you wanted to say?" Menelaus asks.

Antinous stops.

The room has stopped.

From the furthest darkest corner to the nearest eye-down maid, there is silence. Waiting.

Nicostratus's grin is pricking the tips of his ears. Lefteris is trying not to laugh. Menelaus likes that his captain of the guard shows his pleasure at the pain of others. He likes a bit of honesty in his life.

Antinous looks at the king of Sparta and cannot meet his eye. Swallows. Penelope is entranced. The last time he stood this close to her, he was calling her whore, liar, temptress. He was declaring that the loom on which she was weaving Laertes' funeral shroud was a lie, he was exposing her as a harlot, queen of shadow and deceit.

Now he is afraid.

She knows she should not revel in his fear, and yet it is intoxicating. It is ambrosia to her dull and aching heart.

"King of kings," he tries again.

"You want something? Young people today are always wanting, never appreciating what they have. Well, boy? Well? Spit it out!"

Antinous holds out his hand. In it is a brooch. It is shaped like a falcon, and has a bloody ruby for its eye. It has come from the southlands, from the Nile and the places beyond where they say you can pick gold up from the ground as if it had fallen like rain. Antinous's father traded it for nearly a shipload of tin, hoarding it close, waiting for the right time to use it. That time, he has determined, is tonight. He is wrong.

"On behalf of the people of Ithaca ... as a representative of the good men gathered here ... " this is a hasty adaptation of Antinous's speech, which until a few seconds ago was almost entirely about his personal qualities as a potential king, "we wish to give you this insignificant token of our respect and—"

Menelaus jerks his chin towards his son. Nicostratus unfolds from his chair, snatches the brooch from Antinous, holds it up to the light, scratches at it with the rough edge of a thick nail, tosses it to his father. Menelaus catches it with one hand, pulling his fist into his chest to stop the unwieldy thing tumbling should he have missed the trick. Peers at it, holds it up, lowers it into his lap, stares at Antinous, smiles. Antinous looks down, then looks up when looking down is going on a little too long, to find Menelaus still staring straight at him, and immediately turns his gaze back down, down, down, where perhaps the ground might swallow him.

Menelaus's smile broadens into a grin. "Nice," he muses, turning the golden falcon this way and that between his fingers. "Nice. Nice people. Odysseus always said that the thing about Ithaca is that no one would ever say please or thank you, none of the arty manners of more civilised places, none of the pomp and all that rot. Just generous, honest people, doing their best. Loyal, he said. Loyal and, though you might not know it to look at them, basically kind. 'Not into their arty manners,' I replied, 'but then what's the story with you?' But Odysseus, well, he always stood apart, didn't he? Always a bit above everyone else, even his own people. Antinous, was it? Thank you for your thoughtful, *nice* gift."

Antinous bows again, eyes not leaving his own toes, and begins to back away.

"Penelope." Menelaus's voice is big enough, bright enough to stop Antinous in his tracks. He leans over, takes Penelope's hand, folds it round the golden falcon, pushes it away, from him to her. "I want you to have this."

Antinous's eyes flash from the ground to the Ithacan queen. He has never had any problem staring down a woman. The brooch is warm in Penelope's palm, heated by the grip of the Spartan king.

Menelaus rises. Helen covers her mouth as if she might giggle. Nicostratus lounges back in his chair, arms folded; Lefteris is trying not to snort. "You suitors!" Menelaus doesn't have to shout to fill the room with sound. He commanded men in the roar of battle, he made himself heard over the burning of a city set aflame. I would have loved him once, if he had only let himself be open to all the many things that love could be. "You suitors." He lets the volume drop a little, now he is certain he has their full attention. "It is so nice of you to give me gold. So thoughtful. I see what my good friend Odysseus meant about the cunning of his people, I really do – you Ithacans, you always know how to surprise. But it seems to me that you have been here at this good woman's feet, the wife of my dearest brother, eating her meat, drinking her wine, for what ... two years? Three? You come to her palace, you preen over her bed, fawn at her virtues, disparage her husband, who she loves, who *I* loved ... "

This word "love" has not been spoken in these halls for a very long time. It hangs in the air like a spider's web, before blowing away in the breeze. Menelaus thinks he knows what it means when he utters it. He does not.

" ... as if his legacy were some cheap trinket to be bought. As if his kingdom were some plot of dirt for children to scrap over with your sharp, pointed sticks. Look at you. Look at you. Boys raised by women. Traders' sons. Merchant whores. And this,"— he waves towards the brooch in Penelope's hand—"this? You think you can buy a kingdom for what? Little gifts? Odysseus bled for his home. Odysseus slaved on sand and stone, beneath rain and sun and icy winter snow for his home. And all that time this good woman, his beloved queen, the best, most loyal, most faithful woman in all of Greece, waited for him. Prayed for him.

"You." He points – not at Antinous, but at Eurymachus, dressed in his father's finest, lapis lazuli at his neck, sweet perfume in his hair. "Do you have something fit for a king?"

Eurymachus stands. His father, Polybus, was not as quick as Eupheithes was in sensing opportunity, taking steps to try and seize the moment. The consequences of this inaction are now a mixed vessel. Eurymachus looks from Menelaus to the others at his table, his allies, those lesser suitors who know they never will be king but hope perhaps to rise when Eurymachus does, to follow his path to glory. The snapping of Menelaus's fingers draws his attention back to the Spartan king. Slowly he unhooks the necklace of jewels and gold from about his neck, a thing his father bartered from a merchant who had sailed all the way from the mouth of the Tigris in search of Greek oil and silver. He approaches, holds out the prize to Menelaus, who snaps his fingers again and turns and points at Penelope.

Eurymachus steps forward, and carefully lays his offering in her open hand.

Bows.

Retreats.

Menelaus beams. "Right!" he exclaims, patting his hands idly on his out-thrust belly. "Who's next?"

CHAPTER 17

>>>

"Well," says Ourania, as Eos closes the door to Penelope's bedroom behind her, "this is a little unexpected."

A chest of gold and jewels, silver and precious gems lies at the foot of Penelope's bed. It was Eos who fetched the vessel, when it became apparent that Menelaus was not going to stop in his endeavours until every suitor in the hall had delivered some precious item into the queen's hands. The Spartan king's smile grew even wider when he saw it brought in, and he nodded just once as the maids laid it down, before continuing with his demands. A few of the finer pieces Nicostratus had a look at first, nodding and frowning to show his approval or displeasure. Two of the suitors wept silently as they handed over their fathers' rings, their last memorials of a dead relative, the only things they had to give.

"Are you going to return them?" Ourania asks, as Eos recounts these events. Old Ourania, hair an explosion of snow on a face like the crumbled desert, was once a maid in this palace, as Eos and Autonoe are now. But Penelope found it more useful over time to have as her ally a woman who could travel freely and speak her mind, and so Ourania ceased being a maid and become something far more. No one remarks when she enters or leaves these halls, save perhaps Euracleia, who grumbles that Ourania has ideas above her station. Her presence is familiar as old dust, and she proceeds through life with a beatific smile and a little glimmer in the corner of her eye that the foolish might mistake for charming innocence. After Penelope, Ourania is the woman Eos most wishes to be, a giver and taker of secrets and shadows from behind an impenetrable smile.

"You can't return them!" Autonoe blurts, as she folds Penelope's veil over her arm. "This is a fortune!"

All around, the palace slumbers. The music has fallen silent, the suitors have slunk away in misery, Menelaus snores soundly in Laertes' old room. Only the women remain, scurrying by the light of their oil lamps through the dark. The women – and some Spartan soldiers. Menelaus has set them patrolling the wall – "an old soldier's habit, indulge me" – and Penelope finds she has no grounds upon which to object.

"We must note which item belonged to what suitor," Penelope concludes. "Especially those that seemed to have significant value. It is possible that in returning them, we can extract a reward even more useful than gold."

How many suitors, she wonders, will not return to the palace tomorrow? How many will thank her, grovel before her on bended knee to have some item placed back in their palm, a pat on the head and an invitation to leave by the fastest ship they can find, now that Menelaus is in Ithaca? She is fascinated to find out.

She holds one item only in her hand. It is an arm ring, a snake twining towards its own tail. It is of unusual design – a hint of copper, she thinks, about the smelted metal – but not without artistic merit. It came from the arm of the Egyptian, Kenamon. "Does it even speak our language?" Menelaus asked, when it was Kenamon's turn.

"I speak your language," he replied, looking the Spartan in

the eye, "and am honoured to be in the presence of a warrior as great as yourself."

Very few suitors had met Menelaus's eye, save Amphinomous, the warrior's son. The king chuckled. "Look out for that one, Penelope," he proclaimed, as Kenamon bowed and made his offering. "Always more trouble than they're worth, your sexy exotic foreigner."

Helen laughed at that. Her laugh was high as a tiny spring bird, and went on too long, too loud, before she silenced herself with another slurp of wine.

"I will speak to the maids who were present," Eos declares. "Nothing will be lost."

"Good. We must see the rest safely hidden tonight."

Autonoe shoots a longing glance at the chest of glittering wonders. Of all the women of Penelope's house, it is only Autonoe who has even the faintest conception of what these words might mean: wealth, independence, freedom. Even Eos, who wishes to one day take Ourania's place as spymaster and lady of many cousins of uncertain but useful origin, does not consider the word "free" when she contemplates her future. Freedom for her is not safety. It is position. What better position could a slave dream of than to be a slave with power? But Autonoe understands that this thought is the strongest chain of all, the last link that binds servant to master, and she would one day be rid of it. But not yet – not yet.

"How was your exploration of our guests' rooms?" asks Penelope, as the chest is hurried away. "Did you find anything of note?"

"Nicostratus travels with an absurd armoury, a shield as big as I am," Autonoe replies, eyes following the vanishing gold. "And in Helen's room there was a Spartan maid – Tryphosa – who obstructed us. But she does not stand or speak like a maid, she is . . . " Autonoe looks for the words, struggles to find a way to express this other, alien power. Penelope waits, trusting her maid to report the necessary, and to know what is necessary to report. "... she carries herself more like a soldier than a slave. We lit the lanterns in the rooms of Menelaus, Nicostratus, but not Helen. Her maids threw us out before we could have a thorough look."

"Do you know why?" Penelope asks.

"Perhaps her husband is a mite protective of the woman who broke the world," mutters Ourania, but Autonoe shakes her head.

"I'm not sure," she muses. "There were many pots and creams and perfumes – many I couldn't recognise."

"Interesting," muses Ourania, before Penelope has the chance to say precisely the same thing. Eos smiles at this – she too wants to one day speak the words that would otherwise be in the mouth of a queen. Autonoe merely watches. She one day wants to speak the fewest words necessary for people to fear her.

"What do we know about Helen's maids?" asks Penelope.

No one answers. No one knows. They have been taught that the women of their state are irrelevant, uninteresting, as they themselves are.

"Perhaps we should remedy our ignorance."

Eos nods – she will see to it. The maids depart. Ourania remains behind. Old Ourania was at Penelope's side when the queen gave birth, held her hand as the young bride screamed, mopped away the blood and buried the tattered remains of the afterbirth. Neither she nor Penelope would call the other friend – neither has any time for such strange creatures in their lives – and yet how often have they sprawled together by the light of the dying fire and laughed and talked and howled at secret delights and walked upon the cliff before the dawn has kissed the sky and held each other by the arm and smiled to see the merriment in each other's eye. Penelope's first act when old

Anticlea died was to release Ourania from her bondage. Like Eos, neither woman had much conception of what this word "free" might mean.

"So," says Ourania at last. "Menelaus."

"Don't be fooled by all this," Penelope sighs, gesturing towards the laden chest. "He's here for Orestes."

"Of course he's here for Orestes. That Mycenaean he has with him – Iason – and the priest, Kleitos? He found them and the rest of Orestes' court hiding near a temple of Aphrodite. I have a cousin who knows a priestess who says he tortured Iason for three days and three nights in the most unimaginable of ways to get him to reveal where Orestes had fled. Of course Iason doesn't look that tortured, but I imagine someone like Menelaus doesn't necessarily have to get physical."

Menelaus did not have to torture Iason to find out where Orestes had gone. Instead, he found one of Iason's men "stealing", and when the unfortunate soldier would not confess, had the fellow's intestines slowly removed and burned in front of him until Iason got the message. Thus there was no torture – not by Menelaus, oh no indeed. Just the tragic course of justice, which must always be served.

"He's sending out 'hunting parties'." Penelope flops back onto the surface of the bed Odysseus made for her, too weary to even pretend to have the posture and stamina of a dignified queen. "I cannot stop him."

"Does Priene know?"

"Yes. She's ordered the women to hide their bows."

"Good. If you kill one Spartan, you'll have to kill them all, and Ithaca will burn."

"It's only a matter of time before he finds Orestes."

Ourania levers herself down onto the bed beside Penelope, staring up at the ceiling as once, when they were younger, they lay and looked up at the clouds and tried to see prophecies in their spinning shapes. "If he's going to find him no matter what," she muses at last, "why not just give Orestes to him now? If his success is inevitable, is it wise to be someone who opposed it?" Penelope does not answer. "You find the idea of Menelaus's rule distasteful," Ourania tuts into the silence. "But look at it like this: he has clearly just spent the night trying to convince you that he is an ally. You have seen what his generosity looks like. Do you want to see his rage?"

"Of course not. But for all his talk, Menelaus clearly believes my husband to be dead. If he becomes the king in Mycenae as well as Sparta, no one will be able to stop him if he decides to annex the western isles. And the easiest and quickest way for him to do so would be to have someone of his choosing marry me. Can you imagine Nicostratus on Odysseus's throne?" Ourania's face crinkles in displeasure before she can hide her feelings, but in the low light of the lamps Penelope sees it. "Quite," she mutters. "And then what? Perhaps we avert a war – even Antinous and his faction wouldn't dare fight the combined power of Sparta and Mycenae if they imposed a king on us – but the isles would be reduced to nothing but a colony of our neighbours. Our goods, our gold, our people would be lambs to the altar of Menelaus, our independence lost. It is hardly the outcome I have worked for all these years."

"And the alternative?" Ourania asks. "You throw your support behind Orestes, Menelaus brands you an enemy of his people, and what? You are still unable to resist him if he should take the Mycenaean throne, only now he will have even less interest in your comfort and well-being. You are choosing between two atrocious outcomes, I know. But for your own sake, if not that of the isles, perhaps the time is coming to choose the least terrible of the two?"

Penelope has no answer.

There is a knock on the door.

Ourania unfolds herself from the bed, retreats into the shadows. Penelope straightens her gown, calls: "Enter!"

Autonoe sticks her head round the edge of the door.

"You should come," she says.

CHAPTER 18

>>

Pylades.

He has a lovely chin. It's the kind of chin I just want to pinch between finger and thumb, so manly yet so squishy, and goodness what a jaw he can thrust forward when in a bit of a sulk! If only his tastes inclined more my way, I absolutely would, goodness but yes.

The Mycenaean sits in the wine cellar of the palace, flanked by Eos on one side, little Phiobe on the other. He is armed, sword on his hip, and in armour only half shrouded by his cloak. He barely looks up as Autonoe, Ourania and Penelope enter; he affords the women none of the honour of a queen nor indeed a perfectly respectable lady, but glances at the assembled females, then looks away as if already bored.

My appreciation for his jaw wanes. Maybe I'm not as interested in his clasping thighs as I had hoped.

"We found him trying to climb over the wall," Autonoe proclaims. "There were Spartans everywhere."

"Was he seen?" Penelope asks, sharp and hard.

"I don't believe so. I convinced him to return to the palace before he could be." Pylades grunts, and Autonoe clarifies. "I informed him I would scream loud enough to wake the Furies, and that if he didn't come inside immediately, I would tell every Spartan that I had heard him speaking treasonous words against Menelaus."

"Your women are harpy lying whores," snaps Pylades. "So much for the loyal ladies of Ithaca."

Silence lands in the room like a stone. Five women of Ithaca stare down at the one Mycenae dressed in bronze, and he at last realises that maybe he has misjudged the crowd, and closes his mouth.

"Pylades," Penelope says at last, "my palace is occupied by the soldiers of Menelaus. His men spread across the island looking for your king. A king who, if Menelaus finds him, will absolutely be paraded around as a madman, unable to rule in his own lands let alone preside over the might of many monarchs and hold together our frail peace. So I have to wonder – what foolishness could possibly compel you to do something so insanely stupid as to attempt to sneak out under cover of dark when Spartan soldiers roam the night?"

Pylades doesn't answer.

Penelope sighs, moves a little closer, clasping her hands. "If you were going to look for your sworn brother, I will understand."

Pylades raises his head. There is desperation in his eye, tears almost. The sight takes Penelope aback. She does not know the source of this, cannot understand its flavour, its meaning. When the queen of Ithaca sees desperation, she assumes it is of a nature similar to her own – the terror of plots in danger, of schemes gone astray, of the weight of responsibility crushing the soul. For all her qualities, she finds it hard to imagine that the blazon of Pylades' soul might come from any other place. "He is my king," the soldier says. "He is my king."

"And if you lead Menelaus straight to him, he will be your king no longer. Do you understand?"

Pylades' head droops. He is still so young. Too young to consider himself the greatest failure in Greece, the worst traitor who ever lived – and yet here we are. I ruffle his hair, pat him gently on the shoulder.

"Take Pylades back to his room," Penelope commands. "Let us be thankful that no one else saw these events tonight."

They take Pylades back to his room.

He shares it with Iason, his fellow Mycenaean. By morning there will be a Spartan guard set outside it – just in case they need anything, you understand.

Neither man sleeps. Nor are their deeds unseen that night.

I fly to Laertes' farm.

It has been a little while since I looked down on Orestes and his sister.

The Furies shudder high above the house of Laertes, and as Orestes sleeps, they send him nightmares and bitter sweats, cackle at his distemper, lick their lips with blackened tongues at his every groan of despair. They are playing with their prey, feasting on his suffering – but increasingly I begin to suspect that they are not the cause of his pain, merely parasites come to gnaw on the carcass. Nevertheless I dim the light of my divinity as I approach, bow my head from their scarlet eyes as I hurry across the porch.

Athena sits by Orestes' side, Elektra slumbering at his feet. She does not wipe the moisture from his brow, as she was wont to sometimes do with Odysseus, when she thought no other god was looking. She does not quiet the nightmares that roll behind his eyes. She is wiser than to tamper with the business of the Furies, those primal ladies of the burning earth.

"How is he?" I murmur, though she barely stirs on my entrance.

"The priestess of our cousin Artemis does her work well," Athena replies. "He is safe."

"And the Furies?"

"Orestes is safe from mortals," she corrects. "At least, for now."

"I wouldn't be sure of even that," I murmur. "Menelaus will hunt tomorrow."

At this, the goddess of wisdom rouses herself a little from her contemplation of the broken prince, and looks up, meeting my eye. Few of my kin ever meet my gaze, fearing perhaps its enchantment, but Athena has reached a decision, and once she has made her mind up, she is rarely known to change it. "Did you ever love Menelaus?" she asks, with an almost childish curiosity that must be sated. "I know you loved Helen long before you made her your plaything."

"I love everyone," I reply. "It is my gift."

"But still you gave his wife away."

"She was ready to go. I merely guided her towards a potential outlet for her desires."

"And Menelaus?"

I sigh. "Menelaus and his brother . . . were never going to be men of my inclination. They desired, of course. They desired more than most men have dared to dream of – kingdoms, riches, power, vengeance, glory. These are not of any interest to me. They will not bring an end to suffering, they will not grant a man contentment. Love – the love of a soul that learns to fly, to delight in the flight of another – was never on their minds. And so they were never much on mine."

Athena nods at this, a question to which she thought she knew the answer and is pleased to discover that in fact she almost certainly did. "Father complains that mortals blame us for their deeds. He rails against their contradictions – that a people born so free are nevertheless incapable of taking responsibility for their own actions, and the suffering they themselves create. He does not see the contradiction in his own position, that he too does not take responsibility. None of us do. We exult in our power, and never stop to gaze upon its consequences. We may not guide mortals to the choices they make, but as we are their exemplars, the ones set above, we must lead, and we too are responsible. You and I, cousin. We are responsible too. But we always make others pay the price."

I touch my fingers to the cool palm of her hand, and she does not flinch.

I wrap my arm around hers, press close to her, as a sister might, and on that night, as the Furies cackle high above and the seas foam off the shore of Ithaca, Athena does not reprimand me my sentiments.

CHAPTER 19

M enelaus hunts.

Nicostratus joins him in his stolen armour, resplendent and polished.

"Is he so scared of rabbits?" mutters Euracleia, the old
nursemaid. She has strong opinions about how men should
hunt – ideally clad in as little as possible, to demonstrate their
fearless manliness. When she tells the story of Odysseus and the
boar, he wears progressively less and less in each retelling, so
that these days he's barely in a loincloth, wielding nothing more
than a pebble and a bit of string.

Penelope does not grace Euracleia's opinions with a reply.
She has had very little time for the nursemaid for a great
many years, and the old woman's mutterings do not alter this
situation.

Menelaus does not deck himself in armour, but carries an
old sword scarred with time and an oft-battered, oft-sharpened
blade. A slave carries a brace of javelins and spears behind him,
ready to hand to the roaming king. A troop of fifteen Spartan
warriors accompanies him and his son, and nearly twenty men
more will run ahead to scout the rugged land and call out when
they see a suitable beast.

Penelope says: "Let me send good Peisenor with you, a man who knows these lands well."

"Not at all!" Menelaus chuckles. "I was perfectly capable of finding game to feed an army outside the walls of Troy; I am sure we will find something suitable for the evening's feast on your lovely little island!"

"A fast ship to Kephalonia – you can be there before the sun hits its highest point, and the hunting there is glorious, far better than on Ithaca . . ."

"Odysseus and his father loved this little rock, and I respect their judgement! Don't you worry yourself over this, sister – we'll not be a burden!"

With this, the riders of Sparta kick their horses into a trot, while the men of Sparta jog along at their side in a really very impressive and manful fashion that they keep up until just outside eyeshot of the town, where they can slow down to a more sensible walking pace.

"Have the women follow at a distance," Penelope murmurs in Eos's ear, as they watch the procession wind away. "Send me news of where they go."

Eos nods, and slips away.

Helen stays behind, flanked by her ever-present maids.

"Cousin! Oh, cousin!" she chirrups, as Penelope turns to go into the hall. "Will you join me for a little drinky?"

A normal day in the life of Penelope of Ithaca is frankly more dull than I can bear. Hera or Athena might have more time for it, given that it consists of an inordinate amount of counting goats, arguing over the price of oil, negotiating costs with masons and carpenters and so on. There are none of the finer arts of a queenly life, as in listening to music or sweet poetry, the crafting of lovely gowns, or gossiping with wise mothers about the marriage prospects of their fresh, nubile daughters.

Life on Ithaca is, to be frank, an absolute bore. Which makes the arrival of lovely Helen, who always had an ear and an eye for the sweetest things in life, something of a jarring experience for the lady of the palace. Now they sit beneath an awning of blue and white slung between an olive branch and a trellis of sweet climbing flowers, as the maids Zosime and Tryphosa serve wine to Helen in a golden cup, and Autonoe serves very little at all to Penelope in a clay one.

Yet Helen, who was a queen of two lands, and once was considered the wittiest, finest creature to ever discourse on womanly things, has a little something on her tongue that seems to stifle her. For where at supper she chattered freely on all things, an airy burble of empty noise, now her words come stop-start, as if she is trying to converse – of all things – *seriously*. As if she would have some meaningful conference with her cousin and is not sure how.

In Troy, Hecuba, wife of King Priam, once turned to Helen across the table and said in front of all there assembled: "You are beautiful, daughter. But let no one pretend that you are wise."

In Sparta, in the days before Paris came, Helen's sister Clytemnestra, when she was still Agamemnon's beloved wife and queen of Mycenae, howled with laughter at something Helen said, exclaiming: "She would have you think she is a philosopher!"

A woman – a wife – especially a beautiful one, must not be silent. Helen learned that. Silent women are sullen, resentful, scheming plotters. Neither must she be too outgoing in her speech. A loud woman is a nag, a bore, a busybody. A perfect place in between is required, where she might be observed to be participating but be dismissed without a thought the moment matters of any great import arise. This requirement was one of the many things, she found, that Troy had in common with Sparta, and Paris with Menelaus.

162

Yet now she sips from a gleaming cup that her maids refill, and her eyes are wide and her speech a little strange as she says: "So . . . how did Telemachus come to leave Ithaca?" The question knocks the breath from Penelope, almost seems to slap her across the side of the face. Perhaps Helen sees this, perhaps she does not – her eyes are already in some other place – but she adds in an easy exhale: "He seems such a sweet young man."

"He is gone looking for his father," Penelope at last replies, watching the two Spartan maids who watch no one at all from their posts at the edge of this little garden. "To find Odysseus either living or dead. Either way – an answer."

"And if he is dead?"

"Then Telemachus will return and seek his birthright."

"Be king, you mean?" Helen giggles. Penelope manages not to wince at the sound. "Gracious, won't that be something! King Telemachus. Well, I'm sure he can do it. Strong young man like that, I'm sure he'll find a way."

"Naturally he will be looking to his father's noble allies – Orestes, Nestor, your good husband Menelaus – to support him in his claim."

"Of course, of course! My husband is so soppy about Odysseus, he really is. He'll do anything for his son, just you wait and see. Just you wait." Penelope's smile is a frozen thing. She holds her cup to her lips, does not drink, forgets to even mime the action. "And what about you?" Helen asks, laying a hand on Penelope's knee. The Ithacan jerks as if stung by a wasp, but Helen seems not to notice. "Will you marry when Telemachus returns? I imagine you can't, if your husband is dead – at least not without your son's approval. Perhaps a temple life? They say there is real peace to be found serving in a sacred place, a calm that people like us can only dream of. Humility. I often wondered if I should try and go to such a place, but you know how it is – there are too many duties I must discharge, too many responsibilities. Work work work until we drop, no?"

She laughs and holds out her cup.

Zosime refills it, and at once steps away again.

Penelope watches her cousin, head down, eyes up, doing her best not to stare and unable to stop herself.

"My children, of course ... well, it's been so hard for them," Helen muses. "What with both myself and Menelaus gone for so long. They had the best possible education, the finest upbringing imaginable, but you know how it is. Children are forced to grow up so fast these days, don't you think?"

Of Menelaus's children, there are two boys still living – Nicostratus and Megapenthes. Both were born of slaves, and both have sworn that they will drive their stepmother into the sea the moment their father dies.

Only one child of Helen's lives, lovely Hermione, a daughter old enough to remember what it was like to have her mother stroke her hair in the days before the war. She is also old enough to remember how it felt to be left behind.

"How was Clytemnestra when she died?"

The question comes from nowhere. It is pitched as if Helen were enquiring after the nature of some unusual blossom, or wondering what recipes Penelope might use to pickle fish. For a moment Penelope imagines she did not hear it right, but looking from Helen to her maids and back again, she sees only Helen's expectant gaze. Zosime and Tryphosa should turn away, should step a little further back from this most intimate of enquiries, give the daughters of Sparta privacy to speak of their fallen kin. They do not.

"She was ... as ready as I think any soul can be," Penelope says at last. "She knew that for Orestes to be king, she must die. I believe she thought of her son until the last."

"Even though he killed her?"

"Yes. That is my . . . little understanding of the thing."

Helen nods, sips, gazes at nothing much. "Is that why he's mad, do you think?"

Penelope holds her cup like she is clinging to the straps of a shield in a storm of arrows. "Mad?" she murmurs.

"Yes, mad. Isn't that what they're all saying? That he fled Mycenae because he's lost his mind, that it's only that sister of his – Elektra – who's keeping him from being quite publicly insane? That's what my husband says, and he has people everywhere."

"Orestes did his duty and avenged his father's death," Penelope replies, voice like pebbles tumbling on the shore. "Why would he be mad?"

Helen dismisses this with a flick of one long, thin wrist. "Goodness," she clucks, "he killed his mother! His father killed his sister, his mother kills his father, he kills his mother – I mean, the whole family is cursed anyway, isn't it?" That high laugh again; Penelope has to remember not to grind her teeth. "The sons of Atreus! Their great-grandfather fed his own son to the gods, then Atreus fed his nephews to his brother – it's nothing but cannibalism, rape and incest every step of the way; no wonder Orestes is mad! When Daddy told me I was to marry Menelaus, I was delighted, of course I was, absolutely thrilled, but I remember turning to him and saying, 'Papa, are you sure the big warrior man won't just eat me?'"

That laugh again – louder, higher, brighter. Penelope is going to crack a tooth if it carries on like this for much longer. "Do you blame the gods for what happened?" she asks at last, a careful, cautious line of enquiry that she hopes will cause minimal confusion.

"Of course not!" Helen exclaims. "Foul fathers make foul sons! Violence breeds violence. That is the way of things. Breaking the cycle is far harder than continuing it, poor dears."

Penelope frowns. It is possible that there is in these words a hint of something if not wise, then at least perhaps somewhat true, tumbling from Helen's lips. The notion is disquieting. Penelope has not expected to hear a shimmer of either quality from her cousin these many, many years.

Zosime refills Helen's cup. Autonoe does not go anywhere near Penelope's.

There are things Penelope wants to ask.

There are things every mortal breathing wants to ask.

Things like: so come on then, sister, cousin, babe – fess up. Did Paris kidnap you or did you run away with him, seriously now? What were you thinking? What was going through your mind? Was he really all that? Did Menelaus do something, say something that made you choose to destroy the world? *Did* you choose? And what happened when you were reunited with your husband? Did you rend your gown, as everyone says, bare your breasts and weep, beg forgiveness? Did he really order his soldiers to stone you to death, but at the sight of your bouncing bosom they couldn't do it? Did you give him the knife that he drove into Deiphobus, did you make some secret agreement with Odysseus to help the Greeks into Troy, did you . . .

Did you, did you, did you?

It occurs to Penelope that she has a glorious opportunity to ask all these questions. To unpick the heart and mind of the woman for whom the world burned.

She does not.

There are too many answers waiting on the tip of Helen's tongue that it would not be apt to hear. No, not even for the wife of Odysseus, who is waiting still for her husband to come home. For what will Penelope say if Helen replies: ah yes, Menelaus, of course once he was done with killing Deiphobus and butchering the babes of Troy, he raped me, repeatedly, in front of all his men on the deck of his ship, such a mood he had, but you can't really blame him, can you? My fault, you see. It's all my fault. All of it. All the things that people have to do to me. I am to blame.

Or what will Penelope say if Helen laughs and says: gracious, of course I ran away with Paris! Of course I did! I was a *child*. I was a giggling infant girl who had been kept infantilised, taught that I was at my most charming if I was a foolish virgin who demurred and simpered and said "oh yes, sir, how pretty" and bobbed my lovely little head – of course I ran away with the handsome man who said I was a lady! Of course I chose it. Wouldn't you?

What then will Penelope say?

Will she snarl at the queen of Sparta? Spit in her face? Slap her perfect white cheek? Will she scream: whore, harpy, destroyer of my world, my life? You took my husband from me, you did this, you did this, *you are right you are to blame!*

Such an action would be politically unsound. And even if it were not, Penelope finds that she does not have the heart to do it, and is baffled at this conclusion.

So she says nothing, asks nothing. This is the way of things with Helen. This is how it shall be until my lovely lady, fairest of the fair, dies at last, alone, far from home in a place where no one says her name.

Instead they sit in silence, the two queens, the last queens of these lands whose stories the poets will tell.

"I hear," Helen says, to no one, to nothing, to the air, to the sky, to the unrelenting quiet, "that there's a shrine on Kephalonia to Hera, mother of all."

"There are shrines to Hera across the western isles."

"Yes – but not to Hera as the mother of all. There are shrines to her as a wife, as the protector of the household, but I heard this was a shrine to Hera as a creator, as a queen of air and fire, as they say sometimes the mother is worshipped in the east. A shrine only the women go to. Is that true?"

"There are some who have ... old-fashioned beliefs," Penelope concedes. "Many women of these isles worship Hera, Artemis, Athena, not as they are sometimes honoured on the mainland but as ... as gods of a somewhat more elemental sort. As creatures almost equal to or maybe even greater than the men. My husband said it was silly superstition, and of course the priests do their best to stop it."

"And the priestesses?" Helen asks.

"It would not be appropriate for a king's wife to dabble in religious affairs," Penelope replies.

Her cousin nods. "Of course. You always were so much smarter than me."

Another sip. Helen turns her head upwards, half closes her eyes. She is enjoying the play of sun on her skin, the cooling kiss of the breeze. Her neck is long, a few loose strands of hair flick around her face. Penelope is fascinated. She has never before seen a woman of her sort, of royal blood and training, outwardly enjoy the touch of her own senses. These experiences are innocent, of course – warmth and cold, shadow and light playing over the skin – but they are also outrageous, forbidden, enthralling. Helen is enjoying the sensation of being in her own body. She listens to the sea and finds it soothing. She smells the perfume from the tiny flowers crawling up the wall at her back and loves its scent. And strangest of all – she dares to show it. Penelope feels a twist in her stomach, and thinks for a moment it might be envy.

"You are very lucky, cousin," Helen murmurs at last, "to have a place such as Ithaca."

"I thought we were considered an uncivilised backwater," Penelope replies. "Unfashionable, I think, is the kindest word for it."

Helen opens her eyes, turns back to Penelope with wide-eyed surprise. "Not at all! Well, no – yes, of course you *are* a bit isolated out here, and frankly one grows bored of fish, but don't let the poets and the gossips get to you, not at all! You have a lovely purity out here. A lovely quiet, a peacefulness. I know that the land is hard and the sea can be cruel – dearest, how cruel, poor you – but when you sit behind these walls in your quaint little garden, I imagine it is peaceful. So very peaceful, just away from it all."

Penelope looks at this little nook of space, this tiny walled garden in the tangle of the palace, and seems to see it for the first time. She has of course spent some time here before, resting, relaxing after a long day, but that was rare, and rarer still as the years went by. There are so many other places that have required her attention. The vegetable garden, the orchards and olive groves, the muddy fields, the treasury – both the one her male councillors know of, and the other one she keeps a little more hidden. Then there are the secret rooms of Ourania where they conspire to keep control, the tannery and the fisher-women's wharves. She has forgotten to see any of this, any of the kingdom that is ostensibly her domain, as anything other than labour. Even the sea has turned from a silver sheet to a beating threat that brings danger to her shore.

How strange it is to look now, she thinks, and be reminded that this land – even Ithaca – is beautiful. She has only remembered this occasionally in recent months, when the Egyptian, Kenamon, caught in a moment of obscene solitude, might raise his fingers to the cool rain and murmur: "The heavens bless you, my lady."

Penelope has never stopped, in those moments, to ask Kenamon more about what he sees. It is not suitable that a queen and a suitor exchange more than passing words, let alone out of sight, and so busily she has breezed on by, and pretended not to be disquieted by his voice in her ear.

Now I kiss her fingertips, sit between Penelope and Helen and hold their hands in mine, an unseen bridge between the two silent women.

Behold, I whisper, my lips brushing Penelope's cheek. *Behold beauty.*

The sound of the ocean is soft behind the walls that shield them from the coldest gusts of the turning wind. The clouds rush overhead, fat and fluffy, not yet broken by beating against the hard land beyond. Honeybees collect the last of the summer nectar. A lizard the colour of the stones it warms itself against slips away from the shuffling of Zosime's foot, and Helen of Sparta, Helen of Troy, turns her face towards the sun and breathes in the glory of the morning.

Then Eos is in the door, and the moment is at an end.

"My queen," she proclaims – these words only ever pass Eos's lips when there are strangers there who might expect it. "There is word from your illustrious father."

Penelope rides, Autonoe at her side.

She does not ride as a lady should – demure, patient, on a temperate mare. Instead she hitches her gown all the way up between her thighs, bends her head over her horse's neck and gallops across the land by little winding paths known only to the shepherd women and their snuffling dogs. I glance about for my lovely cousin Artemis – these are her hidden ways, the branches that snag and the thorns that bite draw their blood in her honour, sacred mistress of the dappled groves. I heard a rumour that she had been seen hunting about this isle of late, but very few of my kin pay attention to their wayward cousin, save perhaps her brother Apollo, and he only looks out of jealousy.

No sign of her – at least, none I can see, which with the huntress is never quite the same thing.

Eos has gone ahead to warn Anaitis, Melantho is sent into town to alert Ourania, but now Penelope herself gallops for Laertes' farm, sun beating down upon her head through the broken branches and dappled leaves, hair flying from its binds as she races towards the old Ithacan king.

The Furies are waiting, of course, spinning their mischief above Laertes' farm in bitter tastes upon the tongue, in rotten grain and aphid-crawling infestations upon the vine. Yet for all that they howl and clatter and laugh, still they have done no more than these light mischiefs to Laertes, these little insults to the man who hosts their prey, and I think again that perhaps Athena is right. Perhaps it is not dead Clytemnestra, drifting in the grey lands of the deep, who has summoned these creatures. Perhaps their purpose was set by someone else altogether.

Priene is waiting by the gate of Laertes' farm, fully armed, bold as the eagle. Her loyal lieutenant Teodora is by her side, a quiver of arrows on her back, bow held loose, ready to fire. The hidden backwards paths and secret ways of the isle bring Penelope out of a shrouded copse of trees and straight towards the waiting warrior, and as she dismounts, Priene barks her news.

"The Spartans are approaching from the sea road. They will be upon us momentarily."

"How many?"

"All of them."

Autonoe is already leading Penelope's horse inside as the queen marches towards the door of the farm. As she does, the old man emerges, his dirty robe hitched to his knees, his hair tangled about his head. Laertes did consider tidying himself up for his guests, being as they are royalty of the highest sort. That instinct lasted barely one night, when he realised that Elektra and Orestes were so preoccupied with their own business that they barely noticed he was there, let alone bothered to acknowledge him as a king.

"Who's this?" he barks, seeing Priene and Teodora at Penelope's back.

"Huntresses of the island," replies Penelope briskly, barely slowing her stride. "Menelaus is come. I set these women to watch his progress, and they report that he is now heading directly here."

"I imagine he's not just planning on paying homage," Laertes scowls, as Penelope marches inside.

"No doubt he'll say he is, but he has armed men and they will search this farm. Is there anywhere to hide Orestes?"

"Is there anywhere to hide Orestes," mimics the old king with a sour curl of his mouth. "Goodness, let me think – of course not! I had a place once, but oh no, wait, it was burned to the ground when pirates attacked over a year ago, and I haven't had a chance to rebuild it, and even if I had, I am a king, not a smuggler or a *huntress*." He directs the last word to Priene, whose hand still grips the hilt of her less-than-hunter-like blade.

Penelope shakes her head, has reached the door of Orestes' room, bangs on it. "Elektra! Menelaus comes!" The door opens a little bit, Elektra's face grey as the cobweb beyond. "Menelaus is coming here," barks Penelope. "Can your brother walk?"

"I do not know," she replies. "Can't you stop him? This is the house of Odysseus' father!"

"My palace is overrun with Spartan soldiers, my cellars full of Spartan wine, my maids displaced, my musicians sent away from my own hall, my isle thronging with Menelaus's men under the ostensible cover of going for a hunt, and rather than look for boar he comes directly here – no, of course I can't stop him!" Penelope is not used to raising her voice, it is an unqueenly thing to do, but now she is more than a little provoked. "Whatever you can do to get your brother as ... presentable as you can, do it now!"

A scurry of movement behind them – Eos has arrived, breathless and hot, Anaitis at her side.

"Anaitis, good – Menelaus comes and we need Orestes at the bare minimum sober, at the best talking in a calm and regal manner. Can you do anything for him?"

"He has been improving, but he is still weak, the poison . . . "

"Whatever you can do," – Penelope nearly shoves Anaitis into the shadow of Orestes' room – "do it now."

Elektra closes the door behind the priestess, and Penelope turns now to face those assembled. "Priene, Teodora – I need you to hide."

"If Menelaus harms any of this house, I will split him from groin to gullet, you have my oath."

This declaration from Priene, rendered calm and collected as if she were discussing the passage of dusk and dawn, stops Penelope in her tracks. It is, arguably, the single most impassioned, loyal and moving thing this warrior of the east has ever said. Under other circumstances, it might induce in Penelope something almost verging on tears, grateful, astounded, humbled by the lady's vow. Even Laertes, hovering in a corner, has the decency to raise his eyebrows in surprise. However, there is now no time, so she nods once and hopes that is enough to communicate her sentiment on the matter. For Priene at least, it appears to be, for the woman and her lieutenant turn and run, sprinting out of the farmhouse gate and for the shadows of the trees that shelter the land around, while Laertes mutters and calls for a clean gown.

"If I'm going to have to put up with a visit from a king, I might as well look like a king," he proclaims. "I was an Argonaut, you know!"

"Do you have any incense?" Penelope asks, as Eos wets her hands and tries to pull Laertes' thin white hair into something that might resemble a more dignified mop.

"Incense? Why the blazes would I have that?"

Penelope pounds on Elektra's door. "Anaitis!" she calls. "Tell me you have something theological we can burn!"

CHAPTER 20

>>

Menelaus comes to the house of Laertes.

The women of Ithaca – those warriors hiding in plain sight, for who would begrudge a widow the need to carry an axe if she must chop wood, or a daughter her hunting bow for chasing rabbits? – watched as the king and his Spartans headed out on their hunting trip.

They beheld his scouts and his warriors on the single winding road that curls round the harsh lip of the isle, and at every opportunity that Menelaus could have taken to set up camp or head towards some likely patch of earth where boar might roam or even a hardy deer, he did not.

Indeed, the only reason, the women later concluded, that he did not go directly to Laertes' farm upon immediately departing the palace was that his men – even his spies – weren't exactly sure of the way. But make no mistake – he has always had but one destination on this isle, as unwavering as the arrow shot from Apollo's golden bow.

Now even the Furies are hushed as Menelaus and his golden troop approach. They huddle on the walls of Laertes' farm and watch the Spartan king as if he were one of their own. What, I wonder, do their blazing eyes see in this man? The blood still clinging to his hands? The shadows of the dead that spin around him, ghostly fingers reaching up to the winged ladies as they beg in tongueless mouths, with voices that no longer breathe, *vengeance, vengeance, vengeance!*

Laertes and his serving woman Otonia wait by the gate as Menelaus and his men draw near. The old king has never actually met the Spartan – after his adventures on the high seas as a young man, he decided he'd had quite enough of exotic travel and foreign food and would stay put, thank you very much. And it's not like anyone of note had much interest in visiting Ithaca. But a king will recognise a king. The expectation of obedience, the presumption of worth, the willingness to cut someone down for looking at you funny – all the proper kingly traits you might expect are here drawn large in both men. To add to the impression, Laertes has even whipped on his best gown, the one he would wear whenever he visited the palace for his annual dose of suitable fawning-over, and pushed his thin, dishevelled mane of hair back from his face. There has been no time to clean between his toes or rub oil into his skin, but that's fine. The kings of Ithaca know how to play the hearty down-to-earth monarch to the hilt.

A column of Spartans stretches out either side of the dirt track to guide Menelaus to the gate, much as they did when he disembarked from his ship. He slows his horse as he draws within the armoured escort, dismounts, hands the reins to a standing slave, approaches slowly, smiling, head a little to one side, eyeing up the father of Odysseus. Nicostratus sits behind, still upon his horse, armour gleaming, arms folded and eyes roaming over the freshly built walls of the farm as if judging a military fortification.

Laertes doesn't say a word as Menelaus nears, waiting for the guest king to speak even as Menelaus waits for his host to greet him. Thus there is a silence between the two, and it is the silence of two old swordsmen assessing the length of each other's blades, considering the duel before them and whether it might not be easier to call the whole thing off and go home.

Above, the Furies shudder gleefully within their folded wings, and an icy wind blows unseasonably across the field, goosebumping bare skin and startling a flock of crows. Their chill touch seems enough to break the silence between the kings, and it is Menelaus who smiles, puts one hand to his heart and gives a shallow little bow.

"Great King Laertes," he says, "I am honoured to meet you at last."

"You must be Menelaus of Sparta," Laertes replies, not bending an inch. "You're exactly how I imagined. Come inside then, take a load off, if you're coming."

With this, he spins on his heel and marches towards the open door of his house. Menelaus hesitates just a moment. He is – merely as a force of habit – contemplating cutting off Laertes' head. He will not, of course; that would be not only a dreadful violation of all the laws of hospitality, all the sacred commands of the gods, but an absolutely abysmal political move that might put his crown itself in jeopardy. But given that no one save dead Agamemnon has spoken to the Spartan king in this way for a very, very long time, we must at least understand Menelaus's instinctive reaction. Instead, however, he chooses to smile, to laugh – no, not laugh. To *chuckle*. A decidedly different beast. He hooks his thumbs in his belt, waves his son and his captain, Lefteris, with his men to follow, and trails Laertes into the house.

It is but a few steps from the door to the great hearth that warms the old king in winter. Set around this are several low stools for guests, sheepskins upon the floor, and one high-backed chair that is Laertes' own. Stood beside this chair is Penelope, Elektra at her side, facing the door. Eos stands a little in the shadows, water and wine at the ready, a few dates on a plate.

Menelaus sees Penelope, smiles, sees Elektra, and stops in his tracks.

"Oh, Menelaus, you remember your niece, Elektra. Isn't this all cosy and familial?" Laertes says, waving away proffered wine.

"Uncle," Elektra says, with a tiny bow of her head. "I heard you had come to Ithaca. Forgive my tardiness in not meeting you at the docks."

Menelaus's eyes move round the room, counting doorways, considering corridors, before he moves a little deeper inside. He heads straight for the hearth, leans up against it, claiming that sacred space for his own. Behind him, Nicostratus enters, followed by Lefteris and two more warrior men, and suddenly the place is cramped, the ceiling too low for the Spartans' plumes, too tight for the beating of so many hearts.

"Elektra," Menelaus proclaims, "what an unexpected but lovely pleasure."

"Indeed," she replies, light as smoke from the flame. "We had hoped not to trouble kind King Laertes with our presence when we came to Ithaca for our devotions, but it is true what they say – the Ithacans really are the most gracious of hosts."

"Aren't they just, aren't they just? Your devotions, you say, your ... "

"A pilgrimage, of sorts. Ithaca is where, by the judgement of the gods and in the most righteous path of vengeance, my mother was slain. Though it was entirely just that she died, the priests of Apollo decreed that to wash away the stain of a mother's murder, a journey to the great shrines of all the gods would be desirable, before of course at last offering to gracious Athena at the place where Clytemnestra rightly fell. We had hoped to conclude the business privately, but as you are family, I suppose it is fitting that you of all the great kings are here to see it through."

Menelaus's eyes flicker from Elektra to Penelope. "And your kind Ithacan queen—"

"I requested that she keep this matter private," Elektra cuts in, fast. "She is already burdened with so many weighty matters, we did not want to add to her troubles. When kind King Laertes offered to give us shelter away from the prying eyes of men, a place to pray and give thanks to the gods . . ."

"Of course." Menelaus's voice is a polished pearl. "Just as you say – such excellent hosts. Still, that's all done now, isn't it? You've done your praying and made your offerings, I expect, and now that I'm here, well, what kind of uncle would I be if I didn't see that you were done right by? My brother's ghost would haunt me for ever if I didn't keep an eye out for his children. Menelaus, he'd say – I can hear him now, so I practically can – Menelaus, I sailed to Troy for your wife, now you'd better sail to the ends of the earth for my kiddos, the ends of the earth, he'd say. And mind my foolish old man's heart if you didn't have me a little worried for a moment there, niece. When I got word from Mycenae saying you and your brother had vanished, I thought, Menelaus, I thought, you're the worst of men. You're the worst brother who ever lived, the worst uncle, your blood is really properly cursed, just like the priests always said it was, you've let your family down, and nothing's more important than family. But here you are. Camped out on Ithaca. Praying. I'm so relieved I could cry – look at me, I swear there's a bit of water in the corner of my eye. Come here, niece."

He grabs Elektra before she can object, twining his arms around her in an enormous, breath-crushing, rib-creaking hug, her feet nearly lifting off the floor with the force of it. At his father's back, Nicostratus picks his teeth with a long, grubby nail and watches Elektra, whose bulging eyes meet his and immediately look away. Nicostratus grins, as Menelaus deposits his niece back down and turns his attention to Penelope with a waggling finger and a broad grin.

"And you, sister! Very tricksy of you not to mention this,

very loyal I will say, very loyal to your cousin, got to respect that, admire that, but tricksy too, got to keep an eye on that one, Odysseus always said you were the cleverest woman alive!"

Laertes snorts. The sound is rich in mucus and saliva, and just about grotesque enough that all eyes turn to him. "Her? Tricksy?" he barks. "I grant you she's got a good head on her shoulders for the value of sheep and a fine ear for when some merchant is trying to rob her. Good shepherd's eye, good farmer's legs – didn't expect that from a woman of Sparta, not going to lie, but I imagine as she's now lived on Ithaca longer than she did in Sparta, you'd hope some of our ways would rub off on her. But she's no child of Hermes. When news came of royal ships on the horizon, I sent a message to her at the palace – not a word of this to whoever's coming to visit. Princess Elektra and her family have had quite enough of the royal nonsense you people do on the mainland, all your courtly manners and ways, they need a bit of time for prayer – trust me, I know a thing or two about the gods. Not a word, daughter, I said, I know what you're like but you will obey me – and I'm glad I did, frankly, because you know what, seeing you here, Menelaus, pardon my saying so, but seeing you here with so many servants and soldiers and such an entourage, it's a wonder you have any time for prayer at all, there's so many mouths to feed and voices going in your ear. Bit of quiet contemplation. That's what a king needs from time to time."

Menelaus looks at Laertes – finally looks. And at last he sees not just the scraggly, dirty old man in the unfashionable robe, but the man who was once master of all these isles. Not merely the father of Odysseus, but the soldier who dragged the western isles together through bronze and blood while Menelaus and his brother were still babes, exiles from their native land. Sees the cunning old king, cracked yellow teeth and sunken eyes, grinning at him from across the hearth.

"Of course you did," he murmurs, as Laertes meets his eyes, straight and true. "Of course you did." A little louder, for all the room. "Silly of me – stupid really – to think that a woman would be making these kinds of decisions. Very silly."

Their gazes hold a second longer, and there is defiance in Laertes' eyes, an ancient triumph, a flash of the bright cunning that would shine a moment before his blade danced a path to victory. It is Menelaus who looks away, lips curling, a slight nod of his head, but when he looks up again, it is directly at Elektra. "And where is your brother, niece? Where is Orestes?"

"I am here."

Orestes stands in the mouth of the corridor that leads to the private rooms, Anaitis at his back. He is accompanied by a waft of incense, of burning sacred herbs, the smell of hurried prayers carried by his passage. He leans a little against the frame for support, one hand steadying himself, but that movement is slight. With every muscle he holds himself straight, his chin firm, his gaze steady, as the sweat rushes down his forehead, his chest, prickles the soft hair beneath his arms. His eyes are wide and rimmed with red, his hair combed back taut from his scalp, a man's beard struggling to make itself known on his jaw. His gown stinks of salt and clammy dark spaces, but no one will dare say so to the king of kings, the greatest of the Greeks. No – not even Menelaus. Not yet.

For three days and three nights, Anaitis has worked her healing ways upon him. For three days and three nights he has screamed and howled and puked and clawed at his skin as his sister sits weeping by his side. And now Anaitis has given him one last herb and whispered in his ear: "When you feel dizzy, sit before you fall," and so, at last, Orestes stands.

Outside, the Furies snarl, they hiss like feral cats, their feathers standing upon their backs, their ears pricking forward, lips curling back. Their displeasure is a sudden whiff of smoke, a

skipping of the steady beat of every heart within a mortal chest –
no more, no less.

Menelaus turns slowly, takes his time, looks his nephew
up and down. Says, "Your majesty," and bows a little. Even
Nicostratus, a scowl tugging the corners of his lips, briefly dips
his head up and down once in acknowledgement. Orestes does
not return the gesture, does not move, does not detach himself
from his current place of half-leaning, half-standing safety.

"Kind uncle, I hope you have not come all this way for me,"
he says. "If so, it must be proclaimed across Greece that your
love knows no limit."

"Come now," Menelaus chuckles, "Ithaca isn't *that* bad." His
smile turns down a little, thins a little, but does not entirely
vanish from his lips. "You look ill, nephew. Have you inhaled
some foul vapour?"

"The voyage was rough and several of the crew fell sick
during our passage," Orestes replies, quick and simple – ah, the
Furies show their teeth at that swift response and a shudder runs
through his body, barely suppressed. Every word will cost him;
there will be a price to pay. "Thankfully good Laertes, wishing
to protect both our privacy and our prayers, took us in, ordering
his daughter to secrecy." This last is an afterthought, a glance to
Penelope, half forgotten in a grey corner of the room.

"What a kind man – what a good man of Ithaca. But
nephew – I think of you as my son, may I call you son? I could
never replace your heroic father, of course, never dream of it,
but I do hate to think of you so young without my brother's
wisdom, and though I am a mere shadow of all he was, I'd love
to be here for you in whatever capacity I can . . ." Menelaus
crosses the room as he speaks, loops an arm across Orestes' back,
pulls him a little away from the wall. Orestes' feet tangle as
Menelaus holds him against his body and he nearly falls, holds
back a gasp, catches his breath, clenches his fists before he uses

them to grab his uncle for support. Menelaus seems not to have noticed as he leads the half-panting Orestes into the room. "It would warm my heart so much to have you think of my son here, Nicostratus, as your brother ... " Nicostratus is the son of a slave. It is outrageous that he should be considered in any meaningful way kin to the king of kings, but Menelaus appears not to care. "Now I'm here, you must be properly looked after. Prayer is all very well, of course it is, all very well, noble in fact, so noble, your father would be so proud of you both, but I'm not going to lie, there have been questions asked, questions about where the king of Mycenae and his lovely sister have got to. There are things only a father could tell you, of course, about what it is to be a king, only a father, but I feel I owe it to him, to my brother, to you – owe it to you to help you now. To guide you even. As best I can. With what little I have."

The Furies preen, coo, brush their cheeks together lovingly, tongues tasting the air. Orestes half closes his eyes, as if darkness is the price he must pay to stay upright, capable and on his feet. Elektra does not blink. Nicostratus is watching her, grinning. Menelaus gives Orestes a squeeze about the shoulders, a frown upon his brow, a concerned uncle, desperately worrying for his stinking, sweating, shivering kin. Laertes stands by the hearth, straight as the mast of the noble *Argo* when first she set sail. Penelope does her best to appear not to be visible at all.

"Uncle," Orestes says at last. "You are too kind."

The slap on his back that Menelaus gives him nearly sends the young man to the floor. It is only the hasty dart of Elektra to his side that catches him, halts his collapse. Menelaus pretends not to have noticed, already a flourish of activity. "Right, that's settled then! A horse for the king – Nicostratus, you'll give up yours, of course – and we need one for his sister too ... Send word ahead to the palace – Orestes must of course have my room – and break open the finest stores we have on the ships ...

Don't worry yourself, good sister Penelope, we won't trouble a hair on your head – everything must be arranged for my nephew! Everything must be prepared for the king!"

Nicostratus sticks his head out of the door of the farm to pick up this cry and echo it to his men as they scurry to their business.

"For the king!" he calls, and the nearest men take it up.

"For the king!" they holler.

"For the king!" echoes the valley.

"For the king!" cry the warriors of Sparta.

"*For the king*," whisper the Furies as they take to the sky, and laugh and spiral around each other in their merriment, as burning black feathers fall from their beating wings.

CHAPTER 21

‣‣

P enelope, Eos and Autonoe stand in the courtyard of
Penelope's palace and watch other people take charge.

Maids of Sparta seize control of the kitchen – "So as not to
trouble you a jot, hostess, not a jot!"

Men of Sparta bring supplies from Menelaus's ships – "Luckily,
we came prepared to feed a king, not that I've anything against
fish, but you know how it is!"

Soldiers of Sparta ring the walls, man the gates – "There are
people who might wish Orestes ill, I shudder to say it, monstrous, but I have to do right by my nephew."

Euracleia, the old nursemaid of Odysseus, is outraged, on the
verge of tears. "They tell me to mind my busy head! In my own
halls! In the palace of my Odysseus!"

Her distress is only partially alleviated by the arrival of
Laertes, who appears after everyone else has already made it
back from his farm, on the back of a grumbling donkey. "Well,"
he mutters, "if every king in Greece is about to eat at my son's
table, the least I can do is show my face."

He dismounts from his shuffling beast and marches over to
Penelope's side. She nods, smiles, does not know how to say thank
you to the old man. Laertes has never been a kind father-in-law,

but neither was he ever cruel. Penelope did her duty quickly as a wife by producing a grandson for Laertes to harangue about the proper way of kinging, and never dishonoured her husband by sleeping around or getting ideas above her status. The orchards have bloomed and vines have been tended; Laertes' table has never wanted for animals to slaughter or fish to gut. Moreover, the western isles do appear to be defended on Penelope's watch, and even if that defence smacks a little too much of "the blessed huntress Artemis intervened with her divine power in obscure yet deadly ways" for Laertes' taste, he respects the value of a scrappy battle waged in the secret hours of darkness. The honourable valour of the publicly lauded warrior was never the Ithacan way.

"Good King Laertes!" blubbers Euracleia as the old king enters the hall. "You're here! You'll bring some order to the palace! You'll do what's right!"

Euracleia was beloved of Anticlea, Laertes' departed wife, and out of loyalty to her he has always given the nursemaid a kind word or two. But there is a time and a place, so for now he barks: "For goodness' sake, Euracleia! We have the greatest in the lands in our halls tonight! Show some decorum!"

His presence is enough that she pulls herself together for now, only to weep even more extensively when the sun has set and she finds a private moment to do so.

Orestes has already been put in Laertes' room, and it would be dishonourable in the extreme for the king of kings to be moved now. "That's fine," the old man grunts. "I wasn't going to stay anyway."

I am disgusted at this development, of course. The dishonour of the father of the house – the shame of it, of Laertes being displaced from his own room. Were I to lay a curse upon Menelaus and all his brood right now for the insult, none would question me. But though my curse would be righteous, there would be consequences – oh so many consequences – so for now I bite my lip and hold my ire, though my godly wrath flickers bright at the tips of my silken fingertips.

With the Spartans making no effort to change their plans, Laertes must save face, and so . . .

"I imagine after the feast you will be retiring to the temple of Athena to offer prayers for your son, as you are so often inclined to do," murmurs Penelope in her father-in-law's ear. "I will have one of my women attend to you. Ourania – do you remember her? She will wait upon you at your midnight devotions and see that you are . . . accommodated in your piety."

It is rare for Laertes to smile, but rarer still for a scowl not to be upon his lips. He does not scowl at Penelope, but simply nods and says: "Yes. All-night prayers for my son. That sounds exactly like the kind of thing a pious father would do instead of sleep in his own bed, doesn't it?"

Elektra and Orestes arrive. Helen spots them from an unshuttered window, and shrills: "Elektra! Orestes! Coo-ee! *Coo-ee!*"

They do their best to ignore her, but she will not be ignored, rushing down to greet them in the courtyard in a flurry of pearl and jasmine. "Darlings, you're here! You're here!" She kisses Elektra on either side of her face, forgets to bob before Orestes, then remembers and does a shuffling little bow with a cry of "Goodness, so sorry, I mean, your majesty!" before grabbing him by the tops of both his arms to land a squelchy smacker on his cheek.

"Wonderful, wonderful!" she exclaims, as Orestes sways in the heat, on the verge of toppling, Elektra by his side. "Oh, isn't this wonderful, it's a whole family reunion! Darling, isn't this fabulous?"

"Fabulous," Menelaus agrees, dismounting from his steed. "Cosy, even."

*

Pylades rushes to his king's side as Orestes is led into the palace. He throws himself at his feet, kneels, a humble petitioner. Iason and the priest Kleitos follow slower, heads down, the shuffling feet of the shameful. "My king," gasps Pylades, heart beating fast in his bosom, hands clammy as he clasps Orestes' own. "Forgive us. We have failed you."

"No, Pylades, no." Orestes cannot help Pylades stand, he has not the strength for that. But he can at least grasp his blood brother's arm when the warrior rises, give the thinnest, weakest smile into his eyes. "You could never fail me."

"Your majesty," murmurs Kleitos, priest of Apollo. "You look a little pale."

"It's nothing," Orestes replies, every word a breath closer to collapse. "It's nothing."

The women of Mycenae cluster round Elektra, shielding her from the attentions of the flapping Spartans. At their head is Rhene, her raven hair swept back from her angular face, her body inserted like Nicostratus's great shield between her mistress and the Spartan maids. With chin stuck forward and shoulders pulled back, she swats away a Spartan woman who seems to want to fiddle with Elektra's hair, and proclaims one ringing word at a time: "We will see the princess is safely taken in hand."

Elektra does not thank Rhene, though she has often desperately wanted to. She does not know how.

Anaitis has a terrible difficulty getting past the guards on the gate, until Eos sees her and bustles down. "She is a priestess of the island, she is – let her through, *let her through!*"

The Spartans are not used to obeying any woman, let alone a slave. But they do have orders not to upset the locals too badly, and everyone knows that Artemis watches over the western isles, even if no one is entirely sure how. Lefteris sneers at

Anaitis as she passes by, calls after her: "Can't Ithaca do better?" Anaitis seems more confused than outraged by his cry.

The priestess is led to the one place the women can meet that seems at last to be free of Spartan men – the sties. Here a hasty council has assembled of Penelope, Eos, Autonoe, Ourania and Anaitis, among the pigs and their shit, hems hitched and eyes glancing furtive to the door. Anaitis is the last to join, oblivious to the odours of the place as Eos shoos her inside.

"Is Ithaca conquered?" she asks bluntly as the door is pulled to behind her.

Eos sighs, Penelope winces, and: "Yes," Autonoe blurts, before anyone can offer a more nuanced reply. "We are conquered."

"Oh. Without a fight?"

"Thus far," mutters Penelope.

"But I thought . . . Priene, the women . . . "

"Priene's women were raised to defend against pirates who came by moonlight, not against an enemy who arrives by our front door, takes over the palace while bearing gifts and invites everyone to dine at spear-point."

"I see. So . . . are we all going to die?" Anaitis asks.

"Eventually," offers Autonoe.

"That is fair," Ourania concedes.

"Enough!" Penelope's voice cuts through, loud and hard. Neither she nor her husband are much for raising their voices – they were both taught to believe that doing so was a failure of many other, superior leadership skills. At once all eyes flicker to the door, all lips seal as they listen for those who might listen to them. "Enough," repeats the queen, softer, quiet. "The fact remains that Menelaus has Orestes and there is nothing we can do about it at this time. All we can hope to do is ride the coming storm. Anaitis – how is he?"

"Weak," the priestess replies. "Hardly able to stand. I made him drink something that will keep him on his feet for a little while, but when it wears off, he will be weaker than ever. He needs time – that's all. The poison left him frail as a newborn lamb."

"Good luck if you think he won't be poisoned again now he's in Spartan hands," grunts Ourania.

"Is there anything we can do about that?" Penelope turns to Eos, who shakes her head.

"Pylades has been reunited with Orestes – he protests that he was sworn by all the most sacred oaths of heaven to not reveal his king's pilgrimage, and Menelaus slaps him on the back and says he loves a loyal soldier. But this means that all the Mycenaean crew are also united with their king – every soldier, priest and maid who sailed with Orestes from Mycenae. Between Mycenaeans, Spartans, we can hardly get near."

"And the poisoner might still be among them," sighs Penelope. "And we are powerless to intervene."

"Are we?" muses Ourania. "This is still your palace, our island. The Spartans may have occupied it, but they do not know it."

"Menelaus went straight to Laertes' door. He didn't even pretend to look anywhere else. Last night, the feast, the treasure . . . it was all just a game. Playing with us." Penelope's voice is bitter as medicinal bark, black as the forest spider. Menelaus has come, Menelaus has beaten her at her own game – and with ease. With such casual, laughing ease. She swallows down bile, disgust, self-reproach and sickly regret, shakes her head. "This island is too small to hide a mad king, and we cannot win a fight with things as they are. This is not the right place, the right . . ." Her voice trails off. Then: "We need ships."

"The vessel my women fish in is still waiting for you," Ourania muses. "It is always kept fully provisioned and prepared should you need to flee."

"It may not be enough. Ourania, send word to your cousins.

Fishing vessels, boats to Kephalonia, small, fast, as many as we can get. Speak to Priene. How many women do we have under arms on Kephalonia?"

"Maybe a hundred," Eos replies.

"A hundred. And on Ithaca?"

"Perhaps ninety. But there are well over a hundred fully armed Spartans on the isle, and our women were trained to fight pirates, not veterans of Troy."

"Nevertheless, we may be forced to make do. Ourania, is there any word on the warships that Antinous, Eurymachus and their fathers agreed to arm and crew?"

"Their so-called 'defensive' vessels? The word is that they have thus far outfitted only one, which slunk into port on Kephalonia at the first sight of Spartan sails. Didn't want to give the wrong impression to Menelaus, I suspect."

"Good. Autonoe, send word to those two and their fathers. Tell them I request a private audience at their first convenience. Bring Amphinomous as well." That would be the end of it, but then another thought. "And Kenamon. Him too."

"You have a plan, my queen?" murmurs Ourania.

"Not yet. Perhaps. Anaitis, is there any chance you can get close to Orestes, tend to him?"

The priestess shakes her head. "There is a Mycenaean priest of Apollo all about him, a man called Kleitos. He was very rude when I introduced myself. Said that it was charming that the women think they could be useful, but that Orestes was a king and needed the services of physicians who tended to men, not goats."

Now even Penelope has to fight the ugly, unqueenly inclination to roll her eyes. "Very well. Anaitis, join Priene and her women. We may need you to accompany her, if the moment comes."

"I will pray to Artemis," replies Anaitis primly, "as I serve only the goddess – but I imagine she will agree with this course of action."

Funny how often divinities are found to agree with the actions mortals most desire. It is a trait I have often noted, and would find annoying if it wasn't so often quaintly delightful in its unexpected consequences.

"What will you do?" Ourania asks Penelope, as the council disperses.

She sighs, and slips the veil down about her brow. "I will attend the feast, of course."

CHAPTER 22

❯❯❯

The feast.

Watch, yea gods, watch – there has been no feast like it before, nor is there like to be one of its sort again.

Orestes, son of Agamemnon, king of kings, murderer of his own mother, sits in the place of highest honour, yes, next to indeed, right next to Odysseus's empty throne. Laertes sits beside him, at the same height and honour as the empty place where his son should be, Menelaus by his side. They are three equals, three great men next to the absent ghost of the fourth, kings and heroes, warriors and murderers all, drinking wine and meeting no one's eye.

Elektra, Penelope and Helen sit a little below, Helen's chair angled to one side as it always is, equal of course to her fellow queens, but just perhaps a little apart, so that she can tell her stories to the air, not her kin.

Below them, the great and the good whose time is yet to come. Loyal Pylades, who watches his king as if there were a thousand leagues between them. Quiet Iason and the priest Kleitos, making up the highest of the Mycenaean side. Nicostratus, legs sprawled out in front of him as if the only way he could find comfort in his feet was to distance them as far

192

as possible from his skull; Lefteris, who finds the things that unarmed men do funny.

Beneath them – the suitors.

There are far fewer tonight, and none are dressed in finery. A great many discovered sudden pressing reasons why they could not attend the feast. A parent taken ill. An unexpected burst of dysentery. A donkey needing its mane combing – whatever they could, really. Only the bravest, the greatest or those with nowhere else to go have made it to tonight's feast – Antinous, Eurymachus, Amphinomous, Kenamon – and none wears silver or gold. Menelaus looks down upon them and their now more scantily adorned limbs, and his eyes sparkle bright.

And around them, always, but always, the maids.

Maids of Sparta – Zosime and Tryphosa, forever by Helen's side, and dozens more, serving sweet treats from the bowels of Menelaus's ships, strips of beef carved from the freshly slaughtered bull.

Maids of Mycenae – chief among them Rhene, always standing by Elektra's side like the mother tree over its bending sapling, dark eyes glistening as she watches the motion of the room.

Maids of Ithaca – Autonoe and Eos, Melantho and Phiobe, even sullen Euracleia, who hovers on the edge of the hall in the hope that Laertes might see her, might say something kind.

They will not be remarked on when ballads are sung of this night, nor noted in the eyes of any god passing through, but I brush through their souls as I take my place, highest and above them all in the hall, wishing them sensuous dreams of soft kisses and the sighs of half-imagined moist delights, that when they wake in the morning, they may close their eyes and wish to dream again.

There are four other guests of note at the feast, who the mortals all – or nearly all – fail to perceive.

Athena sends her owl. Hera, mother goddess, hates that owl,

delights in throwing objects both physical and unseen at the creature until it flaps away. I think it is really rather lovely, a great big fluffball with wonderful blinking eyes and a chin that was meant for scritching, yes it is, *yes you are*. It perches high in the rafters and watches all below, a sign of her presence that no mortal notes, and yet which blinks down a baleful warning in its yellow gaze.

And above the rafters, on the roof itself?

Why of course, but of course, the three Furies. They sour the soup, burn the bread, turn the wine bitter on the drinkers' lips. No one says anything as they crunch their way through the spoiled meal, slurp the ghastly concoctions poured into their cups. To say anything would be to dishonour their true host – not the Ithacan queen, but the Spartan king who now presides over her palace – and no one would dare. Besides, the Ithacan maids are mildly gratified to notice the thin fungal blooms spreading across the platters the Spartans bring to the feast, satisfied that though their kitchen may mostly serve some variation on a theme of fish, at least it's fresh damn fish.

Thus, all mortals assembled feel the presence of the Furies, but only one sees them, and he dares not raise his eyes to look, lest he go quite, quite mad.

"To Odysseus!" roars Menelaus, and the cups of foul wine are raised in a salute, Menelaus tipping the lip of his first to the father, then the wife, and then at last to the empty chair.

"To Agamemnon!" proposes Laertes, when Orestes does not seem in a hurry to make a suitable toast to match the vigour of his uncle.

"*To Clytemnestra*," whisper the Furies, talons clattering on the high roof tiles. "*Mother of a murdered babe, a murdered daughter, wife of a traitor husband, killer of a king, to Clytemnestra, Clytemnestra, Clytemnestra!*"

Zosime refills Helen's cup from a golden carafe, and Helen raises it in salute. "To my husband!" she proclaims.

Those about her make to raise their cups too, but Menelaus does not. Because he does not, Laertes does not, so Orestes does not, so Elektra does not, so Penelope does not.

Menelaus stares at his wife, her wide dark eyes, and for a moment she holds his gaze, then looks away and giggles. It is the tiniest, smallest sound. She puts her fingers to her lips, as if astonished to have heard it, as if she might be able to press the noise back past those lovely pearl teeth of hers. "What are you doing?" he asks. She doesn't answer. He passes his cup to a servant, leans a little closer. "*What are you doing?*" His voice is a low hiss, a rattle of ashes over a cold fire, but seems to carry across the room. "Are you trying to be stupid?"

"No, dearest," she simpers. "No, I just thought ... "

He knocks the golden cup from her hand. It clatters away, bounces to the feet of the nearest suitor. The wine spills red and glistening, Helen staring at the liquid as it flows as if enthralled, fascinated, as if she has never seen anything so crimson – no, not even blood. Kenamon stares down at the fallen cup, then slowly picks it up, gives it to a maid, who hands it to Nicostratus, who holds it at arm's length as if it were poison.

The slap of Menelaus's hand against Helen's cheek rings out through the hall. In the silence that follows, only the crackle of the hot embers in the hearth can be heard. Even the Furies cease their chittering above the hall, burning eyes turning down to watch the scene. Helen is knocked against the side of her chair, recovers slowly. His second slap is not enough to knock her to the floor, but she falls anyway, hand pressed to the glowering red mark on her perfect cheek. He has not broken her tender, beautiful flesh, and I will wash away the bruises before the dawn comes, but for now, the brightness of blood still flares beneath her skin.

He straightens up, eases back into his chair, gestures for a new cup, more wine. Tilts it again to Laertes, to Orestes. Does not seem to see Elektra or Penelope, let alone his wife as she struggles back into her seat. "To Odysseus," he repeats. "To Agamemnon. To our fallen brothers of Troy."

He drinks.

Laertes drinks.

Orestes drinks. His hand shakes as he holds the cup. Elektra makes to reach for him, to steady him, but Penelope catches her before she can, pulls her back, a tiny shake of her head, the smallest motion beneath her fluttering veil. Elektra clenches her fist, and holds it in her lap.

"To the heroes of Troy!" Nicostratus doesn't bother to straighten as he makes his toast, still sprawled so low in his seat it's a wonder he doesn't slide straight out of it.

"The heroes of Troy!" echoes the room, with the vigour and valour of a wilting daisy.

At the long tables furthest from the fire:

"Try this," Kleitos whispers, offering a pinch of herbs across the table.

Kenamon regards them with some confusion, not sure what the priest of Apollo intends. Kleitos chuckles, a wise man familiar with the foolishness of foreigners, and sprinkles a little of what he holds between his fingers first into his own cup, then into the Egyptian's. The habit of demonstrating that one does not poison one's guests has, it seems, reached even into the priesthood of Mycenae. He raises his cup, tilts it in salute, drinks it down. Cautiously Kenamon follows suit, and then, with relief, takes a longer sip. The wine has turned sour, with a hint of something bloody in the water; no sweet spice upon this earth can undo the taste of the Furies' bile upon Kenamon's lips, but the priest's herbs do at least slightly take the edge off.

Kleitos watches him drink, chuckles, pats him on the

shoulder. "Ithacan hospitality," he explains. "You really have to prepare yourself for it."

Kenamon smiles, but does not reply. He is tempted to defend Penelope, to explain that until Menelaus came, he had not been fed a single slice of fish or cup of wine that was not, at the minimum, perfectly adequate. But he is sitting among the suitors and the great men of Mycenae, and has learned – alas, how he has learned – that when with these Greeks, it is often better to be silent than to offer sincere praise. He thinks this is tragic, a terrible indictment of the state of Greece.

"I bartered for the powdered remains of an Egyptian corpse once," muses the priest, eyes lost on some distant memory. "Fantastic in the treatment of boils and maladies of the blood."

Kenamon's eyes go wide, but he manages to hold himself back from crying blasphemy, blasphemy, you foul violator of the dead! Too many of the suitors in this hall are waiting for him to do exactly that, to start a fight, to violate the sacred codes of hospitality, so they might at last have the excuse they have been looking for to remove him from their game, and his life.

So instead, casual as spring rain: "How interesting. Do many of my people selling the bodies of our interred dead come to Mycenae?"

"Oh, plenty!" chuckles Kleitos. "You should visit, if you live that long."

There is no threat in these words; the priest of Apollo is merely a realist, Kenamon concludes, and for a moment – and not for the first time – he glances round the hall at his fellow grumbling suitors, and sees not men living, but rather the living dead.

He shudders, turns away, manages to even drink another foul sip of scented wine to mask the picture that paints itself upon the hidden darkness of his eyes.

*

In the shadows of the palace as the feast winds down:

Penelope finds Elektra standing just outside the kitchen door, hauling down breath.

The daughter of Clytemnestra is on the edge of panic, here it comes, here it comes, this desperate heaving, this desperate, frantic gasping, gasping, sobbing, she will fall to her knees, dear gods don't let anyone see, almighty Zeus help me, help me great Ares, help me warriors of the heavens . . .

I catch her before she can fall. She did not call my name. Elektra does not pray to the women of Olympus. But I catch her nonetheless, steady her, press my forehead to hers, brush away the heat and terror in her chest. With another tendril of my will I guide the Ithacan queen through the shadows to her side. Music plays and wine is drunk and just this once, by my power, no one will question where Penelope has gone as she takes the young woman's hand.

"Elektra?" she whispers. "Cousin?"

Elektra straightens her back.

This is what a queen must do.

Wipes away a hint of water from her eyes.

Looks to the cloud-scudding midnight sky and prays to Zeus, thinks she hears the Furies whisper her mother's name – *Clytemnestra, Clytemnestra* – thinks she sees her mother's ghost, shakes herself, knows she has imagined it.

"Elektra," murmurs Penelope again. "Speak to me."

"It's all gone wrong," she replies, voice on the verge of breaking, the tears still haunting the trembling of her lips. "Menelaus has Orestes, and my brother is standing now, is talking now, but it's only a matter of time, only time, they will come for him again, the madness will come for him again, it will come and . . ."

She stops herself.

To say more is to break.

Penelope holds her.

Clytemnestra tried to hold her daughter once, but the young Elektra pushed her away, called her whore, slut, harlot, and a dozen other words whose meaning she wasn't sure of but felt seemed appropriate to the task.

Now Penelope holds her, and Elektra, to her surprise, wraps her arms tight around her cousin and refuses to cry, though tears are flowing down her face. That's fine – that's just a physical thing, not crying at all. Not Elektra. Not the daughter of Agamemnon.

Clytemnestra, Clytemnestra! cackle the Furies. *Daughter of Clytemnestra!*

Then from the door: "This is lovely."

Nicostratus stands there smiling, leaning against the frame, picking meat from a bone in his hand. Elektra and Penelope untangle.

"Nicostratus," murmurs Penelope. "Is there something we can do for you?"

He shrugs. "Just enjoying two ladies being convivial."

"Excuse me," Elektra mutters, pushing past Nicostratus and back into the hall.

As she does, his hand drops.

It is casual.

Maybe he was bumped by her passage.

Maybe it was the way he turned to let her by.

His fingers caress her backside.

Pinch.

Squeeze.

Test the softness of her bum, cup the roundness of her flesh, that's so good, it's so good, he wants her to know that when he pleasures himself tonight, he'll think of this moment, think of her buttocks grasped in his wide, clawing hands – but then again, maybe not, maybe she imagined it, it's all so fast, so easy, such a little thing.

Elektra sucks in air but does not stop, does not look back, does not bend, but heads into the sound of music, voices, melody, raised up for her brother.

Nicostratus grins, waves his half-devoured bone at Penelope, turns to follow.

"Nicostratus." Penelope's voice cuts through like the cold night air. He turns to look at her, one eyebrow raised. "I just wanted to say how good it is to see you so loyal to Menelaus. It must mean a great deal to know that he has the dedication and service even of men like you."

Nicostratus's smile is like his father's, and does not waver as he returns to the hall.

And in the morning?

"Well, uncle, I think perhaps my brother and I should set sail," Elektra says.

"Nonsense, nonsense!" blurts Menelaus. "How often do we get to feast together like this? You, me, Penelope, I know it means the world to her having us all here, a little bit of warmth around her fire after all this time, you must stay – another night, I insist!"

"We really must be going," she tries again, but Menelaus wraps his arm across her skinny shoulders, squeezes her tight.

"And where would you go?" he asks, smiling like the sun. "Where would you go?"

There is nowhere for Elektra to run. At his father's back, Nicostratus undresses the Mycenaean princess with his eyes, his wet lips rolling in like a hound before the feast. Of the two whores he thinks his father could give him, he hopes it'll be Elektra. Penelope is old and weak, and though he thinks Elektra is an ugly canker of a woman, he also thinks she'll fight, and he learned from his father to love the sound of a broken scream.

"Hunting!" Menelaus's slap against Orestes' back is enough to nearly knock the young man from his feet. "Let's go hunting!"

"It is surely too late in the day, the sun too high . . ." Elektra burbles, clasping her hands to stop them shaking.

"Nonsense, not at all! Fresh air will do us the world of good, and frankly, dear nephew, you look like you could use the sport!"

"Alas, brother," Penelope slips into the conversation like the soft snake under the door, "I believe my honoured cousin is already spoken for, having pledged to attend my dearest father in his devotions at the temple of Athena."

Nice cool place, the temple of Athena. Lots of benches to sit on in shadows where not too many people will disturb you. Handy if you need a bit of a lie-down. The priests won't mind. Not today. Penelope has made sure of it.

Menelaus's jaw has a little muscle in it that flexes, just on the edge of perception, when he has been holding his smile too long.

"Of course," he exclaims. "How pious. Lovely, lovely. Well then, myself and Nicostratus will go hunt ourselves a nice deer maybe, spear ourselves a fresh hot doe for dinner, and we'll see you tonight for the feast."

He slaps Orestes one more time on the shoulder in the same easy motion with which he turns for the door, but Elektra catches her brother before his stagger can become a fall.

At sunset, Ourania is waiting for Penelope in her room as she prepares to go to the feast.

"I have a cousin . . ." she begins.

"Not now, Ourania," sighs Penelope.

Ourania smiles, a little disappointed perhaps that tonight she will not get to explain how very clever she has been, how very very smart and dazzling and just a little bit sexy, the sexy that comes from confidence, from capability, from being right and knowing it in your heart, from knowing that you're winning, that you can win, that you are worth fighting for – but not tonight. Tonight Penelope is a woman with the greatest men of Greece waiting for her in the hall below, and so Ourania leans in and whispers in her ear: "When you return, I have some secrets to tell you."

Later:

Helen says: "Well, this has been lovely, so lovely, goodness, I think I should retire."

She sways when she stands. Tryphosa catches her by the arm.

Penelope stands too. "May I escort you, cousin, help you to—"

"We will see to her," Zosime replies, a slave cutting off a queen, high, haughty – utterly outrageous! Penelope looks to Menelaus, who doesn't say a thing, and Laertes, who merely raises an eyebrow but makes no other move.

"Lovely feast, lovely!" slurs Helen, as Zosime and Tryphosa lead her away.

Elektra says: "Perhaps we too should—"

Nicostratus hollers: "More wine! More wine here!" silencing her mid sentence.

"I'll need to be about my prayers," murmurs Laertes, to no one in particular. "Seeing how pious I'm feeling these days."

"Goodness, if I was Poseidon and I heard your prayers, I really would think twice about drowning Odysseus at the bottom of the endless deeps, I really would," chuckles Menelaus. Laertes says nothing in reply, but there is that in the corner of his eye that still remembers what it was to hold his babe in his arms, all kicking little legs and bubbling gumless lips, and it has no time for games.

And then, some little while later, Orestes stands.

"I, uh . . ." he says.

Orestes falls.

Elektra screams.

Laertes snatches his legs back to avoid the crashing of the crumpled king.

Menelaus passes his wine to Lefteris, the drink barely touched. Pylades leaps to his feet, rushes towards his blood brother, hand reaching for a blade. "Protect the king!" he cries. "Protect the king!"

It is hard to see what he will protect Orestes from, or how, in these circumstances, but at least he sounds really rather hunky and dashing in his urgency. Iason and Kleitos follow, kneeling by their master's side, shaking him. Rhene and the Mycenaean maids flock to Elektra in a tight wall of womanhood, leaving Penelope pressed into a rather narrow corner by backs and shoulders and shouting men, doing her best not to be squeezed out of existence.

On the floor, Orestes begins to shake, to shudder. From head to toe he rocks, he twitches, he groans, he dribbles; his bowels grow loose, he moans, sweat pouring off him like a river. "Mother, Mother!" he whimpers, first so low that perhaps the hearers did not hear it, then again: "Mother, Mother!" louder this time, and louder again. I reach down to his brow and a hot blast of fire breaks across my skin. I blaze in brief, shocked indignation, spin to rain down absolute perdition upon any creature, divine or otherwise, that dares to interfere with a goddess, let alone one quite as majestic as myself – and see them. The three Furies stand in the door of the hall, their talons extended together as if they were not three creatures at all, but rather many bodies to one soul, pointing directly at the writhing Orestes.

"*Clytemnestra,*" they hiss, and "Mother!" he cries. "*Clytemnestra!*" they chant, and "Forgive me!" he wails. "*Clytemnestra!*" They move forward until they loom above him, their invisible forms bending, flowing around the mortals who crowd about the prince. I see Pylades gag as one reaches through him; hear Rhene choke at the noxious passage of a Fury by her nostrils. Athena's owl has fled. I am alone before the three ladies and their prey, and I . . .

. . . I stand aside.

The Furies bundle Orestes in their arms as he screams and screams and screams, "Forgive me, forgive me, forgive me!" before all the hall, before every great man of the western isles, before his uncle the king, before his sister, before his friends and enemies. "Forgive me!"

It is Penelope who at last elbows through the throng, shuddering at the proximity of the cackling Furies, though she does not know them to be so near. "You, help him!" she barks to Pylades, as he holds his shaking king. "Get him to his room! Fetch clean water, and the priest – where is the priest?"

"I am the priest of Apollo, servant to the king's family," offers Kleitos, slouching forward as if a little embarrassed to be caught in this scene.

"Tend to him!" she barks.

This command causes at least some action, some stirring. Hands lift the shaking Orestes, others comfort the now openly weeping Elektra. Nicostratus sips his drink, the suitors part before the troop like crows before the wolf, Laertes watches with brows raised, and Menelaus . . .

Why, Menelaus sits in his chair, and says not a word, and smiles.

CHAPTER 23

>>>

I n the night, chaos, confusion.

Everyone who can press themselves outside Orestes' room has done so. The corridors of the palace of Ithaca are too narrow for this to be anything other than an incredibly uncomfortable experience.

Kleitos, Pylades, Elektra and Menelaus are gathered around Orestes' bedside. The priest of Apollo is burning a foul-smelling concoction of herbs, intoning dull prayers. Apollo does not answer. Apollo is far more interested in music than medicine these days.

Penelope tries to get into the room, but Lefteris blocks her path, shakes his head. "Best leave this to the priests," he drawls, mouth still circling the half-chewed food he has brought up from the feast below, never a man to let a dying king get in the way of a meal.

"I am the lady of this house!"

The Spartan shrugs. She's said it herself there, hasn't she? She's the lady. What use are ladies here?

With a huff of indignation that would have made her old mother-in-law Anticlea proud, Penelope turns away, casts around for another plan, sees instead an unlikely ally. Laertes

205

has also brought his food up with him, but made no real effort to approach the door, happy to be an onlooker to other people's events. She bears down on him, grabs him by the wrist. "Pious prayers?" she asks.

The old man looks his daughter-in-law in the eye, then mutters: "Fine." She nods in quick gratitude, but as she turns to go, his bony fingers grasp hers. "Careful," he adds, before marching down the hall and shouldering straight past Lefteris before the Spartan can say a word. "What's the matter with the boy, then?" She hears his voice ring out as he marches into the sick room. "Can't take his fish? I know this wonderful prayer to Athena . . . "

Nicostratus waits downstairs, picking at the last of the food left on the tables. Those suitors who dared attend are assembled in anxious little clusters – it would be the height of rudeness to depart the palace when the great king of Mycenae is sick, and might send the wrong message about how deeply and passionately they care about his welfare. On the other hand, there is nothing they can do, and should he die, their presence might lead to unfortunate complications, and so, caught in this trap, they muster and cluster in whispering knots by doors and at windows, in muddy yards and by silent wells. The Spartan warriors who attend are letting no one leave through the guarded gates – they will not say why, and no one dares ask.

"Is he going to die?" blurts Eurymachus to Eos as she marches by at the head of a line of maids with clean water and fresh cloths to wipe his burning brow. "Is Orestes going to die?"

"Of course not!" she barks. "Don't be ridiculous!"

"We may as well do some cleaning, since no one is going to sleep," sighs Autonoe, surveying the muddled mess of the disrupted feast. "Goodness knows what tomorrow will bring."

The Ithacan maids set to cleaning. They are not joined by the Spartans or Mycenaeans, whose dedication to helping about the palace seems to stop at the dirty work. By the low light of oil lanterns the women draw more water from the well, scrub the floor and throw the shutters wide. The shadows flicker and every corner of darkness holds a hushed whisper, an anxious word, as upstairs Kleitos gives commands for this herb or that remedy, this sacred oil to be burned or another prayer to be sung.

"If Orestes does die . . . " whispers Phiobe in Autonoe's ear, as they throw the dirty water from the dishes into the darkness of the vegetable garden.

"He won't."

"If he does . . . what happens to Ithaca?"

A shimmer of light before Autonoe can reply – another little knot of suitors scurry through the dark, see the women, turn the other way. No one will speak where another might hear, so instead: "Keep scrubbing!" Autonoe proclaims.

Menelaus sees Penelope waiting in the hall outside Orestes' room. Puts a hand on her shoulder, shakes his head sadly.

"My poor nephew," he sighs. "I fear he is quite, quite mad." He should close his eyes as he makes this declaration, stare sorrowfully down, or maybe turn his gaze to the heavens in search of celestial intervention to remedy this wrong. He does not. He stares directly into Penelope's eyes, waiting for her answer.

She clasps her hands in front of her. If she clasps her hands, perhaps she will not swallow, will not flinch. "What may we do?"

A moment.

A smile.

A little squeeze of her shoulder.

"Honestly, I don't think there's anything you can do."

And with that, as Spartans guard Orestes' door and the Furies shriek their merriment high overhead, Menelaus, king of the warriors of red and black, conqueror of Troy, goes to bed.

*

The moon turns, and in one shadow deeper than all the rest, in a little room near the locked armoury of the palace, a hidden gathering at last assembles.

It comes together slowly, in nervous scuttles and down winding passages that the Spartan men have not yet realised connect one to the other. Some wear cloaks, pulled up high over their heads to mask their presence. One still wears her veil, and waits stiff and weary by the wall furthest from the door, Eos by her side, a little lantern burning in her cupped hands. If those meeting here did not already know each other so very well indeed, they might not recognise each other at all, so deeply has the dark gathered and so hushed do their voices fall. But they cannot hide from me, who sees all, and I name each of them as they assemble – Penelope and Eos; the old councillor Medon, profoundly unhappy to be out of his bed; Antinous and his father Eupheithes; Eurymachus and his father Polybus; Amphinomous, the warrior who would be king; Kenamon, the suitor from the far-off southlands, cast adrift so far from his home.

There are seven men to two women in this room. It is a proportion that is unusual on Ithaca. None of the men are armed, but none need to be when things are so skewed. It is partly with this in mind that Penelope has invited Kenamon, who has never before attended anything so secret, so hidden, and who perhaps now stands with the greatest curiosity and least fear, not being well enough informed in matters of local politics to feel an acceptable volume of terror. This at least is what Penelope tells herself.

"Antinous, Eurymachus. Amphinomous. Gentlemen all. Thank you for coming," she murmurs as the last man is led into this dark, hidden place.

"What is this?" blurts Eupheithes, before his son can speak. Antinous learned how to be a blusterer from his father, but consequently the only man he cannot out-bluster, cannot out-harangue is the very man who taught him, and who does not understand that the qualities he dislikes in his son are the self-same qualities he cannot perceive in himself. "Why are we here? What is happening? Is Orestes going to die? What does Menelaus want?"

Polybus, father of Eurymachus, joins in with a brief rattle of noise along similar lines. It is not that he has anything to say – merely that if Eupheithes is going to speak on behalf of his son, then Polybus is damn sure he's not going to be left out. "What are you doing about the Spartans? What is the situation with Mycenae? What have you done, woman? What have you done?!"

He slaps his fist into his palm. Eurymachus jumps. Eurymachus is the only one in the room who has cause to associate the sound of his father's flesh hitting flesh with fear, and no one else stirs.

Penelope's eyes in the low light are oily pools, flecked with fire. She watches the men, waiting for them to finish, Medon by her side. It would usually be the place of the old councillor to speak at this time, to step forward and defend the honour of his queen, to demand the attention of those fathers who should be his peers. Tonight he does not. He knows as little about these events as the others here assembled, and unlike the other men of Penelope's court, knows also when to keep his peace.

It is therefore Kenamon who clears his throat and murmurs: "Perhaps we should let the good queen speak?"

Penelope inclines her chin towards him, a bare shimmer of motion, then draws back her veil. Antinous takes in a breath – this is a gesture that very few of the suitors have seen, though many have fantasised of it as an act, a gift, dedicated entirely to themselves. "Gentlemen," she says, pushing her voice through fatigue to hold quiet but firm in the room. "Thank you for coming, and under such unusual circumstances. I thought it best we speak now, tonight, while there is still some . . . confusion, and before the situation deteriorates further. Orestes is currently being tended to by a priest of Mycenae, and has been given a potion that has sent him into a profound sleep. Neither I nor my maids have access to him. Meanwhile, Ithaca has been conquered."

This sparks immediate protest from Antinous, Eurymachus and their fathers. Ithaca has never been conquered! She is mad, she is foolish, she is . . .

"The Spartans in my husband's palace outnumber my men by three to one, and are veterans of Troy. Even if every suitor now took up arms and united as an allied front against them, we would have a very hard fight on our hands to be rid of them. And if we succeeded – if we killed Menelaus – what then? He has come to us as a guest. His men have occupied this palace to serve us. To help us. They are our honoured, heavily armed, highly disciplined, welcome allies. We cannot engage them in open warfare as matters currently stand, nor can we refuse or resist a single command that man may make while he is in this kingdom. So you see – we are conquered."

"You did this," barks Eupheithes, stabbing a chubby grey finger towards Penelope's face. "You let this happen. If there was a king . . ."

"If there was a king on Ithaca, Menelaus would behave precisely the way he has, knowing that man is far too weak, far too feeble to resist him," she replies, too tired to shout, bored already of this argument. "However, as there is not a king, I think we must consider the most likely outcome of the coming few days. Orestes is, as you see, sick. The Spartans call him mad."

"He sounds pretty mad to me," grumbles Antinous, and is at once shushed by Amphinomous.

"Whether mad or not, it is almost certain that tomorrow morning, Menelaus will demand that the king and his sister leave with the Spartan ships to seek ... help. Safety. However he puts it, the outcome will be the same. Orestes and Elektra will become his prisoners, Menelaus will seize the opportunity to become protector of Mycenae in his sick nephew's name – helping out, as he always does, as you see he does here – and once he has secured his position in Mycenae, Orestes will die quietly and we will have a new king of kings. Ruler of the unified kingdoms, the greatest power in the land. Does anyone here disagree with this assessment?"

Antinous and Eurymachus want to, but even they do not. It is Amphinomous who speaks for the group. "Sounds plausible enough. Then what?"

"Well, then Menelaus will conquer the western isles. Properly this time, I mean. Not because he is very interested in us, but because he can. Because my husband is missing and the isles need a king. He will marry Nicostratus to Elektra to secure his control of Mycenae, and I will doubtless be married to some other of his relatives, or a chosen appointee of Sparta whose loyalty he can trust. If I resist in any way, I will be imprisoned until I consent and then quietly done away with once the process is complete. My son will vanish in some unfortunate sea voyage before he can return to claim his throne, and just like that, Ithaca will be a Spartan tributary. And none of you will be king. You, Antinous, and you, Eurymachus – Menelaus will probably have you executed to minimise the possibility of rebellion against his rule. Amphinomous – you will either be recruited to serve in some dangerous venture where you will hopefully die as quickly as possible, or you will be murdered in the night. You are known to be honourable, so your public death is less desirable than a hidden one."

"What about me?" asks Kenamon, and Penelope is surprised. I ruffle his hair. *Bless your heart*, I whisper. *You're adorable.*

"You? You are not important enough for Menelaus to kill.

211

You are a foreigner. If you resist in any meaningful way, of course you will be murdered, but no one will care."

Kenamon has the grace to be only briefly riled, before shrugging it off. "Oh. Well, that is something, I suppose."

It is Polybus, father of Eurymachus, who breaks the slightly awkward silence. "If what you say is true . . . why are we here?"

"Because you have a ship," Penelope replies, cold and simple. "A warship, fully armed, which you have set to patrol the waters around Ithaca."

"I don't," offers Kenamon, but no one cares. The room has turned to ice, ready to crack.

"When I first heard that you had come together to arm this ship, I was of course . . . surprised. Astonished even. Antinous and Eurymachus, Eupheithes and Polybus, sons and fathers working together at last. And Amphinomous, you didn't object, you didn't appear horrified by the idea of your two greatest rivals cooperating, even though that presents the single greatest threat to your safety imaginable. You informed my council that you did this to protect Ithaca, but you could no more protect Ithaca than you could shoot the sun from the sky. Why then this sudden and unexpected show of unity? The answer is simple. You are not patrolling the seas to protect Ithaca. You are lying in wait for my son."

Kenamon's jaw drops. Amphinomous's jaw tightens. Everyone else stands mute, but Penelope doesn't appear to mind.

"Sooner or later, Telemachus will return from his travels, and when he does . . . who knows what manner of threat he might present? Who knows what men he will have convinced to join him, from the court of Nestor, from Sparta and Corinth, Pylos and Mycenae? He doesn't need to have that many loyal soldiers at his back – just enough to convince the other boys of the western isles that he is a true leader, a warrior worth backing – and he could slaughter you all. Best to stop him coming home

212

at all. Best for everyone that Odysseus's son, that *my son*, never makes it back to Ithaca. Just another missing man of my family, vanished without trace."

It is Amphinomous who finally has the courage to raise his head, to look Penelope in the eye. "If Telemachus returns, with men, he will kill us all."

This declaration, without rancour or remorse, breaks open the mouths of the others. "This is your fault!" blurts Polybus, and: "If you had just married before the boy got ideas in his head," shrills Eupheithes, while their two sons try to find something worthwhile to add for themselves, and fail at the task.

Finally Medon cuts through, rolling his eyes, raising his voice – like his former master, Odysseus, the old man rarely lifts it much above a jovial chortle, or a cry for more wine, but he can upon occasion silence the storm. "By the gods!" he proclaims. "Will you just be quiet?!"

Polybus, Eupheithes and Medon were friends, brothers in arms, when they were young. They have forgotten these things. They had sons, and those sons grew up, and the old men forgot what it was like when they valued different things. Now they fall silent, not meeting each other's eyes, until Penelope speaks again.

"Look at you. The would-be kings of Ithaca. Too frightened, too cowardly to face my son yourselves. Too weak to look him in the eye. Instead you send your lackeys out onto the high seas to try to smother him like an infant Heracles in the crib. It is so vulgar as to be almost beneath my contempt. And do not think that I am concerned you will actually threaten him. He knows these waters better than you do, can fight harder than any of your mercenaries will, has his father's cunning and the loyalty of his allies. Even if your ship could find him before he returns, I am confident that he will overcome it."

She is not.

She has a dreadful feeling that the son is as poor at maritime navigation as the father, and hopes this is not the case.

She sometimes prays to Poseidon, who does not listen.

Pray to me, I whisper. *Pray to Aphrodite, who broke the world.*

"Your majesty," Kenamon begins, trying to find some words in the silence, reaching for . . . he does not know what. *Pray to me*, I hiss, nibbling his ear. *I will teach you what to say.*

Penelope raises a hand, bringing him to a stuttering halt. "Kenamon, I do not believe you are complicit in these actions. Antinous, Eurymachus and their fathers are the ringleaders here. Amphinomous knew, but did nothing. The same can be said of many of the greatest of my would-be suitors. Doubtless they did not tell everyone, for fear that someone would have come to me, tried to barter the knowledge for some . . . favour. You were not worth telling – you are an innocent in this. This is also why you are here. I will not speak to these vipers alone. There must be an unimpeachable witness."

This is not entirely true, but Kenamon does not know it. Neither, in a way, does Penelope. She is not herself entirely sure why she has asked the Egyptian here, and is too frightened of what that uncertainty might mean to look too deep.

"If Menelaus becomes king of kings, there will be no Ithaca for you to squabble over. Just this once, therefore, our interests align. I do not wish to be forced to marry some petty chancellor of Menelaus's court; you do not wish to be cut down by Spartans while you sleep. Agreed?"

"Even if we do," mutters Eupheithes, "what exactly do you propose to do about it, woman?"

Anyone who called Penelope "woman" instead of "majesty", "highness", "noble one" and so on would have been imme-diately struck down were Odysseus standing by her side. Not necessarily killed – Odysseus believed in the shock value of a truly grotesque punishment, and knew that shock lost its value if deployed too often – but certainly given good reason to reconsider their speech. But Odysseus is not here, and Eupheithes feels mortality licking upon his heels, so "woman" it is. Medon's glare could set torches alight, but Penelope, if she notices the slight – and she does – shows no sign of acknowledging it.

"The time is coming when we may need to take drastic action. To choose between two kings – Menelaus and Orestes. If we throw our lot in with Orestes and lose, Menelaus will of course kill us all. However, as established, he will kill you all anyway, so that is hardly a concern. Indeed, I could throw all in with Menelaus right now and agree to marry whoever he wishes, and as a wedding gift he would no doubt line up and execute every man I indicated from among you suitors, in whatever way I saw fit, just to show what a generous fellow he is." Penelope enjoys this image far more than she knows she should. She especially enjoys that no man present is quite foolish enough to disagree with her pithy, bloody assessment. Rare – so very rare – that these men pay attention to her words with such dedication and concern. "Well then. For your sakes we must ensure Orestes is safe. Healthy, safe, and king in Mycenae. I am of course just a woman, weak and isolated and alone, but with good counsel and the loyalty of the great men of this isle, it is possible that we can serve and protect the Mycenaean king. To do this, I foresee a time when I may need a fast, powerful ship. Your ship."

Antinous opens his mouth to object, but to his astonishment, his father's hand grips his arm. Eurymachus sees this, and wisely stays mute. Polybus looks to Eupheithes, Eupheithes to Medon, Medon to Polybus. The old councillor smiles. The old men look away.

"What ... precisely are you proposing?"

"Yield command of your ship to Medon here. You all know he is an honourable man."

"A lackey of your husband's – a devoted sot for your son!"

"Yes. He loves my son. Of course he does. But he has also loyally served Ithaca – *Ithaca*, these isles and its peoples – for forty years. He will do what is right. And if in the process the threat to my son is disarmed, then fine. That is the price you will pay for my not going straight to Menelaus now and humbly begging his protection from you and the rest of the suitors. Maybe Telemachus will return with soldiers, and maybe he will try to fight. You will deal with that problem, when it arises, as men, or I will unleash the full force of Sparta on your heads right now, and damn the consequences. Now give me your ship."

This is the first Medon has heard of any of this, and he already feels profoundly seasick. But he will not admit as much while the suitors and their kin study each other's faces, looking for an accord, a way out. Finally it is Amphinomous who says: "My lady, you have us at your mercy, it seems. Though I do not command the crews of the ship in question, what influence I have, what authority I have in this matter, I will gladly yield to good Medon."

This is a fairly meaningless statement, but these are also the western isles, where meaningless statements are often bartered as if weighted like bronze. Penelope nods in acknowledgement of it, turns her attention to Polybus and Eupheithes, ignoring their sons entirely with her questioning gaze.

"This game . . . is dangerous," Polybus at last grunts. "But I fear Amphinomous is right. Menelaus cannot be king of kings. He cannot. He is not . . . valiant. I make no apologies for doing what is right for my son – and for Ithaca. My son is the king this island needs, and it is only your delaying, your insufferable stubbornness that has brought us to this place. But as we are now here, we are forced to cooperate. Until at least these matters are past."

All eyes turn to Eupheithes. Their sons are largely irrelevant

216

in these negotiations, it appears. "Fine," the old man snaps. "Medon can have command. But when Menelaus is gone – if we live that long – there will be consequences to these threats, queen. There will be a reckoning."

He turns and marches for the door. The door is heavy and sticks, which is a little frustrating for the splendour of his exit, but he eventually manages it, Antinous trailing desolate in his wake. Polybus nods, and makes a slightly more dignified exit behind his rival, Eurymachus at his back.

Amphinomous bows. "My lady," he says. "As a man who would be king, I cannot apologise for consenting to a scheme to thwart my enemies. Telemachus will kill us if he has the chance – it is folly to let the lion into the sheep's pen. However, as a man who would also be your husband, I apologise. These actions were considered necessary. They were also cruel. I cannot reconcile or undo that truth, and that is the end of it."

This said, he bows again, and raises his eyes to see if there is some sign from Penelope – an acknowledgement, a flicker of forgiveness – but she is once again lowering her veil, and so with a little sigh, he turns, and slips away into the dark.

This leaves Medon, Kenamon and Eos behind.

"Well," says the Egyptian at last. "This is, uh . . . really all very . . ."

"I am as surprised as you," Medon grumbles, patting the suitor on the shoulder.

"Thank you for attending," Penelope proclaims, not looking the Egyptian in the eye. "It is important that there are witnesses to this event who are neutral to either side."

Is it?

Kenamon is not sure it is.

Medon is almost entirely certain it is not.

Both study the ground, as if they might find some answer in the dust beneath their feet to unravel this mystery.

"Medon, you will speak with Polybus and Eupheithes in the morning about the necessary requirements to take command of the warship. We cannot engage the Spartans in open naval conflict, of course, but we may yet have need of a fast, strong vessel. Be standing by for my command."

Medon has never stood by for his queen's command before. He has of course acted in her interest, given her his best advice, and very much turned a blind eye to actions on her part that seemed more of a kingly bent than a queenly one, however secretly they were performed. But a direct command? He has never heard of such a thing from this queen. He is surprised to find that he is almost pleased by the development. Is it better to be commanded than merely manipulated into Penelope's desired outcome? Perhaps it is.

He smiles, bows deep and low, with a flourish of hand and arm. "My queen," he murmurs. "What an instructive night tonight is proving to be."

"Thank you, councillor. For everything."

He takes her hand. Gives it a squeeze. Smiles again, sees Kenamon still standing in the shadows, nods once, lets himself out.

Now, of all the men, only Kenamon remains.

"I confess," he says at last, "that when I first came to Ithaca to woo you, I did not expect matters to be so . . . complex. I had thought I would tell you enchanting stories of my homeland, offer you fine gifts, tell you a witty anecdote about a crocodile, sing a few songs in a language you could not comprehend – most lyrics are improved upon when you do not understand them, I find . . . " His voice trails off. Eos whispers in Penelope's ear. The queen nods, smiles, turns her full attention to the Egyptian.

"I am sorry we missed the opportunity for you to woo in this . . . eclectic way," she murmurs. "While of course I could never have married you, it would have been nice, I think, to have been seduced with witty anecdotes and exotic music instead of my would-be husbands' less traditional approach of attempting to murder my son upon the high seas."

"That is an odd way of getting a wife, I will admit." Then, serious, sombre, a rare flash of the soldier beneath the strange foreign man, "I did not know. If I had known, I would have warned you. I swear it."

She dismisses it with a waft of her hand. "I know. As I said, your exclusion from these matters was almost certain. It is why I wished you included in tonight's conference."

"Is that . . . why?" He wants to step closer to her, and does not. I nudge him in the small of the back, *go on, go on*, but with all his might he resists me and I do not press the point. "I thought perhaps . . . there was some other reason."

Penelope glances at Eos. Eos looks away. "I will . . . admit," she says at last, "that when considering tonight's events, I thought it might be useful to have . . . an ally. In the room. Someone whose ignorance of our local ways, inability to play at politics and utter powerlessness, if you'll pardon me saying, makes him in many ways above reproach. But also someone who . . . I trust. As much as I trust anyone. Medon, of course, is a loyal and worthy councillor, but he is not a warrior. If matters this evening had gone less well, it would have been . . . it is useful to have . . . Of course I understand if you feel that you have been used, it is . . . but you were so supportive of my son when he was here, and that is . . . Well. I thought. It might be useful. Given the circumstances."

Penelope is out of words.

Penelope is almost never out of words.

Oh, she is silent. A great deal of the time she is silent. But that is not the same thing – not at all. Her silences are merely words swallowed back, a great bellyful of sound waiting to be freed. She has spoken, and now she is silent, and it is an entirely different affair.

"Well," Kenamon shifts where he stands, "I ... am grateful for the trust you put in me. I am ... I am sorry for these difficulties, for Menelaus, for Orestes, for ... I only regret that there is not more I could – not by being your husband, of course, I see that is entirely foolish, it would be ... but as a ... an ally. An ally to your house. If there was more."

"Oh!" she blurts, reaching into her gown. A gold bangle, a snake swallowing its own tail, is produced from within, thrust towards him at arm's length as if it might come alive and start snapping at the fingers that hold it. "I, um ... this. For you. I mean, it is yours. I wish to return it. Do not let anyone see you have it, of course. If you did, I would have to tell them that you snuck into my room to steal it, and you will be immediately drowned – the others won't ask questions, you see, it is useful to them that a potential threat is removed, they'll all want to join in. But I thought ... you are far from home, and this is perhaps of some sentimental value to you, greater I mean than its worth to me ... so please."

She waves it towards him again.

It was a gift from Kenamon's sister, the day he departed his homeland for Ithaca. She pressed her forehead to his, her hand across the back of his neck. "Come home from this madness," she said. "Forget our brother and the things he said. None of that matters. Come home alive."

That was nearly two years ago. Kenamon reaches for the bangle, but does not touch, does not take. His hand brushes the air above it, as if he might feel some of the sunlight that once infused the gold, blazing still from the burnished metal. Then his fingers drop away. "Keep it, my queen," he says. "I do not think I would like to be drowned."

I am here, I breathe. *I am here.*

Penelope hesitates, then draws the bangle back into the folds of her gown, and it is gone from sight, hidden somewhere close to her skin, as if it were never between them at all.

"Goodnight, Kenamon," she says.

"Goodnight, queen of Ithaca," he replies.

They go their separate ways, darting into the shadows of the palace like midnight dreams.

Upstairs, in old Laertes' room, Orestes lies in a stupor of crushed flowers and herbs. But even in his dreams . . .

"Forgive me, forgive me, forgive me! Mother! Mother!"

The skies crack, icy rain that thickens to hail, balls of ice the size of an egg, smashing through straw and beating against muddy walls, tearing up the streets and pounding on the helmets of the Spartans who guard the palace gates. "Mother, Mother, Mother!" howl the Furies as the clouds spin wild above the island of Ithaca, and the gods themselves turn their eyes away.

Laertes drinks wine in the temple of Athena. It is a small wooden affair, notable only for some pillaged gold he and his son stole from other kings a long time ago. He tilts his cup to the crude statue of the goddess set above the altar as outside the lightning flashes and the sky empties its wrath into the pounding streets. "Well," he mutters. "So much for all that."

Antinous and Eupheithes, Eurymachus and Polybus cower in doorways as the heavens fall about them, darting from cover to cover as they scurry towards their ice-pounded homes.

Autonoe and her maids scrub the floors. Melantho and Phiobe try to calm the animals frightened in their pens. Eos shuts the door behind Penelope as she slips into her room, whispers: "No way back now."

In the bedroom of Penelope, that most secret, private place, the old spymaster Ourania sits away from the light and says: "Now let me tell you a thing or two about those Spartan maids . . ."

Lightning cracks across the skies above, but it is not Zeus who thunders now.

Kleitos, the priest of Apollo, presses another cup to Orestes' lips as Pylades and Iason hold him down, a concoction, a brew of herbs; the king spits and gags and chokes, but they keep pouring, tears in Pylades' eyes as Orestes boggles and squirms.

Anaitis stands in the doorway of the temple of Artemis, a bow in hand, and watches the heavens break. Priene is at her side, sword on her hip, and behind her, her warrior women, faces lost to the dark.

I turn from the Furies as they spin the storm into a whirlwind, dim my divinity, hide within palace walls as Orestes screams and Menelaus smiles and the animals shriek and the storm breaks across Ithaca.

In the morning.

Sunlight across a calm ocean.

Quiet in the town.

Quiet in the palace.

A few little fishing boats slip into the waters off the island. They carry more women than usual, their weapons bundled away beneath oily rags. No one questions them – everyone knows that with the men gone, the women must catch their own supper.

Eos rouses the still slumbering maids.

Elektra sits wide-eyed and wide awake in her room, Rhene by her side.

Menelaus is slow to stir, goodness, he mutters, morning already? So much to do.

"Prepare the ships!" he barks. "Food, water, we mustn't miss the tide, come on, you slackers, you layabouts, move yourselves!"

"Brother," murmurs Penelope, as Menelaus centres himself at the heart of a bustling whirlwind of men and bronze. "What are you doing?"

"Gotta get that boy the help he needs. He needs the best – the best – now I know your island has lots of women who know how to deliver a goat, but that just won't cut it, he's my brother's only son, I have a duty, you understand, I know you do."

"You're taking him to Mycenae?"

A brisk shake of his head. Menelaus isn't looking at Penelope as he speaks – not from shame. He just has far more interesting things to look at, far more interesting people to think about, bustle, bustle. "To Sparta. Now, I know what you're going to say, but I assure you, by the time we get there, I'll have sent messengers to Delphi, to Athens, I'll have every priest of Apollo waiting at the palace to see my nephew's all right, see that he's safe. Besides, can't have him going back to Mycenae in that state! People wouldn't think he was fit to rule ... Don't drop that! Are you blind? Where's my son, he should be ... You! Go see where Nicostratus is! Move!"

"Of course," murmurs Penelope. "You are wise and kind as always. Perhaps I should send to Nestor too, it would be good for Sparta to have the aid of its nearest ally ... "

Menelaus dismisses her words with a wave. "No need, no need! This is family, and Nestor – well, I mean, him and me, of course, him and me ... but blood. Blood runs deeper. Blood goes all the way."

"You do not think the other kings need to know? They could be anxious, with Orestes in Sparta. I am only a foolish woman, of course, I only—"

"Quite," he barks, and then catches himself. Turns to Penelope, a huge smile across his lips, puts his hands on the tops of her arms, squeezes, on the verge of another of his famous friendly hugs. "Forgive me, sister. You're entirely right as always, of course. I forgot myself. Of course I'll send messengers to the other kings to inform them that my nephew is so ... unfortunately disposed. They deserve to know. Where's

Nicostratus?" This last, hollered to the room, which has no answer. "In Zeus's name," he mutters, turning to stride from the hall to the crooked creaking stairs up to his son's room.

He does not reach it before the maid he sent to find his son does. It is her scream of purest horror that provokes even Menelaus – who really feels that he did enough physical activity in his youth and has earned the right not to put the work in now he grows old – to run.

Nicostratus wakes.

Though I am somewhat less petty than many of the gods, I do consider it a slight misfortune that of the two people in his room, he is the one who is roused by the screaming from the door. The cool sea air blows in from the wide-open window, the air inside the room as fresh as the sea-swept land without. The woollen blanket beneath Nicostratus's half-naked body is much disturbed by his weight, as if he slept fitfully, and the blood that dried within it has set to a thick black with the texture of old mortar. On the floor, more blood, here pooled, here spread into long lines where feet and arms and bodies moved through it. The outline of a single delicate foot marks its extremity near the door, and there are rags from the empty washing bowl, saturated to a perfect scarlet at the heart of the largest pool. By the door, the golden armour that Nicostratus has so proudly carried with him wherever he goes is disturbed, the great tower shield fallen face-down, so that one can see the hefty straps across its back, and a blade displaced from its resting place and thrust through the body of Zosime, where she lies still, crooked on the floor.

It is this latter, the body of the murdered maid, that induced the scream of heart-rending pain that has pushed even Menelaus into a bit of a jog. Now he stands in the door breathless, beholds slaughtered Zosime, beholds his son rousing himself from his bed, blood across his legs, his chest, his brow, and is for the first time in a very long while silenced.

"Father . . . ?" begins Nicostratus, fumbling for a blanket to cover some of his nudity. Then he too sees the blood, sees the fallen maid, and for a brief, really rather gratifying moment, all the men of Sparta are struck dumb.

Then Helen sticks her head round the door, disturbed by the sounds of terror, sees her maid dead in a pool of thick, sticky blood, gasps, swoons, and faints clean away at her husband's feet.

CHAPTER 24

>>

In the stories of the poets, a dead maid is usually of only passing narrative relevance. What do we know of Heracles' wife, other than that he killed her? What of Ariadne, other than she was a plaything of treason and treachery, abandoned to the whims of gods and the sea?

So it is for Zosime, murdered at the foot of Nicostratus's bed. Her life will be defined by her death, for her death was by the son of Menelaus, and that is far more interesting and important to posterity than the woman who lived, before she died.

But I, who have heard the laments of the dead as well as the living, their mournful wails for the loves they have lost, the ones they will not see again, hear the song of Zosime still. Pity me, she cries, oh but pity me, for I thought I loved a man and he loved me, and I was wrong. Pity me that I was punished, oh so cruelly punished, for my human heart.

Helen sits in the corridor and is fanned by Tryphosa. If her surviving maid shows any sign of horror or regret at the passing of her companion, she does not show it, but focuses instead on her mistress, who swims in and out of sense to sometimes murmur: "Zosime!" and sometimes "My heart!" and sometimes "Poor Zosime!" before seeming to succumb again.

Menelaus holds Nicostratus by the throat against the wall, oblivious to the blood, to his son's nudity. The would-be warrior boy is now a pup, cowering, whimpering, a child before his father's wrath, and why wouldn't he be? He only really knew his father when he was a boy, never had time to learn how to be a man in front of him, and now Menelaus roars and rages, spittle in the face and glistening pink gums: "WHAT DID YOU DO?!"

"I don't know I don't know I came to bed I came to bed I didn't I didn't . . ."

Menelaus slaps his son. Nicostratus staggers, but cannot fall, for his father's other hand is still wrapped about his throat. *"WHAT DID YOU DO?!"*

"Nothing, I swear, nothing, I don't remember, nothing . . ."

Menelaus slaps his son again, and this time doesn't hold on, lets his son fall, kicks him in the gut, kicks him again and again. Nicostratus is a warrior, a fighter, bold and brave, but against his father's foot he cowers, he grovels, he begs, hands above his head, until finally, blood in his eyes and metal on his tongue, Menelaus roars without words and storms from the room, leaving his son coughing and gagging on the floor.

Helen whimpers, and there it is, just for a moment, there at last for all to see – contempt, disgust, revulsion, he has never seen anything as grotesque as his wife's little show, and oh yes, oh yes, he knows it is a show – after all, this woman saw the sacking of Troy! She guided Menelaus to the murder of her then-husband, held his hand as they walked through the streets where mothers, daughters, sisters screamed beneath the weight of the Greek men who pressed them; and now she dares to fall in this place, at this time, as if she has not seen blood? He despises her for this more than anything, and with a snarl breaking across his lips, turns and stalks away.

Slowly, the household of Penelope assembles in the bloody

door. Penelope hitches the hem of her gown a little to avoid trailing it in crimson as she steps cautiously, carefully into the room. "Eos," she murmurs, "kindly take Nicostratus to the temple of Athena. Send for the priest Kleitos to tend to him there. Autonoe – clear this corridor. No one comes in until we have completed our work. I want a full accounting of the movements of everyone who sleeps within vicinity of this room, who came and who went last night. Melantho, kindly escort my cousin back to her room and see that she is tended to."

The order is given, and it is the single calmest thing about this morning, and so it is obeyed.

Penelope stands in the door of Nicostratus's room, hands clasped at her belly, head bowed, a watchwoman to the body and the blood as around her order is imposed. Only when no one is looking does she take a moment to raise her head, offer a brief prayer for the soul of dead Zosime, lower her head again, and despite herself, and with a great pang of guilt at the motion that she cannot contain, smile.

Soon only Penelope and Eos remain on the whole floor, guards set at the stairs, maids waiting below with buckets and cloths.

"Her name was Zosime," Eos says, gazing down at the body of the woman before Nicostratus's bed. "A maid of Helen's."

"Nicostratus?"

"Gone to the shrine of Athena, as commanded."

"I trust the priests there will follow their usual patterns of noble behaviour, and tell everyone they possibly can. Menelaus?"

"He stormed from the palace. I think he was too incensed to have a purpose or a destination."

"He will be back soon. And my cousin Helen?"

"Downstairs, with the Spartans."

"Good. It will not be long before Menelaus calms down

and realises the full implications of these events. We must move quickly."

Here is the inventory of Nicostratus's room:

A golden washbasin – Spartan, of course, not Ithacan – stands on a table furthest from the window. It is empty. A bloody cloth lies still wet in the drying pool of blood by Zosime's bosom.

Three stab wounds drive through from her back to her front. Only one of them penetrated all the way, and there Nicostratus's sword still remains, tip pointing out of her chest, wedged, difficult to withdraw.

There is a stand by the bed, on which Nicostratus has put a single precious ring he believes was gifted him by his father, but which in truth a kindly lordling left him when he was a child, taking pity on the son raised without any loving parents nearby to call his own.

His travel chest of gold and clothes, precious goods and personal effects has not been disturbed, save now by Penelope and Eos, who search through it with some interest. The morning light begins to creep in at the corner of the window. Eos goes to pull the shutter across, the cold of the room still heavy with the weight of oppressive night, but Penelope stops her.

"Leave it," she commands. "Nothing is moved in this room until we are done."

Across the floor, bloody passages, speaking of commotion, movement. Zosime died quickly, but her body was disturbed, dragged this way and that. Nicostratus's discarded clothes lie not an arm's reach from her head, his blanket rumpled and stained. A single footprint near the door is a source of some interest to the women – did it belong to the maid? To some other creature? There is blood on the sole of Zosime's foot, but there is blood everywhere.

"I think we have seen enough," muses Penelope.

There are a few rooms nearby, larger and grander than most in the palace, built for an imagined family of beloved grand-mothers and endless grandchildren who were never born. Nicostratus should not have slept in this place, for the next rooms are those of Helen and Elektra, with Penelope's own cold, thrill-less bedroom a turn away. To have a man so close to these women is frankly uncouth, but when one of the women is a guaranteed whore, a traitor, the great slut of Greece – well, is it so unreasonable that a man should watch over her?

"Just to keep her safe," Menelaus would say, with a gentle pat on the back. "One fella tried to break into the royal palace in Sparta itself just to see her face! Had to have him flayed, terrible business, terrible the way people think they have a right to your wife just because you're famous."

Penelope and Eos stand outside the door next to Nicostratus's room. It is Helen's. Several times Autonoe has tried to enter it, to bring fresh oil for the lamp or clean cloths for her basin, and each time Helen's stern maids, Tryphosa and murdered Zosime, have barred the way. "We are instructed not to be burdens," they would intone. "It is our master's deepest wish."

Penelope refers to her house as Odysseus's house. Odysseus's throne, Odysseus's chair, Odysseus's food. But her maids always said they served a mistress, not a master, even when Odysseus was on Ithaca. Penelope never corrects them. There are nuances here that she has found not entirely unhelpful.

Now Penelope looks at Eos, Eos at Penelope. The maid pushes open the door to Helen's room. The queen steps within.

The air is cold, though not as bitten with sea-breeze chill as Nicostratus's room. There is a mirror of pure polished silver – Penelope stares at it in amazement, or perhaps it is fairer to say that she stares at herself in it. She has not seen her own reflec-tion so clearly for as long as she can recall. What are these lines about her eyes, these strands of grey intruding upon her brow, these bushy eyebrows, these swags of flesh beneath her chin? Some aspects of her visage she finds a relief – fumbling with finger and thumb at her own skin she imagined great craters or hanging flags of ageing flesh, which grew larger in her mind with ignorance. A reflection seen distorted by the rippling of a river's water or in the warped polish of crude bronze is a far stranger, less noble thing than that which the eye perceives in the visage of every other face it may look upon. Penelope is thrilled to discover that in broad strokes at least, the picture she created of herself is largely flawed – she looks perfectly human, perfectly normal, perfectly radiant in her normality. But the details still shock. Do her eyes squint so? Are her ears quite so protuberant? Her jaw so square? For a moment – a dreadful, shameful moment – she wonders how to steal her cousin's mirror, what story she will tell to be able to whisk it away. This is unacceptable. For a woman to contemplate her own beauty is vanity, superficial pride, shallow beyond contempt, the sign of a mindless slut. Of course for a woman to be anything less than beautiful is for her to be ugly, or in the best case invisible and without merit, and that is also unacceptable, but still, but still. The most a woman born without socially acceptable perfection can do is worry about these things in secret, rather than be caught trying.

With something of a shudder, Penelope wrenches her gaze from the mirror.

Helen travels with several chests, and what wonders within! Silks from the furthest east, carried on camel's back across mighty rivers and by triangle-rigged sail to these western isles. Linen and wool, soft as the first blush of hair on a babe's head, dyed the most extraordinary colours – crimson and purple, flashes of orange and crushed green. A mountain of beetles have been slaughtered to create this sunset trim; the urine of many mothers was spilled to set this streak of scarlet. Again, a moment of fantasy sits briefly upon Penelope – what might it have been to be a woman permitted to rejoice in her body, to blaze in bright colour and be honoured, celebrated for herself, instead of having to dress in the loose garb of the waiting widow of a missing king? No one gasps when they see Penelope. No jaws hang slack, no one pulls on their neighbour's sleeve to whisper look, look there, there she is! Instead, the most common reaction of strangers is a sad shaking of the head and a little tut. Oh, is that Penelope? Such a pity. Such a shame.

On a table – a panoply of tools for beauty. Penelope wants to drag every wet-limbed man who has ever dribbled at the sight of her cousin to this place and shout, look, look here! Look at the pastes of lead and salves of wax, the concoctions of honey and sticks of char, the pots and patties of every hue and texture with which Helen has made her face! She grows old, oh she grows old, even Helen of Troy grows old, and she fears it. She is mortally afraid of her own mortality, and what is uglier than fear?

Instead, she sniffs jars of salve, marvels at crystal powders and pumice stones. Some she can name. Most she cannot. Eos lifts a little golden vial, slips the top off, sniffs, wrinkles her nose in distaste.

"What are they all for?" she asks.

"I can hardly imagine. Here." Penelope grabs a cloth with which Helen might sometimes soothe her brow, dips a fingertip of it into one pot, a fingertip in another, until soon the fabric is stained with a dozen different fragrances and oils in neat little patches. Eos slips the piece of fabric into her gown, closes the door softly behind them.

Unlike Nicostratus and Helen's rooms, Elektra's room is almost stagnantly hot, the shutters still drawn. Eos throws them back merely so they can see their way about the place, the little lamp by the bed long since extinguished and stained about its mouth with blackened residue.

"Who changes the lamps?" asks Penelope.

"It should be Autonoe, but she has been prevented in her work by the Spartan maids."

"Ask her who changes them."

A nod from Eos; it will be done, and that is all that needs to be said. Eos is not someone who needs to be asked for anything twice, and often need not be asked at all.

Elektra has travelled without any real accoutrements of a queen. No fine robes, no creams of white lead, no wax or pins to hold her hair in any elaborate form. They find the comb with which she so often caresses her brother's head. They find a golden bangle, kept perhaps for trading in extremity, hidden beneath the pallet on which she sleeps. They find a golden ring set with a single black onyx in a crimson leather bag and a dagger beneath a loose board in the floor. For a while Penelope holds the ring in the palm of her hand, then she returns it to the bag and puts it and the weapon back where they were found.

Then Autonoe is in the doorway. "Menelaus is coming back!"

Penelope and Eos leave Elektra's room at once, easing the door shut behind them. Menelaus is heard before he is seen, blasting past the maid set at the foot of the stairs, who squeaks as he shoves her aside, too set on his purpose to bother to explain his passage to a mere slave.

He thunders up the stairs, bursts into the corridor, beholds Penelope and snarls: "What the fuck have you done?"

CHAPTER 25

>>>

Penelope and Menelaus stand in the council chamber of Odysseus.

At Penelope's back, her councillors. They should be the ones handling this affair, speaking for their kingdom, their king. Just this once, they are happy to let a woman do the talking, let someone else stand between them and the roaring king of Sparta.

"Good brother . . ." Penelope tries again.

"You sent Nicostratus to the temple of Athena! What the fuck were you thinking?"

"I was thinking that your son is suspected of murder and that the temple of the goddess was a more appropriate place to hold him than the palace dungeon."

Menelaus looms. He towers. He distends the space around him with his thrusting chest, jutting jaw. All of this is something of an achievement, as he is not a particularly tall man, but he's never let his physical reality get in the way of making an impression. Warriors have cowered beneath his shadow; grown men have grovelled at the fire in his eyes. Just this once, and to no one's surprise more than Menelaus and the council of Penelope, the woman before him stands her ground.

"The temple of Athena is full of gossips and whores. Now every fucking fisherman in Ithaca knows my son is there!"

"My palace is full of gossips and whores," Penelope replies. At her back, Peisenor flinches, Aegyptius studies his feet and old Medon watches with open curiosity, fascinated to see where this business might go. "The word was out about Nicostratus's . . . status the moment the first woman screamed at the sight of that poor woman's body. Every suitor on the island knows, and I assure you that they will have taken not a breath before telling every person they possibly can. You scare them, you see. They are scared of your terrible and mighty power, and so in their fear do you really think they would *not* take the chance to spread the word of this . . . situation? Given that, it seemed that the least dishonourable thing I could do, on my husband's behalf, was move your son to the safety of the temple."

Not every suitor knew what happened the moment the first maid screamed. But Autonoe made it very clear to the maids who mopped the blood that indiscretion was the word of the day. The first ships are already sailing for Pylos and Athens with whispers of the deed; the next ships to depart with the tide will bring firm confirmation of the fact. Penelope is not displeased at this development.

Menelaus tries looming over her a moment more. Penelope does not blink. I pat the great king on the back, whisper in his ear: *She was raised in Sparta too, little man. She saw how the boys behaved when they were trying to become men.*

Menelaus spins away.

It is a defeat. A deflation. An astonishing sight. I am really quite aroused by it, goodness what a thing. He tries to make it into another motion, pacing the tiny distance of the room, bouncing wall to wall like a bewildered bee, before finally stopping and spinning back, levelling a finger towards Penelope's implacable face.

"We are leaving. Now."

"Of course, brother. As you wish. Though if you do, I fear terribly for your son's reputation." Menelaus quivers like a bow, but does not move. Penelope smiles with the patience of a teacher who hoped that their promising student might solve a thing for themselves, and sees now that they need just a little more help. "So hard for a son to live up to his father, especially a father of such astonishing power as yourself. My Telemachus has suffered for it greatly, of course. I blame myself for his failings, for how he struggles to find a way to be a man in his own right, instead of merely his father's son. And your Nicostratus – no one could doubt that he is a hero, of course, a great man in the making. But he is still introduced as the son of Menelaus, as a scion of your blood, before he is named as a man in his own right. And now he has killed a maid. Worse than that – he has killed the maid of your wife, and while a guest in our house."

Now Menelaus stops.

Now Menelaus looks at Penelope.

Looks at her, sees her, knows her. He has never really known what to make of the women in his life. There have been whores for fucking, wives for business, daughters to sell. Sometimes they have attempted to manifest natures beyond this. Hermione screamed when he said she was to marry Achilles' brat instead of her childhood betrothed, Orestes, and didn't stop until he had beaten her until nearly unconscious. Helen betrayed him – but she was a whore, so that was to be expected. That was just another part of an understood female nature, their inherent but observable weakness and failure. Elektra would doubtless resist too, when her fate was woven, but she would yield. That was what women did.

Penelope, however. Penelope has been something of a mystery – until this moment. Oh, certainly she is no more than Odysseus's wife, just another business proposition. But he has always suspected that she has something more, a creeping, alarming *otherness* that defies normal female categorisation.

Now he knows it.

Now he recognises at last that thing in her that he can name, respect even, understand.

He looks at Penelope and sees the face of his enemy.

And he smiles.

For the first time, Menelaus smiles upon her – not the smile of the king upon the widow, the magnanimous bringer of order or the jovial relative executing a plan. He smiles as he once smiled when Paris stepped forward to the fight, although goodness knows that didn't really work out. He smiles as Achilles once smiled upon Hector, as Agamemnon smiled to behold the walls of Troy.

"There, cousin," he breathes. "There you are."

He straightens up, smile widening, little yellow teeth, nostrils flaring wide. It has been a while since he had a fight – a real fight. He had forgotten the taste of it, the flavour upon his tongue, and now here it is. Here *she* is. Enemy. His enemy, pure and glorious and simple and true.

He had not thought he could be so thrilled to look upon a combatant and see that she is female. When he wins, he thinks, he will give Penelope to one of his sons, and stand at the end of the bed as the boy takes her. Damn, once she is broken and the western isles are his, he might even take her himself, whatever petty oaths he made to dead Odysseus. Penelope has not been beautiful, barely been a woman at all in his eyes, until this moment. It is the single most arousing thought Menelaus has had in he does not know how long. The heat of it is baffling, exhilarating. He nearly sways with the force of it, remembers for the briefest moment what it is to be young and full of fire again.

When Zeus looks away; when Ares has finally lost interest in his sport, I will come to you, I whisper in his ear. *I will come to you and give you desire, such desire, that shall never be sated. You will live a long, long time in your bag of bones, wasted flesh and wilted muscle, fatted only on longings unfulfilled.*

He does not hear me – Menelaus's ears have been closed to the goddess of love for a very long time – but that will not change his fate.

Instead, he takes a small breath, half closes his eyes, steadies himself, and gazes finally, fully upon the face of his enemy. "All right, queen of Ithaca," he murmurs. "Let's see what you have. So what if my son killed a whore? A maid – a slave? He struck her down for treachery. He struck her down for betraying my house. He defended the honour of my wife. Everyone needs to defend the honour of my wife, all the kings of Greece swore to it."

"Perhaps. But I have an associate who has a cousin who has a cousin who told my friend that this slaughtered maid – this Zosime – was not just some casual market slave, no? She was from noble stock, from the house of one of your allies in Corinth, sent to Sparta to seek her fortune at one of the finest courts in the land. Under your protection, she came of child – but not of husband. An embarrassing situation. The child was exposed on the mountains and was not chosen by the gods to survive, but the mother? Well, she could hardly be well married now, nor was it entirely suitable that she be sent back to her noble family, having been sullied by one of your court. What maid, I wonder, feels she can walk into your son's room? What slave would so casually dare to be alone with your noble boy, unless she had some prior ... intimacy with him? The noble men of Corinth might just be able to swallow the notion that their daughter was sullied by the son of a king, but slain? Slain perhaps by the very father of her fate-cursed child? This is too much. Nicostratus's name – his prospects even as a potential king – would be washed into the Styx."

Menelaus's smile has grown, not decreased, with Penelope's

speech. Oh, it is something – it is something indeed – to have a foe worth his attention! He is almost overcome, almost dizzy with it, suffused with the fantasy of what he will do to her when she is beaten, gracious, it is really rather challenging to think through the heat of it. But he is a warrior – he pushes through. "Well, sister," he breathes. "You have done your work."

"I try not to put too much store by rumours, of course, but I feel it is my duty to raise these concerns – for your son's sake. For the sake of Sparta and our long, valued alliance."

"Our alliance," he muses. "Yes. Always got to be thinking about the niceties of these things. I suspect you have a plan? One that doesn't involve me and my men getting on a ship right now, with Prince Orestes, and taking him far from here?"

"As I said, you are entirely at liberty to do so. But with the cloud hanging over your son . . . "

"Spit it out. Let's see what you've come up with, wife of Odysseus."

"If we could clear your son's name – if there were perhaps evidence that pointed to someone else having done this terrible thing?"

"Ah, I see. You think a bit of time, a few weeks maybe, a month – how long were you weaving that shroud of yours for, a year, two? I'm no suitor, queen. I will not wait another summer while you play your games."

"Seven days then. That way people can see that we have done our work. We have thoroughly enquired into this affair to see whether, as it seems, your son has violated every sacred law of hospitality, or if – as I am sure will be the case – someone maliciously works against him. If it turns out to be the latter, I myself will, in shame at the sullying of my house, send word to every king of your son's innocence. I know I am just a woman, but I hope that the good men of Greece may at least put some faith in the oath of Odysseus's wife."

"Seven days . . ." muses Menelaus. "Three. Three days for your . . . learned council to do their investigations. To prove my son innocent and find some other . . . culprit. A Mycenaean perhaps? One of Orestes' men, as mad as his master?"

"Orestes of course will remain in the palace."

"Of course he will. Since things are being done so proper . . . of course. Naturally my soldiers will remain too, to look after him. Ensure that what happened to the slut maid doesn't also befall my lovely nephew."

"Naturally. We cannot be too careful."

"And perhaps when your investigation is concluded, as well as sending a message to all the kings of the land assuring them of my son's innocence in this, we might together see if we can't find an answer to the question of Ithaca. I have too long neglected the home of my good friend Odysseus, let you suffer alone in this place. It is time to remedy that and take responsibility, as a brother should."

"You are too generous."

"You are too wise."

"Well then," Penelope gives a tiny bow, a barest nod of the head, "we have an accord."

"Sister," he replies, and before anyone can speak, squeak, flail or object, he reaches in, holds her fast with a hand below either shoulder, and kisses her once on the left cheek, once on the right, his lips lingering a moment as warm breath tickles her ear, breezes through a loose strand of hair. He should say something. Should whisper some hidden threat from this intimate proximity. But he only breathes. Only breathes. And then, at last, lets go, and with a little twitching of his fingers towards the councillors, marches from the room.

The old men of Ithaca let out the collective breath they did not realise they'd been holding as the door closes behind the king of Sparta.

Penelope turns to face them.

It is Aegyptius who speaks first, which surprises nearly everyone. He stares at Penelope, stares at his peers, stares back at her and then blurts: "What in Athena's name have you done?!"

"I have bought us three days," she replies primly. "Three days to save Orestes from being taken to Sparta, which place he will never leave alive again should he ever see it. Three days to find out what happened to Zosime. Three days to save the western isles." The men stand agape. At last she claps her hands together. "Well, come on then!" she barks. "We have work to do!"

CHAPTER 26

>>>

B ustle, bustle, bustle!
    Blood is washed from the floor.

Helen lies across a couch being fanned by anyone who is willing to take a turn. "My poor heart," she whimpers. "It will break! Surely it will break!"

"There there, cousin," sighs Penelope as she passes by. "I'm sure all will be well."

At this, Helen bursts into floods of tears of such sudden force and volume that for a horrifying moment, Penelope worries that she might actually be witnessing something sincere.

Spartan soldiers man the gate of the palace. They stand upon its walls. They guard its doors. They round up every bleary-eyed suitor and hung-over male who spent the night within its bounds and gather them, stinking and sweating, into the great hall. Menelaus paces before them, grins at Antinous, pinches Eurymachus's cheeks. Even their fathers have been caught in the net, old men swaying and unsteady upon their feet.

None of them, not one of the manhood of Ithaca, fights back.

"What is this?" Penelope demands, seeing the assembled men.

"Sister!" Menelaus exclaims with brightness in his eyes, and a sweep of his arm across the room. "To help in your investigation, I have assembled the suspects. They will not leave this room until we have the man who committed this crime, however long it takes."

"Thank you, brother," replies Penelope, "but I assure you this is not necessary."

"It is necessary," he retorts, quick and merry. "You said it yourself. To catch the man who did this – to clear my son's name – everything is necessary."

Soon, other fathers of the trapped suitors are at the gate of the palace, demanding to see their sons. They thought of bringing spears, swords, rattling against the walls. But the Spartans who stand watch are fully armoured, fully armed, and it does not strike even these anxious parents as wise to provoke the finest warriors of Greece with their indignity.

Medon tries to placate them. "All will be well," he intones. "All will be—"

"What is Menelaus doing? He is not king of Ithaca! He cannot hold our boys!"

"Until we have this matter settled, the noble king of Sparta is assisting in our enquiries . . ."

A roar, a cry of dismay. The palace has been conquered, their sons enslaved, and no one even put up a fight.

Penelope goes to the temple of Athena.

Spartan soldiers accompany her, for her safety, of course. Lefteris insists on it, insists on going with her personally – one woman is dead already, he says, can't risk another little lady getting herself killed.

"Nice place for a wedding," the Spartan opines as they step into the cool interior. "Lucky old you."

Penelope ignores him, heading straight for the darkest reaches of the shrine, the low doorway to the secret place of the priests. Kleitos, though of Apollo's house not Athena's, has been constantly fussing about, approaches now anxiously – is there news, what is happening? – and is brushed aside with a briskness that makes his cheeks flare scarlet.

Within a small square room, Nicostratus is awake, fully sober, pacing in the chamber usually reserved for the priest to receive his offerings – sometimes hard to tell the difference between those and bribes – for various services. He marches, he spins, he snarls when he sees the Ithacan queen. He is washed, but there is still a fleck of blood in the hollow of one ear that he's missed. I find it fascinating, but being as we are upon my sister's sacred ground, I do not look too close nor linger too near.

"What are you doing?" he demands. "Where is my father?"

"Your father is in my husband's palace, interrogating every man within to try and determine your innocence."

"I *am* innocent."

"Of course you are, you are Menelaus's son," Penelope replies. "But to prove this conclusively to the satisfaction of your fellow princes and kings, we must be thorough. Tell me what happened that night."

"I don't need to tell you anything."

"Don't you? I am the wife of the king of these lands. In the absence of my husband, that makes me his representative. Moreover, I am trusted. Unlike my cousins, unlike every other woman in Greece, my word will be respected, honoured. I have given up a great deal to ensure that this is the case. If I swear that you are innocent, it will be taken seriously, for everyone knows that I never take an oath in vain."

Nicostratus tries looming like his father does, and fails. Unlike his father, he does not manage to turn the flawed intimidation into fluid motion, but instead slouches against the wall like the sulky child he is, chin out and shoulders curved; he can't believe how unfair the whole thing is. "Orestes went mad. We got him to bed, then I went to bed. That's it."

"You didn't see Zosime?"

"No. She was probably tending to my father's wife."

"She didn't approach you?"

"No, I said."

"Was there anything unusual in your room, on the way to it? Anything at all?"

"No. I went to my room, I . . . I lay down, and then I woke up."

"You removed your clothes, washed."

"I don't remember."

"You don't remember that?" He shakes his head. He is briefly bright enough to be afraid, before the stupidity of his training kicks back in and he refuses to be anything other than indignant, angry and wronged. "And you don't remember a woman being killed right in front of you?"

"I said – I was asleep."

"Most people wake when someone is being stabbed to death within arm's reach."

"Well I didn't! Maybe I was drugged? Poisoned!"

"Did you drink or eat anything unusual last night?" He wants to say yes. It would be so convenient if the answer was yes. And yet. Penelope sighs. "You were . . . intimate with Zosime in Sparta, yes?"

His eyes flash. "I've fucked plenty of whores."

"But she wasn't a whore. She was the daughter of a powerful man."

"Even queens can be whores, when the time is right."

At Penelope's back, Lefteris grins, nods encouragement to his prince. Lefteris thinks that Menelaus will not live as long as the old king of Sparta thinks, sees how he grows fat, intemperate. A wise captain always has an eye to the future blood.

"She had a child. Your child?"

Nicostratus doesn't answer.

"Who decided to leave it to die? You, or your father?"

He doesn't answer.

Penelope feels she should have a strong sentiment about this. She too was left to die, flung from the cliff by her father, Icarius. She is not aware of any other babes who were saved from their fate by a flock of ducks, as she was, and feels therefore that she should have a certain passionate fire for her fellow cast-aside children of secrets and shame. Yet now she feels nothing. Tired, perhaps. She has been tired for so, so long.

"Please stay within the temple, Nicostratus," she says. "If you leave this sacred place, it will look bad for you."

He scowls at her back as she departs.

On the way back to the palace, she glances aside and sees a man looking at her.

He is standing in the market, examining wool as if he has never before seen the hair of a sheep, an intense frown upon his brow and fingers upon his chin, nodding at some mercantile thought or other. But as she passes, his eyes flash to hers, and hers to his, and then they both quickly look away before Lefteris can see it.

Only once she has crossed within the palace gates, ringed by Spartan bronze, does Penelope turn to Eos and whisper: "Send to Ourania. Tell her that Kenamon is outside the palace walls."

"The Egyptian?" hisses Eos, as she makes a show of fussing with Penelope's veil. "How?"

"I don't know. But we need to get him to safety before Menelaus finds out. Go."

With this, she raises her head again, and seeing a Spartan man with spear standing before her trills: "Oh lovely, I feel so much safer already!" as Eos scurries away.

*

By the afternoon, the stench of the great hall is almost unbearable.

Menelaus has not permitted the suitors to leave.

Nor to sit.

Nor drink.

Nor take a shit.

It is old Eupheithes, father of Antinous, who falls first. Polybus nearly cries out in relief and anguish at it, grateful that his rival staggered before he did, on the verge of collapsing, of never rising again himself. Antinous helps his father stand – there is no harm in showing a bit of filial piety before these men, even as his cheeks blaze with shame. Menelaus is sprawled sideways across Odysseus's throne, grinning. "I once went six days and nights without sleep, fighting before the walls of Troy," he vouchsafes when the next man tumbles. "But that was when men were men."

Among the suitors are the Mycenaean men too. Pylades, Iason, though not the priest Kleitos. They stand at the very front. Menelaus beams upon them as food is brought – for the Spartan king, of course, no others. He is deciding which one he'd like to be the culprit, which man close to Orestes will take the blame. And why not? It makes sense, if you think about it, that a mad Mycenaean king would have the kind of mad Mycenaean kinsmen who'd murder a woman in Nicostratus's bedroom. The logic of insanity – it's a truth all of its own.

Orestes is still upstairs, in his room, sleeping the fitful sleep of poppy and wine. The Furies slumber on the roof above his room, lulled it seems by the same thick ichor that has dulled the prince. Best not to trouble the poor boy with things like this. He's got enough to worry about.

"Where's Elektra?" murmurs Penelope as the women slip through the palace.

"With her maids, praying."

"Find her."

Phiobe nods, departs. Autonoe takes her place, filling the shadow the maid leaves behind. Now more than ever it is vital that Penelope not go unaccompanied. An unaccompanied woman is almost as dangerous as a man. "I spoke to Melitta, Melantho, Phiobe, any others who went near Nicostratus's room last night. The Spartan women keep them away, for the most part – Zosime herself was insistent that our maids stay away from the Spartan halls. They don't even let us change the lamps, except in Elektra's room. But Melantho thinks she saw something, an argument."

"Who? When?"

"Before dinner – before Orestes was taken sick. The Mycenaean, Pylades, arguing with Elektra in the shadows of the stair. She says Elektra struck him across the face."

"Really? That is . . . almost pleasingly unexpected."

"Do you think Nicostratus killed Zosime?"

"It certainly appears that he did."

"Why? And why say he was asleep at the time, when the body was plain to see at the foot of his bed?" Autonoe tuts. She likes clean answers, simple solutions. They save time, and time is one of the very few commodities that is sometimes her own.

"Has the body been removed?"

"Yes, and the room cleaned."

"I would like to speak to Helen's other maid – Tryphosa."

"She is with her mistress."

"I would like to speak to her alone."

"I will arrange it."

"I should also speak to Elektra and – if we can get him out of Menelaus's grasp – Pylades. If Nicostratus is innocent, the people with the most to gain from this murder are perhaps the same ones who will do anything to keep Orestes from going to Sparta. How is our noble guest?"

"Kleitos gave him something and now he sleeps. His sleep is very deep." Again, distrust in Autonoe's voice. The best guest as far as she is concerned is generally speaking an unconscious one, but today any good news just feels like a trap.

They find Tryphosa standing stiff by Helen's side, face grey and hard, looking at nothing, seeing nothing, as if there were in this place nothing new to see.

"Cousin!" quavers Helen from her couch as Penelope approaches. "Oh gracious cousin, good cousin, have you seen Nicostratus? Is the dear boy all right, oh the dear boy, my heart, I just, I don't even . . . "

"Helen," replies Penelope primly, and she thinks perhaps it is the first time she has spoken this woman's name since they were children, called her anything other than "cousin" or "queen" or "that woman". The effect is briefly jarring, but she shakes it off, turns her gaze to Helen's last living maid. "I need to speak to Tryphosa."

Tryphosa's eyes rise slowly at the sound of her name, as if it takes some time for her to acknowledge, to understand – ah yes, that is me they speak of, it is I who is here invoked. She is old, this woman, for a maid to a queen. Younger girls should have taken her place a long time ago, she should be married perhaps, or set to work guarding children, not grown women.

"Tryphosa?" whimpers Helen. "You will not keep her long from me?"

"Not at all," Penelope replies, and then, for her cousin's gaze is so moist and her nether lip so tremulous, she adds again, even weaker than before, "All will be well."

At this, Helen gives a little cry. It is a tiny "ah!", as if she had trodden on a jagged stone with bare feet, a thing that comes, goes, happened and has passed but still, it hurt – goodness, it stung. Before anyone can ask after her well-being, however, she closes her eyes and turns her face away, a dismissal given by one who does not wish to speak of her distress, lest more distress be given.

Tryphosa stands in the shadow of a crumbling wall, Autonoe to her right, Penelope before her. She does not meet the queen of Ithaca's eye, but studies her own feet as if astonished to find that these too can show signs of weariness and the passing of time.

The whole effect is rather disconcerting for Penelope, who was hoping for a more receptive beginning to a conversation. "Tryphosa," she blurts at last, "tell me about last night."

Tryphosa does not raise her head, though her voice is steady and firm. "We took our lady to her room, as we always do. I helped her undress and prepare herself for sleep. Zosime left. Our lady lay down to sleep and I slept at the end of her bed."

"You sleep in Helen's room?"

"One of us will always sleep at our lady's feet," she replies. "It is for our lady's protection."

"And this is all? The queen retired, she went to bed, you slept?"

"That is all that happened."

"Did you fall sleep before Orestes had his ... incident?" A flicker of confusion. A moment of doubt. Tryphosa shakes her head. The question itself is strange to her. "There was a great deal of commotion. Enough I would have thought to catch your attention."

Tryphosa, Tryphosa. She wanted to love when she was young. She yearned for it, pursued it, had many very brief encounters with many very slight people and convinced herself each time that this – why this – this was love. But the more her illusions were broken, the further from her heart love seemed to be. Love was not real; love was not for women such as she, until at last, one night long after her soul had waned and her dreams had shrivelled, she stood beneath the shrouded moon and proclaimed: there is no such thing as love. Just the dreams of children. Those who think they have it, why, they have deceived themselves. They have created a story to hide their pain, they live a lie that will break so easy, so simple. Just the cracking of a butterfly's wings. So let it go.

She served in the house of Menelaus, having no alternative. No husband, no home. The men did not see her as sexual or desirable, and she did not see herself in that manner either. Instead, like the grey statue that erodes in the rain, she became an ornament, a thing seen so often as to become invisible. She was the perfect choice of woman to serve Helen when Menelaus dragged his queen back from Troy, for her very spirit seemed to subdue the fire of love and the ardour of all who met her, snuffing out their light with her dour and drooping countenance.

Yet I, lady of desire, know that to herself, and to the world indeed, Tryphosa lies. For though many creatures both living and dead have turned their faces to the cruel skies and proclaimed that love is a lie and they will have none of it, not their most potent declarations or deeply held beliefs can snuff out the longing of even the most deeply wounded heart.

You will love before your life is over, I breathe into her ear. *In the end, you will relinquish the pain that you have made your own.*

But for now, this woman stands on Ithaca, alone in her heart, and says: "I did not hear a commotion. My lady was asleep before any such business, and I too."

"What about Zosime? Did she seem . . . different to you?"

"She was agitated. It was her turn to lie at our lady's feet, but she requested I take the honour."

"Did she say why?"

"She did not."

"How long have you served the lady Helen?"

"Since she returned from her abduction in Troy."

The women of Sparta have all learned the word "abduction" in the last few years. It has been repeated to them slow and careful by soldiers and priests alike. It is a word that Tryphosa has said so many times it has almost lost meaning, words dissolving into sounds and sounds alone, into the strange shaping of her mouth, a pushing of lips, a movement of air. She thinks she might go mad if she has to say it too many times more. She thinks that perhaps it is a plague, this word, and that the more she says it, the more it will destroy her ability to say, to think, any other words at all, all language stripped away.

"And what are your duties? Besides, I mean, sleeping at the end of her bed."

"All that you might expect when one has the honour to serve a queen. All that I imagine your ladies do," – a little nod to Autonoe – "even on Ithaca."

Autonoe's lips twitch, but she says not a word.

"I imagine my cousin has many needs that must be fulfilled, after her terrible treatment … her *abduction*" – Penelope tries the word out for size in her mouth, also finds it disquieting, bitter – "by such a treacherous people. I am glad she has such good care from you."

Tryphosa nods. This is her duty. Her burden. She will carry it, since there is nothing better in her life to give it meaning, and a great many things that are worse. Is this all? Why then, she will return to her duties, she will …

"I see my cousin is often served wine and water from her own vessel," Penelope blurts, before Tryphosa can turn fully away. "Is this also part of your duty?"

"We tend to her physical welfare, as well as her needs. She enjoys a mixture of herbs and spices that enhance her youth, her god-given beauty, but that others of lesser divinity might find distasteful."

"What herbs, may I ask? Not that I could ever compare for

looks, but I do hope that one day my husband may return and find me not too physically grotesque."

"I could not say," replies Tryphosa primly. "They are prepared by the priests."

Now she is done – now she will depart. She gives a little bob of her head, turns away, but still Penelope has one last enquiry. "Did you like Zosime?"

The question stuns Tryphosa. It astonishes her. It appals her. It is faintly disgusting, uncouth. A queen asking not merely about a maid, but the sentiment of a maid? The affection one maid may have for another, the relationship between two women who are no better than slaves? Queens do not care for such things. It would be undignified, inconvenient for them to do so. It implies that the woman Penelope addresses has feelings. Feels hurt. Knows pain. Is indeed human. And Tryphosa has worked so hard, for so long, to be anything but human.

Yet in this moment, she lets go and allows herself to be, just for a moment, a woman of blood and heart and mind and soul that belong to no one but her. "No," she says. "I did not."

Then she is gone, returned again to her mistress's side.

CHAPTER 27

❯❯

P enelope finds Elektra praying at the foot of the waterfall
that drives itself into a hollow of earth between mossy
stones. She is guarded by her maid of Mycenae, Rhene; a
maid of Ithaca, Melitta; and no fewer than five women of
Sparta who have been sent to "help" the princess in her
hour of woe.

As the queen of Ithaca approaches, an owl flaps away from
the tallest branch of a hanging tree, a beating of white feathers
against the afternoon sun. I blow a gentle kiss after Athena's
flight, but as I do, I catch again the distant whiff of the three
taloned ladies who sit on the palace walls, bloodied teeth and
rotten mouths as they leer over the room of slumbering Orestes,
and turn quickly away.

The command of a Mycenaean princess could not dismiss the
Spartan maids. The presence of an Ithacan queen is just about
enough to force them into a slight retreat, enough perhaps that
the two royal women may consort in low voices at the water's
edge, their words drowned out by the rushing stream.

"Elektra," murmurs Penelope, as she sits herself on the bank
beside her cousin, "may I join you in your prayers?"

Elektra nods once, and together they kneel, their backs turned to all, heads bowed, silent a while in the polite performance of piety until at last Elektra hisses: "How did you do it?"

"Do what?"

"The maid. Nicostratus. How did you make it appear he killed her?"

"Elektra . . . I didn't."

"But then . . . I assumed it was you! Buying us time on this island, I thought . . ." Elektra's voice recedes from a gasp, curling back in on itself as things she believed are now being challenged.

"Cousin," murmurs Penelope, "I had rather thought this crime might have something to do with you."

Elektra snorts, shakes her head. "I would happily have killed Nicostratus, killed anyone I needed to prevent Menelaus putting my brother on his ship, but I could not think how. I am watched constantly – even my maids are watched." She nods her head a little to one side, to where Rhene sits in a charming composition with the Spartan women, chatting as if she had not a care in the world, as if there were not five of them to one of her, as if they did not all carry blades hidden within their gowns. "Are you saying Nicostratus was actually such a fool as to kill one of his own household in your palace?"

"I don't know. Perhaps. Everyone I have spoken to thus far in this matter seems to have slept remarkably soundly during the key event. I don't suppose you were sleeping too?"

"I have not slept well for a very long time," Elektra replies. "And if I do sleep, I have . . . " She stops herself. Anyone may speak of disturbing dreams, though it is generally best to choose in advance the imagery that one wishes to convey when doing so, just to make it clear that the doubtless prophetic ideas that have been planted in slumber are of service to a broader, preferably theological and political cause. But these dreams of Elektra's, these visions that haunt her nights – *Mother, Mother,*

255

Mother! – she thinks she has seen the Furies, she thinks she hears their claws crushing dead men's skulls – *Mother, Mother, Mother!* they cry – and when she wakes, she cannot say what torments racked her, but she knows that she dreads to sleep again.

"While I am sorry for it," Penelope breathes, "it is novel to speak to someone who was perhaps awake. Did you hear anything? Did you hear Zosime cry? The room is very near your own."

A shaking of her head. "I heard nothing. All seemed quiet."

"Nothing at all? And you did not leave your room, were not disturbed?"

"No. Rhene slept in my quarters that night. It was her or accept a Spartan slut at the end of my bed – for my protection and peace of mind, my uncle says. He is monstrous."

Elektra, daughter of Agamemnon, killer of babes, has very strong opinions on who and what may be considered a monstrosity, and once she has reached said opinion will hold it dear. She did not think she would reach this conclusion about Menelaus, is not sure when precisely it became so profoundly held, but now, having it, will never, ever let it go. Another thought strikes her, a thing far more urgent than murder and blood. She grabs Penelope's wrist, no longer feigning prayers. "Have you seen him? Have you seen my brother?"

"I have not been permitted close to him."

"He's in your palace, your guest!"

"Guarded by Spartans, who insist that it is best he be allowed to rest. My women who brought water say that he has been given something by Kleitos to make him sleep, and he does not stir."

"Kleitos," scowls Elektra. "He is meant to be a friend to my family, but increasingly I fear he has thrown his lot in with Menelaus. They do that, these men. They will betray my brother – the true king – in the name of their own greed and cowardice, as if honour was just a dream. As if to be a man was just some selfish ideal sung about by the poets. It was foolish to expect anything more from them. Even Mother knew that." This is perhaps the single nicest thing Elektra has said about her mother in over ten years. Penelope notices it, and is amazed. Elektra does not. Elektra has far too much on her mind to be bothered with redemption. Now the princess turns to the queen, face urgent and pale. "Menelaus cannot take my brother off Ithaca. Whatever happens. If Orestes goes to Sparta, he will not leave it alive, and I will be . . . I will kill myself before I let that be my fate, do you understand? Swear to me you will fight. Swear to me, as we are blood, like you are my . . . I will not be some plaything for my uncle!"

Penelope disentangles her arm carefully from Elektra's grip, tries to smile, cannot. "My husband swore an oath to go to the ends of the world for the husband of Helen, and as a result, I have lived these twenty years without him. I will not swear any oaths, Elektra. Not to you, nor anyone else. But for what it's worth, I am as desirous as you to see Orestes, rather than his uncle, on the throne of Mycenae. For my island, and for my people, I will do whatever I safely can to protect him. But I will not make an oath."

Elektra deflates, but is not entirely displeased. She too grows suspicious of the vows of great men and worthy kings. Necessity seems to her increasingly more important than a nice bit of valorous honour vowed by bloody altar stone.

They return to their prayers. Neither is praying. Hera would be annoyed at not being invoked; Athena would understand but be quietly a little miffed. I ruffle Elektra's hair, smooth down a corner of Penelope's gown, wait.

I do not have to wait long. Penelope is too busy for patience at this time. "You argued with Pylades."

Elektra draws in a little breath, catches herself, exhales. "Of course. Of course your women were watching."

257

"Will you tell me why?"

"No. I will not."

Penelope nods; so be it. She will not press the point further with one she respects. "Menelaus has given me three days to show that Nicostratus did not kill Zosime. He will want me to accuse one of your Mycenaean men, no doubt. Pylades or Iason would be most convenient, though I could perhaps take the opportunity to accuse a suitor and have him removed from the palace. However tempting it is to have Menelaus kill Antinous or Eurymachus, once he was gone I would have to live with the consequences."

"So you are looking for someone politically distant from you to take the blame? Pylades would be your safest choice, of course. Most likely to win Menelaus's favour."

"Quite. Which is why I wonder – do you trust him?"

Elektra considers this. "Yes. He would die for my brother."

"What of the others? Your maids? Rhene ... "

"She was given to me when we were both young. Her father died in the silver mines; her mother sullied herself for bread. We played together in the palace when Daddy was still alive. She owes my family everything."

Penelope nods. "My women will send word. Be ready."

Elektra does not rouse from her prayers as the Ithacan queen rises, but stays at the water's edge, hands clasped, mind flying everywhere and nowhere all at once.

CHAPTER 28

>>

It is Laertes who finally brings an end to the torment of the suitors.

"What's this then?" he barks, swaggering into the sunset hall of men. Several have fallen; many more have pissed their pants. The stench has drawn in flies, the heat makes the air shimmer, a rank odour of perspiring humanity.

Menelaus sits on Odysseus's throne, one leg slung across the side, drinking wine and chewing bones. He has smelled worse, seen worse, spent hours, no, days at a time huddled in the sand next to the bloating corpse of his slaughtered brethren. This? This is nothing. For a real man, this is just an easy afternoon of hearty training.

Laertes is far older than Menelaus, was nowhere near Troy when the battle raged – but he was an Argonaut and a king. He has also smelled the rank decay of flesh, seen the light fade from behind the eyes of men. So with an easy lollop, as casual a disregard for the ranks of stinking manhood in his hall as if he were passing through the sheep market but only looking to trade for cows, he swings into the room.

"Mind if I join you?" he asks, and before Menelaus can answer, a chair is brought and popped down right next to the

Spartan, and with a flop and a groan of old bones, Laertes is in it, gesturing to the nearest maid for wine, wine – yes, I'll have what he's having, thank you, smart about it too, and whatever he's eating will be just fine for me, ta.

Menelaus smiles benignly upon the old man, but there is that in the corner of his eye that is darkened by the Ithacan king's presence. Laertes is brought a platter of meat, cracks a bone, sucks out the marrow, gazes down upon the swaying mass of men. "Suitors," he tuts at last. "Disgusting boy-children, the lot of them."

"Couldn't agree more," grumbles Menelaus. "Shocking what these islands have come to, if you'll pardon me saying, with your son and lovely grandson gone."

"Well, you leave a woman to run things . . . "

Menelaus tips his cup to this sentiment – what else is there to say really? Not her fault, expected a bit too much really, but so it goes, so it goes.

"So what's the plan?" asks Laertes, eyeing up the hall once again. "Wait for one of them to step forward and go 'it was me, I killed that girl in your son's room, please execute me before you cut off my nethers and feed them to the dogs'?"

"Good point," Menelaus concedes, and raising his voice to the room bellows: "If whoever did it comes forward now, I'll execute you *before* I cut off your nethers and feed them to the dogs!" Then quieter, another smile for the Ithacan, "Such thoughtful advice."

Laertes acknowledges the compliment with a polite leer. Above, the Furies are slumbering as Orestes does, snoring in great snuffles of flared red nostril and acidic spit that drips off their curling lips and hisses where it strikes the scarred roof on which they sit.

"Of course, problem is," muses Laertes, "this lot are all such a bunch of back-stabbing bastards that what will happen first is that they'll accuse each other. Antinous will realise that his safest way to survive is by calling Eurymachus out, then Eurymachus will have to accuse Antinous, and everyone who's thrown their lot in will start defending their idiot boy, and then someone else will decide that it's best to try and rally round and accuse someone everyone can dislike, like Amphinomous perhaps, but he'll have favour from another party who will swear that they saw him upon such a time in such a place, and even if they can agree on who to accuse, there's a danger that others will come forward and swear sacred oaths to challenge the claim of these cowardly, miserable, despicable men, and then what a mess that will be. Even my chaste daughter-in-law's oath will suddenly be doubtful if she swears that one of the men who has pursued her is guilty of this crime, because of course people will say she has something to gain from it, that she's tipping her hand rather than following the course of sacred justice. And if you can get a Mycenaean to confess to it, I mean that would be very useful for her, save her a great deal of internal strife, but in such a manner as this? People would worry that it was not true, they would say, what if he was bullied to it? Or worse – what if a Mycenaean did something heroic, stepped forward and attested to the crime in order to save the lives of his fellow men? That would only cast *more* doubt on Nicostratus, not less, make it seem like his daddy was coming to save him by forcing noble, worthy men to take the blame for his travesties. It's so difficult having famous sons, isn't it? That's why I always did my best to let Odysseus get on with it, make his own mistakes. Only way these boys will ever have a chance in life, get out from Papa's shadow. Gracious, this wine is good. Is it your own grape?"

Menelaus does not answer.

Laertes cracks another bone. The sound of his slurping is wet, prolonged, sticky, intense. Marrow drips down his chin. He wipes it away with the back of his hand, tosses the bone onto the floor. "Well," he muses at last, "good luck with it."

He slouches from the room.

After a while, Menelaus follows.

He doesn't say anything as he does, not "stay there" or "you can go". He just stands and leaves, as if he's remembered something more interesting he has to do.

The suitors remain.

The shadow of the day creeps across the floor, and they do not move.

Do not move.

Menelaus does not return, but they do not move.

I glance around to see if any other gods are watching this. Despite myself, I am admiring, awed even, of the power that Menelaus's absence still holds, but divine admiration so often turns to divine jealousy, and the last thing anyone needs at this time is another jealous deity getting riled on Ithaca.

Overhead, the Furies nestle their heads together, preen happily in a half-slumbering state. They can smell the stink of this room, dine joyfully on the waft of suitors' fear as it rises to them, coo to each other in satisfaction at the gentle aroma of humiliation, torment, despair. No other creature either profane or celestial gazes down, so I lean over to Pylades and whisper in his ear: *Be brave, my beautiful one.*

Pylades shudders, head to toe, as if he has walked through cobwebs. Then he takes a step. This motion is powerful, something akin to magic, for the whole room on seeing one move seems to unclench, to groan, to cry out in relief and ecstasy, the great hold the Spartan king had upon them shattered in this simple action. Pylades looks to his fellow Mycenaeans, to Iason and the few men of Orestes' house. He has nothing to say. There is nothing to say here that is not grief, pricked out in thin lines at the bottom of their eyes, and so he too, like the king who will conquer him, turns away.

The suitors, as they regain their senses, are far more verbal.

They start to cry treachery, horror, dishonour, vengeance, cursed spite! The smarter among them begin to fling accusations at each other – where were you last night, Antinous, where you, Amphinomous? I saw this one creeping upon the stair, I saw him afoot with murderous intent, Eurymachus has this nasty look in the corner of his eye and said he dreamed of vultures!

I didn't, whines Eurymachus. I *didn't*!

The whole thing is about to break into full-blown punching, faction against faction, when the maids enter. They bring water, fresh cloths to daub the brows of the men, cups to drink from. They ease one group apart from another, coax them into the light, listen appreciatively to the cries of outrage and say, "Oh no, how terrible, that must be awful for you!" and sometimes manage not to laugh as they do so.

Autonoe oversees the whole affair, before sending word to Penelope.

"The suitors are dispersed," says the maid dispatched to Penelope's room.

"Good," she replies. "Now we just have to settle their fathers."

CHAPTER 29

>>

At sunset, Orestes wakes.

He lies sweating in his bed, screaming: *Mother, Mother, Mother!*

Kleitos, the priest of Apollo, is sent for.

"Well yes, yes," he sighs. "We can keep feeding him the poppy juice, but I fear he will never regain his senses."

"Boy's lost his mind as it is!" tuts Menelaus. "If it's a choice between a loud madman and a quiet madman, I know which I'd choose!"

Overhead, the Furies have stirred as Orestes does too, and now they swoop around the palace hooting and hollering in their delight. Maggots crawl from fresh meat, water turns sour, bugs writhe in clean pallets of straw, woodworms nibble at the supporting pillars of the palace, bread burns in the oven, and one of Penelope's finest ewes drops dead, flies in its eyes.

"Mother, Mother!" wails Orestes, and "Mother, Mother!" cackle the Furies overhead. For one who can hear both at the same time, it is really a rather insufferable din.

Elektra clasps Menelaus's arm, tears in her eyes, desperation on her face. "Please, uncle," she is about to beg – Elektra, daughter of Agamemnon and Clytemnestra, is about to beg! Menelaus

264

sees it, manages to just about restrain himself from licking his lips. She catches herself before she can kneel, droop, fade away, and instead with eyes downcast half whispers, "Please – let me tend to my brother."

"Well," grumbles Menelaus at last, taking his time on his conclusion, "if you can keep him calm, I suppose there's no harm to it."

Elektra scurries forward to the side of her brother's bed, soothes his brow, dabs sweat from his neck with a damp cloth. She whispers, "I am here, I am here," and if there were not men in the room, she would sing to him the old songs, the songs their mother sang in secret before she was no longer their mother. She calls for a clean tunic, she strokes his hair back from his skull with her little comb of polished shell. He seems to see her for a while, grasps her hand, gazes into her, through her, whispers: "Forgive me."

She says that there is nothing to forgive, but is lying and he knows it.

Above, the Furies laugh and spin. Tiles fall from the roof, nearly braining Autonoe as she scurries about her affairs. Black clouds spin on the horizon, a chill wind billows in from the north. There will be rain and thunder again tonight, the land will shake with it. Shepherdesses hurry their herds to shelter; shutters are closed against the night, and in the dark, Eos, Phiobe and Melantho approach the palace gates dragging with them a cart of stinking effluence.

"Stop!" bark the Spartan guards who hold the keys to what should be these women's kingdom. "No one in or out!"

"Our cargo ..." Eos replies, lifting a lid on a barrel to unleash the stench of bowel.

The men recoil. "Are there not pits in the palace?"

"There are, but alas, with so many noble guests, it is quite overwhelmed. So we must take these barrels far from here, before their pestilence corrupts the air."

265

The Spartans hesitate.

They are, of course, not meant to let anyone leave, let alone the tricksy women of tricksy Penelope. Menelaus was quite clear about that. On the other hand, no one likes sleeping next to sewage, and these are quite literally shit-covered women of no merit or station, and so . . .

What's the harm? I breathe in their captain's ear. *What's the good of stopping them?*

"Back before the moon is at its height," barks the soldier in bronze, "or we will raise the alarm."

"Of course," replies Eos, as the gates open before her and the women step out into the tossing, turning dark.

There is no feast that night.

A wall-smashing, sea-bursting storm, a rage of foam and wind and rain and sky that makes old Poseidon a little bit jealous, that even Zeus himself shakes his head at. But they do not interfere – will not interfere tonight. When the Furies make their feelings known, even the gods turn away.

The shutters bang and snap against the walls of Penelope's room, but she hardly looks up, barely seems to care. Instead, busy still, she pulls a shawl about her shoulders, bundles her hair into the same sensible style she wears when holding the sheep for shearing, and marches through the palace to the doors of men.

This should be scandal, but everywhere is watched by Spartans, and she is guarded by Autonoe, so with such eyes upon her, she knocks without hesitation or shame.

The first door she knocks on opens barely a crack, an eye pressed to it.

It is Kleitos, the priest of Apollo.

I have very little time for priests of Apollo. Snotty, the lot of them, and their whole prophetic nonsense is an absolute racket that is barely one time in a hundred, one in a thousand, the direct result of divine inspiration. Kleitos, a goat beard on a rabbit face, does not improve my opinion of the bunch.

"My lady," he blurts, surprised perhaps to see the queen of Ithaca.

"Kleitos. You are treating our great king Orestes, yes? May I come in?"

The crack in the door does not widen. "I am currently at my prayers."

"Of course. But I am sure the gods would understand, given the extremity of the situation."

"I am about certain rituals that are . . . not for females. Forgive me, your majesty."

Penelope's eyebrow arches, but she smiles, nods, practically gives a maid-like bob. "Of course. I will return later."

He closes the door, and the lady of the house turns away.

"Rituals?" mutters Autonoe in her ear, as they move down the gloomy passage, the wind pushing against the walls with bulging fury outside.

"Search his quarters the moment he is not there," replies Penelope briskly.

The next door is answered by Iason, he of the lovely neck and really rather dishy arms. At his back stirs Pylades – Penelope sees a hint of blade being sharpened. Again she raises an eyebrow, but says nothing more as she steps into the room. "Pylades, Iason. I trust you are both well."

Iason grunts, unable to give the lie that good manners would clearly require. Pylades stands, and having already been seen with a weapon, makes no effort to hide it now. "We have not been allowed to see our king," he barks. "Why can we not see Orestes?"

Penelope glances over her shoulder to where the Spartan guard stands, just outside their conference. Autonoe smiles, nods, heads to his side, propping herself in the door frame.

"Hello, handsome," she says to the soldier. "Don't you have lovely arms?"

I paraphrase, but the essence of the speech is there.

The soldier tries ignoring Autonoe, but the effort doesn't last long. Everyone knows the maids of Ithaca are as sneaky as their mistress; but everyone also knows that beneath their crude, rustic manners are naïve creatures of a lonely land just yearning for a bit of cultivated, manly ecstasy.

"Now you mention it," he concedes, "my arms are looking especially nice tonight."

Conversation thus flowing freely without, Penelope turns her attention back to Pylades within. "One question, and one question only: what did you argue with Elektra about?"

Pylades freezes. Iason is confused. Pylades shakes his head.

"My island is conquered, your king is poisoned and captive. To save my kingdom I will not hesitate to do what Menelaus wants and accuse you of murdering Zosime. To save my kingdom. So I ask you again: what did you and Elektra argue about?"

Still no answer.

"Pylades, whoever is poisoning Orestes reached him in Mycenae. You were poisoned in your own city – something that I must admit only casts more suspicion on you. Orestes was poisoned on the road. On his ship. And now in my palace. There are very few people who have that kind of reach. This is the last time I will ask."

Pylades looks to Iason. Iason looks away.

"Well then," Penelope concludes. "I see I have no real reason to protect you."

She walks away, and no one tries to stop her.

Thunder rolls across the sea, lightning cracks, the Furies howl in their merriment.

Menelaus sticks his hand out of the window to feel the rain

upon his skin. This hand – this hand – people cannot imagine the things this hand has done. He still feels the sand before Troy on his skin. He remembers the flow of blood through the dips and rivers of his fingers. He has held the most beautiful woman in the world by her neck, he has crushed a baby's skull with just the strength of his digits, grasped a crown of gold. The things he has done, the things he has seen, touched, clutched at – and now look at it. The ends of his fingers grow clubbed and tender, the back of his hand rises and falls in ridges of wriggling blood and skin, and the rainwater as it washes over him is not so cold as his slowly chilling flesh.

He is growing old, this great man of Troy. Others do not say it, hardly dare see it, but he was never the fool. He knew the lesser kings spoke of him behind his back, mocked him, the husband of a faithless wife, the fool who could not keep control of a woman – of a girl! Now he feels the years tugging at him, pulling at his heart, and when he is gone, who will be left?

Menelaus does not like his children. He barely knows them, and absence has given him a cruel clarity about their many, many failings. If anything, the only one he considers even remotely blessed with a bit of spunk is Hermione, his daughter. At least she screamed and cursed and went for him with her nails when he said she was to marry Achilles' son. At least she took the beating without flinching or saying sorry when he smacked it out of her. His sons – he sighs to think of it – his sons crumble and grovel and beg the moment he raises his fist to them, as if that will make him stop. As if that will make him love them.

The palace shivers in the storm.

This time when Penelope knocks on the door of the priest Kleitos, her polite rap is drowned out by the thunder, so she tries again. Kleitos opens it all the way, the smell of thick incense like burned amber wafting out as he does, smiles, says: "Ah, you came back."

Penelope blinks past him into the gloom of his room. There is but one square window, set high and off to the side, a remnant of a previous attempt to build walls in this palace that then fell, or were moved, or were put in the wrong place to begin with, until there was no definition or order left to the place. Outside, the rain runs sideways, blazes a brief, eyelid-bursting white as lightning bursts across the sea. A single oil lamp is barely a flicker of light against the squall, burning amid a table of herbs and ointments, salves and scents that would make Anaitis gape.

"Of course," Penelope murmurs, looking past Kleitos to his medicines. "I was wondering if there is anything you lack? Anything that would aid you in your tending to our noble king?"

He bobs, he smiles, he is all ingratiation and good manners after his previous rebuffing. "You are such a thoughtful hostess, thank you. But I came well supplied with all manner of precious goods that I doubt grow about your island. I will see that Orestes has the best of care."

"There is a priestess of Artemis hereabouts who has some skill with medicinal herbs – perhaps she might be of use to you?"

"That is very generous, of course," replies the priest, voice moving like water down a familiar, well-polished path of stone. "But I doubt a lady of the hunt has the expertise that my vocation brings."

Penelope's smile is little white teeth in a thin pale mouth. "I'm sure you're right. Well then. If as you say you have everything, I will leave you to your devotions."

This time, Kleitos waits politely for Penelope to walk several steps away before closing the door.

*

The moon is not quite at its highest point when Eos and the accompanying maids return to the palace. They are soaked to the skin, shivering and blue-lipped from their ventures. The Spartans inspect the cart they haul, the barrels they carry – stinking still but empty at least of their foul contents.

They do not question the maids, nor inspect every cask. One sniff of that is quite enough, thank you.

"Goodnight, noble gentlemen," Eos says as they are let through the gates. "Goodnight."

CHAPTER 30

A fter the storm, dawn brings with it the smell of life.
I find Artemis sitting on the steps of her temple, sheltered by groves of trees. She is putting a new string in her
bow. Her bare toes curl into the soil, the muscles down her
back ripple, there is a single cracked shard of leaf in her storm-
soaked hair. She has been running wild and free through the
thunder and the rain, not caring if gods or Furies summoned
the tempest. I wonder how her skin feels to touch – which parts
are still burning hot from her excursions, which frozen by the
night. It would be a scintillating pleasure to find out, but alas,
Artemis is not interested, and I do not ask people who are not
interested, even when their nipples are quite so firm and their
fingers quite so dextrous.

"Sister," I say, staying a polite distance from the steps of her
holy ground.

"Hello," she replies. "I am stringing my bow."

"I can see that, and how very taut and long it is."

"There will be blood. It will be tonight."

"You are certain?"

Artemis does not grace me with a reply, but twists her face
into a curl of astonishment – disbelief even – that I or any

other fool living cannot smell the prospect of blood about to be spilled. Athena would never disfigure her features with anything so animated; the goddess of wisdom's contempt is ice and disdain, rather than the expressive bafflement of Cousin Artemis at the sheer blunder-headed ways of her kin. I sigh, step a little nearer, and when she does not bare her teeth at me like a bloody wolf for my intrusion, say: "I had heard you were sometimes about in these parts."

She gestures loosely towards the forest. "Women armed with bow and blade protect the island. They murder men who come here meaning harm, hunt them like deer through the night, kill them with a single blow, an arrow through the throat. It's really good stuff."

"And the matters of . . . policy? Of kings and queens?"

She blinks at me, momentarily confused, then shakes her head, clearing it of strange notions. "The women hunt any who threaten them, and I hunt with the women."

She has not thus far refused my presence, so I ease myself down onto the step below her – this is after all her sacred space, not mine. She doesn't seem to notice or care. I flick a beetle off the top of her foot, and when she does not immediately lash out in indignation, I breathe: "And what about the Furies that circle Penelope's house?"

"They are here for the boy who killed his mother," she replies briskly. "The mother was beloved of Hera. She cared about the politics stuff too."

"Do you think you risk angering them if you help the women in their fight?"

"The Furies don't care for anyone except Orestes. They do their thing, I do mine. They are old, creatures of the earth. They are simple in their desires. I respect that."

She tests the string in the bow, sights at an imaginary target, muscles moving in her arm, her back, her neck, effortless control. I lick my lips, turn away, contemplate the scudding morning sky. "Well then. Tonight you say there will be blood? I will take your word on it." I rise, make to leave.

"Do the others know you're here?" she asks. "On Ithaca, I mean? Zeus grew jealous when he found out Hera was interfering, and now she's stuck on Olympus pretending she likes dinner parties for the family. Do they know you're here?"

"Athena does; I'm sure some do," I reply at last. "But everyone knows I'm too vain and silly to be a problem. Just sending Penelope gorgeous dreams of other men, no doubt. Nothing quite like the ecstasy of a passionate woman who finally, after too long yearning, not even pleasuring herself, lets herself go."

I may as well be speaking the language of the great southern tribes as explaining matters of forbidden longing to Artemis; so says the wide blinking of her eyes. I smile patiently, resist the urge to pat her on her bare, rolling shoulder, murmur: "Well then, well . . . "

"I saw that Spartan woman's here." Artemis does not know how to hide her questions with a smile. She thinks, then she speaks, eyes fixed on some other place, feigning disinterest. Athena would be appalled at her lack of nuance, but I find the whole effect somewhat liberating. "Helen. Her. I just assumed you were here for her, because she's vain and silly too. Funny how they blame the silly ones for all the things the strong ones do."

I smile benignly upon my divine cousin, resist the urge to give her a squeeze on her really rather magnificent right arm, and in the shape of a dove take once more to the skies.

Athena is not at her temple, but rather standing upon the cliff, looking out to sea, her brow furrowed as if her gaze were cast far off, to some place beyond the horizon.

"Athena," I say, landing with a soft sigh by her side.

"Aphrodite."

"You are looking to . . . oh. How charming."

I follow her gaze, far across the water, far across foam and rock and hidden depth of lurking creature and spinning storm in distant sky. I hear the nymph's cries, her sensual delight mingled with bitter tears as for the last time, indeed the very last time, she lies with her lover on their feather bed. Odysseus has not been a tender lover to Calypso for far too long, but today he honours her body, her pleasure, her needs as if they were meeting for the first time, learning the mysteries of each other's sex for the first time, holding her close when they are done so she can wrap her slim, dark arms tight about his shoulders, before at last he rises and heads towards the sea.

Then she stands silent upon the beach, tears on her cheeks and no words more upon her lips, as Odysseus pushes his raft into the water.

"So it's done, is it?" I ask. "Odysseus will come home?"

"Not done," replies Athena, turning her gaze at last back to these nearer seas. "Poseidon will find out soon enough, and he will raise a storm against him. But he will not defy Zeus – the storm will batter but not kill Odysseus. He will be shipwrecked one more time, and I will go to him and guide him through the very last of his travels, until he returns to Ithaca."

"Just in time to find it burned to the ground, Menelaus king and Orestes dribbling in a buried room in Sparta, no doubt."

"Indeed. Just in time for that."

"I saw Artemis stringing her bow."

"She does so love a hunt."

"I take it Penelope will make her move tonight?"

"She has to. There is no time left to delay."

"And will you help her, when the moment comes?"

"I must watch Odysseus," she replies, the frown deepening.

"I must see that he is safe, and bring his son back too. Telemachus must not be far when his father finally returns. It would not be . . . poetic." She shifts a little, back straight as her spear, eyes anywhere but on mine. "At Troy, we were on opposite sides. You even took to the battlefield to defend your precious pets – I did not see that coming, and I can predict almost anything. My gift is not prophecy, as Apollo's is, but I can judge, and do not like it when my judgements are wrong. The goddess of desire, on the field with a blade. Remarkable. Unpredictable."

"What is love if it does not fight for love?"

Her lips curl; there is that in this sentiment that she finds too trite to tolerate, and yet also nothing in it she can refute. "I have been forced to consider that my paradigms are . . . flawed. We women of sky and fire, we goddesses, we are so mighty, and yet if we learn anything from old mother Hera, it is that the brighter we blaze, the more the men line up to make us fall. Our power will be suppressed, subdued, and we will be turned from creatures of immortal majesty to cowering wives and simpering whores, adjuncts merely to a story told by a man. A story about a man. The poets will tell Odysseus's story for millennia, and when they do, they will speak *my* name. *I* will be his guardian protector. *I* will be the one who brings him back to his love. Men will pay homage to me. But even here I must still be secondary. It is . . . the victory that I can win. Sometimes in war that is the only victory you can have."

A little sigh, a little tilt of her head, like the owl that is her creature, still watching the horizon. "I have been observing Helen. I have been observing you. I begin to see that perhaps there is some small protection in being the fool. The giggling girl who understands nothing and thinks only of carnal pleasure or temporary satisfaction. That being the fool is in fact . . . wise. Safe. An intelligent, capable, living human – such we may hold accountable for their actions. But a simpering girl?" She closes her eyes, squeezing them tight; she is struggling to comprehend this, to accept it, to believe it, and yet the evidence, the hard evidence ... goodness, it is something when a goddess of wisdom is having a hard time with a simple idea!

She shakes her head again, opens her eyes, steps from the cliff to walk upon the waiting air, turning her body as she goes so she does not have to look at me, head down, her light gathered tight about her, hidden from the gaze of Olympus. "I know you watch over Helen. I think perhaps you will watch over Penelope too." Then a thought – a question that no one but I can answer. She is fine with that; she considers the domain of these things to be so trivial, it does not bother her that it is beyond her reach. "Does Penelope love Odysseus?"

I take my time answering, savouring the experience of her ignorance and my insight. "Will your poets care what the answer is?"

She considers only briefly. "No. Not at all. It is necessary that she loves him, and that is what the story will say. But I find myself ... curious as to the woman's heart."

"So does she, sister. So does she."

At last Athena looks at me.

So few of the gods look upon me, and fewer still of the goddesses. But she does now, and she smiles, and salutes me with a short raise of her spear, before she takes flight into the sky in a beating of feathered wings.

In the palace, the Spartans watch, the maids cook, Penelope prays.

Or rather, she kneels at a little private shrine, and when people ask to speak to her, Eos steps between and says: "My poor mistress is distraught with grief for her husband and her son, and prays for their swift return to save this house."

Menelaus sends Lefteris to interrupt those prayers, but the

maids whisper ahead of his coming, and so, as he marches towards the back of the kneeling queen, someone other than a maid intercepts him.

"Honoured guest," says Medon, inserting first his belly, then his chin, and finally his whole rounded self between the Spartan and his queen, "may we help you?"

Lefteris has killed many men, including the old and the unarmed. He looks Medon up and down and concludes that this one will be a bleeder – but he is a bleeder who in this house, at least, it would be politically unhelpful to slay. So he stops, looms over the man, rolls saliva round his mouth, flicks his bottom lip out between knowing teeth and says: "Menelaus, king of Sparta, wants to know if your queen has reached any conclusions on the murder of the maid Zosime, and reminds her that tomorrow morning he will sail."

"Naturally my queen has set her whole council of learned men to solving this terrible matter," Medon replies easily, "and now she prays. Her life has been hard, you see, without a husband for so long. She is easily overcome with weakness and devotion."

Lefteris's scowl does not know if it is a smile, a leer, a growl, and so sits somewhere between all of these. But he does not push the point, spins on his heel and storms away.

Medon waits for him to go, then kneels by his queen's side.

"Whatever you are going to do," he whispers, "you had better do it tonight."

"Have you seen my husband's revered father?" she replies, eyes still closed in her contemplations. "I realise I have been quite neglectful in my filial piety."

Her husband's revered father, Laertes, is in one of his favourite places in the palace – the pigsty. Gotta love a pig, he says. They're smart, they're capable, good-natured if you do right

278

by them, and they give excellent fat when slaughtered. He would have more on his farm, but oh no, oh wait, yes, now he remembers – his whole villa was burned to the ground by pirates, wasn't it? And though new walls rise above his freshly moulded home, he lost his favourite pig in the slaughter and it still hasn't been replaced. So now he inspects his son's pigs, and goodness they are nice, and maybe his daughter-in-law might consider sending that one his way sometime soon, no . . . ?

"Revered father," Penelope intones, as a Spartan leans against the doorpost, watching them, "you can of course have any pig you like."

Laertes turns from his inspection of the animals to scrutiny of the watching Spartan. "Oi," he barks. "You – piss off."

"I am to guard the lady Penelope," the soldier replies, without rising from his slouch or showing even the slightest interest in the royal command. "I am to keep her safe."

"I am Laertes, father of Odysseus, sometime king and hero of the *Argo*! You think she isn't safe with me?"

The Spartan just blinks at him and does not move. The old king grins, yellow teeth in glistening gums. "Course. Guarding a woman – she's grateful for that. She's grateful for your protection, for your master's protection. But me? Guarding a king? That's something else entirely. That's the kind of thing other kings get nervous about, start talking about, not right, they say, not right at all. I may not have gone to Troy, boy, but I was getting pissed with Nestor while you were just a fantasy in your mother's eye. I was shitting round the back of Theseus's palace and getting hammered with fucking centaurs while you were still a toothless little shit sucking on your mother's titty. You can guard a queen all day long – queens need some guarding. But don't think for an instant you can get away with guarding a king."

The Spartan hesitates, then stands a few paces further off. There is nowhere for Penelope and Laertes to go that isn't around the pigsty, of course, no harm in giving them that bit of space, but for now at least their voices will not be heard.

Laertes turns to his daughter-in-law. "All right," he hisses. "When do you run?"

Penelope steps round a sow, gown hitched carefully above the stinking ground, eyes averted, doesn't immediately answer. Laertes slaps his hands together, a crack loud enough to startle even the placid animals at their feet. "Come on, girl! You can't let Menelaus ship that idiot boy Orestes off to Sparta, and you can't delay any longer! Means you've got to get him and you out of the palace tonight – so spill."

Penelope glances again to the watching soldier, moves into the darkest, stinkiest corner of the pen, looks Laertes up and down. He stares back, and it occurs to her that her father-in-law has known her considerably longer than her husband ever did, and that once she'd done her duty by having a son, an heir to the kingdom, he stopped treating her like a wife and perhaps even started regarding her like a human being, albeit one he wasn't very interested in. Laertes is not interested in many humans. He finds them far more tedious than pigs. "Tonight," she says at last. "Preparations are under way."

"Saw your maids sneaking out last night with a cartful of shit," he muses, approval in his voice, a certain almost regal satisfaction in the straightness of his back. "Preparing that ship your Ourania keeps, yes? Sending word to your little army of women?" Penelope stiffens, but he at once waves her reaction away. "I may be old, but I'm not stupid! Pirates 'slaughtered by the arrows of Artemis', *please*. I've seen women prowling around with their 'hunting bows' and 'woodcutter axes', and yes, they chop down a tree when they need wood, but no one burns that much kindling. Can you do it? Can you get Orestes out?"

"I believe so. Orestes, Elektra, myself. But I need you to stay here."

"Of course you do," he replies, and there is a certain satisfaction in his voice, a certain glee to be plotting again, to be conspiring, reminds him of being young – those were the days. "You need someone to protect the ones you leave behind. Once you flee, Menelaus will torture your council, butcher your maids, unless good old Laertes is there to stop him. Course I gotta stay behind."

"Do you think you can? Stop him?"

"He's a bully, but he's not king of kings yet. He wants the rest of Greece to get in line, he'd better not start by murdering Odysseus's old man, no? I can keep him from torturing your women. Won't be able to keep him from killing you, though, if he catches you. It'll be 'Penelope the slut queen of Ithaca ran away to have a secret tryst with some man' and 'Penelope the whore had that maid murdered in Nicostratus's room to hide her terrible lustful secret' type thing. Won't be able to do nothing for you then, except maybe kill you faster than he will."

"Well, I'm sure I'll appreciate that, if it comes to it."

"You'll need a distraction if you're gonna get to that little escape boat of yours."

"There was a storm last night."

"And?"

"I have observed that after violent weather, the wind often blows out to sea. It is as if the land herself exhales all that was battered against her – have you noticed that?"

Laertes spits in a corner in reply – of course he has, he's a bloody king, doesn't she know? Then, a little more thoughtfully: "Did Nicostratus do it? Did he kill the girl?"

"Possibly," she replies, then corrects herself. "Probably not."

"Pity. Who did? One of ours? You'd better just blame a Mycenaean and be done with it either way."

"I'm not sure. Many people slept far more soundly than I feel they should have; as soundly as it seems Orestes himself does when the poppy juice is upon him. I have the beginning of an idea, but . . . there are more things I need to do." She bows respectfully to her father-in-law, turns, then stops. "Tonight. Stay close to Menelaus. Make sure he sees you always by his side."

"Where else should a king be?" Laertes replies, patting a pig casually on the backside as it passes by.

Later, Penelope walks round the flower garden that the honey-bees like to feed on, in pious contemplation. You can tell it's pious contemplation because she moves slowly, dangling her fingers in leaf and petal, eyes half closed, head angled in such a charming way as to catch the sun on one side of her face, enjoying perhaps the contrast between light and shadow, heat and cold.

Her Spartan watchers follow at a polite distance, and she does not mind.

She passes beneath the olive tree whose branches have woven themselves into the very wall of the house itself, outside the bedroom where she sleeps alone by moonlight. She drifts beneath the closed shutters of Orestes' room, hears the faint sobbing of Elektra from within, the louder prayers of Kleitos over the king's shuddering form. Thinks she hears something else too – talon and wing of bat, accompanied by the stench of decay and blood – but she turns and it is gone. She wanders beneath Elektra's room, hears nothing, beneath Helen's room, beneath the open shutters of the room where Zosime was slain. They are trying to blow away the smell of blood and death, but it has a way of lingering even when blasted by the salty breeze of the sea. Her fingers dally with the stems of a bush of fragrant herb that smells of autumn nights and sullen dreams, and as they play, she eases it back to see in a little hollow that dents the greenery a glimmer of broken clay.

She does not stop to pick up the broken oil lamp, nor remark on it, but merely continues in her wandering, as one lost to reverie.

A knocking on a door.

It is Penelope, knocking for her cousin Helen.

"Cousin," she calls. "May I enter?"

Helen's door is opened by Tryphosa. Tryphosa has not been given time to mourn Zosime. It has not occurred to anyone that she might need it. Mourning is for people of leisure, people who have time for important feelings. I brush her cheek with my fingers. Later she will weep, in the dark when no one is looking, and I will be there, holding her close in my arms.

But for now there are things to do and services to perform. Helen sits at her long table of unguents and ointments, adorning her cheek. "Who is it?" she shrills through Tryphosa's guarding shoulder in the door.

"It is Penelope, cousin. May I come in?"

"I'm not quite decent, actually!"

Helen is fully garbed, but she is not fully made up. One half of her face is smeared with white and pink, the brow painted into a solid charred line. The other half is the gently wrinkling skin of the almond, beautiful, fascinating, warm. I caress it, I kiss it. Age is coming upon Helen and she could be perhaps even more resplendent than when she was a young flower, growing into a body that belongs to her and her alone. But no – no. She conceals her skin, she paints over it, she will be a body for other people's viewings again, for men to fight over and kill for, an adjunct to another's story. I sigh and drift away.

Penelope still stands by the door, face to face with Tryphosa. She is not going anywhere.

Helen sighs, hastily applies the merest superficiality of make-up, the minimum required to be seen, and gestures Tryphosa to stand aside. "Yes, what?" she barks, and seeing the slight start in Penelope's face at the briskness of her tone, smiles, simpers and adds: "So sorry, I'm still terribly upset by this whole horrible thing with Zosime. Have you caught the monster who killed her?"

Penelope slips past Tryphosa, approaches her cousin at her table, eyes running over its heaving contents. The golden carafe of water and wine from which Helen alone seems to drink stands by her, an empty cup at its side. Helen's lips are stained crimson as she smiles. "You believe Nicostratus to be innocent, then?" Penelope enquires. "Though he was found with the body, covered in blood?"

"Dear Nico, I mean, lovely Nico, he's such a well-meaning boy! But he does have a terrible temper on him and his mother was, well, how can I say it . . . she had ideas above her station." Helen follows Penelope's gaze, flicks her wrist at Tryphosa, a stool, a chair, bring something for my cousin, quickly now! A stool is brought, Helen takes Penelope by the hand, eases her down beside her, the two women now sitting before Helen's remarkable, perfect mirror. Penelope catches a glimpse of her own reflection, looks away, but Helen studies her – not in her face, but in her reflection, an act that has the convenient advantage of letting Helen study her own face at the same time. "Lovely," she breathes at last. "Charming. I do envy you, you know – your authenticity." She brushes a stray lock from Penelope's brow, twirls it round her finger to make it curl a little more, lets it hang loose, doesn't like the effect, pushes it tenderly back behind Penelope's ear.

Penelope sits, hypnotised by her cousin's ministrations. Every day Eos helps her arrange her hair in some suitably comely yet sensible manner, but this is something else. A memory stirs – of being a child, a girl in Sparta, of Helen braiding her hair again and again, trying out fabulous knots and glorious weaves upon her scalp, of laughing, of being innocent and free for just a little, little while. Even as a child, Helen was told by all who saw her what a pretty thing she was, what a beautiful woman she would grow up to be. A prophecy uttered so many times must be fulfilled. No one told Helen that she would grow up to be royal, regal, wise, learned or revered, so it didn't really occur to her childlike mind that these might be aspirations to seek. The games of dressing-up and playing with hair became serious lessons, Penelope scolded if she moved, mocked for her plain garb, sallow complexion. But there was a moment, before the children became girls and the girls became wives, when Helen played with Penelope's hair as if they were family, gone as quickly as a summer's day.

"Zosime had Nicostratus's child – did you know that?" Helen exhales this secret as if she were pronouncing on the quality of a fig or the colours of a sunset. "She was really quite smitten with him. Charming, really – though of course she could never marry him, it would have been a terrible idea, she was quite below his station. Her father was furious when he found out, demanded that dear Nico 'did right' by his daughter. So my husband, being a good and loving man, kept Zosime at court even though she was, well, I mean, one doesn't want to use the word 'spoiled', but there it is, and put her into my service in the hope that he could find a good match for her somewhere. Someone who'd take her. Poor dear, she really was terribly unlucky. Terrible bad luck."

Helen parts a strand of hair from the mass on Penelope's head, pulls it this way and that, experimenting with some other look, seeing how this or that alignment of locks changes the shape of her cousin's face. Nothing seems quite satisfactory. It is possible that rustic authenticity is the only style that will really serve for the Ithacan queen. Penelope lets her play, allured, enticed, bewildered by the touch of fingers on her scalp, the furious contemplation being focused on her face. But no – no! It is really no good. Helen gives a puff of disappointment and lets Penelope's hair hang free, turning her face back to the mirror to continue her own ministrations, another layer of char, another layer of lead.

Penelope breaks from her reverie, from the memory of being a child, from the present of being seen as an object of even some potential beauty. She watches her cousin a moment in the mirror, then reaches past her for the golden cup. "May I have a . . ."

Helen's hand catches Penelope's, fast and hard. There is a look in her eye that is something of Athena's kind, nothing of my lovely demeanour, but it is as gone as soon as seen. She lets go, her fingers leaving white indents in Penelope's skin as the Ithacan pulls her hand away, and smiles. "So sorry, cousin," she titters, "but I have been taking my medicine. Let me call for a clean cup for you."

She turns to Tryphosa, but Penelope cuts her off before the command can be given. "No, not at all. Not at all. My apologies. I will trouble you no further, I just wanted to make sure you had everything you needed."

"We are very well supplied, thank you. You are, as they say, the perfect hostess."

"If you are sure. The wind can be cold at night, I can have them bring down the finest sheepskin for your bed – oh, do you need a fresh lamp? I do not see . . ."

"Tryphosa has me entirely cared for, thank you. She is so good for me."

Penelope rises, nods, glances at Tryphosa, sees nothing living, nothing that dares to be alive, in the old maid's face. "Well, cousin," she murmurs. "If you are sure, I will see you later."

"I will be praying to Hera," Helen replies primly. "The goddess of wives."

Penelope just about manages not to choke on her own phlegm at this fervent declaration, as she lets herself out of the room.

CHAPTER 31

›››

S o the sun sets across Ithaca.
It is time.

Even I am a little excited, a little giddy to see how this night's events will play out.

There is no feast served in the palace, no formal gathering of men, but there are still suitors, guards, soldiers, kings and maids to be fed, and so in the kitchen, steam, smoke, busy busy busy, bustle bustle bustle!

Lefteris, captain of the Spartans, prowls the wall. He does not look outwards for threats, but rather inwards, master of a prison, keeper of chains.

Nicostratus paces in the temple of Athena, and does not let the presence of divinity muffle his curses.

Orestes lies sleeping in his chamber, Elektra at his side. Kleitos prays. Pylades and Iason have not left their rooms. It is not considered wise to do so – the Spartans set to watch them have made that clear. Everyone, it seems, needs protecting, times being what they are.

Menelaus, Helen, Penelope and Laertes eat together in the great hall. It is quieter now that the suitors have had their mirth broken. A bard sings of Jason and the Argonauts, of the

Golden Fleece and lovely, wronged Medea. The song has been requested by Menelaus, a nod of respect to Laertes. Laertes' eyes glint in the firelight as he nods back. He knows the lies that this poet sings, but doesn't care. They are lies that have served him well, served his house, and if he were any less wise than he were, he doubtless would have taught himself to believe them to be true long before now.

"Well, Hecuba, you see, Hecuba had this theory that once you had given birth to enough boys, every mother needs to have a girl, that this is how you complete the set, you see, that every woman is incomplete until she's had a female . . . " Helen burbles away, drinks wine from a golden cup, and no one marks her.

"How are your . . . *investigations*, my dear?" enquires Menelaus through a mouthful of churning, gummy meat. "Do you have someone ready to accuse?"

"I have nearly concluded, brother," Penelope replies, picking at her plate. "I am certain that justice will be served to every-one's satisfaction."

"Your wise father-in-law pointed out that it might bring some problems for you if you accuse the wrong person," Menelaus muses, scraping a handful of gristle up between a fingerful of bread. "I just want you to know that anyone who gets in the way of your accusation, anyone who says anything to you, I've got you. I'm at your back."

"How kind, brother. You are always so understanding of a woman's needs."

Menelaus grins, and in his mind he's a young man reborn, he's vibrant and vigorous and can go all night, fuck yes, fuck, a fucking enemy, fucking his fucking enemy, that's just the thing, that's just the thing to prove he's still got it, she'll be quivering like a butterfly beneath him at the end, she'll be groaning with the ecstasy of being conquered, being enslaved to a man like him by the time he's done, just you wait and see.

He briefly wonders if anyone can see the physical signs of his arousal, but no, everyone is far too preoccupied avoiding each other's gaze. Not that he'd care if they did – it's the kind of virility that marks out a real man among men.

"By the way," he proclaims, and goodness, he's been waiting for this moment, fuck, it's so good it's a miracle he doesn't just grab her right fucking now and show her what he's all about, "my men went out hunting this morning – to do their part, of course, you understand, to ease some of the intolerable burden of our stay. They found a boat in a little cove near the palace, looked like an abandoned fishing boat of some kind, maybe something smugglers might use. Lovely little thing, be such a shame if it was lost – they've pulled it inland a bit to protect it from the sea, set a watch just in case its owner comes back. So trusting you rural folk are, just leaving things like that lying around."

"You are most considerate," Penelope intones. "I am sure whoever the boat belongs to will thank you."

"Just doing our bit to help however we can."

"Of course, brother. Of course."

Menelaus watches Penelope, and she does not sweat, or flinch, or show any reaction, and that just makes him harder for her than he was before.

Funny thing, speaking of boats . . .

"Fire, fire!"

The boy who is sent running up from the docks is a Spartan warrior in training. He has been beaten, kicked, cut, blasted with shame, chased by dogs, left to starve on the mountainside, and having survived all these things, he knows that enduring pain and suffering is what makes a man. To admit to distress is cowardly and weak, and so bare-footed he runs with burns on his back and ash in his throat to the palace gates, which are barred from within, to shout: "Fire, fire!"

Lefteris ceases his study of the innards of the palace long enough to turn and consider the outside of it, and there he does indeed behold a conflagration raging. Down at the docks, two of the Spartan ships moored in the harbour are already fully ablaze, and a third has begun to catch and billow. Across the quays people are rushing, running, scooping up seawater to hurl from pots, but it is already far too late for the first two ships, and all labours are being directed to soaking the third, smouldering vessel before it too catches alight. The glow stains the walls of the town red, bounces off the hard stone of the bay, makes the sea blaze like a crimson mirror – but the gentle breeze blows the sparks out towards the water, away from the land. I consider adding my soft breath to its passage, protecting the harbour further, but no. Why draw attention to a thing that is already going well?

Lefteris is a veteran of Troy. He remembers when the Trojans burned the Greek ships, that bloody night that nearly broke the army of Agamemnon, that left grown men weeping upon the scars of the sea. This is why his next judgement is perhaps a little rash, for with the memory of flame at his back and smoke in his eyes, he turns to his men and orders: "Open the gates, you fools! Get to the ships!"

The men obey, and this order is given even before word has reached the great hall where royalty sits – fire, fire!

At once Laertes rises, demands to know where, where, what is burning?

This is all very good and impressive, a nice bit of kingly concern from the old man, and it is big enough and loud enough that for a moment Menelaus does not stir. Fires happen, and he is far from home – he is sure it will not bother him too much.

Ships, comes the answer! There are ships ablaze in the harbour!

Now Menelaus rises, startled like an animal that suddenly realises it is being bled alive by the bugs that cling to it. "Fetch the men! Guard Orestes' door. You!" He stabs a finger to two of his guards. "Watch the queen!"

"I will accompany you to the docks," Laertes proclaims.

"I don't need some fucking old man!" Menelaus roars, and then at once tries to swallow back the words he has just screamed to Odysseus's father, mutters a half-apology. Laertes smiles, waves it aside, he's heard far worse, but if you think a bit of bad language is keeping him from sticking to Menelaus's side, you have another thing coming.

"I should come too," Penelope says, rising from her seat. "See to my husband's people."

"No!" snaps Menelaus. "Your father will see to Ithaca. You must stay safe, in the palace."

She sinks slowly back into her chair, nods once. Helen leans over and squeezes her hand. "I'm sure they'll be all right," she whispers. "My husband is so brave."

Penelope does not reply, as she watches Menelaus and Laertes bustle from the hall.

Chaos and motion, motion and chaos!

Spartans run from the palace towards the harbour – quick, fetch more buckets, use whatever you can find, your helmet will do! – to throw water upon the blazing vessels.

This does not mean all Spartans leave the palace. The women remain, and Lefteris is careful to ensure the proper protection of all within by keeping back some thirty fully armed men, just in case, as he says, the blaze should spread in a terrible and unexpected way towards the palace walls.

Menelaus storms down to the shore to direct the efforts, Laertes at his side. The old king is having a remarkably pleasant time of things, for every time Menelaus shouts, "You, fetch water!" Laertes will echo immediately, "More water!" Or if Menelaus should cry, "Don't waste your efforts there, help here!" Laertes will at once repeat the same command, but with a word or two out of place. The effect is to produce an ever-deepening frown on the Spartan king's face, and the increased pulsating of a fat vein in the side of his neck, but having shouted at Odysseus's father once, it would be profoundly uncouth to shout at him again, and so gleefully Laertes continues in his antics, savouring every second in the high heat of a Spartan flame.

The suitors flock to the gates of the palace, demanding to be let out and see – but no, no. They are shoved back, ordered to return to their rooms, to watch from windows there. Outrageous, they holler – unacceptable! These are the men who would be kings of Ithaca! Someone shoves someone else, someone else shoves back. No one is ready to actually draw weapons and fight – they might get a scratch if they do that, someone might be hurt, someone might literally die! But they rage and roar and curse the Spartans who keep them from their manly destinies, until at last the Spartans lower their spears and order them back. Pure insult! The greatest violation of the rules of hospitality that can be conceived! But then again, the Spartans' ships are blazing and Nicostratus is accused of murder and a maid is dead and Orestes is mad and all things considered ... maybe it is time for the suitors to cut these warriors a little slack, no?

Slowly the suitors retreat. What is noticeable about this whole affair, however, is the three suitors who are *not* present in the scuffle, the three who should in fact most likely be leading it. Where are Antinous, Eurymachus and Amphinomous?

Let us cast a divine, all-seeing eye through the palace – and there they are. They are waiting against the palace wall near the latrines, huddled without torchlight in the shadows, blinking in silent darkness. As they wait, Melantho slips from the darkness towards them, a coil of rope in her hand, a short, crude ladder used for climbing olive trees over her shoulder. These she gives to the suitors without a word, and at once they lay the ladder against the wall and start climbing. On the other side there is a steep drop to the edge of the cliff, but no – look again, for there is a ragged, thin little path, barely more than a foot-shuffling ledge against which these suitors may scurry, heading away from the palace and into the chittering dark of the Ithacan night.

Thus, by the reflected light of the fire in the bay, the first three escapees from the palace of Odysseus make good their exit into the dark.

Who next?

Penelope retires to her room. Two Spartan soldiers stand at her door. A Spartan maid is sent to attend to her.

"Absolutely not!" barks Eos. "We have our queen's well-being quite in hand, thank you."

She slams the door in the woman's face. A Spartan soldier pushes it back again. Eos's mouth falls open. "How dare you?!" she shrieks. "*How dare you?!*"

"For your lady's protection," he grunts in reply.

"Darlingest, what's happening?" trills a voice from down the hall. Helen sticks her head out of her door, sees the soldiers, the maids, approaches, concern and anxiety on her brow. "Dearest Penelope, is everything all right?"

"Quite all right, thank you," Penelope replies. "Your thoughtful husband sent this kind maid to attend to me, but as *my* maid was saying, I am quite well looked after."

"Oh *gosh*," Helen exclaims. "This won't do at all! Excuse me!" She barges past the Spartan maid in the door, glares at the guard, barks: "I am going to tend to my poor grieving cousin!" and slams the door in their faces.

They do not knock again. Helen presses her back to the door she has just closed against their watchful eyes, beams brightly and exclaims: "Well go on then, I assume you're going to escape now? Off you trot!"

Penelope's jaw drops.

It is not the most dignified of expressions, but at least she is not alone in her reaction, for Eos also stands agape, blinking uncomprehending at the Spartan queen. Helen tuts and flaps them towards the window. "Come come, now! Spartan ships don't just catch fire by themselves. Whatever you're planning is clearly happening tonight. Come along!"

Penelope gains a moment of composure, a glimmer of calm. "You seem . . . very sanguine about this, cousin."

"Well of course! It's all really rather thrilling, isn't it? When my husband said we were visiting Ithaca, I will not lie, I thought, how dull. How backwards and tedious and dull. But actually it's all been much more exciting ever since we got here! Now I'm not going to ask how you plan on sneaking Orestes and Elektra out past their guards, but I'm sure you've got a lovely plan for that too. Oh – but my husband was absolutely not bluffing about having found your little escape vessel, please do steer clear of it. I assume you have another way off the island? Of course you do. Always scheming with that clever little head of yours!"

Eos looks to Penelope. Penelope looks to Eos. Then with a shrug, Eos marches straight to the window and whistles down to Autonoe, who waits below with knotted rope that now she throws up to her fellow maid.

"What about you?" asks Penelope, as Eos starts to tie the rope to the olive tree bed. "The guards saw you come in here, they will know you helped us escape."

"Nonsense!" Helen replies. "I am drunk! I came in, I passed out, I snored in a light, fluty manner that is more charming than it is grotesque, I was stirred only by the shaking of whichever maid is sent to check on you in the morning. Observe!"

She flings herself like a giddy child onto Penelope's bed, closes

295

her eyes, and honest to goodness, starts to snore. It is not a light, lyrical snore. It is the snore of the wine-swilled drunkard, the profound snuffle of an alcoholic wretch. And as soon as it has begun, it has ended, and Helen sits bolt upright again, beaming with charming delight. Penelope still stands dumbfounded, so Helen flaps her towards the window. "Off you go then! Fly along! Don't get caught!"

"Cousin ... Helen ..." Penelope begins, but Helen cuts her off.

"Cousin," she declares, and there is not a whiff of wine about her, not a shimmer of delirium in her eye, not a simper of the child in her voice. Rather, for the briefest moment, there is a woman, beholding another, in a private place illuminated by reflected firelight. Penelope stops herself recoiling, and instead almost leans in, studying the sudden sobriety upon Helen's brow, the age about her downturned mouth. For a moment she is sure, she is certain, that when Menelaus slew the last of the Trojan princes, it was Helen who handed him the blade. "There is no time," Helen says. "Really – no time at all."

This final declaration made, she shuffles a little deeper into Penelope's bed, shrugs a sheepskin over herself against the cold night air, closes her eyes and lies as still and contented as the sweetly slumbering babe.

For a moment Penelope is too dumbstruck to speak, let alone move. Then Eos puts her hand gently on the queen's arm, and together they go to the window, grapple onto the rope that hangs from it, and let themselves out into the swirling shadows of the burning night.

There are two more critical people to extract from the palace of Odysseus, and they are not going out of a window.

Orestes lies curled against his sister's side, as Elektra strokes his brow, kisses his fingers, combs his hair. Her maid, Rhene, stands by with clean water and cloth. Kleitos prays in his room below. No fewer than five Spartans guard Orestes' door, the corridor that approaches his bed.

Penelope has considered many subtle schemes with which to distract these men, but they are the undistractables. Nothing is parting them from Orestes' side, and with great reluctance, she has been forced to accept this reality. This is why, on leaving her bedroom window, she does not head directly to the palace walls. Instead she slips, unseen at last by any but her maids and the gods, free to move without hindrance in her own home, to the deep part of the palace where just one Spartan guards just one door.

This man Autonoe now approaches, bringing water, wine, a few scraps left over from the feast.

He takes them without question, waits for Autonoe to be gone before taking a sip, a nibble. He does not need much to sustain him – he is a warrior of Sparta, one of the greatest military men in the world! It is with this in mind that Autonoe has not been subtle about the drug she has poured into his cup, smeared across his plate, rubbed into the chunks of fish he now chews. The concoction, as it comes upon him, does not make him immediately fall, but rather makes his face flush hot, his fingers turn to ice, his bowels churn, his world spin. He staggers, he catches himself, his ears roar, he falls, he crawls on hands and knees, he thinks he will be sick. He makes it out into the cool night air to retch, and it is while he is there, struggling to stand against the swelling torment of his own burning skin, that Autonoe, Eos and Penelope slip past him to Pylades and Iason's room.

The two Mycenaeans are inside, already fully armed, though quite what for they do not know. They too were perhaps planning some brave rescue, some heroic act of valour and desperation. They make ready to charge when the door is pushed back, but stop themselves on seeing the women in it.

"Pylades," Penelope proclaims, "I hear you are willing to die for your king." The soldier straightens, nods once, jaw hard, shoulders back, a really rather lovely display of noble manhood. "Tonight may be the night where we put that to the test. Come."

They follow her through the palace. Swift and sure they move through its spider's web, its maze of broken halls and cruel shadows. At the foot of the stairs that lead up to Orestes' room, they stop. A Spartan lies sprawled across the bottom, half draped over his own shield. Pylades prods him carefully, and he groans, but does not stir.

At the top of the stairs, another of his colleagues, and then two more, all fallen, eyes lost to some distant place, gasping, gagging, one lying cheek-down in his own vomit. At their feet, spilled cups of wine, half-eaten food. Pylades takes in all of this, raises an eyebrow in what he wishes was disapproval, but he cannot entirely disapprove. Penelope steps over the bodies, knocks on Orestes' door, hears no reply, eases it back.

Inside, caught in the light of a single lantern, a scene of shadows and thin dancing light. Orestes lies in his bed. The maid Rhene is huddled in a corner, as if the walls might swallow her whole. A single Spartan man stands in the centre of the room, his blade laid across Elektra's throat.

This man's name is Ploutarchos, and it will not be spoken by the living ever again. He did not eat the food or drink the wine that was brought to him by the Ithacan maids, for he had a slightly loose stomach from bad fish the night before and was wary of eating too readily again. Thus when his comrades began to fall, he staggered one to the other, cried, poison, poison, help, help! But no one answered, his fellow men rushed to the docks, or drunk in their cups, or otherwise distracted by the maids of Penelope. Even the Spartan women did not answer his call, for at the moment that the dishes were being sent to their men, Phiobe in the kitchens spilled a whole bubbling pot of broth over the foot of another woman, who still sits on the floor screaming, howling in pain, her sisters gathered round her – oh no, such a shame, I'm so sorry, Phiobe cries, I'm so sorry! Phiobe, of all Penelope's maids, is the best at turning on the tears, at blubbering and saying how sorry she is, and goodness it is a sight to see.

Thus Ploutarchos found himself alone, and with enough good sense to realise that this could only mean one thing. Into Orestes' room he has burst, ready to defend himself and do something ... he's not sure what, this is really the kind of decision-making he's not qualified for ... but *something* to stop whatever it is that is coming for the Mycenaean king.

He cannot harm Orestes, of course.

A Spartan killing the king of Mycenae would be war, retribution, mayhem. Every king in Greece would turn on Menelaus at once should that happen. Orestes must be seen to be alive and mad, not murdered by his uncle's hand. So as hurting Orestes is off the table, and as no one is interested in murdering a maid, he has done the one violent thing that is left to him: he has caught Elektra by the hair and pulled her from her brother's side, and now holds her pressed against his body, sword at her neck.

This is the scene Penelope observes as she pushes open the door to Orestes' room, and for a moment she is still, silent. Then Pylades sees the same over her shoulder, and at once draws his blade and snarls: "For the king!" He makes to charge straight in, to lay down his life in a manner that is also not very clear to him – there is a great deal of heroic motivation happening at this moment, and a certain lack of common sense – but Penelope stops him, drives her hand between him and his prey, holds him back.

"Soldier of Sparta," she says, soft as midnight, calm as the evening dark, "what are you doing?"

Ploutarchos has no idea what he's doing. Ignorance was beaten out of him as a child, along with sorrow and regret – he can admit to none of these things lest he is beaten again, and so instead he tightens his grip across Elektra's chest, pulls her a little harder against his body, grits his teeth, thrusts forth his jaw.

"You hold the princess of Mycenae," Penelope continues. "You are violating Agamemnon's daughter, your king's niece. I ask you again – what are you doing?"

Ploutarchos is not trained in answering to a woman, but something has to give in this moment. There are at Penelope's back two armed men of Mycenae, and it is true that his hostage is also his master's niece, and so ... "My brothers have been poisoned. Poisoned by your maids."

Penelope licks her lips. She is looking for a cunning strata-gem, but in the circumstances it is hard for even her to concoct a speedy excuse for why there are four collapsed Spartans at her back, armed men by her side. Ploutarchos sees this. Elektra does too. It is perhaps this understanding that settles Elektra on her path, for she moves her hand a little within her gown, and plucks from a hidden place a dagger. It is the same dagger that Penelope had seen hidden beneath the floor; the kind of blade a princess should never carry, and which all princesses should. She does not have the space to drive it hard or far, but she does not need to. Her thrust, as she rams it into Ploutarchos, slips all the way in between the muscle at the top of his thigh and the lower curl of his belly.

He gasps but does not scream – screaming is also unaccept-able for a warrior – but neither does he do what he thought he might and cut Elektra's throat. Even in agony, there is a part of him that knows this is a foolish plan, a pointless plan, and so his arm for a moment grows limp, and Elektra grabs it with both hands, hauling it from her neck. She cannot move it far, but she does not need to. Pylades at once shoves past Penelope, nearly knocking her to the ground, and adds his strength to Elektra's own. There is a moment of struggle, confusion, gasping. A blade nicks flesh; blood begins to flow. Then Pylades hauls Elektra free from Ploutarchos, and as the Spartan staggers back, Iason steps in and drives his blade through the soldier's side, splitting rib, lung and chest.

Ploutarchos falls, and only the dead now will speak his name. Elektra staggers away from Pylades' arm, one hand pressed to her neck. There is blood on her fingers. Penelope starts towards her, but she waves her away. "It's nothing!" she gasps. "My brother!"

Penelope nods to Eos, who at once steps to Elektra's side, holding the lamp up to better see the princess's neck. Rhene too rises from her corner, wipes tears from her eyes, draws down a shuddering breath, does not look at the dead Spartan where he lies but instead tears cloth from her gown to press into Elektra's wound. It is indeed not deep – the last scraping of the blade across her skin as the sword was dragged away – but it bleeds and will leave a glorious, lovely white scar that in future years lovers could trace their fingers over and marvel at the story it tells, if Elektra was inclined to that kind of flirtation. She is not.

Pylades moves to Orestes' side, shakes him softly where he lies – above, the Furies rattle and squawk at the disturbance – and there are tears glistening upon his cheeks, pity breaking in his heart to see his king so fallen, so weak and so pale. Orestes' eyes are sunken into his skull; bones protrude through pale, sallow skin. His eyelids barely flicker to see his friend, but he smiles. Pylades nearly gasps; Elektra looks away. Orestes is light as a bag of sticks when Pylades lifts him from his bed.

"I take it we are escaping?" Elektra rasps, flapping away the women who attend to her bleeding neck and snatching the cloth from Rhene's hand to press hard against the wound herself.

"If you are willing," Penelope replies.

Elektra scowls, prods the fallen Spartan at her feet with her toes, raises her chin as once her mother was wont to do. "Now," she commands. "*Now.*"

The fire is still blazing in the docks as the five women and three men slip down to the garden of sweet flowers near Penelope's hives. There are still five Spartans guarding the gate. They have not drunk wine nor eaten food – they will not do so until dawn comes, for they have their duty and will not be distracted.

Instead Autonoe guides the little group to where the ladder the suitors used to flee is still waiting against the wall. Manhandling Orestes up takes both Pylades and Iason, grunting as they try to manipulate the king, who groans and stirs in their arms.

"What has Kleitos given him?" Penelope whispers to Elektra, as the men work.

"I don't know. Nothing I have seen before," Elektra replies.

With a heave, the men get Orestes up onto the wall, then start lashing him to Pylades' back for the drop down the other side, as if he were a babe to be carried in a winding sheet. I pull the darkness a little tighter about their forms; breathe a distracting perfume onto the wind that carries towards the Spartans by the gate.

Elektra climbs, then Rhene. As the maid reaches for the ladder, she stumbles, trips in the shadows. Penelope catches her by the arm, steadies her, nods, smiles reassurances – though the gesture is lost a little in the dark.

Pylades, Orestes on his back, has just made it down the other side of the wall when the scream comes from within the palace. It is the cry of Spartan women, who at last have left the little drama that Phiobe has created in the kitchen to check on the well-being of their men, only to find them poisoned, fallen, slain. Help, help, they cry, help, we are betrayed!

In a few moments those guards who are not intoxicated will burst through the door to Orestes' room to find him gone, will thunder to where Pylades should be under guard, and will in grossest violation of all the sacred rules of the land break down Penelope's door to find Helen sleeping groggy upon her bed.

"Oh goodness," Helen will slur. "I must have had a bit too much to drink . . . "

Then they will cry help, treachery, help, fetch the king! And the fastest of their number, a boy of some thirteen years of age, will race down to the harbour to tell Menelaus that he is indeed betrayed, that the witch queen of these islands has spirited away Orestes and his sister, help, help, raise the men!

The news will only come as some surprise to Menelaus. He too knows that Spartan ships do not just catch aflame, but in his arrogance – and with more than a taste of the fires of Troy still at his back – he thought the burning of his fleet more of a priority than keeping a personal eye out on some tricksy queen. Goodness, he is learning about his enemy tonight, isn't he?

All this then is unfolding as Pylades with Orestes on his back slithers down the rope to that precarious cliff edge, and starts sliding along it, one hand pressed into the wall at his side for safety, one hand drawn across his back to steady the monarch strung to it. Iason follows, helps Elektra find her footing. Penelope is next, and though she has a reasonable head for heights, she does not look down, down to the roaring sea below, down to a skull cracked and limbs smashed, down to the fall into the dark. Instead she fixes her eyes on the distant point where the ledge grows to a wider path that grows wider still as it weaves away from the walls, and to a single light that flickers there in the distance, inviting.

Rhene comes after, but as she peers down the rope she is to descend, she sees the raging seas below, and begins to shake, to tremble, to toss her head from side to side, to crawl back the way she's come. Eos grabs her by the arm, hisses: "We go now, or not at all!"

"I can't," whimpers the Mycenaean. "I can't. The fall ... I can't ..."

"Then stay!" snarls Eos, who has at the best of time limited sympathy for dawdlers. "Pray that Laertes can protect you too!"

With this, Eos starts to ease herself down. Autonoe pauses, as if she might say something kind to Rhene. She leans in to give the Mycenaean a reassuring smile, to press her forehead against Rhene's own – comfort, sister, comfort, she seems to say. She is not known for her generous nature, for her kindness, but these are extraordinary times. She squeezes Rhene's hand, then hesitates.

Perhaps it is the unusual nature of the gesture. Perhaps Autonoe is surprised at her own delicacy, her own compassion. Her nostrils flare; perhaps it is something else entirely.

Whatever it is that discombobulated her, it is already passing. Now Autonoe draws back, smiles again, with something now in the corner of her eye, and slips down the rope on the other side of the wall.

For a moment more the Mycenaean lingers on the wall, looks to the left, to the right, as if casting about for any alternative, any path that may redeem what she has to do, and seeing none, edges down the rope after the others and into the waiting dark.

CHAPTER 32

>>>

Penelope, Elektra, Pylades, Orestes, Iason, Rhene, Autonoe and Eos.

These are the eight who shuffle one cautious step at a time away from the shadow of the palace of Ithaca into the night.

The Spartans are mustering, assembling in the courtyard. Menelaus has given up on saving the three ships, but they at least managed to push the vessels out into the bay, towards the open sea, carried by the wind that most fortuitously seems to have encouraged the flames to spread towards the Spartan ships and away from the town.

Very tricksy, he thinks as he marches back towards the palace. A very tricksy Ithacan queen. Odysseus said she was smart, but Odysseus was a fool when it came to women. He'll show her what it is to be owned by a real fucking man.

I turn my gaze from him in disgust as he musters his men. "Spread out!" he commands. "Find them!"

They churn through the palace, strike the maids who get in their way, overturn tables and chairs as if eight people might somehow be crouched under a stool, kick open doors, punch a suitor in the gut, break another's nose, until Laertes steps forward and roars: "YOU WILL ACT WITH RESPECT IN MY SON'S PALACE!"

Menelaus turns to strike the old man, but stops himself.

The father of his sworn blood brother glares into the Spartan king's face, dares him to do it, dares him to be the man who raises his fist to an old king of Greece, an ancient ally of his house and the house of Agamemnon. Dares him to be the one who starts that fire, begins that war. Menelaus lowers his arm, and Laertes grins. "Right," he drawls. "All the suitors, all the maids, all the council of Odysseus. They're Ithacan. They're under my son's protection. That means that until his wife is found, they're under mine, yes?"

Menelaus lunges forward, his chest pressed to Laertes', pushing the smaller, older man back. Laertes is surprised for a moment, staggers, nearly loses his footing, just about catches himself before he falls. It is not a strike to the face; it is not a drawn blade. It is merely Menelaus taking up the space that he feels he should rightfully own. "When I find your son's wife," he hisses, "I'm going to take her with me. I'm going to take her to Sparta and she is going to be the guest of my house. Her, Orestes, his little sister. They are all going to be treated to my hospitality. Do you understand, old man? Do you take my meaning?"

Laertes blinks up into Menelaus's face, then slowly, thoughtfully, he spits. He doesn't spit at Menelaus – instead he aims a globule of saliva and phlegm onto the floor at Menelaus's feet, smiles and says nothing at all.

In the darkness beyond the palace walls, eight figures hurry towards a light.

Ourania waits, her little lamp held aloft. At her side stands Priene's favourite lieutenant, Teodora, a bow in her hand and a quiver on her hip. Ourania inspects every face as they stagger into the small circle of light, taking in each in turn without emotion, until at last she sees Penelope and allows herself a slight exhale of relief. Even the short slither along the wall's edge has started to bedraggle these travellers, mud at their hems and wind in their hair. Ourania pulls off her shawl and winds it round Penelope's shoulders, and the queen does not object. Pylades begins to unstrap Orestes from his back, that Iason might take a turn carrying the load, as Teodora proclaims:

"There are armed Spartans guarding your ship. We can attack them if you wish, though most of our forces are already off this isle."

This is a flat declaration, delivered in the same brisk tone that Teodora has so often heard Priene use on military matters. Teodora is confident that if the women attack these Spartan men, the Spartans will die. But she is fairly sure too that some of the women in her small troop will fall, such is the chaos of fighting in the dark. This is the reality; Teodora is never shy about things that are real.

"No," Penelope replies. "I have another way off the island. We must get to Phenera."

"There will be Spartans on the road," warns Ourania. "Menelaus has given up trying to save his burned ships."

"We always knew that would be only a brief distraction. Teodora, can you scout ahead?"

Teodora nods once. This land is her land, every stone and trail is known to her, every branch and leaf. She turns and retreats swiftly into the dark, and as she does, I feel another move with her, run with her, a brush of branch bending beneath bare, hard feet. Artemis bounds along with her beloved warrior women tonight, guides Teodora through the dark, revels in it, gives out a little cry that some think just a turn of the distant wind, but which others may hear as the howl of the wolf.

"You have a plan?" Elektra barks, as Ourania starts to follow the shadow of Teodora down the grubby little trail.

"Of course, cousin," Penelope replies, not raising her eyes from the path on which she carefully treads. "Of course."

The moonlight that guides them is thin, but the clouds have parted after last night's storm to reveal the blanket of heaven, a gift of starlight. No colour shines in this world, save for the occasional flicker of a lamp left burning by the women of the isle to guide them along their way. As Teodora runs ahead, swift and sure, Ourania leads the party behind her. She too carries a lamp, but she does not unveil it save occasionally to point at a stream that crosses the little track and give warning, or to call out softly in the dark: this way, come come, this way.

Creatures of night and mist dart away from the group as they travel. A startled deer, perhaps, or a bewildered hare. An owl is silent overhead; I strain my ears to hear Artemis's footfall as she bounds through the night, but even I cannot find the huntress just by listening. The travellers do not talk, do not raise their heads from the study of the darkness through which they move, do not whisper of fearful things. Teodora reappears from the forest, presses her finger to her lips: down, down. They drop into the dirt, press shoulders and backs into stone, smother the light, wait and do not breathe. There is a road, such as Ithaca has, not a few steps from them, and now with the clattering of bronze and the smack of shield a group of men jog down it, Spartans guided by a captain with a lantern. He thinks he has seen some of the lights the women have left to guide the way, wonders what they are, has a mind to strike into the interior, to brave the unknown places of the isle – but no, look. Even as he tries to make his mind up, a lamp goes out. A woodcutting woman of the isle has felt a certain urge to extinguish the flame before it can draw too much attention, and at her side stands Artemis with arrow notched to string. The Spartans shake their heads – no point trying to fumble around in the darkness to find a light that is no longer there. After all these royal escapees – guests, rather – have nowhere to go.

The group waits in huddled silence for the Spartans to pass, before Teodora again emerges to gesture them on. Quick, quick, this way, quick!

They follow the path of a dried stream, polished stones in a thin cut through the land, heading now down, down to the sea. Even mortal ears can catch it, the breaking of foam on ragged stone, and the thicker, shallow sucking of the tide reaching up a thin curl of sandier shore where a boat might wait. They cannot follow the bed of the stream all the way down, for it crashes into the edge of a cliff where after rain tumbles a thin waterfall, so instead they turn to hug a thin path that zigzags down to the shore. Here there is almost no cover, for the cruel wind has bent back the scrubby vegetation to little more than a shin-scratching irritant, and so the group picks up pace, their backs framed against starlight.

They will think it is this same starlight that betrays them, but Orestes, who groans and moans in his intoxicated slumber, is the only one of the mortals who knows that it is not. Then I see them, the three hags sitting upon the burned white branches of a crooked, salt-blasted tree. They grin at the sight of me, cackle and clap their claws in delight at their little trick, tilt their heads as if listening for a pleasing note. The Furies lick the air, and I too smell it now, the stench of sweat and musk of men – an aroma that I have found more than pleasing on many an occasion, but which tonight I would happily avoid.

So it is that as our little gaggle of royal runners reach the lip of a hill that rolls down to a ruined bay of burned-out houses, they hear again the sound of armour and the stamp of feet, the sound of male voices rising in sudden urgency. Teodora is at once by their side, calling out without pretence of discretion: "Spartans! Move!"

Ourania does not need to be told twice, but pulls her hem up high enough to reveal her bony old knees and runs. Penelope and Eos gallop along behind her, all regal dignity forsaken as they slip down the sandy path towards the shore, while behind the Mycenaeans struggle to support the weight of Orestes as they scramble through the dark. Elektra is not used to running head-first down a steep scrap of crumbling path; Rhene nearly falls and cries out, but is caught about the arm by Pylades, who drags her back to her feet, supports her as Iason lugs Orestes down the slope.

Behind them – movement, a flash of bronze, and a voice cries out, raised in alarm. A flicker of torchlight, another, brandished aloft. There are only four Spartans, without shields – a small scouting party perhaps, lighter and faster than their more cumbersome brethren. They did not expect to see anyone come this way tonight; the majority of Menelaus's men are arranged around Ourania's little fishing boat in its hidden cove, rather than all the way out here, by the remnants of a pirate-burned town. They were half slumbering, half asleep, lulled perhaps by the cool sea air or the soft scent of crumbling leaves wafted from the woods, but one thought he dreamed of bat wings and ebony claws so woke with a start and . . . well, here they are. Here they are, and here they come.

Below, in the bay of a town once called Phenera, a ship is waiting.

It is not the ship that Menelaus expected.

Rather it is a warship, square-sailed and proud. Firelight flickers on the beach around it, and moving at its base are not the women we are used to seeing running through the dark, but the shadows of men. Towards these now our little group tumbles, Teodora leading the way, bow in hand, calling out: "Ready the ship! Ready the ship!"

Her voice carries faintly over the wind, but before I can push it on, Artemis is there, lifting the sound, throwing it towards the hearers below, who look up and, seeing the figures descending towards them, start stirring, start working about the beached prow of their vessel. Ourania is the first to reach them, staggering straight out into the foam towards the rope slung off the bow of the ship, hauling herself gracelessly up the side. Then Eos and Penelope, but they do not immediately climb, but turn and call out to their companions – come, come on! Come quick!

Elektra stumbles in the dark, nearly falls. I catch her by the elbow, lift her up, urge her on. The Furies are spinning high overhead now, the air giddy beneath their wings, the sail of the ship snapping and twisting at their passage. Iason is at the back, half dropped beneath the weight of Orestes, and behind him, the Spartans.

It is Teodora who concludes that they are not going to make it, so it is Teodora who stands by Penelope, notches an arrow to her bow, draws, aims, fires. The arrow should have struck straight into the soft thigh of the nearest Spartan as he barrels towards Iason's back, blade drawn – but the Furies beat the air and the shaft goes wide. At once, Artemis is by Teodora's side, a scowl of distaste on her lips, her brow so deeply drawn she looks as if she is trying to smother her own nose. She steadies Teodora's arm as the woman draws back her bow for another shot, but again the Furies beat their wings, and even with divinity in her limbs, Teodora's arrow misses its mark.

Iason falls at the edge of the bay, breathless beneath his burden, and Pylades steps between him and the Spartans, blade drawn, ready to defend his king. Teodora throws down her bow and draws daggers from her belt, runs towards the Mycenaeans as the Spartans begin to circle them. Elektra pulls her little blade from within her gown, but Penelope catches her by the hand before she can rush into the fray, shakes her head, drags her towards the side of the ship.

"My brother!" Elektra cries.

"You cannot protect him!"

These are words that should break Elektra's heart. They are the words that have been hanging over her for . . . she does not know how long. Now she hears them on a sea-turned shore, salt between her toes and fire in her eyes, and she finds that her heart does not break. Perhaps, she thinks, she hasn't a heart left to be broken.

Iason is still trying to disentangle himself from the weight of Orestes when the first Spartan lunges for Pylades. The Mycenaean turns to knock the thrust away, tries to get a chop at the attacker's hands in reply, but it is all too quick. These are men used to war – they understand that the best fight is the one you can get through in haste, and they leave nothing of themselves exposed. They do not, however, expect Teodora to come barrelling up from the shore, knives drawn to thrust at the exposed armpit of one who has his back turned to her. They do not expect her to stab, stab, stab again and again into his flesh until he is collapsed groaning beneath her weight, his lifeblood gushing into sand. One aims a blow for her head on instinct, and Pylades steps through to block it, though he is as surprised as anyone else at these developments.

Only now does full, ugly combat break out, a spinning eddy of feet and blade as each tries to find an angle past the other's guard, lunging and leaping back and slashing at skin and flesh. No one cries out – no one gives a heroic battle cry. This is a business of life and death, and what breath there is must be saved for fighting. Pylades blocks blow after blow, keeping his sword always in front of him, his body always safe behind his guard, but he cannot find space against the onslaught to attack back, cannot catch a moment where a parry might turn into a counter, and already he is exhausted, struggling to keep balance as his feet twist and turn in the churning sand. Teodora for her part darts away from the man she has slain as another Spartan tries again to split her in two, but one of her knives is lodged deep in the corpse and she only has one left. The longer blade of the Spartan whistles by her throat, comes back again and nearly takes off her hand at the wrist as she tries to slip by it with her remaining dagger.

Priene told her never to fight like this – never alone, never so close – but her arrows went wide and so here she is, backing away a step at a time when she knows she should be trying to go forward, trying to find a way past the slicing guard of the Spartan, to take away the distance that now is his friend, not hers. She attempts a lunge, but he knocks her back with his free arm, a blow that rings through her jaw and ears and sends her scuttling on all fours into the dirt.

I reach forward to catch his wrist, a moment of distraction, just the briefest moment – and then the Furies are all about me. I shriek and curl away as they dive, talon and claw and wing and charred feather across my face, suffocating, beating me down. They do not draw blood – even the Furies would hesitate before nicking the skin of a divinity such as I – but they smother me in their blackness like a swarm, driving back the light of heaven, a suffocating stench of acid and metal, rotting flesh, pestilence and decay, festering heat and throat-constricting cold all at once beating from their wings. I cry out and try to push them away, but they just spin me tighter, pulling at my hair, catching with claws at the loose fabric of my gown. Through it all I think I hear Teodora cry, smell mortal blood through the heady cloud of chaos the Furies spill.

Then Athena is there. She blazes, she burns, she holds her spear aloft and her shield close by her side. Her face is shrouded from sight by her golden helmet, her gown billows about her feet as she floats above the ground. Mortals do not see her, for this sight is for the ladies of the earth and the pit alone, but she crackles with thunder and lightning, the only creature besides Zeus who would ever dare wield them. The Furies spit and shriek before her, snarling, claws tearing crimson gashes in the air itself; they spin upwards into the sky, releasing their claws from my gown, fire in their eyes and the night rippling sickeningly about their wings.

"Enough!" Athena roars, and when the Furies do not answer save with spits of yellow pus that scars the earth where it falls, again she raises her spear, and again it gives forth a burst of celestial light. *"Enough!"*

In the light I see again Artemis upon the shore, her bow drawn, fingers pressed into her cheek, arrow notched to fire. The huntress clothed herself in shadows; now even those are burning back as the thunder crackles from Athena's arm.

"HE IS OURS!" the Furies shriek. "HE IS OURS!"

"That remains to be seen," Athena replies, and goodness, it is just one of the sexiest things I think I've ever seen, the calm confidence, the stillness of her tone, the way nevertheless her voice just carries. I always knew she had a certain special quality, but seeing it is really something else. "You will have what is owed to you, ladies of the night – but first we must see *what* is owed."

"You cannot stop us," snarls one, and then at once the next picks up her words, voices mingling, three as one. "You cannot defy us – cannot steal our prey!"

"And I will not. But it must be certain that what you say is yours is rightfully given. And anyway," – Athena's lips twitch in a smile, barely visible through the thin line of her helmet, and I melt a little inside to see it – goodness, it's really quite something to see the goddess of wisdom being pleased at her own cleverness – "you will find that this fight is done."

The Furies glance down at the mortals, still locked blade to blade. Teodora is bleeding, a thin slash across the top of her arm, struggling, staggering back from the man who presses against her. Pylades beats back a blade from one man, but his movement has grown sloppy, he is wide open, and there it is – a kick from the side that sends him staggering, knocks him to one knee, barely catching himself to duck under the next blow that comes for the side of his head. A blade swings down and Pylades will not get there in time – but Iason catches the arm before it can complete its journey, throws himself bodily on top of the Spartan warrior who was an instant from severing Pylades' throat. Iason has a blade, but has not had time to draw it, and so for a moment the two men wrestle on the ground, grunting and rolling as each struggles to get the point of a weapon into the other's flesh.

I do not see what it is about this scene that could so entertain Athena. It is Artemis who alerts me, her gaze flashing to the edge of a ruined house that hems the bay. There another man moves, running with bare feet over the soft earth, no armour on his chest nor helmet on his head, but a short stabbing sword in one hand and a curved knife in the other. I recognise him, and have to resist the urge to squeak as, with a silent sweep, he comes behind the Spartan who is looking to kill Teodora and slices through the back of his legs without seeming to even slow down.

The Spartan tumbles, his feet useless lumps at the end of leaden limbs. Teodora looks down on him and considers, if only for a moment, mercy. It is only a moment. His life ends quickly, her blade through his throat.

The Spartan who kicked Pylades to the ground is the next to die. He doesn't even hear the man approach behind him, will not know what name to give to the boatman when he reaches the river of the dead, or who to blame for the knife that comes across his neck. The last Spartan falls to a group effort – hauled off Iason's chest by Pylades, held down beneath the Mycenaean's knee, stabbed to death by the man with the curved blade.

The Furies shriek and spin into the air, rising to pinpricks of darkness that stir blackened clouds about them in their rage. Athena lets her light go out, her divinity fading as she returns to walk soft upon the earth. Artemis croons over Teodora's bloody arm as the warrior woman limps towards the edge of the sea. For a moment I think my huntress cousin might be about to lick the wound, wonder if it's only the presence of more civilised goddesses such as myself that restrains her.

Then Elektra is running to Orestes' side, calling out to winded Iason, dizzy Pylades – is he safe, is he safe?

The Mycenaeans recover themselves, groggy, bloody, exhausted, help Elektra haul Orestes up again and towards the ship. This just leaves the last warrior standing, blood on his hands, sprayed across his cheeks, pooling about his toes. It is Penelope who approaches him in the dark, Eos at her side.

"Kenamon," she says politely, eyes anywhere save the slain warriors at his feet.

"My lady," the Egyptian replies, with a nod of his head. He is still breathless, shoulders rising and falling fast, weapons drawn.

She smiles at his courtesy, looks up into the dark at their back as if searching for more men about to beset them – or perhaps no. Perhaps that is not it at all. Perhaps she is saying goodbye to Ithaca, listening one last time to the night of her isle, just in case she never hears it again. Then, barely looking at him, she holds out her hand to the Egyptian.

He slips his curved knife onto his belt, and with fingers still soaked in Spartan blood, he takes her hand. Then, without a word, she leads him towards the waiting ship.

CHAPTER 33

‹›

"Goodness, an Egyptian not in the palace?" Ourania had exclaimed when word came to her of Kenamon free in the market of Ithaca. "We had better hide him before some Spartan gets a bright idea."

"I was out for my morning walk," Kenamon spluttered when Ourania's ladies swept him up and bundled him away. "I like to stir before the dawn."

"Isn't that just charming, isn't that delightful?" Ourania replied. "You have such lovely hair."

"And you do . . . what precisely for the queen?"

"I protect suitors for whom Penelope has a slight soft spot from being tortured and gutted by our Spartan guest!" she explained. "May I offer you some fish?"

This was the beginning of the process that now sees Kenamon of Memphis upon a Greek warship in the smallest hours of the night, covered in Spartan blood, sailing away from Ithaca.

He is not, however, the only suitor upon its decks.

"Fuck!" shrills Antinous, as he gazes back towards shore, where already the busy gulls are beginning to explore the cooling corpses of the slain Spartans. "He killed them! You killed them!"

"They were attempting to kill the personal guards of the Mycenaean king," Kenamon replies politely, as Eos brings him water in a bowl to wash the blood from his arms and face. "I thought it perhaps best that they be prevented, yes?"

"I would have helped," offers Eurymachus from his corner, and immediately:

"Shut up, Eurymachus!" barks Antinous.

"My compliments, sir," says Amphinomous, from where he stands nearest the prow, huddled in a thick cloak against the cold night air. "You fought well, and with speed."

Well yes – why yes. These three, the most powerful suitors of Penelope, the most infuriating thorns, one might say, in her side – they now stand in an uneasy knot on the deck of this ship as it leaps across the water, watching by reflected firelight as Ourania binds the bloody wound on Teodora's arm, as Elektra soothes her brother's brow where Pylades and Iason have laid him down, and as Penelope, queen of Ithaca, watches them in return. They should really go to her, do a bit of bowing, a bit of "we are glad to see you well, my lady", but even Amphinomous, the boldest of them, can't quite meet her eye this night.

So instead, Penelope goes to them.

"Gentlemen," she says, "I am glad to see you made it safely to this vessel."

The three are perhaps grateful for the rolling of the deck beneath their feet as it hides the unease with which they shuffle foot to foot. At last Amphinomous says: "My lady. Your escape was not without incident, I see."

"No. I am grateful that one of your number was able to intervene, albeit heartbroken that matters took a violent turn," she replies, nodding towards bloody Kenamon. She doesn't sound heartbroken, it must be said. When Eurymachus swallows, a knot moves all the way up and all the way down his throat.

Antinous, however, is never one to let someone else take any glory whatsoever, so blurts:

"You are lucky we had this ship to aid you, queen. What would you have done if we were not here for you?"

Penelope turns her gaze to him slowly, as if she needs to build herself up to this moment like the coiling snake preparing to strike. When at last their eyes lock, he nearly stops himself from flinching – but not quite. "Why yes," she muses. "How lucky I was that you gentlemen and your fathers had equipped this fine ship in such secrecy. What excellent fortune that the selfsame vessel you prepared for the hunting-down and murder of my son can now be put to most convenient use."

It would be kind at this juncture to turn imperiously and drift away.

Penelope is not in a kind mood.

She lingers a moment.

Lets them cringe a moment.

Considers the sky a moment.

Considers the wind a moment.

And only then turns and leaves them shivering together at the prow.

The Furies are somewhere high in the sky as the ship beats its way through the dark.

Artemis watches us from the cliff on the shore, uninterested in nautical matters.

Athena studies the heavens from the stern, the wind tugging at her hair. The wind would never be so daring and bold if she did not permit it. Perhaps she too is sensual after all; perhaps she loves to have the feeling of movement about her scalp, wonders if this is what it feels like to have a hand run through your locks, to have touch against your skin. It breaks my heart to know that it is only the wind that is permitted to caress her lovely flesh.

I lean against the rail with her, follow her gaze upwards. Say at last: "You defied the Furies?"

"Not defied," she replies. "Merely made enquiry as to their rights. There must be rules. Even for the profane. Even for the divine. They will return soon. We must be ready." Then she looks down the deck, towards Orestes, bundled in his sister's arms. "He must be ready."

On the eastern horizon, a sliver of grey, the faintest kiss of approaching dawn. I turn to greet it, bless it with kindness and soft illumination. Athena follows my gaze, then turns her face away.

"I will see you again on Kephalonia," she says. And then, careful, cautious, a word she does not like to use, a word she is trying out for size, she adds: "Sister," and is gone in a beating of feathered wings.

CHAPTER 34

> >>

Rosy-fingered dawn caresses the sky like a familiar lover, still enamoured with the curves of this most radiant, resplendent world.

In the palace of Odysseus, Helen falls to the ground, pressing her fingers to her jaw. The bruise will swell before it retreats, but she will angle her face just so, just so, and paint over the mark. In Sparta, Menelaus almost never hits her where it shows – it sends the wrong message to his court. He likes to keep the bruises to her ribs, her belly, her buttocks, her legs. He has learned how to target her just so, just so, to get his message across but leave room for doubt in all who see her that she was ever struck by more than a breeze and a whim.

"Fucking drunk," he snarls. "Fucking whore."

Helen stays down, softly weeping.

She continues weeping until he is gone, until Tryphosa has also left to fetch some water to wash her mistress with. Then she stands. Rearranges her hair loosely in the perfect reflection of her mirror. Smooths down her gown. Presses her fingers into the tender place where tomorrow there will be vibrant purple smears of pain. Presses a little deeper, until there are different tears – tears of a different nature – welling in her eyes. Sighs.

Lets go. Sits at her stool and waits for her maid to return, to help adorn her for the coming day.

On the shores of a village once called Phenera, Lefteris stares at the dead bodies of his murdered men. He does not have the same romantic ideas of what it is to have an enemy as Menelaus does. An enemy is simply a job. They are simply work to be done. Notions of vengeance, retribution, honour, justice – these are for the kind of men of whom the poets speak. Lefteris will not be spoken of by the poets. He will simply get the job done.

"Take their armour and blades," he commands. "Burn the bodies."

His order is obeyed. These are men of Sparta, after all. Devotion is their cause.

On a ship leaping between the thin waters that separate Ithaca and her sister isle . . .

Kenamon sits apart. The last time he was on a ship of this nature, it was leaving his homeland, speeding north from the place where lived his heart, his family, his hopes and his dreams. It was a vessel headed for Ithaca, carrying with him nothing but sorrow and shame.

Now he sits, bloodied, upon a ship sailing to Kephalonia, and the swell of the sea and the beating of the water remind him of just how far he has come from home.

Then Penelope is by his side, Eos and Autonoe a discreet little wall of womanhood standing guard, backs turned to them, keeping away the eyes and ears of the suitors gathered, already bickering, at the helm.

"Kenamon."

A little nod – neither of them has slept, both are wearied of words bartered in the thin morning light. Penelope glances past her maids, checking again that no male eyes observe them, then with a little smile huddles down at the Egyptian's side, pulling a shawl tight against the cold wet breeze, her shoulder bumping his as she adjusts herself in this folded nook of ship. He is surprised, but does not know what to say to this, so merely sits with her, enjoying the thin warmth her body gives off at his side. After a while:

"It seems I must thank you once again for a timely military intervention."

"Not at all, I—"

"No. Please. You saved my son when pirates attacked, many moons ago. Now you have been instrumental in protecting me once again, not to mention the king of Mycenae."

"Ah yes. Your king of kings. He does not seem . . . well."

"He is not."

"And yet you protect him?"

"Should I not?"

"Forgive me. I merely mean that . . . of the options available to you, you appear to have chosen a reckless one. As my blade can perhaps attest."

Penelope scowls briefly, before the expression is replaced by a flicker of surprise – she is amazed at herself, astonished to have caught herself so open in her features next to anyone, let alone a man. She composes herself, and he waits while she does so, enjoying the shape of her flickering brow. "If we have learned one thing from Troy – and I do not think we have – it is that forging alliances with bullies and butchers may seem like the greatest path to safety now, but in the long run it will absolutely wound you. All of Greece swore to honour and uphold the righteous claims of Menelaus and Agamemnon, because frankly if they did not it would make them enemies of these two barbarous men. And look where that oath got them. As dead on the beaches of Troy as surely as if they had died defending their palaces. At least there they would have died for something

323

more than just ... " A loose gesture, encompassing what? Agamemnon's ambition? Troy's bloody walls? Helen screaming as Paris pulled her away by the hair? Helen falling joyously into the arms of her one true love? Helen, a giggling girl who didn't take the time to think about anything much too particularly? What is it that this loose flick of Penelope's wrist encompasses? Maybe all of it. Maybe nothing at all.

"So you are choosing to resist while you can, on your own ground."

"That is roughly the aim, yes."

"I cannot fault you for that. As you say, better to die at home."

Kenamon's eyes are on some distant place, his nostrils filled with the memories of a far-off land. Penelope sees it, wonders perhaps at the visions his mind unfurls. "Kenamon ... when we first met, I chose to trust you, because it was clear that you had nothing to gain and nothing to lose. You will never have the power to be king, and as you are so far from home, so far from ... I know I have taken certain things for granted. I am not ... I am not used to thinking about these things as a woman, instead of a queen. You are ... I wanted to thank you. Again. Thank you."

So tongue-tied with this Egyptian! If they were to make love right here, right now, it would be "is this all right?" and "are you sure you're comfortable?" and awkward fumbling at each other's clothes while trying not to giggle.

Kenamon sees it too. His heart sings of it, and there is a moment here where perhaps ...

But the ship knocks against the waters of the sea, and Kenamon's heart is sailing home again, bounding across the ocean to Memphis, to the southlands of his birth, to a tongue that is familiar and people he calls family. And the ship knocks against the waters of the sea, and Penelope is being torn apart and cast into the waves where her husband most probably drowned, is being murdered by her son as Clytemnestra was, called whore, temptress, harlot, her severed limbs cast into the crab-clawing deep.

Such images will shatter even the most lovely of mature sensual fantasies, and so, with a little exhalation of breath, Penelope turns from Kenamon, and Kenamon studies his feet, and she rises and returns to the prow of the ship, where all eyes might once again behold her standing apart in her contemplative, endless chastity.

And on the island of Kephalonia, as the fresh sun rises over the new day?

Priene stands on a shingle beach, watching as the warship presses its oars cautiously into the bay. Hidden upon clifftop and behind the great rocks around are twenty women, all armed with blades and bows, the fisherwomen and shepherds, widows and never-to-be-wives of Penelope's little army. A hundred more are scattered across the isle, waiting to receive their orders, to string their bows and hunt something a little more substantial than rabbits.

Priene is not of these isles. She is not of these people, swore once to murder every one of their kind that she found. But whether she likes it or not, she knows these women, is learning to even love them, and understands that in their own strange way, they now are her tribe. Though those on the boat cannot see her little army, she knows that her women see all, that they see her, and look to her as captain.

For now, though, Priene waits as the ship pushes up onto shore, hand on the pommel of her sheathed sword, chewing the flesh of dried fish as she waits for the people of the vessel to start to disembark. Anaitis stands beside her, the priestess of Artemis also now carrying a bow, a quiver of arrows, a heavy bag of herbs strapped to her side. These women crossed the water together several nights ago, as many women have come, answering Penelope's call.

Pylades is the first to slip down the rope from the side of the ship and onto Kephalonia's shore. He looks around at the isle, the bigger, more luscious and generally more lovely sister to little Ithaca, and is clearly unimpressed. But he is hardly in a position to complain about almost anything that is given to him at this time, so with barely a glance at Priene and Anaitis, he busies himself with helping Elektra down the rope, then more gingerly, with Iason and Amphinomous to help support his weight, Orestes.

The voyage from Ithaca to Kephalonia is short, a bare whiff of water between the two isles. But even this voyage has rattled young Orestes, who now swims in and out of wakefulness, cries again for his mother, for forgiveness, sometimes gags as if he might choke, stares through popping eyes, chews his own swollen, ravaged lips. As soon as the Mycenaean king is on the beach, Anaitis rushes to his side, barks: "What has he been given now?" and when no one has any answer tuts and shakes her head, disappointed more than angry at the ignorance of these men. She kneels between Elektra and Rhene, jostling them out of her way, oblivious to the status of the princess. Sniffs the air, catching a scent of something unexpected as she does, then shakes her head and presses her hand to Orestes' forehead, his throat, his wrist, muttering dismay. Just this once Elektra lets herself be supported by the elbow by her maid, stares at her brother as if he were already dead, says not a word.

Antinous and Eurymachus, as they disembark, look at Priene with confusion. A woman, armed, is an anomaly, a thing they cannot understand. They should really ask questions at this juncture. Questions like "who are you?" and "where did you come from?" and "why does no one else seem bothered by a woman carrying a lot of knives waiting for us on this shore?" But to ask questions would be to admit ignorance, and ignorance could be construed as weakness, and weakness is unmanly – so they do not.

Amphinomous, as he gratefully steadies his sea-shook legs on solid land, looks at Priene, takes in her manner, her stance, her folded arms, the slow rotation of her mouth as she chews down another piece of early-morning fish, and is bright enough to be briefly afraid. He too should ask questions, but perhaps senses how little he will enjoy some of the answers that could be given.

Eos helps Teodora from the vessel, the lieutenant's arm now wrapped in torn swathes of cloth. Priene raises her eyebrows to see this, approaches Teodora as the younger woman walks towards her captain, stops before her, assesses, says at last: "Did it bleed too long or go too deep?" Teodora shakes her head. Priene nods, satisfied. "Well. You will tell me about it later."

There is a place here where kindness might be. Teodora can see it, longs for it. Priene is on the verge of giving it, an expression of something . . . she's not sure what. Something that speaks of . . . tenderness? But it has been too long, too long, she's not ready yet, and so a jerk of her head it will have to be, with the hope perhaps that at another time, at a later time, there will be more to say.

Penelope is flanked by Autonoe and Ourania, Kenamon a polite distance at her back. He, like Amphinomous, has a feeling that any questions he might ask about this current situation would produce answers he does not want to hear. He wishes to be close to Penelope, feels a strange and urgent desire to protect her. And yet he does not want to be so close that she will have to lie to him, have to change her speech to shield him from things she does not want him to hear. So he stands a little off, out of earshot, courteous, silent. He hopes that one day she will tell him her secrets. It surprises him how much he hopes for that.

"Priene," says the Ithacan queen, as she approaches her captain.

"Queen," replies Priene briskly. "I see you made it off Ithaca more or less unbloodied."

"Indeed. There was a little skirmish, but it was resolved satisfactorily. My compliments to the women who set Menelaus's ships ablaze. I was impressed at the force of the conflagration."

Priene shrugs. She saw the Greek ships burn before Troy, as Menelaus did. But she saw them from the other side of the lines, and thought it made for a spectacular sight, and a terrible tactical decision. Her relationship with fire could be classified as ambivalent.

"We have set up camp near the shrine of Hera." Priene is all business – this is a military matter, and it is pure courtesy that keeps Penelope informed of the decisions she has made in this regard. "We can muster nearly a hundred already, and more come to us – though our movements will be observed if we raise too many under arms. We have observed twenty Spartans on Kephalonia, almost entirely around the town and harbour. They are not currently going into the countryside and no ships have yet arrived from Ithaca warning them of your flight."

"Are we able to kill them now?" Penelope asks, with a calmness that would turn the stomach of any suitor. "Before word arrives from Ithaca and puts them on guard?"

Priene considers it. "We could burn their garrison down, but the fire would spread and injure many in the town. We need to lure them out from behind their walls, and I don't think we can do that before word reaches them."

Penelope clicks her tongue in the roof of her mouth. It was an optimistic idea and she knew it. It is gone as easily as it came. "Very well. Let us strike into the interior and make camp." She raises her voice a little, to catch more ears. "Antinous, Amphinomous, Eurymachus, here, please."

The suitors slink over, doing their best not to stare at Priene. Penelope smiles upon them. It is a smile that in some ways resembles that of her cousin Helen when Helen wants something done. In Helen's mouth it is innocent, bright, dazzling, sincere. For Penelope it is a flash of teeth, a wolfish grin. Not everyone is going to be a total charmer.

"Gentlemen. For your safety and security, I suggest you take shelter at the temple of Zeus, further inland."

"The ship—" begins Amphinomous, but Penelope cuts him off.

"There are several skilled sailors of my acquaintance on Kephalonia who will ensure that your vessel is kept safe and out of Spartan hands. After all, we may need it again, no?"

The suitors look to each other. On the one hand, they want to argue. Arguing is their natural state of being. Even being given an order – and this is definitely that – by a woman is cause enough to bicker, even if the order is the most sensible thing they've ever heard. On the other hand, Priene stands by Penelope's side, and Teodora too, and there is something about the whole situation that just this once, for the first and quite possibly last time, makes them hesitate.

"My lady." Amphinomous bows.

Penelope graces them with a single flash of smile, and turns away.

They look one to the other, and then in sullen silence begin to shuffle up the beach.

Kenamon follows, always on the outside, not one of them.

"Not you, Kenamon," Penelope barks.

The men stop.

They turn.

She gestures towards where Orestes lies, Anaitis bent over him still, muttering in discontent at all she sees. "It is clear to me that the king is in need of suitable protection that I and my poor women . . ." another flash of that smile; it has something of an edge to it now, that knife's point between pleasure and pain, "my poor, weak women . . . cannot provide. Kenamon has proven himself useful with a blade. He will remain."

"I can—" Eurymachus blurts, and:

"Shut up, Eurymachus!" snaps Antinous.

"Is this wise?" Amphinomous enquires, voice pitched at a forced politeness. "A foreigner, a stranger – however good with a blade – close to the king? Close to you?"

Penelope's smile has tasted blood, it has hunted beneath the moon, it is Artemis, it is Athena, it is the arrow, it is the blade. It is nothing that I know. She directs it now to Amphinomous, who looks away, then turns to Elektra, who meets her eye. "Cousin?" she asks.

Elektra holds Penelope's gaze for a moment, then turns to the suitors. "The Egyptian stays with my brother," she barks. "I command it."

The suitors bow their heads and slowly march away.

CHAPTER 35

>>>

The shrine to Hera is little more than a nook carved in a cave, but it smells of power.

Hidden power, old power, the power that the mother once held to herself. High in the hills of Kephalonia, shrouded by olive groves and shadowed by great grey stones, there are no marble pillars or golden statues, no bowls of silver or marks of fame to draw the eye. Rather there is a thin, clear stream running down a shallow brook, and crimson leaves billowing in a soft inland breeze, and carvings scratched into the wall, old, older than even the first scratching of the thunderbolt of Zeus. Images of mothers, bellies swollen with child; of daughters dancing; of wives running naked across the land with spears held high. The deepest parts of the cave smell of time and blood, and the images raised to Hera are not of some many-chinned matron, but of a huge-breasted creator goddess from between whose legs life itself comes to be. I linger on its edges, smell the prayers, taste the blood that has been spilled in sacrifice and childbirth before this rough altar, wonder for a moment if Hera is looking down, if she remembers what it was like to be this lady of stone and earth, before she was reduced to being merely Zeus's wife.

At the mouth of the cave, Priene and her women have made camp.

With the suitors gone, there is no pretence about how many have rallied to Penelope's cause. Pylades and Iason gape to see it; Elektra's jaw is grimly set as they traipse between tents and under cloth awnings, past long, rough tables where the women sit, the stones where blades are sharpened. The youngest in Priene's army is a child of thirteen, whose mother sold her when they could not afford to feed the rest of the sisters screaming at the table, and who fled from a master who said he liked the way her woman-liness grew. This girl now runs like the deer, like the huntress herself, across the isles, bringing messages wherever Priene needs them brought. No one told her she couldn't, and so she runs all day and all night, oblivious to the consensus view among the wisest of the lands that this is clearly impossible for a girl to do. The oldest is a mother of more than sixty years' age, with claw marks on her thigh and silver lines across her belly and back from growing great with the daughters who will never be wives.

These women – nearly a hundred assembled – turn to stare at their queen as she enters the camp, salt in her hair and mud on her gown. They do not bow. They do not kneel or show any deference. They are here because it is necessary. It is necessary that they fight, it is necessary that they have a queen to fight for. Necessity has always been the word by which these islands live.

Orestes is laid down upon a woollen blanket beneath an awning open to the soft breeze and the smell of cooking fires. Elektra does not kneel by his side, does not brush his brow, does not weep. Instead she turns to Anaitis and says: "Will my brother live?"

Anaitis glances at those who will hear her answer – Penelope, Elektra, Rhene. Pylades too wants to be part of this conversation, but the priestess instinctively turns her back to him, until Penelope stands a little aside to give the man room. "Perhaps,"

Anaitis concedes. "He has been given drink that makes you sleep as if you were walking the edge of death, but you must take it often. The waking can be as dangerous as the falling asleep."

"Can you do anything?" Penelope asks.

"I can give him herbs to help ease the process. But as before, what he mostly needs is time. Time without medicine. Time without poison."

Elektra glances to Penelope, then quickly looks away. "Orestes was poisoned while in my palace," Penelope sighs. "He was recovering, and then he was not."

"Well that's not a surprise, is it?" blurts the priestess. "All those people, all those Spartans?"

"I will guard him now," Pylades proclaims. "I will not sleep."

"That's stupid," Anaitis retorts. "Even if you could stay awake, which is absurd, who's going to fetch his water? Make his food? Wash his clothes? You standing guard is meaningless against poison."

"I will fetch his water, his food," Elektra proclaims. "I did it in Mycenae and I will do it here."

"You did it in Mycenae, and in Mycenae he was poisoned." Penelope's voice is low, almost kind. "Your respective devotions are lovely, but demonstrably not the way."

"Then what do you suggest? That we let my brother die?"

"If I was going to let your brother die, do you think I would have abandoned my own city? I have made my choice. We will do what we can. Hopefully we have left behind any other threats to Orestes' well-being by fleeing the palace."

Penelope says these words calmly, but Elektra scowls, arms folded, shudders as if bitten by a cruel north wind.

The women go about their labours in the camp.

Teodora sets guards; Autonoe joins the women in fetching water.

Elektra goes with them, as if perhaps the spring itself from which they now draw has been in some way poisoned, as if the whole world is tainted black against her. But Elektra, for all that it is she and she alone who wishes to fill her brother's cup, is not used to carrying heavy things, and as she sways a little beneath the weight of fluid, Rhene catches her arm and steadies her, before wordlessly taking up her burdens.

Autonoe watches this a little while, and then, when Elektra is returned to her brother's side and Rhene stands alone, she approaches and says:

"Doesn't it make you angry?"

Rhene is surprised, confused, caught wringing out a cloth of cool water to bring to her mistress. "Angry?"

"The way Elektra treats you."

"She treats me no differently from how your queen treats you."

Autonoe's lips twitch, for there are secrets here, understandings and accords, that she will not say out loud. Instead: "She risks your life. With the poison. All this ... doting on her brother, all this madness. Tell me she hasn't ordered you to try his food or drink from his cup before he tastes it. Your life worth less than his."

Rhene lays her cloth down in its crude clay bowl, as if too preoccupied to both move her fingers and think the thoughts now upon her. "Would you not drink the cup, to save your queen?" Autonoe snorts her contempt at this idea, but Rhene's eyes turn to her, deep and forever dark. "I would," she says simply. "For my queen: I would."

Autonoe has no idea what to say to this, but again her nostrils flare as the Mycenaean maid turns away, and she shakes her head a little, as if trying to dislodge a fly tangled in her hair.

Penelope is given a tent nearest the mouth of the shrine. It is an easily defendable position, Priene declares, and away from

334

the cooking fires and latrines. In Priene's opinion, there is no higher honour that can be given to any creature living than to be in a defensible position that isn't too likely to catch on fire and doesn't smell of pee.

Penelope nods in acknowledgement, though she doesn't fully understand the courtesy her captain has here bestowed; pushes back the rough canvas to enter the musty interior. Some straw has been strewn upon the ground. Someone has left a little wooden figure of Artemis, bounding across the land with bow in hand. This is perhaps intended as a kindness, a courtesy to the queen, a sign of the blessing and good fortune that will befall this little women's army. Penelope picks it up, feels for a moment as if she might cry, as if she might weep, fall down. She is incredibly tired, incredibly hungry. If she sits, she does not think she will stand; if she falls, she knows she will never rise. When did she last sleep a whole night through? She cannot remember.

The privacy of the tent; the sudden quiet of the moment. There is almost a permission here, a granting of space to the Ithacan queen, who now clutches the image of the huntress so tight her bones might burst from her hand, drags down shuddering breath, squeezes her eyes tight and in a jolt of terror thinks there might be tears upon them.

Then Eos is by her side, as Eos always is, catching her by the elbow – and then more. More than just a maid should. Eos puts her arms around Penelope and holds her as the queen shakes and refuses to bend. She tries to speak, to say ... something, anything. But she has spent so many years saying nothing, feeling nothing, being nothing but what is needed to be, that now, when the words are desperate to break forth, she still cannot do it.

She cannot do it.

Her mouth moves, her hands shake, she holds onto Eos with

all her strength, and she cannot say a word. No, not even such as:

What have we done?

What have *I* done?

What will happen to us now?

I'm sorry. I'm sorry. I'm sorry.

Because, of course, Penelope has looked in Menelaus's eye, and she has seen what lurks within. She has seen him light up at the sight of her, seen him lick his lips, heard saliva pop behind his gums. But even when he is done with her, he will keep her alive. Can't kill the wife of Odysseus – at least not publicly. Not in any way that would arouse suspicion. He'll keep her alive, and once he has conquered her, he'll grow bored. He'll grow bored because conquest is what excites him, and conquest cannot last forever. Penelope will live, an old maid on some withered island, but her maids?

Oh yes, her maids.

Eos and Autonoe, Melantho and Phiobe, what will Menelaus do to them when all this is done? Nothing, of course. It won't occur to him. They'll be left to his guards, to his men. Not to the soldiers of Sparta the real spoils – not a kingdom, not the gold of Ithaca, not her tin and amber and rich flowing waters. They will not fight and die for that, not at all. All the soldiers have to look forward to are the meagre scraps from Menelaus's table, and naturally, the maids. The screams and tears, the begging and horror of the broken women of Ithaca will not feed these men, they will not give them worth in their master's eyes, they will not bring them happiness or contentment or rest from fear. But at least they'll feel something. If they win – when they win – the men will feel something.

Penelope stares into Eos's eyes, and Eos stares back.

They know the truth of each other's hearts well, these women of Ithaca. They have seen the lowest of one another's spirits, heard the cracking of each other's souls. Eos holds Penelope,

336

and Penelope holds Eos, and for a while that is all there is, as each refuses to weep.

I wrap them in my arms.

Usually I'd be all for letting it out. Having a good old bawl on the floor, a proper "woe-is-me" girls' session, followed by a nice bit of self-care and a massage. But we are in a military camp, hidden on an island on the verge of war. Even I, who otherwise would be the first to bring the scented oils, understand that there is a time and a place.

Then there is a cough at the mouth of the tent, and immediately Eos and Penelope move apart, stand straight, always straight, eyes dry, mouths set.

Autonoe enters. She looks one to the other, sees all, and just this once, judges nothing. "All right," she says. "Hear me out. I think someone smells funny."

In the evening, a detachment of Spartans arrive on Kephalonia's shores.

They are only a reinforcing party of thirty. That is all Menelaus can spare, given he is now faced with the dubious challenge of searching the whole western isles, from tiniest rock to sprawling isle, for his missing Mycenaean king.

They do not come by Spartan warship. After the fire, there are only three vessels worthy of putting to sea, and Menelaus needs those scouring the waters for any trace of missing Penelope. Instead they come by a commandeered merchant vessel, whisked from under Eupheithes' furious nose. "For the good of good King Orestes," Lefteris proclaimed, sword drawn, tip turned towards Eupheithes' neck. The Spartan captain did not think to enquire of Eupheithes where his son has gone. He simply didn't understand enough about the isle to know to ask.

A fisherwoman of the town reports to a weaver, who reports to the mother who tends the sheep upon the hills, who tells the girl waiting by her door, of the strength and disposition of the Spartans come now to Kephalonia's shores.

The girl runs to the shrine of Hera to tell Priene, who marches to Penelope's tent and proclaims: "Fifty Spartans in all, garrisoned for tonight. They'll spread out and start searching the island tomorrow, no doubt."

Autonoe has come and gone, so now only Penelope and Eos hear Priene's news.

"In strength, or in groups?" asks the queen.

"If it was me, groups of no fewer than fifteen, with a small force left behind at the garrison."

"Who leads them? Not Menelaus?"

"No – Nicostratus."

"Interesting. I thought Menelaus would release his son from the temple sooner rather than later. I didn't think he'd send him to Kephalonia. You can kill any Spartan you like, but if we can take Nicostratus alive, that would be helpful."

Priene considers this. "He may not be uninjured."

Penelope dismisses the thought with a waft of her hand. "So long as no one can say we killed the son of Menelaus, I have no concerns whatsoever as to what happens to his knees."

Priene nods once, briefly. She isn't a huge fan of taking people alive, or at least possessed of injuries that won't absolutely kill them in the coming few days. The care involved in such an operation is always messier and harder to manage in the heat of battle than just a clean bit of slaughter – but at least she knows she has options. She leaves to gather her forces. There are traps to be laid, ambushes, brutal skirmishes in the silver twilight – nothing that the poets will sing about.

In the sullen darkness of her tent, Penelope sits on a pile of straw. Eos sits next to her. There is a closeness here that would never be seen in the palace, shoulder to shoulder in the gathering dark of cold night. The formal distance between the women is habitual, a needful show, but these things grow a little absurd when imminent destruction is on the line. Eos says: "I would comb your hair, but . . . " A little gesture, to indicate the tragic truth that of all the womanly accoutrements Eos could have escaped from the palace with, the only one she brought with her was a hidden blade. Penelope swallows down an inelegant snort of laughter, shakes her head. "I asked Rhene if Elektra might lend me her comb, but the woman's response was remarkably uncharitable," the maid adds, clicking in disappointment.

Penelope turns her gaze to Eos with a slow widening of her eyes, their darkness glistening half lost in the tent. "What?" Eos blurts when her queen doesn't speak, though her breath comes fast and light. "Was I wrong?"

Penelope grips the maid's hand. "That's how," she breathes. "That's how."

At once she rises, brushes back the flap of the tent, is briefly bewildered on stepping outside to realise that she doesn't know exactly where to go in this camp, is unfamiliar with the chittering night. However, Teodora has been set to keep guard over her, and now approaches from the edge of firelight, bow in hand, eyes constantly turning to the shadows beyond their hollow dwelling, head inclined a little to one side as if she, blessed of Artemis, might hear running feet through the busy night.

"My lady?"

"The tent of Orestes and Elektra. I must see it now. Eos – fetch Autonoe and meet me there."

Penelope is at her most gloriously attractive in one of two modes: in early autumn, skin glistening with sweat as she labours at the harvest, sun glistening in her dishevelled hair, a woman of business, a woman surrounded entirely by women who labour with her too; not a queen, but a farmer who loves the earth upon which she treads and gives thanks for its bounty.

Odysseus never saw her like this – she was too busy being a queen when he was still king on Ithaca – but goodness, he would have found it really quite a sight to see his wife laughing and singing the songs of the women as they washed their hot feet in the cold river at the end of the long harvest day.

Her next most attractive mode is indeed a queenly one, but it is not one of holding court nor sitting in council, nor of hosting tedious feasts and waving at the common folk as though to say why yes, yes, it is I, how special that must make you feel. Under those circumstances she keeps in a modest, subdued vein, head down and eyes up as befits a woman of service – service to her husband, service to her people. It is only on those rare occasions when she perhaps plays a skilled opponent at tavli and sees a cunning trap, a clever little move, and cannot stop herself, cannot suppress the beating of her heart and the twitch of the smile on her lips, that she shimmers. She glows with excitement, and take it from me, excitement and arousal are often of the same fluttering breath, the same licked lips, the same wide eyes, the same hot flushed cheeks. Odysseus saw this in his wife, before he sailed to Troy, only once. But there was never enough time in the day for games, and then he was gone.

This then is the light that now shines upon Penelope's face as she picks her way through the ragged camp sheltered beneath the rocks of Kephalonia. It is the look of one who has seen the way, and knows it, a beauty that shines through mud and knotty hair and weariness and the weight of encroaching time.

Pylades is sitting in the dirt outside the tent of Orestes, a rock guarding the door, sullenly refusing to sleep, though his eyes will betray him long before his spirit does. Rhene approaches from the nearby stream, a jug of fresh water in her hands; Iason sleeps on a nearby bed of moss. I caress his brow, let him slumber a little deeper, an easy rest to reward the really rather manly excursions of his day.

Pylades does not rise at Penelope's approach, is too much of a dullard this night to see how beautifully she shines in the spinning firelight. He looks past her to Teodora, then stirs a little as Eos and Autonoe approach. This gathering of women arouses the curiosity of others – eyes turn towards the tent, breath is caught, there are people in the camp not so weary as Pylades to see a certain something about Penelope that speaks of action.

"I will see Elektra now," Penelope says.

Pylades opens his mouth, though divinity knows he has nothing worthwhile to say. His words are cut short by the tent flap pushing back and Anaitis sticking her head out. "What do you want?" she demands. "I am trying to attend to the patient!"

"Just a few moments of his sister's time, nothing more," soothes Penelope.

Anaitis blinks this information into her skull, nods once, disappears back into the tent, and then with a near shove expels Elektra from it, having as little interest in the princess disturbing her labours as any other who might venture into her domain.

Elektra glares at Penelope, the habit of one who does not like to be taken from her brother's side – but since Penelope is a queen and not fit for glaring at, she directs her ire with a flash of heat in her cheeks to Pylades, who looks away.

Penelope catches her cousin by the wrist. Elektra nearly jumps, nearly lashes out at the intrusion, but stops herself, hesitates. Though the grip is strong, it is not wounding, nor a threat. Merely an anchor, an invitation to be steady, to be here, for the two hearts in two bodies to perhaps now feel the strength of the other's pulse, and briefly beat in unity.

"Your comb," Penelope breathes. "May I see your comb?"

"What?"

"Your comb. The one with which you brush your brother's hair. The one you use to soothe him in his troubled sleep."

Penelope does not let go of Elektra's wrist, and now perhaps the princess is relieved at this, senses the strength that holds her up as with her other hand she reaches into her gown. She nearly drops the little object of polished shell, fumbling as she puts it into Penelope's open palm. Penelope turns it this way and that, holding it up to the firelight, then softly calls: "Anaitis?" Movement inside the tent, then the priestess appears again, lips shaping a decidedly disrespectful enquiry that she just about restrains in the face of so much royalty. Penelope beams at her, serenity upon her brow. "Would you examine this, please?"

Anaitis considers the comb held towards her, opens her mouth to blurt something that would be decidedly unpolitic, and stops herself. The same idea that has now nested itself in Penelope's head slips into the priestess's too, and though it would be delightful to take some divine credit for this act, I will admit that it was all their own lovely cognition. Anaitis takes the comb. Examines the sharp ends of every tooth. Holds it up to her face. Sniffs it. Brings it to her lips. Licks it. Rolls the taste around her mouth. Looks up at Penelope. Smiles. Nods, just once. Hands the comb back to the Ithacan queen.

A circle of women has formed around this scene, drawn by a story they do not understand, a mystery unfolding that calls to them as the poets have always called to every ear that bends to hear. Penelope lets go of Elektra's wrist, and the Mycenaean staggers, nearly seems to fall, catches Penelope's hand in her own, holding on now, holding tight. Stares into her eyes. Whispers: "Was it me?"

Penelope nods, and Elektra seems for a moment to buckle. She bends, she breaks, she twists over her own belly as if punched, she clutches at Penelope's shoulders, at her chest, falls into her arms, and at last, in child-like heaves, in gasping, snotty sucking snorts of air, she weeps like a child in a mother's embrace.

CHAPTER 36

>>>

O nce, when Elektra was sixteen years old, a serving boy touched her. Their lips, their tongues, their flesh tangled behind the stables. He caressed her nipples, worshipped her belly, ran his tongue, his fingers between her thighs. She rocked and writhed in ecstasy and then – at the moment when she might have burst in passion and delight – kicked him away. Tumbled from his grasp, gathered up her clothes and fled from that place. He was rather confused by this development, even more so when two days later he was sold to a smith in a faraway town.

For her part, having dispatched her could-have-been lover, Elektra wept and prayed before the altar of almighty Zeus, begging forgiveness. Not for having consorted with a boy per se – she was enough a child of Agamemnon to know that marriage vows were at best loosely ambitious things. But for having enjoyed her body, exulted in her flesh, dabbled on the very rim of ecstasy. Women should not do such things, she knew. Her mother had cried out in delight to be worshipped upon by Aegisthus; her aunt Helen had betrayed the world when lured by the passionate promise of Paris and his agile, firm body. The delight of women was sinful, cruel, unnatural. The gods proved this, for lo, any god could take any woman he wanted and she would be punished for his deed, as was the natural way of things. So Elektra prayed that when she was married, as surely she would be, her husband would push her face-down into the marriage bed, as her father was said to have done unto his wife while his conquering men stood by and cheered, and do his business upon her until she bled, and she would bear the pain. The women of the house of Agamemnon were nothing if not made to endure.

Orestes was fifteen when he first lay with a woman. It was considered a useful part of his education to be introduced to the nuances of female flesh by his tutors in Athens, who were a bit disappointed that he hadn't availed himself of his pleasure in this regard already. And so one night he was taken to a shrine raised in my honour and the attentions of a really rather fabulous woman of my creed were negotiated, who promised with her art all sorts of wondrous delights and secret ecstasies.

"No no no!" retorted his teacher. "You hold her down like this, and then you enter her like this, and you just do that until you are done!"

Pylades was there too that night. His sexual education was of far less importance than Orestes', given that the need for him to produce an heir was going to be of less political significance, but since they were boys of the same age, it was considered apt that Pylades too should get a taste of manly affairs. Besides, their teachers said, it was unhealthy for men to contain their essences for too long, especially men who would be warrior kings.

So Pylades did his business by Orestes' side, and the two boys did not look at each other as they went about their work, and did not look, and did not look, and did not look.

Thus did the children of Agamemnon leave their childhoods behind.

*

On the island of Kephalonia, many years later, a small circle of women – and a few passing men – sit around a fire. Penelope holds the comb in her lap, Anaitis to her left, Autonoe to her right.

"Henbane," Anaitis proclaims, to the assemblage of light-reflecting eyes. "The priests of Apollo burn it in their so-called oracles, make their priestesses inhale the smoke. I have seen it used as an oil too, dripped into food or rubbed into the thin places of the skin to bring about prophetic dreams. It is easy to take too much – there are some who have died from it. But in small quantities it brings about visions. Some might say madness."

"Everything Orestes drank – everything he ate – was eaten or drunk by someone else too," Penelope adds, as Elektra watches her across the dancing flames. "In Mycenae, on the road to Ithaca, in my palace. He did not drink from any special vessel as Helen does, he was not fed food that others might not eat. And yet he was poisoned. Touched by something unique to him – something that only he might be touched by."

Elektra has cried her tears away. Now more than ever she sits still and stiff, as her mother did – so much of Clytemnestra in her daughter, even more now than there was before. Clytemnestra once swore never to be seen to be weak, to never show her tears before the eyes of men. Elektra too will take that oath, is already weaving it into her heart, not knowing it is the same one her mother carried with her to the end.

"Pylades was poisoned too, in Mycenae," Elektra whispers. "And my maid."

"Yes. But that was before you fled. Easy enough to coat a cup, a washing bowl, something intimate to Orestes. The water with which he washed his face; the cloth with which he cleaned his skin. Even the bed in which he lay. Once he was on the road, that would become far more challenging to sustain, and so we see, perhaps, a change in tactics."

345

Pylades stares at nothing, though many around the fire stare at him.

"It would take a long time, and have to be done regularly," Anaitis muses, for her own curiosity more than the ears of the hearers. "But the teeth of the comb, used often enough, will brush along the surface of the skin, allow the oil to penetrate. A patient poison, but effective, as we can see."

"How did this happen?" Elektra's voice is a bare breath. She has to cough and try again, pushing her words out louder, more powerfully, performing the act of the wronged queen – better to be a wronged queen, better to be Clytemnestra, than to be the foolish girl who nearly killed her own brother. That child must die, that child must never be seen again, anything but that, anything but a guilty girl weeping at the cruelties of this world. *How did this happen? I kept the comb about me at all times. It was our sister's . . . it is a family . . . How did this happen?*"

"You slept," Penelope replies with a shrug. "Even you had to sleep. You changed your clothes. You bathed. Only a few moments are needed to coat the teeth with oil and return it to its place."

"But how?" snaps Elektra, voice rising again, a little closer to terror, a little closer to breaking; she draws in a shuddering breath, pulls it back. "How?"

"You guarded access to your brother, not to you." Penelope is trying to be kind. She used to try and be kind to her son, Telemachus, and he hated her for it. Now she is not sure how to sound kind without also getting it wrong. "Though you waited upon your brother, women waited upon you. In Mycenae. And in Ithaca." She extends one hand politely to Autonoe, sitting impatiently by her side. "Tell my cousin what you told me."

Autonoe has no qualms about meeting Elektra's eye. She would have made a glorious queen if she had not been sold as a slave. "The priest. Kleitos." Elektra's lips curl in distaste, but she holds back her bile. "We went to visit him, to examine his rooms, suspecting that he was not of your cause. He did not let us in the first time we knocked, said he was at his prayers. But when we came again, he admitted us. I wondered then what he'd been hiding – or who. Who might have been visiting this purveyor of oils and ointments in the palace. There was a smell in the air, an incense perhaps used for some religious rite – or the appearance of one. We don't have fine incenses like that in Ithaca, but the memory of it stuck in my nose. And I smelled it on her." A finger extends, without particular malice or regret, towards Rhene.

The Mycenaean maid has been sitting quietly on the edge of the firelight.

A maid's place is always to be quiet on the edge of the light.

"Elektra," murmurs Penelope, "which maid was it who was poisoned in Mycenae?"

"Rhene." Elektra's voice is a ragged stone, sticking in her throat. "It was Rhene."

"Rhene and Pylades. The only two people apart from Orestes to be affected. We assume of course that they maybe ate something, drank something Orestes did, but what of the alternatives? Either that they are . . . intimate with your brother, close, shall we say . . . or perhaps that the poisoner when she first began her mission was not yet so skilled as to not accidentally poison herself."

No one gasps. No one cries "for shame!" or faints. There is no one to perform this for now, just the cold truth unravelling at the bitter end. Rhene looks at Autonoe, and seems almost to nod, one maid to another, an acknowledgement of equals more important perhaps than to acknowledge these nearby queens.

"Rhene?" Elektra breathes. "But you love me."

No one loves Elektra. Even Orestes, when he is sober, finds it hard to love his sister. He tries, of course – it is his brotherly

347

duty – but duty cannot melt the heart, nor bring about one's sincere, kind desire by wishing alone.

Rhene looks upon Elektra, and there is almost pity in her eyes – a pity that sits but a blink away from contempt. Then she looks upon Penelope and, loud and calm, says: "When they kill me, you will ensure it is quick."

Pylades is the one whose breath catches, who reaches for his blade – but his hand is steadied by Eos, who shakes her head, commanding patience, silence. He is used to demonstrating his loyalty in significant, heroic ways, but this is not the time or place.

Penelope considers the maid, then nods. "Yes. There will be no barbarous cruelties enacted here."

Rhene raises her chin to the shadow of Priene, standing on the edge of the circle, where light meets dark. "She'll do it. She's a warrior. She'll be fast."

Elektra should protest, should scream for torture, sacrifice, foulest retribution, should demand to eat her blood! But Elektra is silent. Her tears are over; she will not weep again. I caress her hair, squeeze her tight, and she does not feel me, is gone too far even from love.

Penelope looks from Rhene to Priene, shakes her head. "I will not order her to be an executioner."

"Will you?" Rhene asks, fixing Priene now with her gaze.

Priene considers, arms folded, staring long into the maid's eyes. Then nods. Rhene smiles and looks away.

Elektra, now near fit to burst, knuckles white in her lap, breath fast and thin, blurts: *"You swore to love me!"*

Rhene seems almost surprised by this, by the absolute conviction in her mistress's voice. "Yes," she says. "I did. I promised your mother that whatever happened, I would love you. Your mother insisted on it. She took me by the hand, stared into my eyes, made me swear to protect you, to keep you safe. I would

348

do anything for my queen. Anything at all. So I swore it. For her. For Clytemnestra."

Elektra throws herself towards Rhene, fingers out, hands turned into claws, nearly setting herself aflame with her abandon as she leaps across the fire. Teodora grabs her before she can reach the maid, pulls her back, hissing and snarling, gathers her into her arms. Pylades steps between them, helps Teodora hold the Mycenaean down as Elektra screams: "*I trusted you I trusted you I trusted you how could you how could you how could you!*" Her words become mumbled, distorted, dissolve at last into an animal scream, a shriek of rage and horror, of purest despair, that cracks the night. The Furies, twisting overhead, mimic the noise, echo the shriek across the isle, across the sea, turn the waters red and crack the stones, until at last, hollowed out and gutted of all sound, Elektra collapses in Pylades' arms.

"Priene, Teodora, Eos. We should walk a little way off with Rhene, I believe," says Penelope.

Rhene rises quickly, smooths down her gown, nods to Priene as the woman slips out of the dark to stand by her side, Teodora taking up position by her other arm. Elektra turns her face away and Pylades holds her still, jerks his chin towards Iason to follow the knot of women as they move away from the fire.

I catch a whiff of starlight and spin it a little brighter about them as they walk into the woods. Teodora finds the way over rough stones and through snapping branches down to the edge of the stream, where the hanging trees and rocks part enough to let through the shining eye of heaven. Priene stands at Rhene's back. Eos stands by Penelope, Iason some few paces off, silent, a witness to this scene but not part of it.

Rhene raises her chin to the sky, closes her eyes, lets herself bathe in this night, in the breeze, in the beauty of the air and the weight of her own lovely flesh. Penelope watches her a moment, then says: "For my own curiosity. If you will. Did Menelaus ask you to poison Orestes?"

Rhene only half opens her eyes, answers as if already dead, already in a far-off place where the mist rolls over fields of broken wheat. "Not directly. But he owns Kleitos, and Kleitos knew me of old. She saved me, you know. Clytemnestra. She saved us all. I was just a child when she found me, already destined to be some ... some old man's whore. She took me in, washed my face, combed my hair, dressed me in her daughter's clothes, rubbed oil into my skin. She was ... she was so very beautiful. When Agamemnon was in Mycenae, the women were just ... flesh. To be thrown from one dog to another like an old chewed bone. But when he sailed to Troy, she put an end to it. Enforced the old rules, ordered that any man who took a woman without her consent, even the lowest slave, be punished for it, not the maid. The men hated that, used it against her, but we ... I ... loved her. Men give women power, and women sacrifice the women around them to appease men. Not Clytemnestra. She was a real queen. She could ask me to do anything – anything at all – and I was grateful to serve."

The Furies are spinning overhead, trying to catch again the sound of Elektra's scream, mimicking, playing with the noise – but they can't quite get it right, shriek, *Mother, Mother, Mother!* Then I realise that there are others watching too, peeking down into this place of starlight. Artemis stands, toes in the stream, bow unstrung by her side, head bowed as if she would fall into the running water. Athena, too, waits on the edge of the clearing, her helmet set at her feet, spear driven point-down into the ground. They have come – not for Penelope – not even for Elektra or her brother or the Furies raging overhead. With a start of surprise, I realise that they have come for Rhene. For an unsung maid, the goddesses come.

"But you swore an oath. To Clytemnestra. To protect her daughter."

Rhene nods, sharp and brisk. "I did. Elektra will never understand her mother's love. Clytemnestra saw that her daughter was lonely, and asked me to play with her. So I did, and for a while I think there was a kind of friendship there. I very much wanted to be Elektra's friend, if it made Clytemnestra happy. But Orestes swore an oath to avenge his father, and so he killed his mother. The only people who care about oaths are warriors and kings. No one cares what a slave woman says."

I put my hand on Rhene's shoulder, breathe strength into her spine, steadiness into her chest. Her love burns bright and glorious; *Clytemnestra, Clytemnestra, wonderful Clytemnestra*, sings her soul. While the queen lived, Rhene never expressed it, never dared tell the queen of Mycenae thank you, thank you, you radiant one, I would be yours for ever. Only when Clytemnestra was gone did Rhene at last, in the loss of the thing, let it consume her. What could matter more than love?

Autonoe whispers: Perhaps banishment, perhaps . . .

Eos replies: No. We both know it cannot be.

If Priene does not end this business tonight, then Pylades or Iason will end it tomorrow, or Elektra the day after, and they will be cruel. They will be so cruel, these sons and daughters. They will think, perhaps, that the torment of another may in some way alleviate the pain of their hearts, and they will be wrong.

"Do you know who killed Zosime?" asks Penelope, a question to which she does not expect an answer.

Rhene shakes her head; she has no reason to lie now.

"No," sighs the queen. "I didn't think so."

Eos holds Autonoe's hand when Priene draws her blade. The captain of the Ithacan band hesitates a moment, stops before the Mycenaean maid, looks her in the eye. "Sister," she says. "I think, were I you, I would have done the same."

Rhene nods, an acknowledgement of a truth, nothing more, and does not look at Priene's blade.

The screaming of the Furies has stopped, I realise. As Priene levels her blade, I look about for the three bloody hags, the taloned ladies of fire and pain, and see them – not spinning in the sky, not cackling in merriment, but standing now silently on the edge of the grove, wings furled across their hunched bodies, eyes glistening like the heart of the flame.

They are still now, heads bowed – come not to mock, not to cackle or feast on tragedy, but to honour a daughter of their own.

As Priene strikes and Rhene falls, I hear a sound I think I never shall again as goddess and Fury alike raise their voices in mourning song for the soul of the departed maid.

CHAPTER 37

>>>

L et us recount the passage of three days.

Spartan bands spread across the island, but of the women they find no sign. Kephalonia is far larger than Ithaca, though the smaller isle commands the greater. Menelaus has not brought enough men to conquer all the land – he thought it would be enough to take the palace, and now he pays for that misjudgement.

Priene sends scouts out to watch the progress of the soldiers in their bronze plate as they clatter between orchards and over rough, stone-poked fields. The scouts go as precisely what they are – the herders of goats or gatherers of firewood, the bringers-home of oil and women who beat copper and tin. They can stand not three paces from the Spartan men and watch them with mouths agape, and be in their own strange way invisible.

"Beware the women!" Menelaus instructed his son before sending Nicostratus across the water from Ithaca. "They're sneaky! They're on her side!"

Nicostratus nodded and said yes, Father, of course, Father, but he didn't understand. Of course he knew that Helen had gone to Troy and brought about the war that broke the world, but that was just another story. The Helen he knows is a blubbering drunk drooling at his father's feet, and so the imprecation to consider the women of the isles as some sort of meaningful threat is anathema to the fundamentals of Nicostratus's mind.

Thus he marches through Kephalonia, demands to know where's the queen, who's seen the traitor Penelope – and lo and behold every woman he asks this of cowers and grovels and says, oh goodness, oh no, dear master, oh please don't hurt us, good sir, spare us, we are but humble widows and old maids, and this fulfils Nicostratus's expectations, and therefore must be true.

Priene hears all this from the women who run through the forest to bring her news. She plans, she prepares, she counts spears, she counts bows and blades, she sits upon the brow of a hill that looks down towards the sea and wonders just how serious Penelope is about the order to bring in Nicostratus alive.

"It would be really very bad indeed to kill the son of Menelaus," repeats the Ithacan queen over a dinner of snared rabbit cooked upon the open flame. "Really very, very bad."

Priene sighs, but finds to her surprise that even she can just this once see the long-term tactical merits of not killing every Greek she comes across, despite her natural inclinations.

Anaitis tends to Orestes.

I see Artemis walking sometimes with her priestess, as Anaitis gathers herbs from the forest; see too how quickly the footprints of the women fade into the earth as they move about the camp, how the trees bend in to hide the light of their midnight fires. Artemis, whose chastity is a running joke in Olympus, who is mocked because she cannot be conquered, derided because she does not care to be dishonoured – the gods in their cups forget sometimes how many ways there are to love. I see it in her now, as she steadies the knife of a child who is learning to skin a hare; as she breathes a little more warmth into the hidden campfire; as she runs at Teodora's side by the light of the setting

354

sun, crimson in her hair, freedom in her laughter. She loves, she loves, oh with all her glorious heart does she love; brighter and more beautiful even than Athena's love for Odysseus, hotter and more beautiful than Paris's desire for Helen, Artemis loves the women of the wood, her people, her sisters, her heart's kin. She would bleed divinity for them; she would stand naked before snarling Scylla in their name. And yet, because her love is not some sexual thing, because it is not the thing that the poets stroking their beards will make ballads of, she herself does not know it is love. Her joy is not spoken of by the spinners of stories, not sung by the music-makers, and so she does not perceive it even as happiness, as delight. She lives merely in this moment without a name, and will recoil in wounded horror if I whisper the truth in her ear: that she most deeply, and most truly, loves.

Eos tends to Elektra.

Elektra does not leave her tent.

Does not tend to her brother.

Does not go near him.

Eats when told to eat.

Drinks when told to drink.

Says nearly nothing.

Shows no sign of weeping.

Sleeps a great deal, poorly.

Wakes tired, and with a low, restless pain she cannot shift.

Eos says: shall we walk? And in silence they walk.

Eos says: shall we bathe by the stream? And in silence they bathe.

Then in the evenings, Eos returns to Penelope and says: she eats, she drinks, she walks, she bathes. Yet she is as a ghost who drinks the waters of the River Lethe, forgetting all things and herself.

Penelope hears all this without remark, then thanks Eos when she is done, and retires to her tent to think and pray.

Her prayers are, for the first time in really quite a long time, real.

She has spent so much time praying for the show of the thing, displaying piety in public places and invoking the gods whenever she needs a moment to collect her thoughts, that to actually pray for something real is a somewhat clunky, unfamiliar experience. But she gets on her knees and does her best.

She prays to Athena, for the martial wisdom to defeat her foes.

She prays to Artemis, to keep the women of her little army hidden and safe, and that her priestess might be wise in her ministrations to the Mycenaean king.

She prays to Hera, for regal strength.

To Apollo, for the quick recovery of Orestes.

To Poseidon, for bad seas to trap the Spartan ships in port, but good winds to carry her back to Ithaca, when the time comes.

She knows she should pray to Zeus, but can't think of anything worthwhile she might want from the old thunderer.

She prays to Hades. It is considered incredibly bad form to pray to the god of the dead, to offer up libations in his honour, to even invoke his name out loud in this breathing world. But Penelope sends her thoughts down below the earth regardless, to ask for comfort for those departed, and those whose time to depart is yet to come. She prays that when she too reaches those distant fields, the spirits of those who greet her will be compassionate to a fellow sister of the damned.

She does not pray to me. She cannot imagine what possible merit there could be in giving up prayers to the lady of love.

On Ithaca, Helen prays, and her prayers are Aphrodite, Aphrodite, Aphrodite! Never was I so sorrowful as when I was your plaything! Never so small, never so diminished! Aphrodite, Aphrodite, you sold me as flesh, you sold me as skin, as sex, you made me a thing to be toyed with, a mockery of faithfulness, you broke the world in my name, oh goddess Aphrodite, you

356

broke the world. Give me your power again. Give me your love. Let the world love me. Let the world tear itself asunder for me again.

I close my eyes and let her words wash through me. The prayers of mortals all carry a different flavour, a different scent from the mouths of those who utter them. The men rarely offer up their voices to me; it is unmanly to desire, to need, to long for companionship or to be afraid of loneliness and regret. Away with it! Away with foolish yearning! The prayers of maids are naïve and fanciful, the prayers of the old wives often soured with regret. But Helen – her prayers are nectar and honey, they are the caress of warmth against cold skin, the brush of fingers upon the brow, the taste of tears upon the tongue. They fill me, they fulfil me, my love for her blazes so bright I sometimes fear it will crack me apart, unbearable, intoxicating, my beautiful one, my broken one, my love, my queen.

Three goddesses there were who bathed in the waters of Mount Ida as Paris leered upon us, Zeus at his side. Three Furies there are who spin above the tent of Orestes. Three queens there were in Greece – one beloved of Hera, who killed her husband and died. One who is wed to the beloved of Athena, whose husband even now sets forth in his little rough-hewn boat again. And one who is mine, and whose name will live for as long as there is love, for as long as hearts beat throughout eternity.

Then Athena is by my side. She puts her hand upon mine, and it is a shock like lightning. I feel tears in my eyes, turn to her, open my mouth to say sister, my sister, are you ready at last to be loved? To show love, to feel love, be of love, my love, my beautiful Athena?

But she shakes her head, as if dismissing any thought other than her own, and breathes: "It is time."

*

Thus it transpires that on that third night on Kephalonia, Orestes, son of Agamemnon, son of Clytemnestra, poisoned by the maid who loved his mother, compounded by the priest who served his uncle, saved perhaps by the priestess of some backwards isle, stirs in his bed. Opens his eyes. Gazes round the shell of cloth that encases him. Tries to speak, finds his mouth is dry. Takes a few sips of the water that Anaitis holds to his lips. Tries again to find words, to find meaning, and utters a plea that seems to come from the depths of his soul: "Mother, forgive me."

"*He is ours, he is ours, he is ours!*" the Furies cry.

"Not yet," Athena replies.

"*He is ours, by blood and by right he is ours, no more delay!*"

"Not yet," she repeats, holding her spear tight, the helmet drawn across her eyes. I stand by her side – well, maybe a little behind – and from the forest Artemis appears, arrow notched to the string of her bow, to stand shoulder to shoulder with her.

"Forgive me!" cries Orestes to the night, and the Furies howl, claws out, wings beating pestilence across the night sky.

"Forgive me," whispers Elektra, to the cold hollow of her soul.

"Mother!" wails the prince.

"Mother," whispers the princess.

"*HE IS OURS!*" shriek the Furies. "*FIRST THE BROTHER, THEN THE SISTER TOO!*"

"Not yet," repeats Athena, and as the Furies snarl and show their teeth, she raises her spear, lightning crackling round the tip of it, and points towards another part of the camp. Towards Penelope's tent, into which Anaitis now ducks, moving with purpose. Athena grins, the same snarl of satisfaction I have sometimes seen on Penelope's mouth. "Not yet," she declares. "There is still one last judgement to be made."

*

The tent of Penelope is crowded that night.

Ourania, Eos, Autonoe, Anaitis, Elektra. There is hardly enough room for a queen and her maid, let alone this assemblage of women, but they squeeze in as best they can and try not to knock their heads together too hard as they shuffle away from the flap.

"Orestes is mad," Anaitis says.

Elektra does not stir, does not object, does not rouse herself at this, so it falls to Penelope to raise a questioning brow. "I thought he was awake. I thought you were tending to him, that he was no longer being poisoned."

"He is. I am. He has not had contact with the poison on the comb for several days, and I have been astonishingly skilled and excellent in my care," replies Anaitis with the same flat composure her patroness is wont to manifest when explaining just how good she is with a bow. "However, on waking, he still calls out for his mother, for forgiveness. What do you think the priests of Apollo do when they burn that plant in their prophetic groves? They don't just shove any virgin girl in there and say 'pronounce on prophecy'. They choose nice, impressionable youngsters with a profound devotion to their patron, explain to them very firmly in clear language what the issues are, advise on possible desirable outcomes, and *then* make them inhale the fumes of the burning shrub."

"I'm not sure I take your point."

"My point is that the women who give their pronouncements are already very appropriately primed to have an exceptional religious experience. Do you really think the outcome would be the same if they took some . . . sex-crazed girl with an obsession for . . . kittens . . ." – Anaitis is struggling to think of things that are anathema to her very nature. Vivid imagination is not her greatest quality – "and expected them to deliver prophetic pronouncements in a suitable manner? No. One must prime the person whom one is influencing, coax them into a suitable state of being and *then* provide the fumes."

"You are suggesting that Orestes was already primed to have a certain . . . complicated emotional state before he was poisoned? And that this experience merely pushed him to the edge?"

"Quite. As I said: he is mad. All the drugs did was bring out this state that already existed."

"*He is ours, he is ours!*" shriek the Furies, but they are now circling, watching, waiting for this conference to conclude.

Penelope looks to Elektra, and Elektra looks at nothing at all. I reach towards her, but Athena grabs my hand, pulls it back. Neither goddess nor Fury will decide this moment. Instead we must watch. Infuriating! I bristle at the indignation of it, pull a little against Athena's hold – but she is unrelenting.

The Furies spin but do not speak, do not cry out, do not spit venom onto the cold earth.

Rhene drifts through the underworld, calling out for her queen, her love, Clytemnestra, Clytemnestra!

Clytemnestra thought she saw the ghost of Iphigenia by the waters of the river of forgetfulness, but when she reached her, she was not sure if it was her child or no. She is already finding it hard to remember her name, in this land of the dead.

Poseidon has returned from his feasting in the far-off southern lands to find Odysseus fled from Ogygia. In fury he scours the seas to catch at the little raft the Ithacan king has made with his sea nymph's favourite axe, and now he pours down the ocean upon Odysseus's head, tosses him from peak of towering wave to trough that seems to scrape the seabed itself, glimpses of broken bones and fire-cracked sand. He would kill the man in a moment if he had his way, but no – no. Zeus has pronounced. Odysseus will survive this storm. Odysseus will be free.

Menelaus prowls the halls of his sometime sworn blood brother. Sees a fresco showing Odysseus and the wooden horse, a painted monument to the lost king's cleverness. Helen, skin white as snow, golden hair about her round, innocent face, gazes down from the city walls.

Menelaus looks to the left. Looks to the right. Sees no one watching. Draws his blade and scrapes it across the loose plaster of the wall, across those painted eyes and down those painted lips until his blade is blunt as a plank of wood and the ochre on the wall is shredded to thin pale dust about his scuttling feet.

Helen sits by her perfect mirror, tugs at her lower lip, hates the way the skin has dried, hates how on the inside of her mouth she can see strange nodules, little imperfections in her wet flesh. No one else will see them, even know that they're there. But she will. She will know.

And on Kephalonia, while the goddesses and Furies alike look on, Penelope sits in silent contemplation, her council assembled about her, the moon hidden high overhead.

Then she stands.

Marches to the mouth of her tent without a word, followed by her council of women.

Picks her way through the camp.

Strides to the door of Orestes' tent, where Pylades wearily keeps his endless guard.

Barks: "Stand aside!"

He stands aside.

Penelope grabs Anaitis by one hand, Elektra by the other, and pulls the women in.

CHAPTER 38

>>

In the darkness of Orestes' tent, three women and a man.
But no – no.

These are merely the figures that mortal eyes can see.

Look again, and observe. They bend the space around them,
distort the senses to find their accommodation, but here they
are. The Furies have come, they stand now at the head of
Orestes' bed, and in this place they are more like women than
I have ever seen them before. Their wings are folded, their
curling tongues inside their mouths, their fingers bent to hide
the talons. They are a maid, betrayed and violated by one who
swore he loved her. They are a mother, beaten for bearing only
girl-children into this world, until she bled no more. They are
the widow who heard not a kind word in her life but served
regardless, because it was her duty, and whose corpse was robbed
the moment she died. I see them all, for just a moment, have to
fight the urge to raise my hands towards them, to call out, my
sisters, my lovely sisters! But then one snarls, as if sensing the
faintest glimmer of my compassion, and I turn my face away.

On the other side of this assemblage stand the goddesses. We
too warp space and perception to find our place at the foot of
Orestes' bed, Athena at our centre, the leader of our little pack.

We too will watch, as the Furies do, to see that nothing interferes in this night's business save mortal hands.

Penelope kneels by Orestes' side, brushes the hair back from his head, smiles on her cousin.

He blinks himself blearily to wakefulness, seems to see her, takes her hand. "Mother," he whispers.

"No," she replies, gentle, kind. "Penelope. It is Penelope."

He is briefly confused, then seems to see, nods, squeezes her hand tighter. "Penelope. I remember now."

"How are you?" He doesn't answer. The question should not be asked of kings – kings must always be all right, it is their duty; and yet he is human too, and there are tears in his eyes. "You've been ill," Penelope adds, before he can weep and make things even more awkward for them all. "Poisoned at the orders of your uncle, Menelaus."

"My uncle?"

A little nod, a little sigh. "He wants you mad. He wants his brother's throne."

"Perhaps he should take it. I am not strong like he is. I am a weak man."

Elektra should step forward now, bark *of course not! Of course you aren't!*

She does not.

"You've been calling for your mother," Penelope breathes. "For Clytemnestra. 'Mother, Mother!' you cry. 'Forgive me.'"

Orestes holds Penelope's hand so hard it hurts, but she does not flinch or pull away. "Forgive me," he whispers. "Forgive me."

Penelope looks to Anaitis, who shakes her head, to Elektra, who does not move at all, then back to Orestes. "Orestes," she says at last, "what do you think forgiveness is?"

He doesn't know. He thought perhaps he should, and he doesn't, shakes his head dumbly.

"When my husband went to war, he stood on the dock and

363

held my hand and asked that I forgive him. There was a prophecy, you see. It said that if Odysseus went to Troy, he would not return for twenty years. We both knew this. 'Forgive me,' he said. 'I do what I have to do.'"

The Furies stir, but Athena glares at them and grips her spear a little tighter. Orestes gazes up into Penelope's eyes, but she is no longer looking at him, but back to some distant memory. "Of course, my husband had no choice; no choice at all. As a king, he was Agamemnon's sworn ally, pledged to come when the king of kings commanded. He had taken the oath he himself had proposed at Helen's wedding, to come to her husband's aid should another try to claim her for himself. His duty was clear and there was, therefore, nothing to ask forgiveness for.

"But of course, there was another oath betrayed the day my husband left. His oath to me as a husband. As the father of our child. He swore these oaths too – as a man he pledged himself to me – but a husband is a far lesser man than a king. Achilles disguised himself as a woman and hid on a far-off island to avoid sailing to Troy, knowing he might die. Odysseus feigned madness to avoid his summons, ploughed a field while gibbering – but it was, to be frank, one of his less impressive schemes. Easily seen through. A nice touch to add to the story of his cleverness, nothing more.

"The day my husband left he at least had the grace to not say any particularly foolish thing, such as 'the war will be short' or 'I'll be back before our son is a man' or such nonsense. Instead, he held my hand and said 'forgive me'. Forgive him for doing what had to be done – I mean, what woman would do less? Of course. Of course. But also: forgive him for what was yet to come. For twenty years in an empty bed. Twenty years without companionship, without comfort, twenty years besieged in my own home, raising our son alone, the sun will rise and the sun will set day after day after day, year after year, unrelenting, the winter, the summer – 'forgive me'. Forgiveness for a marriage vow betrayed. Forgiveness for a barren home. Of course I kissed him on the cheek and said how brave he was, said that there was nothing to forgive. And with my forgiveness in his ears, he sailed away. All very . . . poetic.

"I have had a long time to think about that moment. My forgiveness, so broad, so vague. What wife would not grant it to a man going to war? I forgave him the things that must be done, and I forgave him our marriage vows, and I forgave him the duties of fatherhood. Thus with conscience unburdened and heart at ease, he sailed away. No doubt he also felt regret, but what a great gift my forgiveness bestowed upon him, a salve to his wounds. What an unconscionable robbery I performed that day upon my own existence. Because of course, here is the thing – he never said sorry. He did not take my hand and look me in the eye and say, 'Penelope, my wife, I am sorry. I am sorry that I must leave you. I am sorry that I am going to let you down. I am sorry for the burdens I will put upon you. I am sorry for the child I abandon by your side. I am sorry.' That would have been his gift to me, of course. His apology, bestowed on me. But that's not what happened. He asked *me* to forgive *him*. For me to bestow this gift upon my husband. Even in that moment – that tender moment, that tenderest of moments, a moment the poets look to as the act of greatest devotion from a man to his wife, that needful farewell – he did not give unto me, but *took*. Took my forgiveness, and not just a bit of it, not just the necessary part. Took it for all things that had been, and all that might be yet to come. I hate him for that sometimes. I really do."

Orestes stares up at Penelope and barely breathes, does not move. Even Elektra has roused a little from her stupor, stares down upon the Ithacan queen, lips parted, shoulders rising short and fast about her chest. The Furies cluster together as if for comfort, preening against each other. I feel Athena's divinity warm beside me, smell the forest about Artemis's bare toes where they curl into the earth.

Penelope sighs, shakes her head – let it go. Let it go. Turns her attention back to Orestes, away from this distant place. "So you see, cousin. You lie there and ask for forgiveness. You call out 'Mother, Mother!' but your mother is dead. You killed her. You, your sister – and me. You may have held the blade, but we all helped you drive it through her heart. All of us. It was the needful thing. We all would have perished if you had not done it, and she knew that. She forgave you, for what it's worth. That is blitheringly obvious to anyone with eyes to see. She forgave you long before you killed her – as a mother she forgave you. It was one of the more astonishing things I think she ever did, and she lived a really rather remarkable life. The only thing that interested her more than her own survival was yours, and for you to survive she had to die. She knew that. I think you know that. I think you saw it in her eyes, the night you killed her. Which then raises the question – what exactly are you asking for?

"My priestess here thinks you're mad. She thinks the madness began before the poison took you, that it merely brought to the surface that which was already there. It is said that when a child kills a parent, the soul of that parent will summon the Furies, unleash the ancient hags from beneath their prison in the earth. Clytemnestra, though – she doted upon you. Adored you in a way I find . . . shameful. Shameful in that I cannot love my own son as she loved you. She embarrasses me as a mother. Her love makes mine feel small. Whose forgiveness are you looking for then? Hers? Your sister's? Mine?"

Orestes does not answer, so Penelope gestures briskly at Elektra, pulls the Mycenaean princess down by her side. "Elektra," she snaps, voice hard enough to jerk the princess to full attention, eyes raised for the first time in days. "You were betrayed by your maid, who loved your mother, who you helped kill. They are dead. They cannot forgive you. You have made mistakes, been used and used others. Used your brother. But you did not poison him."

Elektra now looks at Penelope, stares into her, through her, as if tied to her by a rope. Cannot look away. Penelope sighs, shakes her head, pats Orestes absent-mindedly on the back of his hand. "It would be convenient, of course, if we could forgive ourselves. My son ... when I think of my son, I find myself ... confused. Wrapped in as much guilt as love. I look back at my life and tell myself that the choices I made were the only ones that could be made, the only thing to be done. This is true, of course. It is also a lie. There were words spoken that could have been expressed some other way. There were secrets held. Judgements made. I cannot change them now. I run through my memories again and again, and every time they grow more distorted, the truth vanishing into fantasy. I tell myself that I was a woman alone. I tell myself that I did the best I could. I tell myself that we are merely mortal. Fallible. Flawed. In this way I forgive myself. And of course I never shall. When a parent dies, when a mother dies, we never truly forget that grief. It stays within us, deep below, and on top of it we put more of our lives lived, more experiences, until it is so weighted down by the matter of our days that we are astonished to find that one unremarkable new moon we look inside, and there it is, bright and brilliant as the day it was born. This is the way with grief. With guilt. With regret. All we can do is honour the lessons this brings, look honestly upon who we were and what we have done, and try to do better when the next sun rises. Forgiveness does not change that. Especially the forgiveness of the dead. So tell me, Orestes ... whose forgiveness do you seek?"

He has no answer. Elektra kneels by his side, clasps his hand between her own, as if praying.

"The trick, I find," muses Penelope, "to living with a pain that cannot be reconciled, a grief, or a fury, a rage that you think will burn you from the inside out, is not to dwell on all the reasons why your life has ended, but to wonder what it might become now. I am a widow queen. This is my trap, my curse. My power. My grief is a knife. My anger is cunning. Having been denied the purpose intended for me – to be a wife, a loving mother – my purpose is to be a queen, to serve not myself, but my kingdom. *Mine.* The land that is entrusted to *me.* Not to my husband's ghost. Not to some . . . poet's picture of Odysseus. But to me. I will live and I will take all that has been put upon me and I will make of it something new. Something better.

"You want forgiveness, Orestes? It will never come. So either crawl into your hole and shrivel now, die now, or seek repentance for doing the needful thing. Make your repentance your strength. Build life over the ashes of your butcher father, your murdered mother. Where Agamemnon slaughtered Iphigenia, raise a shrine for unmarried girls, a place of safety in her name. Where Clytemnestra slew Agamemnon, set up courts of justice to bring back harmony to your land. Where you slew Clytemnestra, cast libations into the sand and make upon those shores treaties of peace, an end to bloodshed. Someone must end this story. It may as well be you. Either live with that fire in your heart, or die in shrivelled, blackened grief. No one will forgive you. No forgiveness will ever be enough. And no one but you can make your actions the apology that the dead are owed. Repent and live – and stop asking the dead to take the pain away. They cannot. You will live with it, and that is all."

So saying, she stands, brisk and quick, brushing the hand that clasped Orestes' own down her gown as if stained with some sticky stuff. Nods once to the prince, once to Elektra, once to

Anaitis, and then looks round the tent one more time, as if she might see those of us here assembled, as if she smells the blood of the Furies, feels the warmth of our divinities. Artemis is already turning away, bored, slipping back into the warm night that holds her, but Athena and I remain as Penelope pulls back the fabric door of the tent and strides away without another word.

After a moment, Anaitis follows, and now only Elektra and Orestes remain.

Look at them, ye Furies. The last children of a cursed house. I kneel by their side, and Athena does not stop me, nor do the Furies rouse in hissing revenge. I breathe a little warmth into the coldness of Elektra's fingers, wipe a single tear from Orestes' eye, knocking it down his cheek. Brother and sister hold each other's hands in silence, and do not speak, and do not wail or shout or lament. All that has already been spent, by fathers and mothers, grandfathers and grandmothers, generations of weeping flowing back and forth through time, a torment set upon the children of this house even before they were born.

Elektra presses her brow to her brother's, skull to skull, and for a moment there they remain. Then she pulls away, smiles, is not used to smiling, immediately buries it beneath a frown, a face of stone, lest it be something too daring, too bold and presumptuous. Orestes squeezes her hands between his own. "Sister," he murmurs. "I'm sorry."

"No, you don't—"

"No," he cuts in, sharp and quick. "For Pylades. For what I wanted to do. For everything I've done to us. To you. I am sorry."

Now, for the very last time, Elektra weeps.

I hold her tight as she sobs into her brother's hands, stroke her hair from her salty eyes, wipe the snot from her nose with the hem of my gown, shake her a little when she stops, hold her again as she falls weeping one more time. She weeps for her sister, for her father, her brother, herself. She weeps for the childhood she was not permitted, for the daughter she could never be, for the princess she dreamed of, for the woman she has become. She weeps too for her mother, for the mother Clytemnestra was, for the mother Elektra prayed she would be, could have been, and never was. She weeps for herself, honest and true, and Orestes holds her close and says, I'm sorry, I'm sorry, I'm so so sorry.

Athena steps between the siblings and the Furies, and the three creatures of fire and earth curl away from her presence. "We are done here," the goddess proclaims. "We are done."

"*He is ours,*" whispers one, but there is no conviction in it. "*He is ours!*" whimpers another, and from the last, a bare hiss of air over cracked tooth: "*He is ours.*"

"Orestes it was who summoned you, Orestes it was who put your curse upon himself. His mother did not do it – it was he himself. And it is done." Then Athena removes her helmet. I am so surprised, I stand, retreat from Elektra's side, unsure what it should mean that the warrior is unmasking before these creatures of violence and blood. Athena lays her shield aside, holds out her hands, palm up towards the Furies, a gesture of peace. Her voice is soft, almost kind when she speaks – I cannot recall when I last heard compassion in her tone. "Sisters," she murmurs. "Ladies of the earth. There will be shrines raised to you." The Furies snarl at this – "*hypocrisy!*" hiss their rolling tongues, "*lies!*" spit their crimson eyes – but Athena doesn't seem to feel the heat of their rage, nor flinch from their flexing claws. "There will be shrines," she repeats. "You will be honoured. Worshipped even. When justice fails. When there are no laws. When wives kill husbands and husbands daughters and sons mothers, when the world is nothing but madness and blood, the people of these lands shall pray to you. They shall pray – not for vengeance, or retribution, or blood for blood, but for justice. Justice that shall not be denied. They shall pray for a power that cares nothing for kings – no, not even for gods. The great levellers. When all else has failed them, they shall pray to you. I proclaim it now, and it shall be so."

The air rings with the pronouncement, the earth shudders beneath her feet. I at once am the white-winged dove upon the stirring air, darting for the shelter of the nearest trees, and not an instant too soon, for lo, I see the clouds of heaven part overhead and feel the eyes of the gods turn to gaze upon this little place, drawn by the force of Athena's divine creed. Zeus shrugs in the heavens, a ripple of lightning playing across the sky. Hades sighs beneath the earth, a tumble of rocks tipping from the nearby cliff to plunge down in a clatter of black. Poseidon grumbles at all things Athena does in general, the seas surging in a sudden bitter squall of salt against the shore, but no one stops her. Not tonight. Not as she stands over the son of Agamemnon, the Furies cowed before her, divinity ringing in her command. Even the petty mortals feel it, the changing in the wind, the rolling of thunder, the twisting of the sea, for they huddle closer together, clasp hands, lean into the safety of their little fires.

And at last, with all the eyes of heaven upon them, the Furies give a final shriek, scar the earth with their claws, beat upon the twisted air with their leather wings, and depart. They do not spill blood as they go, nor rain down pestilence. They do not tug at the hearts of the creatures below them, nor slaughter the cattle, nor burn the tender trees. Instead they spin one last time through the churning sky, shrilling to the air that holds them, clicking and snapping at the sky, before turning their faces to the earth whence they came and diving down, down into the wounded fissures of the gaping deeps.

CHAPTER 39

>>>

The next morning, at first light . . .

The Spartans have not come to this farm before, but they are ready to do their usual business. To kick and rummage, to steal food, to pummel any who stand in their way. Any men they find, they beat, but there are few enough men on Kephalonia. Any women they find, they leer at and threaten, promise to take them back to their little barracks by the sea, promise to show them what a real man is like. This at least would be their usual way, but in truth they have had a hard time finding anyone to do anything to. They are not strong enough in number to meaningfully occupy anywhere, and they know it is only in the absence of men and a meaningful militia that their stomping across the island has not been resisted. They are indeed little more than a wandering gang of bandits, in both demeanour and numbers, hunting some missing queen and some mad prince through deserted farm and empty village, the people already vanished like night.

This farm then. Another empty place. The grain stores have been emptied, there are fresh tracks from the cart that pulled it away. There is no firewood in the hearth, as if even the sight of kindling might prove too provocative. The sheep are gone, herded away to the other side of a nearby craggy hill. There is no one to threaten, no one to interrogate, and nothing worth the Spartans' time to steal.

They mutter and grumble among themselves, wonder whether they can be bothered to strike a flame to burn the place to the ground, and in the midst of this conversation are entirely unprepared for the arrows that rain down upon them.

The arrows are not much use for the killing of armed men in heavy bronze, although two do indeed fall in that first volley to some lucky shafts shot from the forest's edge. The rest cluster in confusion, duck behind the corner of the house, peek their heads out to try and see their attackers.

"It's ... girls!" blurts one, a little bolder in his examination than the others. And indeed, where farmland meets the thin cover of trees, a line of women stand, bows drawn and arrows notched, taking their time to find their targets, relaxed and patient. Their patience should be a warning – the soldiers should really sense something of the huntress about these calm ladies, but alas, they are not really primed for that degree of contemplation.

So it is that they resolve to charge. They are veteran enough to understand that covering even the short distance between them and the women is going to be a tiring business in full armour, but that's all right. They will move behind their shields, run a little to motivate each other and encourage the general sense that it's all right to head into a falling hail of arrows, walk a bit to get their breath back, and in this systematic way chase and slaughter the foolish women who have the gall to attack them.

One – one of the more intelligent of the group – opines, "There are at least as many of them as there are of us, do you think—"

But he is drowned out by a general chorus of manly

confidence and mockery, as the little group of Spartans hoist their shields and charge.

The distance between the men and the women is not much. Long, uncut yellow grass brushes against the Spartans' legs, their thighs, tickles their hips in a way that under other circumstances I might find amusing. They run towards the women, who at once lower their bows and dart away, weaving between the thin-trunked trees, before stopping and turning to fire again. Then the Spartans march behind their shields, but another falls limping to a lucky shot through his thigh as the rest of the arrows bounce off thick metal. Then they run again, and again the women retreat, swift, unencumbered, darting away in a silent, ordered line. This pattern unfolds until the men are nearly all at the edge of the wood, sweating, grunting, aware already that this battle plan is not really working out for anyone, but not possessed of the imagination to do much else.

It is there, right on the edge of the trees, that the other group of women emerge. They rise from the long grass behind and to the side of the Spartans, their arms and legs and faces covered in mud – less to serve as disguise and more as a cooling repellent against the many insects that would otherwise nip and nibble at them as they lay in wait. They carry javelins, which they throw into the Spartans' backs from not twenty paces away. Even the breastplates of the warrior men cannot resist such a weight of weapon flung so near, and those who do avoid the initial hail of death are not equipped to fight six women bodily crashing down on top of each individual man, wrenching the helmets from their faces, kneeling on their legs, their arms, their chests, their backs while their little knives find a dozen ways to slip through the gaps between metal plates.

Of the fifteen men who go to the farm that day, only four survive, and two are dead of their wounds by morning.

*

And then, in the afternoon . . .

Nicostratus, son of Menelaus, stands before the fine villa near the harbour wall that he and his men have borrowed for the good of Ithaca, to which Sparta is such a loyal ally, and looks for the troops who have not returned. Of the fifty Spartan men now on Kephalonia, there are only six stationed with him now, the rest having been sent out in groups of ten to fifteen to seek missing royalty.

That evening, not a one returns home.

Nicostratus has not hated a place more than these western isles, knows in his heart that his father will make him king of them if Menelaus gets his way. Nicostratus would rather be king of an anthill than this accursed place, cannot bear to think of having to put up with the ugly old harpy Penelope as his trophy queen, and will of course never dare say any of this to his old man, will die instead mute and bitter in his sullen, terrified resentment.

The sun speeds towards the horizon, blood in the sky, blood in the water. The local people of this wretched port are closing doors and shutters, shooing children inside. Funny that – and then not so funny. Nicostratus looks again and sees that the streets are deserted, the little fishing boats that were tied off the wharf have slipped their knots and splashed gently back out into the darkening seas; even the door of the meagre temple to Poseidon is drawn and barred.

Nicostratus is a miserable little shit with all the tender love-making skills of a broken pot, but he is at least soldier enough to recognise a problem when it arises. He draws his blade. "Spartans! To me!" he cries.

The six men of his personal guard gather, weapons ready and eyes questioning, tight about their prince. They look for the threat that has so alarmed their master and see . . . nothing. Long streets of empty. Alleys and passages of void. Hear silence where voices should be, only the fat gulls busy calling out over some squabble of fish bones.

When raiding the southern lands, Nicostratus learned that this was precisely the moment when a sensible warrior got back in his boat and sailed hard for open waters. But his boat is no warship, rather a commandeered vessel of Eupheithes that even now – ah yes, even now – appears to have been cut adrift and bobs some little way out in the mouth of the harbour. And even if it were not, there is only one place for Nicostratus to go, and that is where his father is. Nicostratus is not sure when it became more desirable for him to die in glorious battle than to look his father in the eye, but it would be of thin comfort for him to know that he is at least not the only man of Sparta who feels that way.

The Spartans huddle together, shields up, weapons drawn, and wait for disaster to unfold.

There is the clop–clop–clopping of hooves.

The slow rumble of a cart.

The reflection of torchlight plays across the end of an empty, silent street.

The men turn to the sound, biding their time, saving their energy for a fight.

When Orestes appears, he should be riding a magnificent, noble beast. But magnificent, noble beasts are hard to find in the western isles, so instead he rides a donkey. It is in fairness one of the more noble of its kind, and with a reasonably pleasant nature compared to many of its kin. The animal enjoys having its ears stroked and the crooning attention of some of the women of Priene's army, who though prepared to split any invader from skull to crotch with all manner of weapons if provoked are also indulgent of any furry creature with gooey eyes and the merest whiff of a social sensibility that crosses their path.

Thus then: six Spartans, armed, and at the end of the path they guard, the son of Agamemnon on an ass.

Orestes is pale, thin, worn, but still manages to sit on this lumbering beast with something resembling the dignity of a king. Athena props him up in his saddle, tilts his chin a little higher. I ruffle his hair, smooth a touch of something bright into his sallow skin. Artemis chats merrily with his ride in the tongue of beasts, far more interested it seems in the animal than the man.

The effect is at least enough to make Nicostratus hesitate as he recognises his royal cousin, perhaps sensing without knowing the touch of divinity that walks with the king. Then the rest of Orestes' entourage appears, and Nicostratus' blade wavers.

First, Elektra and Penelope, who have at least gone to some effort to brush the leaves from their hair and scrape the worst of the mud from their fingernails. Then Pylades, Iason and lovely Kenamon, fully armed, leading the cart upon which ride five Spartan men, bound hand and foot, stripped of their armour down to the merest cloths around their nethers – I take a little moment to enjoy the resulting scenery – and in another larger cart pulled behind them, piles of glinting bronze, stained with blood. The women struggled a little to work out how best to arrange the breastplates and bracers of their slain enemies, trying various configurations to make the stack neat. In the end, they largely gave up, and instead have lashed the armour together around bales of hay to offer both the impression of a more bulky haul of stolen weaponry and a little structural stability to the whole display.

It is with this latter cart that the rest of the women come. Priene walks at their head, sword in one hand, dagger in the other, drawn, ready to indulge in her favourite pastime of killing Greeks. Teodora marches at her side, arrow notched, and behind her are the women of this army, nearly fifty strong, javelins and bows and axes and spears. The rest of the women now join them too, marching from the opposite end of the street, spilling in from alleys and scrambling over rooftops to encircle Nicostratus and his knot of men. None of them have washed, as the queens have. The blood of Sparta is still damp in their tunics; their hair flies wild about their earth-scrubbed faces, their teeth are bared as that of the wolf. In silence they assemble, encasing the son of Menelaus in arrow points and bloody blades, waiting for their command.

Orestes stops some two spears' lengths from Nicostratus. Drops from his donkey's back, is steadied a little by Pylades as he lands, draws up straight, pulls away from Pylades to stand on his own two feet. He is unstable, breathless, on the verge of falling. It is therefore all the more majestic that he does not. By will alone – and perhaps a little strength of the gods – the son of Agamemnon looks upon the son of Menelaus, looks round at the arrayed mass of armed women, looks back to the Spartan men.

Says simply: "Cousin. I am so glad to see you here. It is good to know that my uncle cares so much for my well-being that he would send his most beloved son to check in on me."

Nicostratus does not surrender that night.

Surrendering – let alone to women – would be an outrageous insult, impossible to bear.

Instead, as is the way of things, he is invited to enjoy a certain Ithacan hospitality.

"Your father has been so good in looking after me," Orestes declares, voice hoarse where he pushes it through to a quality his body does not yet want to sustain. "It is an honour to return the favour. Here – you don't have to wear such weighty armour or carry such a heavy blade. Let these kindly women help you with that."

Orestes is master of Mycenae, Sparta's nearest and dearest ally.

Son of Agamemnon, king of kings.

It would be dreadfully rude to refuse his hospitality.

CHAPTER 40

>>

At night – a feast.

It is a real feast, strange to Penelope's eye.

The women of her army gather in the villa the Spartans used as their base, and drink and eat and cook together over the open fire and sing. Not the songs of the poets, the bearded men purchased by wealthy kings, but women's songs. Bawdy ballads and mournful dirges, ancient love songs and naughty ditties about stick-legged boys. Orestes' donkey somehow ends up in pride of place in the centre of the yard, bedecked with flowers and cooed over by scuttling children. Teodora joins hands with Autonoe, and before anyone can object, the two have formed a dancing circle of ladies, knives bouncing at their hips, spinning and laughing round and round the fire. Eos is a flare of activity about the villa's kitchen, exclaiming in despair at the disorderly way of things until at last Ourania sits her down and explains that everyone seems to be feeding themselves perfectly adequately and perhaps Eos should consider taking the night off too.

Nicostratus's men – those who live – are bound in the storeroom, their toes nibbled by rodents, their door guarded by dogs. Nicostratus himself has been cordially led to a room to rest himself, food brought to his door, everyone most attentive, most respectful, as befits a noble guest of such thoughtful hosts.

"Good cousin, you look pale," Elektra barked when he opened his mouth to object. "Perhaps you should have a lie-down."

Orestes sits, Pylades by his side, aloof a while from the dancing and the noise. When at last he tires, he says as much, leans over to Penelope and breathes: "I think I should rest. For all that is to come."

There is a weakness here. A falling-off, a fading-away. It is dishonourable to be weak; it is unmanly to be weary from all that has gone before.

There is strength here too. A truth, a trust, a reality. In time, reality conquers all.

Elektra skulks in shadows, watches her brother be led away to his rest, listens to the music, picks at the food, and then at last takes the empty seat by Penelope's side.

For a while they watch the dancing, soak in the sound of voices raised in merriment. Priene is shoved to the front of her women, called upon to sing, sing, sing! She does not know any songs of the Greeks. Her songs are of the eastern grasslands, the steppe and the women riding with wind in their hair. She thinks she should sing of Penthesilea, of her fallen, beautiful queen, and is astonished to find that the song is in her, is upon her lips, this secret, broken thing trying now to be heard again. It would end the evening not badly, not in cruelty, but in sorrowful contemplation of the other thing that is true, of the truth that this army of women came together in loss, and victory is a hollow, fleeting thing. It is important, Priene thinks, that soldiers sing songs of the fallen, harden their hearts to death, learn to mourn, learn to grieve.

Then she looks at the faces of her muddy women and thinks: not tonight.

Tonight instead she sings a song of the eastern fires and the mother goddess, teaches the women to raise their voices in chorus, mouths tangling over the foreign words. The women of Troy would have found this song easier, recognised something in its tune. But they are dead, even though their music lives.

Elektra and Penelope sit together a while as the women sing with their captain, until at last Elektra says: "Orestes sent Pylades to negotiate with my uncle." At once Penelope sits up straight, frightened, face draining of liquor. But Elektra shakes her head, adds quickly: "Not now. Before. Before all this. Back in Mycenae, almost immediately after he was crowned. My brother was betrothed to Hermione, Menelaus's daughter, from a very young age. They were meant to marry, but after Troy, Menelaus promised his daughter's hand to the son of Achilles. It was a source of great dishonour, great insult. Orestes should have demanded Hermione as a gift brought before him on the day he was crowned, made it clear that he was indeed his father's son, king of kings. But he didn't. That showed weakness. He knew it too. He sent Pylades to Sparta to negotiate – I thought perhaps to negotiate regarding Hermione's wedding. But no. Not at all. My brother instead offered me to Nicostratus as a match to seal our houses together. Bartered me to that . . . creature like a piece of meat.

"When I found out, I was so angry, I was . . . but I was also relieved. It was the correct thing to do. A strong decision. My brother was selling me and it was . . . the appropriate act of a king. But Menelaus never gave an answer. He hummed and hawed and said he'd make up his mind soon – an outrageously rude reply, a gross provocation to do anything other than grovel in gratitude when a princess is offered to the son of a slave! But by then I imagine he already had Kleitos's loyalty, Rhene . . . Rhene in the palace, already had his eye on taking the Mycenaean throne in his own right. He didn't need to marry his son to me. He'd get what he wanted anyway, and far sooner."

She sips thin wine, doesn't enjoy the taste of it, drinks anyway. "The night your women saw me arguing with Pylades ... I blamed him, of course, for selling me to Menelaus. I appreciated the wisdom of the act, and was angry. Was both forgiving and enraged. I forgave my brother. Took my rage out on Pylades. But that is not all. Pylades, you see, loves my brother. Loves him. More than any man." Penelope nods at nothing much, but Elektra clasps her arm, fingers digging into flesh. "No. Listen. Pylades loves him. And Orestes loves Pylades. More than the love of boys who together have become men. Do you understand me?"

Penelope nods, slow and careful, and Elektra's fingers unwind. The princess of Mycenae turns her gaze back to the dance, to the spinning bodies of the women, her voice still low, for her cousin alone. "When all this is done, Orestes must claim Hermione as his wife, to prove that he is strong. He must own her. Have children by her. That is his duty. But he loves Pylades. Swears he will never give him up. And Pylades ... I begged him to walk away. This ... childish thing they think they share ... it will kill our king, destroy the very man he swore to love. He understands, of course. I tell him that his greatest act of love would be to leave without another word. He says that the greatest act of love there is is to love against all adversity, to be brave for love. That's why we argued. And that is why Orestes will be the very last of his line."

The songs are sung, bare feet pound on polished stones, wine pours, women laugh and Elektra's voice is stone. "I love my brother. I hate him too sometimes. I was proud when he sold me to Menelaus. I was proud of him. I thought that when Nicostratus ... when he did what he had to do to me ... maybe then I would finally make my father proud. My mother, of

383

course – she would have been appalled. Outraged. She would have told me to kill Nicostratus on our wedding day, to drive my dagger through his eye. Impossible things, of course. Impossible things. But in her way ... it was love. My brother loves, you see. He loves with all his heart. I hate him for that. Sometimes. I do hate him for it."

Elektra sighs.

She has nothing more to say.

Does not want advice, insight, promises or forgiveness.

Her words are spoken, her business done.

She stands, nods once towards the Ithacan queen, and turns away from the fire.

CHAPTER 41

>>

K enamon, sing, sing!

It is Ourania, a little drunk, who grabs the Egyptian by the arm and pulls him into the circle of women.

The women should be suspicious of this suitor, this strange man in their midst – but not tonight. He has fought for their queen, he has proven himself an ally time and time again, he has marched with them, slept by their side and shown nothing but the height of good manners. He helped them fetch water from the stream, didn't complain too much about the cooking, carried firewood to the camp and now, as he too gets a little into his cups, has started telling strange foreign stories about exotic creatures called crocodiles and hippopotamuses, as well as a few utterly flat-footed jokes that seem to the women even more hilarious for being so badly told.

Priene has sung! She has sung her songs of far-off lands, now Kenamon, sing! Teach us your songs of the fattened river and endless sands!

Oh no, really, I couldn't, I mustn't . . .

Don't be such a tedious bore! There are no men left here to judge and we promise we don't care, look at us! We are barely women now, we are barely recognisable to the people of our own lands as creatures they can name and own. You are safe with us, outsider, you are safe with our family. So sing!

He sings.

He has a dreadful singing voice. I flinch, but the women don't seem to care.

He sings a child's song, a parable about a lion that hunts the naughty boy who strays too far from home. The women shrill, tell us, tell us, what is that? What does it mean? Is it a story about warriors? About love? Has your land burned for a woman, did your Pharaoh crack the world in two for the love of his bride?

Um. No. It is about a lion . . .

What's a lion?

It's like a very big cat.

That doesn't sound so bad.

I don't think "big" is the right term, um, let me think . . .

Ourania has fallen into a drunken stupor. Priene and Teodora are nowhere to be seen. Eos went to find a room suitable for her queen to sleep in, and there was this one with a lovely soft bed, so she laid her head down and, well, whoops . . .

Autonoe tucks her fellow maid in, drifts around the house snuffing out the lanterns, brings water to the women set to keep guard on the edge of the roof, looks over the sea to the darkness of Ithaca looming, waiting with its back to the horizon. Elektra sleeps in a room far from her brother's bed, and does not dream, and does not wail in the dark. Pylades peeks out of the door of Orestes' room, sees only Iason slumbering on his guardian's chair, closes the door to shut out the world and lays himself down on the bed beside his king, feeling the slow and steady breath of his brother, his master, his heart's twin, his Orestes, rising and falling in the dark.

Kenamon sings of home, and later in the dark he will pass Penelope as she retires to her bed, and their shoulders brush in the narrow, unfamiliar passage of this place, and their fingers too, and they look at each other in the silent dark and see only the glistening brightness of the other's eye.

And as dawn breaks across the sea, another voice rises, too salt-bitter and sea-scarred to sing, and calls out for home, home, home. I see Athena move beside him as Odysseus lifts his head from the ruins of his raft and blinks a little life back into the gummy balls of his eyes to greet the dawn as it shimmers across his back. Home, he whispers, gazed fixed on the endless sea.

Home.

The next morning, a warship sits outside the harbour of Ithaca.

It is the same vessel in which Penelope fled from her island, the suitors' ship, sent out into the dark and now recalled by fire-light to these busy seas. On its decks are women, some wearing Spartan breastplates, another the bronze bracers pillaged from a Spartan corpse. They are few, those who wear this armour, for it is ill-fitting and Priene doesn't approve of fighting in any gear that you are not fully competent in. The only concession she has made to the garb of her warrior women as they stand upon deck is that they may paint their faces in fearsome stripes of bloody crimson and muddy ochre, may weave their hair into filthy crowns and howl like animals, a bitter song to greet the bright, welcoming day. They take turns to beat the drums of war, hammering out their savage noise, and at the helm stands Orestes, his sister on his left, Pylades on his right. In the middle of the deck are piled the remaining plundered goods of the slaughtered Spartans of the isle, a gaudy display of glinting riches that is visible even from the palace walls where now Menelaus looks down upon them.

"Order the men," he commands, "every soldier we've got, to form up by the harbour."

Lefteris obeys, and in neat ranks and rows the Spartans still remaining on the isle assemble in the harbour, spears held tight, shields pressed to their chests to greet the incoming ship. The drums pound and the oars press into the water as the vessel edges its way towards the quay. A line of women, arrows notched, gaze down from the side of the ship to the assembled Spartans, who do not blink.

Menelaus takes his time to saunter down to the water's edge, fingers hooked in his golden girdle, sword at his side. He does not hide behind his troops, but steps forward, easy, confident. This? This is not a battle, his loose shoulders proclaim. This isn't even a little skirmish. This is just ... silly people flapping their blades around, little more than a courtly dance, a slightly rowdy dinner. Menelaus has seen battles. Menelaus knows what real fights are.

Orestes and Elektra appear at the rail of the ship, but no ropes are thrown nor gangplanks lowered. Instead Orestes calls out: "Uncle! I believe you misplaced your son?"

Pylades has his sword to Nicostratus's throat as the princeling is brought forward. Menelaus's smile twitches, recovers, cannot hold the easy curve of his lips, falls away. His frown is long and slow to gather, his voice an unfurling of a banner when he finally speaks, addressing not Orestes or his sister, but Pylades. "You hold your sword to the neck of a prince of Sparta, *boy*. You had better be careful with your fucking blade."

"Your son is suspected in the murder of an innocent woman in the king of Ithaca's house," retorts Orestes, voice ringing across the water. "I was surprised to find him roaming free."

"Orestes," Menelaus replies, tilting his head back a little to gaze up at the king, "you've been sick. Why don't you come down, let the priests have a look at you?"

"No thank you, uncle. I am, as you see, perfectly well attended to."

"By women. Muddy women with dirty bows. Slaves and widows. Whores and orphans, no? Whereas I ... " An easy shrug, a gentle encapsulation of the finest of manhood around him.

"Nicostratus." It is Elektra who speaks, easy, taking the time to enjoy the moment. "Kindly inform your father what has happened to the rest of your men."

Nicostratus does not want to die. Neither does he want to ever again look his father in the eye, nor speak out loud of failure, or defeat, or humiliation. Caught between these two states, he flaps, his mouth churns, his eyes boggle, his knees go weak. This may not be fluent, but it is expressive enough. Menelaus's jaw tightens. He looks again at the muddy women on the deck, considers their bows, remains unimpressed – but perhaps a little less so.

"I see," he murmurs. "Well then."

A thought strikes him. His eyes search the deck once again, flicker to Orestes, to Elektra, pass straight over his son without even slowing. He rocks forward on his heels, rocks back, feeling the weight of his ageing body move, feeling the creak in his joints. Steadies himself. Looks Orestes in the eye. "And where the fuck is Penelope?"

CHAPTER 42

>>

T his feels familiar.

Comforting even.

A certain closing of our circle, a satisfactory knot in the yarn of our tale.

Where the fuck indeed is Penelope?

Why, she is on Ithaca. Of course she is. She has come by little fishing boat, slipping into the same bay where Ourania has for so long kept her once-discovered escape vessel. As everyone gathers at the dock to make a fuss over Orestes, his sister and their unexpected little band of armed women, Penelope and her companions slip onto the isle, Teodora as their guide, and back along the same muddy clifftop path that they took some days ago.

No one speaks.

No one looks too closely down to the bay, where even now Nicostratus stands with a sword at his throat.

Their eyes are fixed on their destination – the palace, the walls, the end of the road.

The rope by which they descended the walls is gone, but that is no trouble, for neither are there guards on the palace gates, all the Spartans down by the busy quay. Instead the doors have been thrown open, and standing in their hollow frame are two figures we know well. Medon has been listening to Laertes discourse on the breeding and butchering of pigs for what feels like the best part of his elder years by the time the women arrive, cloaks drawn above their heads, dust scudding beneath their feet. Laertes keeps blathering on until the moment Penelope stands directly in front of him, determined to conclude on a very important point before at last turning to acknowledge his daughter-in-law. He spins saliva round his mouth, licks his teeth, surveys her up and down and says at last: "Well, you took your time getting back here."

"My humble apologies, Father. There were Spartans to kill. Kings to save. Princes to kidnap and so on."

Laertes has had a thoroughly tedious time, a prisoner in his own palace. He has not been harmed, nor has he been honoured, but he has been curtailed, dismissed, confined and generally speaking treated in a manner not befitting a great and noble sometime-king. The only reason he tolerated it with something resembling a certain resolute humility was for this moment, and it is at this moment that he finally permits himself to grin. "Here to make the bastard pay, yes?"

"That is indeed my plan. Shall we?"

He gestures her within, a grand sweep of his arm and a little bowing of his head, as once he welcomed her to these walls when she was barely a child, a youthful bride to his strutting son. Medon moves to stand beside her, head cocked on one side. "Princes kidnapped?" he politely enquires. "Spartans slain?"

"It has been a strenuous few days," she replies lightly. "Albeit remarkably dull during those periods when all one can do is wait around. Ah – I see there has been some light damage to one of the frescos. We will have to attend to that."

Laertes pats the scarred wall as they pass it, slashes across Helen's painted brow, crumbled plaster across his son's noble visage. A little dust falls away, and he wipes his hand on his thigh before proclaiming: "Maybe an opportunity to reconsider some of the decor? I'm as fond of images of my son being valiant as any proud father, but Ithaca's history is so much longer, so much more."

Spartan women peek their heads round doors as the royal entourage descends deeper into the palace, look for Spartan men, see none. Ithacan maids are emerging from the yards, the laundry, the kitchen to form a wall of womanhood that shields their queen as she moves into the palace, and there is something in the way Melantho holds that heavy pan, a certain intention in how Phiobe clutches her chopping knife that makes the Spartan women slip back at the Ithacans' approach. One woman makes a run for the front gate, but Teodora is waiting there, Eos by her side. They do not threaten, do not proclaim "stop or die!" – nor do they need to. Teodora has her sword drawn, and plays with it loosely, as if working out a little stiffness in her stabbing wrist, while Eos stands calmly by remarking on this nice thing she could do with Teodora's hair.

Thus unmolested and unannounced, they reach the foot of the stairs up to the royal quarters, even as Laertes muses: "Perhaps a painting of other great voyages? After all, there was at least one Ithacan who sailed with the *Argo*, if you take my meaning . . ."

"Thank you, honoured father," Penelope intones. "You are of course entirely right, and your learned counsel is greatly appreciated. As soon as we have saved our island from Spartan invaders, we must absolutely reconsider the decor. Now if you will excuse me . . ."

She gives a little bow, and alone, climbs the stairs.

Here are rooms with more than enough history to fill a ballad.

This room here, where Anticlea, the mother of Odysseus,

wept and drank herself to death over her missing son, shrieking at all who dared try to help her: *YOU WILL NEVER KNOW MY SORROW!!*

Here is where Zosime died, washed in her own crimson blood.

Here the room whose very walls are twined with the olive tree, where baby Telemachus first cried, where Odysseus lay by his wife's side after Eos had washed the blood away and said: *thank you for giving me a son.*

Here is Helen of Sparta, Helen of Troy, sitting by the open window gazing down to the sea, a golden carafe by her side, a golden cup empty in her hand. She has not adorned her face today. Not daubed charcoal across her brow, painted in blackness about her eyes. She has not woven her hair into a high, aching plait, nor rubbed crimson into her cheeks. Instead she sits as innocent in her features as the child she once was, as the girl who did not know that it was not her place to laugh, or to scrape her knees, or raise her voice in song. Nor is she a girl either, for though she looks down to the sea, her eyes see far beyond, to a past, to towers burning, to lovers slain, to children living and dead, the screams of childbirth, the weeping over bones, the first gasp of dawn as life comes back again, as life keeps going, keeps going, keeps going, holding on.

She is beautiful then. She is my Helen, my queen, my fairest one. She is the innocent and the knowing, the hopeful and the wise, the lover who lost, the lover who dreams, the one who plays the game and the one who breaks vulnerable beneath the weight of living. I rush to her, caress her cheek, cry out Helen, Helen, my lovely Helen, and she closes her eyes at the touch of me, catches her breath at my familiar embrace, seems for a moment gasping, on the edge of tears, overwhelmed by too much of too much, by all that she is, by all that she feels, loves, desires and has seen.

My queen, I whisper. *My love. My mortal self. My Helen.*

Then Penelope stands in the door, and Helen opens her eyes again, sees through me, beyond me, sees her cousin. Stands and says: "Ah. You made it. Shall we?"

CHAPTER 43

≫≫≫≫≫≫≫≫≫≫≫≫≫≫≫≫≫≫≫≫≫≫≫≫≫≫≫≫≫≫≫≫≫≫≫≫≫

Helen and Penelope progress around the garden.

It is a very small garden, meant to grow flowers pleasing to bees, herbs pleasing to Autonoe in her kitchen.

They walk arm in arm. As they walk, they conspire.

Helen says, yes, of course I can do that. Of course I can. I was just waiting for you to ask, really.

Penelope says, I thought as much, cousin, but didn't wish to presume. Didn't wish to ask until I was sure.

Tsk tsk, Helen chides. Tsk tsk! We are cousins, are we not? We are blood. You should always know you can count on me.

An accord is struck.

A deal is made.

Helen returns to her rooms, to make a few scant preparations.

Penelope gathers up her maids, her father-in-law, the men of her council, and proceeds to the dock to meet the kings of Greece.

At the harbour, the kings of Greece are having a thoroughly awkward time.

"Nephew, won't you come down from your ship?" Menelaus asks.

And: "No, thank you, uncle, why don't you join me on board?" Orestes replies.

"I'd love to, nephew, but my men, you see, my men are awful protective."

"That is understandable," Orestes replies, "given your age."

In this really rather uncouth manner things could proceed for a while, until Penelope arrives.

The fact that she arrives from behind Menelaus, from the palace itself, causes a great deal of consternation. Trained warriors who should know better jump at her approach, parting in an uneasy, broken formation as she breezes through. But she is not armed, not accompanied by more fiendish women of blood and bow – Teodora is tactfully elsewhere – and she smiles radiantly upon both Orestes and Menelaus as she approaches.

"My dear cousins," she exclaims, bright as the noonday sun. "What on earth is happening here?"

Menelaus's face is a heavy frown away from a full growl, his jaw working back and forth in his skull as he seeks to control his really rather strong sentiments on the appearance of this queen at his very exposed back. "Queen Penelope," he mutters. "Fancy seeing you here. And with your aged father-in-law too. How nice."

"Goodness, is that Orestes, king of kings, son of Agamemnon, master of Mycenae and all-round healthy-looking chap standing upon that boat?" Laertes drawls, arms folded and eyes sparkling as they look upon Menelaus. "Well, better not keep him waiting, terrible bad form. What will people think of the hospitality of Ithaca? Come on down, lad! Come have a drink!"

In the end, they assemble in the hollow halls of the palace. Nicostratus remains on the suitors' boat, Pylades' blade at his throat. Lefteris stays below, a contingent of soldiers at his back, watching his captive prince. Elektra meets the Spartan's eye, smiles from the ship, does not look away as her brother descends with Iason by his side. She cannot be part of what follows – it would not be seemly for a woman of her status to get involved.

Eos waits for them in the great hall of the palace, a table already laid with wine, bread and, of course, fish. She offers Menelaus a cup as he marches through the door, and he knocks it from her hand. The crude clay shatters on the ground. Eos sighs. She has laid out only the poorest goods of the kitchen for this little diplomatic engagement, but even so, she regrets needless breakage.

Helen has also descended, pacing anxiously back and forth across the floor. As Menelaus enters, she flings herself upon him, drapes herself about his neck, cries, "I was so frightened! I was so ..."

He shoves her away. She falls. No one offers to help her rise again. She shuffles away a little from the table, then picks herself up, murmurs: "I'll go to my room ..." wobbles away, unregarded.

There are chairs set for four. Menelaus takes one, Orestes another, Laertes the third. The last should really be taken by a councillor of Odysseus, but before they can move, Penelope slips into it, folds her hands in her lap, smiles at the men, takes a cup that is set before her and raises it in salute.

"To my father," she proclaims, tipping the vessel Laertes' way. "To my honoured guests. Let us give thanks to the gods."

Orestes sprinkles wine on the floor; Laertes tips a splash from the lip of his cup, then drains the rest down. Penelope bows her head in prayer – and does not pray. Menelaus does not lift his drink, does not touch the food, does not even look upon the wine he is offered.

Penelope prays a nice long time. Laertes should be the first to interrupt this piety, but he is enjoying how much her protracted silence is infuriating her Spartan guest. Orestes should be the next to speak, but he is − of course − embraced in his own prayers, his own entirely sincere devotions.

I shall repent, Mother, he prays. *I may not be a hero, but I shall be a better man than Father was.*

Menelaus's fist slamming into the table rouses Orestes from his contemplations, a roar of rudeness that echoes through the hollow hall. "What the fuck do you think you're playing at?" the Spartan snarls − not at either of the kings assembled, but at the pensive queen. "What the fuck do you think you're doing?"

Laertes raises an eyebrow. Orestes waits, enjoying perhaps the opportunity to save his voice, his strength, still so thin about his bones.

Penelope looks Menelaus in the eye, looks him up and down, and is for a moment the most beautiful mortal thing upon this land, even though Helen herself is not a minute's scamper away. There is a word here for her beauty − a word like power, or victory; or perhaps even more arousing still, there is that in Penelope that is *untamed.*

"Cousin … *brother,*" she corrects herself. "I must report some shameful things." Laertes leans back in his chair, ankles crossed, arms folded, an entirely willing audience about to enjoy a thoroughly good show. "There has been a terrible con-spiracy against you. A plot against your whole family. A priest of Apollo, Kleitos − I think you know the man − has schemed with a maid of Mycenae to poison our dear cousin and king of kings, Orestes. The maid has confessed and is dead, executed for her crimes, and the priest will soon be found, interrogated, tortured and made to confess the names of any and all parties who induced him to his heinous crimes. No doubt he will spread terrible lies to try and excuse his actions, but we all know who was really behind our noble cousin's poisoning. The same man who in his vaulting ambition would plot to take a crown. The same man who thought he could by strength and cunning seize perhaps not just the throne of Mycenae, but the western isles themselves. I refer of course to the captain of your guard, Lefteris."

Laertes' grin is going to crack his face asunder. Orestes is a plaster prince, looking forever at some unseen point.

"Lefteris," Menelaus growls. "You abscond from your own palace, you kidnap my son, and then you return to blame ... Lefteris."

"Indeed. After extensive investigations, it is clear to me that you have been betrayed from within by one of your nearest, dearest soldiers and friends. He has had access to the priest Kleitos, access to the maid Rhene, and indeed access to your dear Nicostratus. It was to shame Nicostratus that Lefteris murdered the maid Zosime while your beloved son slept, to make it appear that your own heir – dare I assume he is your chosen heir, of all your excellent children? – was unfit for the throne. I know how close Lefteris is to you, but I think my husband once remarked that the most dangerous blade is the one you cannot see."

Menelaus looks from Penelope to grinning Laertes, from Laertes to Orestes, then back to Penelope again. "No," he says.

"No?"

"No. You come here with your ... your women. *Women*. I have this island. I have this palace, I have—"

"My women killed or captured every Spartan who set foot on Kephalonia, and suffered not a scratch in doing so. You may have heard rumours of some pirates who set upon my land – forgive me, my husband's land – last year, urged on by a suitor who sought to marry me? They were all slain, cut down by the arrows of the blessed goddess Artemis. Their corpses were left tied to their ships, displayed for all to see, guts hanging out for gulls and crows. Of course, it is needful that the goddess protect us from pirates. No one would take seriously an island defended by women and girls. And you, brother – you are the great Menelaus of Sparta. You bested Paris, set the fire that made Troy burn. You cannot be beaten by widows and girls. Not you. And so you see, you haven't been. When you leave this place, which you will, you will tell no one what happened here. Your men who died were lost at sea. They perished in the fires when your ships most unfortunately and unexpectedly burned. They were not slaughtered by women. That would be unbelievable. Unacceptable. And so it did not happen. You say you have your men, and you do. I have this island. I have more swords, more spears, more bows, and my women . . . do not fight with honour. I have the protection of the king of Mycenae, his vow to assist me in all I do, and soon I shall have a fleet of Mycenaean vessels pledged to protect the waterways of the western isles, and they . . . they shall be welcome guests, brother. They shall be guests who know their place."

Orestes raises his chin a little at this, nods to Penelope, nods to his uncle in confirmation. Penelope's smile is thin, weary, a knife's edge. She leans her elbows on the table, her chin upon her knotted hands. It is most undignified for a lady. I lick my lips to see it. "I have your son," she says. "I have Nicostratus with a knife to his throat. A little misunderstanding, of course. He was confined to the temple of Athena, from which he most regrettably fled when our dear cousin Orestes was visiting sacred sites on Kephalonia. Thinking perhaps his flight portended some guilt, our good Mycenaean friends captured him again, and are holding him prisoner until his innocence can be proven. I now believe he *is* innocent of the murder of Zosime, and so you see, we can have this whole little misunderstanding cleared up and everyone on their way home in a satisfactory manner."

Menelaus has known defeat, of course.

On the beaches of Troy, before the city walls – years of grinding, gutting defeat.

He has known the shame of being a cuckold. The way people look at him, the man who cannot keep his wife, cannot keep a woman, cannot satisfy a woman, tiny little man, laughed at by a woman, cuckold, cuckold, little cock, tiny flaccid little penis, little quivering man.

No wound on his wounded body ever cut so deep as when Helen left, the way the kings of Greece all stood at his back and whispered to each other: there he is. There is Menelaus. There is the man too weak to keep his wife.

Oh, Menelaus has known defeat.

Next to that, this . . .

. . . this is just a little skirmish in the road.

"Nephew," he muses, eyes fixed on the Ithacan queen. "If what this . . . wise wife says is true, it seems that someone I trust has gravely injured you. If this is . . . if it is the case, I must ask your forgiveness."

"Thank you, uncle," murmurs Orestes. "I appreciate your sentiment, as I am sure you appreciate that forgiveness is mine alone to give."

Menelaus's eyes dart at last to Orestes, who stares calmly back. The old Spartan grins, but the smile is gone as soon as it appeared. He nods down at his hands, licks his lips, churning over words, thoughts, plans.

Then Orestes says: "You will send Hermione to me, of course." Menelaus's head snaps up, but the Mycenaean king is unblinking. "She was betrothed to me as a child. It is suitable and appropriate that our households continue in close harmony. After all, what could be more wonderful for your daughter than to marry the king of kings? Nicostratus will return to Sparta and my sister will seek an appropriate husband where she will."

Menelaus considers.

Menelaus has known defeat before.

In the end, a daughter is not so high a price to pay.

"Well then," he muses. "Well then. Isn't this all turning out snugly and familial."

"Indeed," Orestes declares. "I will have my men arrange the details with you."

He rises, sways for a moment, catches himself on the edge of the table. Menelaus's eyes glitter as he watches him walk, slow, crooked, towards the door. Laertes rises too, joins Orestes, a hand loosely poised by the young king's elbow, not quite touching, merely by his side. "Have I told you about when I sailed on the *Argo?*" he trills, as he leads Orestes into the light.

Now, only Penelope and Menelaus remain.

They watch each other, *enemy, enemy,* across the table.

Menelaus stretches, long and slow, joints creaking, back cracking as he bends. Then relaxes back into his chair, loose, legs long. Says: "You know I'll get him. In the end. Just because he's sober now doesn't mean it'll last. Marrying my daughter just makes it easier for me to make my claim when he finally loses it. Regent, perhaps. Kind Uncle Menelaus stepping in, as is his wont. Then your ... little gaggle of girlies won't mean shit. Soon as Orestes cracks again, your protection will be gone. Then I'll be back. Looking after the wife of my dear friend Odysseus, heard rumours of some cult of crazy women, dangerous, sacrilegious, I heard. A thousand men. Five thousand. As many as it takes. By the time we're done, there won't be a single fucking cunt we haven't fucked in the whole western fucking isles."

He grips the table as he speaks. His face is flushed, hot, sweat beads his brow. The room is watery at the edges; he draws down a raggedy breath. This too feels like defeat, but something more, something else, something he can't quite ...

"Orestes will be mad and his sister will be some ... some fucking rag for some fat ... some pig farmer ... and once they're done, I'll send Nicostratus to your ... your bed. I'll watch him do it, I'll watch, and when he's done, I'll ... "

His breath comes faster now, too fast for the words to flow, gasps between each thought, blurring between each idea. Penelope stands, and she is too tall, too grave, there are reflections of her in his eyes, winged creatures with fury on their tongues and talons about their fingers. She leans in, and the world seems to lean with her, studies his face, says in a voice that rings through his skull: "Brother? Are you quite well?"

He reaches out for her, but misjudges the distance, overbalances, topples from his chair.

He is on the floor, panting, clawing at the earth for stability, weak, spinning, gagging, gasping. Penelope steps round the table to peer down at him a little closer, just out of the reach of his limp, loose arm. "Brother?" she calls out, sing-song, voice booming and far away. "Brother, are you hurt?"

He tries to speak, to call her whore, slut, bitch, to tell her all the things he's going to do to her, he's thought about it all, you see, in intimate detail, her cunt, her mouth, he's going to show her, no one will call him a cuckold, no one will laugh at him, he's fucking Menelaus, he'll show them all.

Instead, from his lips, a mewling. A little whine of sound, a dirge of voice. He tries to speak again, and the sound goes ah-ah-ah and nothing more.

Penelope sighs, squats down on her haunches before him, shakes her head sadly. "Oh dear. You seem to have come over with a certain something of your dear nephew's affliction. I wonder how that could have happened. They say the children of the house of Atreus are cursed. But poison is such a woman's tool, don't you think? Something used by cowards and weak little whores, not great kings."

He tries to turn his head to the door, to call for his guard, for Lefteris, but Penelope grabs him about the chin, pulls his head away, face towards hers before he can speak. Leans in close. "Brother?" she trills. "Brother, can you hear me? I want you to listen very closely. I want there to be no room for doubt. I can reach you anywhere. Do you understand? You may not be scared of my women with their bows, but the other women – the ones bringing you water, the ones cleaning your clothes, the ones you fuck, the ones you hit, the ones you don't even notice standing in the corner of your eye – they are everywhere. We are everywhere. We can reach you no matter where you run."

She shakes his face a little side to side, enjoys how his body flops limply with the movement, how his whole form seems to shudder like a jellyfish in her grasp. "You are going to leave Orestes alone. He is going to be king in Mycenae, and you in Sparta, and there an end of it. You will not take your brother's throne. And you will not take mine. If you try, you will be the same dribbling, pissing, shitting wretch of a man you tried to make your nephew, and if you think the crows were hungry for Orestes' flesh, just imagine what they'll do to you when you are too weak to defend yourself. No. You will grow old and you will die, Menelaus of Sparta, the man who burned the world to catch his beautiful, unwilling wife. You will live out what days you have left quietly, in peace. That is what the poets will say of you. That is all there is to be said. Goodbye, brother."

So saying, she lets Menelaus go, stands, marches to the door, looks out at the crowd assembled in the courtyard. Spartan maids and Ithacan too. The king of Mycenae, the father of Odysseus, the suitors at the gates, the councillors of Ithaca. They look to her and she takes a moment – just a moment – to enjoy their stares. To look back as if she were a queen.

It is, alas, only a moment. With a little sigh quickly hidden, she bows her head, presses her hand to her mouth and exclaims, "Oh help me! Our dear Menelaus is taken sick!" and just to reinforce the point, swoons softly into Eos's waiting arms.

CHAPTER 44

>>

There is business to be done.

Menelaus is carried on a litter to a Spartan ship, as Helen weeps and wails by his side.

He is loaded on deck, groaning, spittle running from his mouth, while the women scurry to load supplies and the soldiers look around, a little confused, for something resembling leadership.

Lefteris says, "It's poison, it's fucking—"

And Orestes barks: "Seize that man as a traitor to my uncle's crown and mine!"

The nearest men who might obey this command are not Mycenaeans at all, but rather the suitors of Ithaca. They will not be permitted to vent their indignity, their hollow pride and broken vengeance on Menelaus – but violence is how their fathers taught them to make their feelings known, and so Antinous tries to kick Lefteris in the nuts, but misses and stubs his foot on the warrior's thigh. Eurymachus pulls rather unproductively at Lefteris's hair. Amphinomous is the only one who manages to organise some rope and a team of men to sit on the Spartan's back as he is bound. He does not object when Kenamon politely suggests they gag the soldier too, before he can scream any more obscenities in front of the women.

Lefteris cries out: "Menelaus! *Menelaus!*" But his master cannot hear him.

Kleitos is found hiding behind the latrines near the temple of Athena. He is thrown grovelling at the feet of Orestes and Elektra. Orestes looks upon him, but is too tired to pronounce hatred, forgiveness, anything at all of meaning. Instead the young king prays to Athena, prays to Zeus, prays to anyone who will listen for rest, ease, peace, mercy.

Only I hear his whispers, and I cannot answer his prayers.

Elektra, however, is having something of a second wind, and it is she who kneels by Kleitos's side and whispers into his ear all the terrible things she is going to do to his bodily parts if he does not make certain swift and wise decisions.

Kleitos listens, then howls: "It was Lefteris! Lefteris made me do it!"

For his cooperation, the priest is tied up with stones and pushed off a cliff the next day. His skull is smashed open on the rocks below, before the water can drown him. Lefteris's tongue is cut out by Eupheithes to silence his lies, and the pit dug within which he is to die. Antinous and Eurymachus stand side by side to throw the first stones upon him, their fathers waiting next in line.

With the number of conscious Spartans in a position of authority growing thin, it is with Nicostratus that Penelope, Elektra and Orestes sit on a warm evening as the tide turns.

"Cousin," declares Orestes, staring at some point far beyond Nicostratus's face, "you came to Ithaca to do me great service, but it was not needed. I am, as you can see, quite well. Unfortunately, while you were here, three of your ships were lost to foul weather and unexpected flame, and many of your noble colleagues drowned. Your father was also taken sick, and so hastily you are returning to Sparta to see to his recovery. You will send your sister to me immediately upon your return, as was pledged by our ancient bargain. As to the matter of the maid murdered in your room, it was Lefteris who did it. I will attest that this was the finding made to any who may enquire, and your reputation will be ... clean. At this time."

Nicostratus is not as smart as his father, but he is not a dolt.

When he saw Menelaus dribbling on the deck, reduced from a warrior to a stinking old man, he had this overwhelming urge, this sudden and profound desire, to urinate all over his father's face. He has no idea where it came from, and is relieved that it passed without him acting on it, but heavens know he will have a hard time restraining his bladder on the voyage home. Something about the sloshing of water day and night, he concludes. Something about that.

"Of course, my king," he says, and bows to Orestes, son of Agamemnon, before turning his face towards the sea and the waiting horizon.

This leaves only one Spartan of any notable seniority bustling around the palace of Ithaca.

Helen flaps as the maids carry her trunks down the stairs, shrills: "Oh do be careful! Do be careful with that, oh goodness, they're just so clumsy!"

Penelope watches from the open door of Helen's rapidly emptying room, head on one side, hands clasped before her.

"Oh, a sea voyage – again," sighs her cousin, as the last of her gowns are safely delivered to the waiting women in the hall below. "I do get such a terrible tummy, you know, and salt – I mean, salt can do wonders, but too much of it, and with the sun as well, dreadful for one's complexion, the ageing! I mean, Penelope dear, I hope you don't mind me saying, but this coastal life and all the time you spend pining in the sun, you really should think about this sort of thing, you know."

Tryphosa and Eos have wrapped Helen's perfect silver mirror in thick pads of raw wool, then tied the bundle with rope. Even so, they now carry it to the waiting ship between them as if it were delicate as the butterfly's wing, miraculous in its existence.

For the briefest of moments, Helen and Penelope are alone.

"Cousin," calls Penelope softly as Helen turns towards the stair.

Helen looks back, already fluttering with her sea shawl to ensure it lies in the most fetching manner possible across her long, pale shoulders. "Cousin?"

"I know you killed Zosime. I am not entirely sure why."

Helen giggles. It is what she does when she is going to be hit, beaten, struck down, kicked, assaulted, violated, mocked. It is habit. It is instinct. It is a sound that buys her a little time before the blow.

Penelope flinches, and the sound dies on Helen's lips.

Helen glances down the stairs, glances up, sees no one, and in an instant, the child is gone. Now only two women stand together, watching each other in the cool afternoon light. It is Helen who holds out her arm, says: "Would you walk me to the ship, cousin? One last time?"

Penelope and Helen walk together through the evening town, arm in arm. The maids of Ithaca keep all people who might draw near at a distance, a shield of discretion around the moving queens.

"I have done you a disservice, cousin," Penelope says at last. "I have ... misjudged you."

"Not at all!" Helen trills. "Not at all. If anything, cousin, you have been the flower of hospitality."

"I have treated you as a fool. As the child you pretend to be."

"And I am grateful for that. My life would be . . . so much harder," she sighs, "if anyone were to behave in any other way."

"You killed Zosime."

"I did, poor dearest. I felt really quite awful about it at the time, but you know how these things are. We women sometimes have to do awful things, don't we? How did you know it was me?"

"I didn't, for the longest time. I suspected Elektra or Pylades – a Mycenaean at least, desperate to try and keep Orestes out of Menelaus's hands by any expedient. But I could not see how either of them could have done it. I never even considered the possibility that it might be you, until the night we fled the palace. You helped us then – thank you for that – not as some simpering idiot playing a silly game, but as a woman fully aware of everything that was happening and making the deliberate and thoughtful choice to act against her husband's interests. That changed everything."

Helen squeezes Penelope's arm a little closer, nuzzles her cheek up towards the Ithacan's shoulder, a fondness between family, a familiarity that is Helen's gift and brings nothing but bewilderment to Penelope. "Tell me the rest – I do so love to hear about myself."

"Your make-up; your tinctures," Penelope murmurs. "When I searched your room, I took samples of each, showed them to my priestess. There were many there she did not know – and some she did. Powders for beauty, powders for pleasure. Oils that can cause vivid dreams, or which can bring about the most profound of sleeps. And it struck me: so many people on the night of Zosime's death slept so very deeply. Anaitis says that sometimes the priests inhale the fumes of their sacred drugs – and the oil lamp was missing from Nicostratus's room the morning after the murder. We found it later, in the garden, thrown it seemed on purpose from an open window. Why would one attempt to hide a lamp? Indeed, the cold wind had been allowed to billow freely through his room, no shutter closed, as if to blow away the scent of some distasteful odour from the night. The only conclusion that seemed to fit this tale was this – that the oil that burned in the lamp was not of the purest sort.

"What if Nicostratus then was telling the truth? What if he had gone to his room, and fallen immediately into a deep, profound sleep, lulled by the light itself? The only other person who had the same experience seems to have been Tryphosa – your maid. And then I remembered – the lamp was missing from your room too. It was too much to be coincidence."

A turn of the corner, past the temple of Athena, past the houses of old Eupheithes, aged Polybus, the sea glistening below, reflecting the evening sun.

"Nicostratus kept an absurd suit of armour in his room; a large shield too. Not large enough for a grown man to hide behind, perhaps – but for a woman? There was a footprint in the blood, small and slight – perhaps Zosime's, but then how could Zosime have left a footprint in her own blood if she was already fallen? And you left the feast that night before everyone else; we all saw it, and Tryphosa confirmed that you were in your bed fast asleep. When Orestes started raving, all attention was upon him – including that of Elektra, the next most plausible suspect – the ideal cover perhaps for one to prepare a crime. You changed the oil in the lamps, in both your room and Nicostratus's. Swapped it out for one of your ... lulling tinctures, so that all who inhaled the scent might fall into a deep, thoughtless sleep. I don't know how you resisted its allure – some sort of scented mask, perhaps, or another counter-agent from your collection ..."

"A crushed flower, to be exact," Helen chirrups, eyes bright in the afternoon sun. "Its drops upon the eyes produces these extraordinary dark pupils, as well as roaring headaches, a racing heart . . . and a certain resistance to the narcotic odours of the oil."

"You have clearly made a study of these things."

"I have; when one is too foolish and silly to do anything useful about the palace, there is really not much else to keep oneself occupied. Indeed, when your lovely son Telemachus came to visit, I may have slipped a certain something into the wine so everyone at his welcoming feast had a really rather luscious time. Yes, yes, you can thank me later, I'm fabulous, I know."

Penelope nods, regret clenched in her jaw, her heart beating a little faster – *Telemachus, Telemachus!* But no, now and as always these are thoughts for another time. Let it go. "So you change the oil in the lamp in your room first, lulling Tryphosa into a profound sleep. While she slumbers and everyone is preoccupied with Orestes, you slip into Nicostratus's room, change the oil in his lamp too, secrete yourself behind that absurd shield of his and wait. When at last he returns from everyone fussing over Orestes, you only need for him to inhale long and deep for the sleep to come upon him, and then you may do whatever business you wish. What I do not understand is why, in those circumstances, you chose to kill Zosime."

Another corner, and here there is a sudden smell of purple flowers, the rich odour of the last blossoms of a hot, high summer. Helen pauses to sniff the air, to enjoy the perfume, waft it around herself as if it might cling to the back of her lovely, perfect fingers before the cruel sea washes it clear again. Then a sigh, a tug on Penelope's arm, and off they go again, back into the fish-stinking turns of the path.

"Menelaus drugs me," Helen says, true and simple as the boundless sky. "Or rather, he has his women do it. Ever since we got back from Troy. He said that I wept too much when I was sober, talked too much when I was drunk. I was actually rather relieved when my maids started spiking my wine. It took away ... so many unpleasant things. And everyone seemed to find it so much easier to talk to me when I was a fool. A foolish person, you see, has not made choices. She has not considered consequences. No one could expect anything from someone like that. Not forgiveness. Definitely not defiance or regret. You have to be awake, you see, to feel anything. It was easier for everyone to keep me asleep.

"Of course, after a while the concoctions my maids were feeding me began to have no effect. It was easier to pretend to be sloshed, of course – much easier for everyone involved. But Zosime, bless her, was beginning to sense there might be something a little bit off with the whole business. She was always so desperate to get back into my husband's good graces, just so earnestly alert. On the night my husband had his little tantrum about ... goodness, I can't even remember what now, it was all so silly ... I dropped my cup. The drug they feed me forms little crystals in the bottom, really quite distinct once one knows what one is looking for – well then, imagine my shock. My surprise. No crystals! No play of colour in the firelight. That's when I knew – Zosime had stopped giving me the medicine. Clearly she was testing me, seeing if my behaviour changed without the drugs upon my lips.

"Well, darlingest, my behaviour has been very consistent these last ten years! Drink or no drink, this is just how I am these days, but of course, if Zosime knew – if she told anyone that this whole thing is, how might one say it? Well, a little bit of an act? A little bit like, one might say, dressing oneself up in widow's garb to keep the attention of difficult people away – that would be very awkward indeed. It might lead my husband to wonder just what else might be a teensy bit of a put-on, and I couldn't be having that. Clearly Zosime needed to go. Thankfully, before she had a chance to tell anyone about her suspicions, dearest Orestes had his little incident and I had the perfect opportunity. Zosime had been Nicostratus's lover, you know. She was always going to go to him first."

"So you never intended to kill Nicostratus – you were waiting in his room for Zosime."

"Quite! He was unconscious long before she managed to finish her duties and open the door. Then it was just a case of grabbing one of his swords and . . . well, how shall one say it? Doing the deed."

Helen speaks of this as a naughty girl might speak of a flirtatious tumble with a comely shepherd boy. All a little unfortunate, a little regrettable, but well . . . but well. Helen of Troy is not one to linger too long on the regrets of her life.

There is a furrow in Penelope's brow that suggests she does not entirely see it that way. Helen puffs, nudges her in the ribs, tuts and flares her cheeks. "Don't be so sullen, cousin. You know it's all gone well really! Zosime's death bought you time to do that lovely business with Orestes, you have your funny little island back, and my dear husband will be . . . well . . . he'll recover, of course, but he'll not necessarily be quite so . . . you know."

"If you could have poisoned Menelaus earlier, why didn't you?"

Helen presses her hand to her mouth in horror. "I? Poison my husband?"

"You were willing to do it when I asked. You were quite expert, may I say, in throwing yourself upon him with your poisoned needles when he came into the hall."

"Poor dear Menelaus." Helen shakes her head. "I will admit that sometimes his behaviour has been . . . boorish, to say the least. But if I had done anything in Sparta, struck back in his own palace, who do you think he would have suspected? Maybe not little me at first, but sooner or later – sooner or later. This

413

way, though, he knows who poisoned him! You did! Clever Penelope poisoned him, and well, if he keeps on falling sick in Sparta, it's clearly because you have women everywhere. You do have women everywhere, don't you, dear? Everyone knows you do, though no one dares say it out loud. My husband will live, keeping his really rather pestilential sons from the throne, and he will be ... managed. Manageable, shall we say. No one will look twice at me, not now everyone is looking at you. It's all worked out really rather wonderfully, hasn't it?"

Penelope stops.

Stares into her cousin's eyes.

Stares so deep she wonders if she can see all the way through to her soul.

Tries to see.

Tries to understand.

To make sense of all that is before her.

Shakes her head.

Turns away.

Stares down at the ground, up at the sky.

"Do you regret anything, cousin?" she asks at last, to the vaulting heavens above. "You murdered a woman, not in passion, but calmly, with great care, in my house. Drove the blade through her heart. You live with a man who hits you whenever his blood is up. You broke the world. Do you regret any of it?"

Helen sighs, takes Penelope's hand in her own. "Dearest one," she tuts, "when you helped Orestes kill my sister, his mother, did you feel ... regret? Of course you did. Of course. You're such a softie deep down. I'm sure a lot of people would feel a lot happier in themselves, with their own guilts and failures, if you did a bit of gown-rending and hair-pulling and 'woe is me' and generally took responsibility for the cruelties of this world. It would make the lives of everyone else involved so much easier, permit them, perhaps, to ask fewer questions about their own part in this fateful event. Tearful Penelope. All her fault. It would be a great service to so many people if you could just . . . be that for them. Be the one who carries it all. Let everyone else off the hook. But my darling, tell me – tell me true. How does that serve *you*?" She sighs, brushes the words away, lets go of Penelope's hand for the very last time. "Regret," she concludes. "Everyone feels it in some way or another. Poor Menelaus – he is really rather consumed by it, not that he'd ever allow it to show. That's part of his problem, you see. But ultimately, if one is to live a more fulfilling kind of life, it can only ever be a step on the road."

CHAPTER 45

>>

A nd so the ships set sail from Ithaca.

I stand upon the cliff, Artemis by my side.

The Spartan ships unfurl crimson sails. Nicostratus orders the men to beat the drums. Helen dribbles a spoonful of broth between Menelaus's open lips. "Poor lambkin," she coos. "Poor dear."

The Spartan king is already recovering, of course. It would be folly to set to sea if he were on the verge of death. But it will be a long voyage and, thinks Helen, who knows what setbacks her beloved husband might experience. He is getting old, after all. None of them are young any more.

"It's all right," she declares, wiping sweat from his brow. "You can count on me."

Further out across the waves, the Mycenaean vessel of Orestes turns towards the east, brother and sister standing together on the prow, Pylades at their back, watching the ocean. The sea is easier to gaze upon than each other. There is a wedding waiting for Orestes when he comes home – a long-promised marriage to Menelaus's daughter. No one will ask Hermione what her opinion of this may be. No one really cares to know.

"You know, you've got really nice hair," I say to Artemis, as she waves farewell from atop the cliff.

The huntress turns, surprised, immediately defensive, suddenly embarrassed. She opens her mouth to tell me to get lost, to go away, to keep my poisonous opinions to myself. Then stops. Hesitates. Reaches up to feel a lock hanging loose near her brow, as if only just considering it. "Do I?" she asks.

"Oh yes. Absolutely gorgeous. It frames your face perfectly, and your body, I mean, gracious, the muscles, the arms, the quiver, the nudity – the statues really don't do you justice."

"Well that's because if any man dared look upon me, I would carve out his eyes and feed them to my bears," she replies primly.

"I know," I sigh, wrapping my arm across the warm line of her broad back. "And don't ever let anyone make you change."

In the palace of Odysseus: the feast.

The suitors are having an absolutely wonderful time.

More wine, more meat, more everything! Bawdy songs, fun songs, songs of delight – sing that song about how Menelaus lost his wife, sing that song about how he pissed his pants and ran away, sing!

For a brief evening, enemies are allies, rivals are friends. Antinous wraps Eurymachus in his arms and exclaims: "We showed those Spartans, didn't we? Coming here, making it large, we showed them who's in charge!"

"Well, actually, I um—"

"Just shut up, Eurymachus, shut up shut up shut up! *MORE WINE!* Everyone, more wine!"

By the light of a flickering torch, Laertes dismounts the grumbling old donkey he has ridden back to his farm. Ourania and Eos are in a cart behind him, laden with trinkets and gracious goods bestowed by the fathers of the suitors, in thanks to the man who quite possibly saved their sons' lives.

"Where do you want all this stuff?" Ourania asks, but Laertes is already kicking off his shoes and looking round for his favourite, second most soiled robe. Being king for a little while was fun and all, but there's a reason he likes the simple life, the familiar hearth, and no one questioning him when he wanders around without anything about his loins and eats with his mouth open.

"Leave it anywhere!" He gestures loosely from the already closing door of his farm. "I've got all the rubbish I need!"

By the docks:

"It's sinking quick, it's going down, we should fetch help, we should—"

"No, Aegyptius. No."

Aegyptius pauses in his frantic gesticulation to stare into the eyes of old Medon, who stands patient and content upon the quay. Then he turns again to look out into the bay, where yes indeed, the warship – the only warship left in the harbour – is now grimly listing to one side. It is the ship, he seems to recall, raised by old Eupheithes, wise Polybus and their suitor-children, to patrol these coastal waters. It did some service for the queen, and now that the queen is back in her palace, it seems to have met an inexplicable fate. Funny how that keeps happening, he muses.

"It's going to clog up harbour traffic if it just sinks there," he says at last.

"Yes, I believe it will."

"Going to make a terrible impression too, a fine vessel like that being the first thing you see when you come into port."

"I hadn't thought of it that way."

"People will look at it and think . . . so much for the sailors of Ithaca."

418

"Indeed," Medon muses. "One might say that it will be something of a warning. I wonder how the suitors will take it. Given it was meant to be their ship."

Aegyptius nods, clicks his tongue in the roof of his mouth. "Funny old thing."

"Funny indeed," Medon concurs.

The two men stand together a while longer, as they watch the vessel sink.

"Oh, Kenamon, I, uh . . ."

"My lady, I didn't realise you were going to be in this garden at . . . uh . . ."

"No, apologies, I'm actually . . . well. As you see. I was just heading to bed."

"Of course. Sorry. Excuse me. I will . . . um. Let you. As you say."

"Yes. Thank you. As you say."

The Egyptian stands in the door before the Ithacan queen.

She says: "The songs you sing . . ."

Even as he blurts: "I hope I don't disturb you by . . . Oh . . ."

The gods are not watching this garden tonight. I blow a departing kiss to the two of them, frozen in awkward darkness, and slip away.

The hour is so late it has become almost early, the warm breath of dawn pricking the eastern horizon. I open my hands to greet it, spin dreams of desire, of hopes fulfilled and trust made sacred, of skin upon skin in vulnerable ecstasy, of cries of delight and coos of deepest tenderness. I scent the morning air with sweet perfume, bid the petals fall in crimson sheets from the bending flowers, send flocks of birds scattering into the sky in a chorus of sweetest song, kiss a passing nymph upon the lips as she rises from the riverbed, turn my face towards the sky and my beneficence towards all, call out: lovers, lovers, lovers! May you be loved! May love come to you all!

With white feathered wings I beat my way skywards, scattering the scent of a lover long gone, the taste of sweet fruit, the sound of muffled moaning half heard through a thin muddy wall. Lovers, I cry! To all of you love, and love to you all!

I scatter the clouds so that the first light of dawn may pierce through eastern windows and blaze golden upon the warm skin of an upturned buttock, a gently curving breast; that eyes as they open may be dazzled by the radiance of all that has gone before, entranced by all that is yet to come. Lovers! I cry. Be my celebration! You will never bleed more than in my name, you will break the world and mend it again, you will die by my hand and by my hand you will live once more, come sing, come soar, come celebrate! I am your goddess, I am your lady clothed in white, I am . . .

Then I see him.

Tossed upon a southern shore.

I nearly tumble from the sky, have to catch myself upon a twisted finger of wind, steady my wings on the air to take a closer look. He lies sleeping, curled up in a corner, treasure arrayed all about him, the ship that carried him hither already pushing back into the waves. Athena is there by his side, gazing down, caressing his cheek so softly – *love, my beauty, love*, I cry, but I do not give the thought voice, do not dare to let her hear me, let her know she has been seen in such tenderness. Yet it is love, even here, even for all that it portends, all that will be broken and all that will be remade.

I turn my gaze away and beat back towards my palace, my bower, my laughing nymphs and lovely maids, as far below on the shores of Ithaca, twined in the arms of his goddess Athena, Odysseus wakes.

The story continues in...

The Last Song of Penelope

Keep reading for a sneak peek!

Meet the Author

Siobhan Watts

CLAIRE NORTH is a pseudonym for Catherine Webb, a Carnegie Medal–nominated author whose debut novel was written when she was just fourteen years old. Her first book published under the Claire North pen name was *The First Fifteen Lives of Harry August*, which received rave reviews and became a word-of-mouth bestseller. She has since published several hugely popular and critically acclaimed novels, won the World Fantasy Award and the John W. Campbell Memorial Award, and been shortlisted for the Arthur C. Clarke Award and the Philip K. Dick Award. She lives in London.

if you enjoyed
HOUSE OF ODYSSEUS

look out for

THE LAST SONG OF PENELOPE

by

Claire North

The third book in award-winning author Claire North's Songs of Penelope trilogy, a "powerful, fresh, and unflinching" (Jennifer Saint) reimagining that breathes life into ancient myth and gives voice to the women who stand defiant in a world ruled by ruthless men.

Many years ago, Odysseus sailed to war and never returned. For twenty years, his wife, Penelope, and the women of Ithaca have guarded the isle against suitors and rival kings. But peace cannot be kept forever, and the balance of power is about to break....

A beggar has arrived at the palace. Salt crusted and ocean battered, he is scorned by the suitors—but Penelope recognizes in him something terrible: her husband, Odysseus, returned at last. Yet this Odysseus is no hero. By returning to the island in disguise, he is not merely plotting his revenge against the suitors—vengeance that will spark a civil war—but he's testing the loyalty of his queen. Has she been faithful to him all these years? And how much blood is Odysseus willing to shed to be sure?

The song of Penelope is ending, and the song of Odysseus must ring through Ithaca's halls. But first, Penelope must use all her cunning to win a war for the fate of the island and keep her family alive, whatever the cost. . . .

CHAPTER 1

>>

Sing, O Muse, of that famous man who sacked the citadel of Troy, and after wandered many years across the sea. Great were the sights he saw and many woes he endured as he tumbled tempest-tossed, always seeking one destination: home.

Sing his song down the ages, sing of heartbreak and cunning devices, of prophecies and honour, of petty men and their foolish ways, of the pride of kings and their fall. Let his name be remembered for ever, let his story outlast the high temple upon the mountain peak, let all who hear it speak of Odysseus.

And when you tell his story, remember: though he was lost, he was not alone. I was always by his side.

Sing, poets, of Athena.

CHAPTER 2

>>

O f the many kingdoms that make up the sacred lands of
Greece, it is generally agreed that the western isles are the
worst. And of the western isles themselves, comprising many
parts of some diverse merit, everyone concurs that Ithaca is
the pits.

She rises like a crab from the sea, black-backed and glistening
with salt. Her inland forests are scraggy, wind-blasted things,
her one city little more than a spider's town of twisted paths
and leaning houses that seem to buckle and brace against some
perpetual storm. By the banks of the twisted brooks she calls
rivers there are shaggy goats who nip at scrubs of grass that
sprout like old men's beards between the tumbled boulders of
a bygone age. At the mouths of her many coves and hidden
bays the women push their rough boats onto the grey, foaming
sea to catch the morning harvest of darting silver fish that play
against her shores. To her west are the richer, greener slopes of
Kefalonia, to the north the bustling ports of Hyrie, south the
generous groves of Zacynthos. It is absurd, those who account
themselves civilised say, that these richer lands should send their
sons to pay homage in backwards little Ithaca, where the kings
of the western isles have built their crooked excuse for a palace.

But look again – can you see? No? Well then, as I am mistress of war and cunning I will deign to share something of my insight, and tell you that the wily kings of these lands could not have chosen a better place to set their throne than on the back of mollusc-like Ithaca.

She sits like a fortress in a place where many seas meet, and sailors must travel beneath her gaze if they wish to ply their wares in Calydon or Corinth, Aegium or Chalcis. Even Mycenae and Thebes send their merchant vessels through her harbours, rather than risk a voyage through the southern waters where discontented warriors of Sparta and Pylos might plunder their barks. Not that the kings of the western isles have been above a bit of piracy in their time – not at all. It is necessary that a monarch occasionally demonstrate the power they can wield, so that when they choose *not* to wage war, but rather invite in the emissaries of peace, peace is especially grateful and cooperative in light of this merciful restraint.

Other accusations levelled against Ithaca: that its people are uncultivated, uncivilised, uncouth, with the table manners of dogs and a repertoire of poetry whose highest form is little more than a bawdy ditty about farts.

To which I say: yes. Why indeed yes, these things are true, and yet you are still a fool. Both things may be true simultaneously.

For the kings of Ithaca have made something really rather useful of their ruggedness and uncultivated ways: behold, when the barbarians of the north come with cargoes of amber and tin, they are not shunned at the mouth of the harbour, nor berated as ignorant strangers, but courteously they are led into royal halls, offered an inferior cup of wine or two – most wine on Ithaca is appallingly sour – and invited to speak of the misty forests and pine-dark mountains that they make their home, as if to say well, well, are we not all just salt-scarred children of the sea and sky together?

The civilised dolts of this world gaze upon the merchants of the west where they stand upon the shore in dirty robes, chewing fish with open mouths. They call them yokel and crude, and do not realise how easy this opinion makes it to prise silver from the greedy fingers of men dressed in silk and gold.

The palace of her kings may not be fine, no marble columns nor halls steeped in silver, nor why should it be? It is a place for business, for negotiations between men who append the word "honest" to their names, just in case anyone might doubt. Its walls are the island itself, for any would-be invader would have to steer their ships beneath jagged cliffs and through hidden shallows of biting stone before they could land a single soldier on Ithaca's shores. Thus I say: the kings of the western isles made canny, shrewd decisions on where to lay their heads in this rough and ragged land, and those that condemn them are dolts, for whom I have no time.

Indeed, Ithaca should have held for ever, defended by stone and sea against all intruders, save that the finest of its men sailed with Odysseus to Troy, and of all those who went to war, only one is now returned.

Walk with me upon the stone-glistening shores of Ithaca, to where a man lies sleeping.

Shall I call him beloved?

This word – this "beloved" – is murder.

Once, a long time before, I came close to saying it. I laughed in delight at the company of another, cried praise upon her, smiled at her jests and frowned at her sorrows – and now she is dead, and I her killer.

Never again.

I am shield, I am armour, I am golden helmet and ready spear. I am the finest warrior of these lands, save perhaps one, and I do not love.

Well then, here he is, this man who is everything – nothing – everything to me.

Huddled, knees tucked to his chest, head buried in the nook of his arms as if he would block out the bright morning light. When the poets sing of him, they shall say that his hair is golden, his back broad and strong, his scarred thighs like two mighty trees. But they shall also say that at my touch, he was disguised as a crooked old man, hobbled and limping, his great light diminished in a noble cause. The humility of the hero – that is important in making him memorable as a man. His greatness must not feel unobtainable, unimaginable. When the poets speak of his suffering, hearers must suffer with him. That is how we shall make a tale eternal.

The truth, of course, is that Odysseus, son of Laertes, king of Ithaca, hero of Troy, is a somewhat short man with a remarkably hairy back. His hair was once an autumnal brown, which twenty years of salt and sun faded to a dull and muddy hue, crackled with grey. We may say therefore it is of some colour that has been so much overgrown with disarray, shorn with stress and faded with travel that it is hardly a colour at all. He wears a gown that was given him by a Phaeacian king. The negotiations as to the quality of the gown were fantastically tedious, since Odysseus's hosts had to insist that please, no please, their guest must be dressed in the finest, and he as guest had to reply that no, oh no, he couldn't possibly, he was a mere beggar at their table, and they said yes, but yes you are a great king, and he said no, the greatness is yours oh great one, and thus it went for a while until eventually they settled upon this middling garb that is neither too fine nor too drab and thus everyone could come away feeling satisfied in their social roles. The slaves had fetched the gown long before the agreement was struck, of course, and laid it ready out of sight to be presented. They have too much to do in a day to waste time on these performances of civilised, song-worthy men.

Now he sleeps, which is an apt and suitable way for the wandering king to return to his island, indicative perhaps of the weight of the journey that he has experienced, the burden of it, the crushing passage of time, which now shall be redeemed by the peaceful breezes and sweet perfumes of dearest Ithaca and so on and so forth.

Vulnerability – that too must be a vital part of his story, if it is to live through the ages. He has performed so many vile and bitter deeds that any opportunity to embody some sense of the innocent, the man cruelly punished by the Fates and so on is absolutely essential. Throw in a few verses about meeting the hollowed form of his mother in the fields of the dead to really emphasise his qualities as a valorous man who keeps striving towards his goals despite the burdens of a creaking heart – yes, I think that will do.

That will do.

I do not expect you to understand these things. Even my kindred gods barely manage to think more than a century ahead, and save Apollo their prophecies are flawed, cripplingly naïve. I am no prophet, but rather a scholar of all things, and it is clear that all things wither and change, even the harvest of Demeter's field. Long before the Titans wake, I foresee a time when the names of the gods – even great Zeus himself – are diminished, turned from thunder-breakers, ocean-ragers into little more than jokes and children's rhymes. I see a world in which mortals make themselves gods in our places, elevate their own to our divine status – an astounding arrogance, a logical conclusion – though their gods will be vastly less skilled at the shaping of the weather.

I see us withering. I see us falling away, no matter how hard we rage. No blood will be spilled in our honour, no sacrifices made, and in time, no one will even remember our names. Thus do gods perish.

This is not prophecy. It is something far more potent: it is the inevitable path of history.

I will not have it, and so I put mechanisms in place. I raise up cities and scholars, temples and monuments, spread ideas that will last longer than any broken shield, but when all else fails I will have one more string to my bow – I will have a story.

A good story can outlast almost anything.

And for that I need Odysseus.

Now he stirs on the beach; naturally the poets will report that I was here to greet him, a good moment for Athena to appear at last, a revelation of my role, my support – let's not call it that, let us call it . . . divine guidance – my noble presence that has always been with him. If I had appeared too soon it would have made his journey easy, a man overly aided by the gods – that wouldn't have done at all – but here, on his home shore, it's just the right moment, a kind of catharsis even – "Odysseus at last meets the goddess protector who has all this time guided his trembling hand" – it is the perfect narrative beat to insert myself into . . .

Well.

If the poets have done their work, I hardly need to recount this business further. If they have sung their songs as I intend they shall, then their audiences should now be tearing up, hearts fluttering, as Odysseus finally stirs, wakes, sees this land that he has not set eyes upon for some twenty years, struggles to understand, cries out in rage against betrayal, against the perfidious sailors who spoke so gently only to abandon him once again in he knows not what cursed place. The poets too can then describe how he slowly calms, steadies himself, looks about, smells the air, wonders, hopes, sees at last my divine form, standing above him.

I shall say, "Do you not know this place, stranger?" in a manner that is both irreverent – I am after all a goddess, and he a mere man – and also gently fond, and he at last shall cry out: Ithaca! Ithaca! Sweet Ithaca!

I will let him have his moment of passion, of purest delight – this is also an important emotional part of the overall structure of the thing – before guiding him to more practical matters and his still unfulfilled duties about the land.

This shall the poets sing, and when they do, I shall be at the heart of it. I shall appear when it matters the most, and in this way, debasing though it is, I shall survive.

I loathe Odysseus for that, sometimes. I, who have wielded the lightning, reduced to mere adjunct to the tale of a mortal man. But loathing does not serve, so instead, I swallow my bitterness, and work. When all my siblings are diminished, when the poets no longer sing their names, Athena will endure.

The poets will not sing the truth of Odysseus. Their verses are bought and sold, their stories subject to the whims of kings and cruel men who would use their words for power and power alone. Agamemnon commanded the poets to sing of his unstoppable strength, his bloody flashing sword. Priam bade the poets of Troy raise their voices in praise of loyalty, piety and the bonds of family above all else, and look where they are now. Wandering through the blackened fields of the dead, slain as much by the stories they sang of themselves as by the blades that took their lives.

The truth does not serve me, it is not wise that it be known.

Yet here my dual natures tug upon me, for I am the lady of war, as well as wisdom. And though war is rarely wise, it is at least honest.

Truth, then, to satisfy the warrior within my philosopher's breast.

Listen closely, for this is the only time I will tell it.

A whispered secret, a hidden tale – this is the story of what actually happened when Odysseus returned to Ithaca.